Praise for *A Royal Pain*

An NPR

"A delightful love story... ..."
—*Publishers Weekly*, starred review

"Filled with clever characters, witty banter, and steamy sex, readers won't be able to put it down."
—*RT Book Reviews*, 4 ½ stars

"Fresh, funny, and engaging, with Mulry's lavish descriptions of fashion an added bonus."
—*Booklist*

"Megan Mulry's vivacious Bronte is every Englishwoman's nightmare—the straight-talking, hot-blooded all-American girl who bags the Duke!"
—Hester Browne, *New York Times* bestseller

"*Sex and the City* goes to London. *A Royal Pain* is often laugh-out-loud funny with super sexy overtones. It is a wonderful debut that shouldn't be missed."
—Catherine Bybee, *New York Times* bestseller

"A whole new twist on trans-Atlantic romance—sexy, fresh, and delightfully different."
—Susanna Kearsley, *New York Times* bestseller

"Take one sparky, sailor-mouthed American girl and one handsome English aristocrat. Put them together and watch the sparks fly. Sizzling fun!"
—Jill Mansell, *New York Times* bestseller

Praise for *If the Shoe Fits*

"Both flirty and intense, and combining a luxury fashion setting with the English aristocracy, this love story will elicit many
a contented sigh among romance fans."
—*Kirkus Reviews*

"The romantic tension entices the reader from the very first
page and never flags."
—*Publishers Weekly*

"This sexy, sparkly story, with its witty dialogue and likable
characters, is a fun, lively read. "
—*Booklist*

"I thoroughly enjoyed If the Shoe Fits and think that Mulry
has a great way of tapping into strong emotional stories and
characters that readers can love."
—*One Literature Nut*

"A rollicking, laugh out loud, feel good novel that will leave you
with a smile on your face."
—*Harlequin Junkie*

"Mulry does it with such a great voice and such fabulous characters that it still feels fresh and wonderful. Highly recom-
mended."
—*Devourer of Books*

In Love Again

In Love Again

Megan Mulry

Published by Megan Mulry
www.meganmulry.com
ISBN ISBN-10: 0989997502
ISBN-13: 978-0-9899975-0-8

I'd rather have roses on my table than diamonds on my neck.
—Emma Goldman

Being a princess isn't all it's cracked up to be.
—Princess Diana

Chapter 1

CLAIRE LOOKED ACROSS the table at her perfectly turned out sister-in-law and then beyond to the wet streets of Mayfair. To the uninformed observer, both women were perfectly turned out, she supposed, sitting there lunching at C on a rainy June afternoon.

"It's just so hard to believe, I guess," Sarah said. Her American voice always seemed animated and vivacious when she spoke to other people, but Claire got the feeling that Sarah—and, lately, everyone else for that matter—chose words carefully when speaking to her. Claire Heyworth Barnes, the Marchioness of Wick, had become fragile.

"What is?" Claire brought her attention back from the passing taxis on Davies Street.

"Just that after so many years—what has it been? Twenty years? You and Freddy are no longer you-and-Freddy. You were just so... established."

Claire smiled, but it wasn't anything—her lips lifting up, nothing more. "Established, yes, that's exactly what we were. My mother made sure of that. By royal decree."

"Well, you *were* married by royal decree, weren't you?" Sarah made a tentative reaching motion with her hand, as if to comfort Claire, but she didn't end up making contact. Nobody touched her, not really. She had withdrawn so many years ago that it had become a habit, the physical and emotional isolation. Years of behaving a certain way, just because that was how she always behaved—without wondering about the why of it—meant that even genuine affection felt awkward now, like false intimacy. The human touch was foreign to her.

Claire tried. She reached her own hand across the white tablecloth and patted Sarah's. "No need to worry, darling. I was eighteen when I got married, so I'm still—perhaps—able to *re*establish. Thirty-eight isn't horribly over the hill these days, is it?"

"Over the hill?" Sarah grabbed Claire's hand and laughed. "You're gorgeous."

Claire was embarrassed by the younger woman's effusive praise. Did people actually say things like *you're gorgeous* and mean it? All those years of silence and lies with Freddy had unhinged her. Claire knew she was unstable—or at least Freddy had always told her she was a wreck—but maybe she wasn't all that bad. Maybe she was just out of practice. Or had never been shown that type of emotional generosity in the first place. Except perhaps that one time, the summer before Freddy.

She had seen the hints of what it meant to touch, and be touched by, someone. Not just the physical contact, but to laugh when he laughed, to see things and turn to face each other at exactly the same moment, to see that the other person saw the same thing. Not just the landscape or the Roman ruins or the herd of galloping wild horses across the Camargue, but really *saw life* in the same way.

"What were you thinking just then?" Sarah asked, releasing Claire's hand. "You had the softest look on your face."

Claire waved her off. "Oh, nothing, just an old memory from a summer vacation when I was a teenager. Let me get this." Claire picked up the leather case holding the astronomical lunch bill and reached for her credit card.

A few minutes later, the maître d' returned to the table sporting a doleful expression.

"I'm sorry, Lady Wick, but there seems to be a hold on this card."

Sarah started to reach for her wallet.

"No," Claire said quickly. "It's my treat."

Claire paled. He had actually done it. The solicitor had warned her that Freddy's legal team could freeze her assets—depleted as they were—temporarily. Or indefinitely. Or permanently.

She recovered, reaching into her purse. "Very well." She slipped four crisp hundred-pound notes into the leather folder and handed it back to the maître d'. "Thank you, Guillaume." The Frenchman bowed slightly. Claire retrieved her useless piece of plastic and resituated it carefully into her immaculate—equally useless—wallet.

"Come to the shop for a few minutes, will you? I've got all the summer shoes in stock," Sarah suggested.

"Oh, I don't know…" Claire's sister-in-law owned several boutiques that sold exorbitantly expensive shoes. Sarah had married Claire's brother, Devon Heyworth, six months ago, and they spent most of their time in London, occasionally returning to the United States to visit Sarah's family or to check on her other two stores in New York and Chicago.

Usually, Claire would have leapt at the chance to take a stroll through the boutique and look at some of the high-fashion stilettos or sandals from Sarah's newest collection. Not that Claire really had a clue about high style, especially compared to the two fashionable American women her brothers had married. Claire's style was more what her mother described as classically unassailable. Practical. Living in northern Scotland with the usually absent Marquess of Wick for twenty years had not done much to foster any sense of fashion. She stuck to Harris tweeds and soft Pringle cashmere sweaters.

"Oh, please!" Sarah beamed. "There's a pair of strappy heels I would love for you to try."

"I just don't think—"

"Let's go!" Sarah declared.

"Oh, all right." Claire picked up her (practical) Mowbray canvas purse and followed Sarah out to the sidewalk. The rain had stopped and some of the lights around Berkeley Square were beginning to sparkle in the dusky evening of early summer.

Sarah slid her arm through Claire's and started walking. "This is really ridiculous, you know."

"What's that?" Claire turned to face her as they crossed Davies Street and walked along the northern edge of Berkeley Square.

"This not being able to say what everyone is thinking. I mean, what happens if Freddy goes to *jail?*"

Claire didn't reply.

"As well he should," Sarah added, "for all of his treachery!"

Claire winced. She loved these American women and all their brave honesty, but sometimes it was simply too much. Was it really necessary to be chatting idly about treachery and prison as they strolled past the dappled plane trees of Mayfair? It was so grim.

"Really, Claire." Sarah stopped them both at the corner of Bruton Place.

"What?"

"Everyone in your family is so afraid that you're just going to smash into little pieces if we talk openly about your situation. What are you going to *do?* You're a thirty-eight-year-old woman. Your finances are…a shambles. I simply won't allow you to move back in to your mother's Mayfair townhouse after your bastard husband squandered your massive fortune. As Devon would say, it's just *not on!*"

Claire felt the all-too-familiar press of tears, then reached out and hugged Sarah. The younger woman squeezed her hard in return.

"He's just not worth it," Sarah mumbled into Claire's ear. "*Fuck* him."

"You sound like Bronte!" Claire laughed as she wiped at her eye with the tip of one neatly trimmed pinkie and pulled away.

"I know." Sarah laughed too, but kept her hands gripped on Claire's upper arms. "But even I see the occasional use of the warranted epithet. Freddy warrants more than the occasional epithet."

"I can't just walk away, Sarah. If I were on my own, of course I would have left him years ago, but there was Lydia, and I thought…" Claire paused. "At the very least, I owe it to Lydia to fight for her portion. I just don't believe he could have burned through all of it."

"You think he's hiding it somewhere?"

Claire took a very deep breath. "I don't know. But that's what the lawyers are trying to figure out. Do you have wine at your shop?"

"Of course!" Sarah put her arm back through Claire's, and they continued down the narrow lane to the lit-up Sarah James boutique. The little bell over the door jingled with old-fashioned cheer as the two women entered. The salesgirl, a recent graduate of Central Saint Martins, stood up quickly to greet them.

"Oh, please sit down, Shelly. This is my sister-in-law Claire."

Sarah never bothered with formal introductions, since she'd never been able to get her mind around the difference between a marchioness and a March hare in the first place. Dukes, earls, and viscounts were as interchangeable as spaniels and corgis.

Claire was finally starting to see the wisdom in such an approach. After decades of her mother's incessant drilling about the importance of royal forms of address, who was related to whom, and who didn't deserve the slightest attention, Claire was starting to think that Sarah might be on to something.

"Hello, Shelly. Nice to meet you." Claire reached out and they shook hands. Claire wished her own daughter Lydia had an ounce of the commitment and ambition that this young woman seemed to possess. *Oh, Lydia.*

Sarah must have caught a glimpse of Claire's dwindling cheer.

"We'll be upstairs getting drunk," Sarah proclaimed and swept out of the retail portion of the shop and up the industrial metal stairs at the back that led to her atelier on the floor above.

Claire shook her head at Sarah's audacity. As she followed her up the stairs, she realized she was actually jealous. What must it feel like to say what you think without the constant second- and third- and fourth-guessing about the ramifications of every syllable? If Claire asked Freddy where he was going, she was accused of smothering him. If he showed up with a shooting party of twelve men, unannounced, and she wasn't prepared with a cellar of port and boxes of Cuban cigars, she was accused of being an inattentive layabout. Claire had spent the past twenty years trying to please someone who had been lying to her from the day he met her.

Nobody could have known, Claire finally conceded. Even his own mother, the Dowager Marchioness of Wick, one of Claire's mother's closest friends, had recently pronounced that her son was a rotter.

Sarah pulled open the hidden refrigerator and whipped out a bottle of champagne. "I feel like celebrating!"

"Really? I feel like crawling into a hole and never coming out."

"Claire! Stop it! You're free! *Free!* Think about it. When was the last time you were really free?"

Damn if that image of a nineteen-year-old Ben Hayek holding her hand as they looked out over the Roman ruins in Arles didn't pop into her head again. They'd known each other for a grand total of three measly months. Twenty years ago. That was probably the last time she felt free.

"Well?" The abrupt *POP!* of the champagne cork served as a loud prompt.

"Well, what?" Claire asked, stalling.

Sarah poured two flutes of champagne as she spoke. "When was the last time you felt free? Just totally spin-in-the-sunshine, kick-off-your-shoes freedom…"

"Oh, I don't know…"

"Yes, you do." Sarah handed her the champagne flute. "You just got that same look in your eyes that you got at the end of lunch. There was someone before Freddy, wasn't there?"

"Well, not in the way you mean."

"You mean, you didn't sleep with him?"

Claire cringed. "Must you be so graphic?"

Sarah burst out laughing. "Graphic? *Sleep with?* Let me get Bronte to stop over on her way back from work and give you a little graphic."

Claire started laughing too. Her other sister-in-law, the Duchess of Northrop, also known as plain old Bronte, preferred a four-letter word to any other, whether the situation called for it or not.

"Oh, fine!" Claire smiled. "Call her. Let's get drunk and put the pieces of my *fucked up* life back together."

Chapter 2

"YAY!" SARAH SQUEALED. She pulled her cell phone out of her purse and hit the speed dial for her best friend's number.

"Hey, it's me. Can you come over to my office after you leave Mowbray's? ... How much longer? ... Okay...mm-hmm..." She took a sip of champagne while she listened. "Okay, perfect. Yes, I'm here with Claire, and we're going to get her back on track. Roll up our sleeves and tell her what's what...mm-hmm...yes, she even said the word *fuck*..." Sarah burst out laughing. "Okay, see you soon, sweetie." She clicked off the cell phone and turned back to Claire. "Okay, first things first. Who's the dream man?"

Claire set the champagne flute down on the glass tabletop in front of the Breuer chair she was sitting in. "He was nobody. Just a summer...thing."

"Like a swoony, oh-my-god-I-can't-believe-I-met-my-dream-man-while-backpacking-through-Europe thing or...just a thing?"

Claire smiled. It was impossible not to. Sarah had the strangest combination of raw innocence and infectious mischief. "I guess, at the time, I thought he was just a thing. But it stuck. Does that make sense?"

Sarah stared out the floor-to-ceiling windows that lined the southern wall of her office. "I don't know if it's wrong to talk about your brother in this way, but yes. After I met Devon, it just never stopped. I tried to forget him and get over it and move on, or whatever. But he just stuck." Sarah smiled. Now that she was happily married to the devil, it wasn't worth wondering why he had stuck. He just did, and it had all worked out. But Claire?

"I don't know," Claire began, twisting her champagne glass and trying to speak honestly for maybe the first time about her ruinous marriage. "Everything was as it was supposed to be with Freddy. His mother. My Mother. The marquisate. I was the daughter of a duke. He was a marquess. Everything was as it should be."

"What's that supposed to mean?"

"Oh, don't pretend that your stepmother didn't have…hopes… for you and Eliot. You know exactly what I mean. It just all fit together, for the families, for both of us." Claire sighed. "I know it sounds antiquated and stupid to your modern ears, but it was just the thing. To obey."

Sarah looked at the woman she had come to think of as her older sister. Claire was technically her sister-in-law, but being an only child, Sarah had wholeheartedly embraced her husband's family as her own. She thought of Abby and Claire and Bronte as her sisters, and Max as her brother.

"All right. I won't pretend to be clueless about the power of parental approval. I'm sure your father and mother encouraged you to get along with Freddy. But seriously? He's just so lame."

Claire snorted. "I guess he looks that way now, but twenty years ago, he was pretty debonair. He wasn't all slithering and slick like he is these days. He had the occasional nice thing to say. But you're right. I knew he was all wrong for me. Yet, my mother convinced me that I was too young to know what was right for me and that I needed to rely on my elders to point me in the right direction."

"How awful."

"Oh, stop. What's done is done. I married the Marquess of Wick. He has a castle. I thought he was charming and rich. I suppose at the time, he *was* rich. But that's all come to a finish now. Even so, let's not pretend that he didn't have something to offer back in the nineties. As my mother would say, *moving on!*"

Sarah took a deep breath. "Okay. Moving on. Tell me about Mister Summer Vacation."

"What's the point?" Claire asked.

"The point is, I need to know what type of man actually piqued your interest when your mother and everyone else in the world weren't watching. Was he quirky and academic? Tall, dark, and handsome? Smooth? Bumbling? What?"

"Oh, I don't know. When you say it like that, it's hard to describe. He was just, so kind, but sort of adamant too."

"Oh, Claire. You really liked him."

"I think I loved him."

Sarah watched as Claire tried to repress a shudder of pleasure. Even after all these years, apparently the mere thought of him still brought on a physical reaction.

"What happened to him?" Sarah pressed. "Was he just some backpacking ne'er-do-well?"

"Oh, I doubt that. He was American and smart. And he was on his way to some prestigious American university. California somewhere. I don't remember. But he was so…intense. And he seemed to fancy me for some bizarre reason."

"Why would someone need a bizarre reason to fancy you?" Sarah asked.

"Oh, stop. I was pale and shy and, oh…" Claire waved her hand in front of her face. "Just a wallflower."

Sarah set her champagne glass down on her desk and circled around to her chair so she could look at her computer screen. "What's his name?"

"What? Who?" Claire asked.

"What is Mister I-Fancy-You's name?"

"Well, it's been so long…"

Sarah stared at her sister-in-law with one eyebrow raised. "Are you really going to pretend that you don't remember every little thing about him?"

"Okay, fine. Ben."

Sarah stared with ridicule and impatience. "Ben what?"

"Benjamin Hayek. Satisfied?"

"Very." Sarah grinned and started tapping the keys of her computer. As she waited for the results to come up, she asked, "He's American, right?"

"Yes. Well his parents were Lebanese, I think, but they were American."

"Oooh. Lebanese. Sounds exotic."

"This is mortifying. I feel like we're stalking him," Claire mumbled.

"Stalking? You have no idea. This is like the tippiest tip of the iceberg. We haven't even begun to plumb the depths of all the gritty details. Are you seriously expecting me to believe that after all those years alone in Scotland, you never *once* logged on to Facebook or Googled him, just to see what he looked like or where he lived?"

Claire shrugged. "There was no Facebook in the mid-nineties, obviously, and later on, well, I thought I was in a committed marriage, remember? And in any case, I tried to tamp down my curiosity about such things. What would have been the point?"

"The point?" Sarah laughed and took another sip of her champagne. "The point is that it's fun. You can see if he's turned into a pudgy, smug father of three hideous brats or if he's got a toupee and an ant farm." Sarah paused. "Okay, there are a few Ben Hayeks." She hummed and tapped a few more keys. "I'm assuming he's about your age?"

"Two years older, I think."

Sarah kept typing and clicking. "And what did he do for a living? What was he studying when you met him?"

"I don't know what became of him. I think he wanted to be a doctor or something. He was pretty tall. And he had dark hair. His eyes were green."

Sarah hummed suggestively. "I'll say."

"You'll say what?"

"I'll say he's tall, dark, and handsome and has killer green eyes. Is it this guy?" Sarah turned her screen so it faced out toward where Claire was sitting.

The four-by-five-inch portrait stared at her. The dark hair was combed into a far more adult style, the green eyes had creases around the edges, and the mouth had a firm set that was the result of experience. And he was wearing a doctor's white coat.

Claire leaned closer to the screen and realized her breath was shallow.

Sarah smiled and said, "So, I'll take that as a yes." She swiveled the screen back to face her. "You have excellent taste in men, Claire. Sheesh. He's awesome. Look at that bone structure."

Claire actually blushed and was still blushing when Bronte burst in.

"All right. What have I missed?" She threw her enormous Prada satchel on the floor near Claire's seat and leaned down to give her a kiss on the cheek. "How are you doing, honey? What's the latest on *Le Bâtard*?"

Her sisters-in-law had taken to referring to Freddy as *Le Bâtard*. It had started out as a joke over drinks at Dunlear Castle a few weeks ago, when Bronte decided she no longer wanted to refer to him by name and asserted from that day forward, she would only call him *Le Bâtard*. "Because," she had said, "it sounds dastardly and villainous."

Claire looked up at Bronte, there in Sarah's office, taking in her barely contained energy, her vitality. "Well, it looks as if his solicitor or the courts have frozen all of our assets."

"Are you fucking kidding me?" Bronte was in the midst of pouring herself a glass of champagne. She finished pouring, then paused and placed one hand on her hip, turning to face Claire. "How is that even possible? Your legal system is a shit show."

"Oh, it's possible all right." Claire looked up at the ceiling, pretending she was interested in the plasterwork rather than staving off tears.

"Don't you dare cry about him!" Bronte barked. "He's such a douchebag."

"Bronte!" Sarah cried.

"What? It's the truth." Bronte shrugged at Sarah then turned to Claire with more concern. "I know you know he is. Don't you?"

"Yes. Of course." Claire sighed, because even now she had to force herself to face facts rather than the idea of what she had always believed her life was supposed to be. "But—"

"But nothing," Bronte interrupted, thinking she was being supportive.

"But Bron, seriously, he's the father of my only child. All those years that I thought he was…decent."

Bronte pressed on. "That's what makes him even more reprehensible. Think about it. *All those years*. All those years of you doing your good works and helping your father and mother and tending to Freddy's whims. And what's the thanks he gives you?"

"I know," Claire said, willing herself not to weep, to be practical. "But if it was all a lie to him, then it was *all* a lie. My life—" She choked and took another sip of her champagne.

Bronte sat in the chair closest to Claire's and pulled her free hand into hers. "Your life has *not* been a lie. He's the bastard for making you think so. You have a beautiful home. You have a beautiful daughter."

Claire smirked.

"Well, Lydia is salvageable," Bronte hedged. "She's a bit of a handful, but she has spunk. And she is half you, so she knows the difference between right and wrong. Maybe Abby will set her straight."

"At least I don't have to worry about her for a while." Claire's youngest sister, Abigail Heyworth, had started a foundation to educate young women in sub-Saharan Africa, and Lydia had been recruited into service after she announced she was dropping out of university following one lackluster year. Lydia was traveling around different African villages with her Aunt Abby for the summer.

"Exactly. Focus on yourself," Sarah chimed in. "Get a job."

An abrupt silence descended over the bright office. Night had fallen outside the dark wall of windows, and the interior sparkled with the tiny halogen ceiling lights against the chrome-accented furniture. All three women sat frozen.

"What?" Sarah finally cried. "Like it's a four-letter word or something? Repeat after me. J. O. B. Job."

Bronte smiled and swirled her champagne glass slowly.

Sarah must have noticed that she hadn't taken a sip. "Why aren't you drinking your champagne, Bron?"

"No reason." But she still didn't take a sip.

Claire clasped her hands. "Oh! Are you going to have another baby?"

Sarah sputtered. "Wait? What!"

Bronte smiled and looked a bit sheepish. "Two babies, actually."

"What? Twins? Oh, that's the most wonderful news!" Claire leapt up and hugged her hard. "Why didn't you tell us straight away?

It's so much more exciting than my dismal divorce. You are quite terrible for keeping it from us."

"It's all pretty new. We haven't told a soul."

Sarah hugged her next and suddenly started crying.

"Oh my god, Sarah!" Bronte grabbed her by the shoulders. "I'm not dying. I'm pregnant. Why are you crying?"

"We're not all as emotionally cut-and-dried as you are, Bron, all right?" Sarah grabbed a tissue off her desk and started dabbing at her eyes.

"Oh, sweetie. I'm sorry." Bronte pulled Sarah into a tight hug. "I'm such an insensitive idiot."

"I'm fine. I'm fine." Sarah finished drying her eyes and took a deep breath. "Whoa. Okay. Totally fine." She took a sip of champagne. "All better." Claire and Bronte stared at her as she collected herself. "What?"

"Are you and Devon going to start trying soon?" Bronte asked point blank.

Sometimes Claire wondered how these women made it through the day without emotional flak jackets. It was like open season on life's most intimate details. She stared harder into her own glass of champagne and tried to be invisible.

"What? No, of course not. You know neither one of us wants to have kids right away. I'm just happy for you." At least Sarah's voice was starting to sound normal again. She gestured around her cluttered office, full of sketches and work orders and leather samples. "Does this look like the office of someone who is trying to have a baby?"

Bronte stared at Sarah. "You don't really expect me to answer that, do you? We all know you're going to be checking on the factory work orders when you start dilating."

"Would you stop? We're not trying to have a baby. I swear!"

Sarah laughed and the hint of tension left the room. "Not that I don't mind lots and lots of practice—"

"Stop!" Claire pleaded through her burgeoning laughter. "He's my brother. I don't want to think of you two having lots of *practice sex*—" She nearly squeaked out the last two words.

The door swung open just as she said it and Devon Heyworth— the brother in question—popped his head in. "Hi, ladies. Awkward moment?"

"Oh god!" Sarah walked over to the door and gave him a quick kiss on the cheek. "Did you have a good day at work?"

He nodded and gave her a firmer kiss on the lips. "I did." He looked over her shoulder. "What are you all up to?"

"Drinks with the girls. I love you. Now go away."

"Hi, Claire. Hi, Bron."

"Hi, Dev," they both answered.

"All right then." He kissed Sarah again. "I know when I'm not wanted. I'll get dinner started. Because, you know, I want to make sure I've got lots of nutrition for tonight's practice sex—"

"Get out!" Sarah laughed as she slammed the door in his face.

The sound of his receding laughter as he dashed up the stairs to their loft apartment echoed through the room. Sarah had a silly smile on her face as she walked slowly back to where Claire and Bronte were sitting.

Watching Sarah and Devon's loving banter, Claire wondered if she would ever feel that comfortable in her own skin, much less in a relationship with someone else. It seemed utterly incomprehensible— the teasing, the everyday intimacy.

Sarah sat down and took another sip of champagne. "Sorry about that." Then she was back to business. "Okay. So. Where were we?"

Bronte settled more comfortably onto the long sofa and put on her best bossy expression. "Claire was needing to get a job. J. O. B. That's where we were. And I couldn't agree more."

Claire stared into her glass, then finally spoke. "I am unqualified to do anything."

"That's patently ridiculous," Sarah said. "You're Lady Barnes—"

Claire shook her head.

"I mean… Marchioness Claire of Wick—"

"You're getting warmer…" Claire smiled this time.

"Or Lady Wick. Or whatever! I'm no good at titles—you know that. But in terms of getting a job, your title has to mean something. Plus, you need the money."

Claire looked down at her Chanel suit and her outrageously expensive jewels. They were all family jewels on loan from her mother, of course. The clothes too. Whenever Claire came into town, she raided her mother's closet and jewelry drawers. The former Dowager Duchess of Northrop, lately styled the lowly Mrs. Jack Parnell, had always enjoyed the latest fashions and would shake her head at Claire when she would arrive in her serviceable wools from Scotland.

Sarah smiled again. "Not like you *need* the money to put a roof over your head or clothes on your back, but you need your *own* money. Back me up, Bron."

Bronte stared at Claire—lost in thought—then snapped out of it. "Of course, of course. But I'm more interested in what you really *want* to do with your life."

"I thought I was already doing something with my life." Claire sounded small and defensive, even to her own ears. "You know, being a mother and a wife and a…decent person," she added lamely.

"Oh, dear," Bronte said, "I didn't mean it to come out all judgmental and accusatory like that. I'm so sorry."

Claire felt the press of tears again. "I'm trying not to be a baby about this, though it probably looks that way to you two superwomen, but I'm just a person. I never wanted to build an empire or transform an industry." Sarah and Bronte took the hits. "It wasn't easy creating a beautiful life in the wilds of Scotland. And I think I did a pretty good job of it."

The younger women tried to regroup. Bronte launched in first. "Of course you did. The castle is splendid. You spent years renovating it and making it gorgeous and all of that—"

Claire opened her mouth to speak, but Bronte stopped her.

"And I don't mean *all of that* in a dismissive way. Honestly, I don't. But admit it. You were hiding somehow. You were up there at the northernmost tip of the known world. Kind of tucked away."

"I guess you're right. But—" Claire sighed. "But nothing. You're right. I was. But the real world feels so busy and crowded and overwhelming."

Sarah had walked back behind her desk and leaned over to print up the image on her screen. She pulled it from the paper tray behind her a few seconds later and brought her glass and the picture back to where the other two women were sitting.

"Well, well, well. What have we here?" Bronte asked, taking the picture out of Sarah's hands with a low whistle.

"Oh, stop that, you two." But Claire craned her neck and tried to get a better look at the picture as she said it.

Bronte looked up. "Would you like me to make more room on the couch so you can get closer?"

Claire laughed. "No, but do hurry up and pass it here when you're finished gawking."

Sarah and Bronte shared a quick glance then passed the picture of Dr. Ben Hayek to Claire, who pretended not to be all that interested.

But she wasn't able to repress that slight lift of her lips that probably let her sisters-in-law know that the fire and passion that had once burned in a young woman's heart might not have been entirely doused after all.

Chapter 3

BEN REMOVED HIS gloves, stepped onto the floor pedal of the stainless steel garbage can, and tossed the disposable latex in as he left the examination room. He was on autopilot, as usual. The molar removal he'd just performed barely registered in his brain. Unless he was playing his guitar at the jazz club in the East Village or working on an emergency at the free clinic downtown, he merely passed through life these days. Nothing seemed to resonate. Nothing seemed to stick. Even his marriage had just sort of faded away. He and Alice were still friends. They still went to the movies together. No drama. No tears. Just married. Then not.

Apparently, Alice believed there was "more to life," whatever that meant. Ben thought an apartment on the Upper East Side and a thriving dental practice would have been enough for someone. For Alice. But if he was honest with himself, it wasn't enough. Not in the sense he was beginning to realize. It was way more than enough to satisfy his basic needs. Clothes. Cars. Country house in northern Connecticut. Or it should have been.

He had accused Alice of suffering from the Dissatisfaction Disease. Nothing was ever going to be enough. She had argued, quite convincingly, as it turned out—she hadn't made partner at thirty-six for nothing—that it was Ben who was suffering. She was cheerful and loved their life. He was the one who had turned into some weird, mopey version of himself. After nine years—the final two of which saw Ben pretending it was just a rough patch—Alice filed for divorce. He didn't even blame her, really. He *had* become mopey.

Still, there had been other problems. One of the main reasons Ben had decided to become a dentist was to give himself enough time to devote to a family. If he'd become an orthopedic surgeon, as he'd originally intended in undergrad, he decided it would probably limit his ability to be an attentive and loving father, like his own parents had been. He wanted that. A home filled with children and laughter and life. Alice had said she wanted that too. But.

But a few years into their marriage, he felt like he was the only one on the baby train. The more he questioned Alice about when she was going to go off the pill, the more she resisted. *Once she graduated from law school,* she said. Which had sounded perfectly reasonable at the time. *Once she became an associate.* Again, seemed logical in the moment. *Once she made partner.* Yes. He understood. But by then, he felt like he was having to try too hard. And if he had to try that hard to get Alice even interested in talking about having a baby, he didn't really see how she was going to be interested in the actual baby.

Life just wasn't turning out the way he'd planned.

Ever since he was a kid, Ben had been led to believe—he believed—that if he tried hard enough and worked hard enough and studied hard enough, then there would be a pot of gold or brass ring. Not anything to do with money or prestige, but a loving home that made everything else worthwhile. Eventually, after things began to fade with Alice, he figured he was probably spoiled by all the love in his childhood. So many doting older sisters and two loving parents hugging and supporting each other and telling him how much they loved him—and each other—all the time.

Eventually, he realized the futility of trying to re-create something that probably didn't even exist anymore. Loving families were such a cliché. He lowered his expectations in hope of a day-today life that was at least pleasantly satisfying. Ben knew he couldn't pin it all on Alice, though. He just remembered being happy at some point, of having the feeling that happiness wasn't a pretense. But it had been a long time ago and was probably just youthful ignorance.

He went into the next examination room and gave a quick look at a patient who was in for a regular checkup. All good. Next.

And so his day progressed, with the occasional emergency that made him use his brain for perhaps seventeen seconds instead of the requisite four seconds, and on and on it went. He got home that night and made himself one of those organic pasta and vegetable microwave dinners and watched the Knicks game. Maybe something would happen eventually. Or not.

"This is the dumbest idea in history." Claire stood in front of the mirror in Bronte's New York City apartment, Claire's new temporary home. She was wearing a navy blue skirt and matching jacket, and her long, wavy blond hair had been whipped into ramrod-straight submission by Bronte's favorite hairstylist. Bronte stood behind Claire and patted her shoulders and smoothed the skirt along her hips.

"You look amazing. You're going on a job interview. This is what you're supposed to look like."

"I feel like such a fraud. What do I possibly have to offer one of the top interior designers in the world?" Claire turned to face Bronte, unable to stand another second of that imposter in the mirror.

"Stop it. Seriously. You're the Marchioness of Wick—"

"Actually, I've been thinking about it and I want to go back to Lady Claire Heyworth." She looked down at her clasped hands thoughtfully. "I can't bear to be associated with Freddy, even if we aren't technically divorced."

"You will be soon enough."

Claire looked up hopefully. "You don't think it's duplicitous or dishonest, do you?"

"Of course not. You're still Lady Claire, the daughter of a duke. There's nothing dishonest about that. It's a technicality."

Claire had a momentary worry that her sister-in-law's moral compass didn't always point to true north, but Bronte was right in any case. Claire's name at birth had always been hers to use, no matter her marital status or what the British courts ruled.

"And Lady Claire's even better!" Bronte exclaimed. "Who's ever heard of a marchioness in Manhattan anyway? Everyone loves all that lady-this and lady-that."

Claire rolled her eyes. "Bronte."

"I'm not kidding. The plummy accent. The highbrow contacts. The accent!"

Claire frowned. "I get it, I get it. But I don't have any highbrow contacts. I've been holed up in Scotland for nearly twenty years, remember?"

"Oh, that's just untrue. You're related to the queen, for fuck's sake. Enough with the self-deprecating silliness. Or…" Bronte's eyes lit up. "Better yet, keep it up. Boppy Matthews is going to love all that!"

"All what?"

"All that hesitant *Oh, Viscount Linley, you mean David?* that you're so good at."

"Bronte. You're awful."

"I know. I'm the worst. But it's all true, and you know it. If you saw *David* at a party, you wouldn't turn in the other direction, now would you?"

"Well, I suppose not. But I wouldn't offer him a swatch of Scalamandré silk fabric either!"

Bronte burst out laughing. "Bull's-eye! Don't you see? Only you know Viscount Linley, *and* you know that he would know Scalamandré fabric to begin with. And all of that *is* what it's all about. It's just all too good. Now off we go."

Claire sighed and gave herself over to the ongoing pushing and prodding of her relentless sister-in-law. Bronte had offered her old apartment as a temporary stopgap until Claire got on her feet. For some reason, her brothers—who had always dismissed Claire as a doll-like version of their mother—had taken up her cause now that her wretched husband was no longer in the picture and their overpowering mother had moved to France with her new husband.

When Bronte had first suggested giving over her New York apartment, Claire tried to argue that taking charity from her sister-in-law was no better than taking charity from her mother, but Bronte had howled, "Claire! Living in a Georgian mansion in Mayfair and pretending you need a job is preposterous! Living in a modest one-bedroom apartment in Gramercy Park is something else altogether. Plus, New York City is all about new beginnings. How could you ever have a fresh start in London, for Christ's sake? Every maître d' in Mayfair knows your bank details!"

So Claire had spent the rest of the summer closing up the majority of the castle in Scotland, leaving only a few areas open and accessible to the public, and put the staff on notice. Freddy had already moved permanently to his rooms at the Albany many months before, and they'd both agreed to communicate solely through their attorneys. Despite years of lies and disdain, Freddy was still refusing to agree to the divorce, forcing Claire into the very unfamiliar position of aggressor.

Her brother Max had insisted on helping her hire the best attorney, and she'd reluctantly agreed. She hated having to depend on everyone, but Max convinced her that there was no way she could have burned through all her assets, and he was just as interested in ferreting out the truth about Freddy and their shared finances as she was.

She had felt mildly guilty about closing up the castle and effectively leaving her daughter homeless, but the twenty-year-old Lydia hadn't visited Scotland in nearly a year. As she'd driven away from Wick Castle for the last time, Claire had realized it was much easier to shut down twenty years of one's life than it had been to build it. The thought was far less depressing than she'd anticipated.

On that final trip to Scotland, she'd packed up two large suitcases of clothes, half of which Bronte and Sarah had summarily removed from the luggage during her stopover in London. The three of them had been at Northrop House in Mayfair, trying to sort out what Claire would need for her new life in New York.

"That's hideous," Sarah said about her favorite brown jumper.

"You'll never wear that in New York," Bronte said about her much-loved yellow mackintosh.

"Those are the color of puke," Sarah said about her dearest wellies.

"What the hell is *that?*" Bronte cried.

The item in question was one of her great-grandmother's bed coats. It was a pale blue lacy thing, of no sartorial use whatsoever. It was just old and pretty…and had been worn by the Queen Consort, Mary of Teck. And Claire loved it.

"Give me that!" Claire demanded.

"It looks like a spider got wasted on blue gin fizz and wove it in a drunken frenzy," Bronte said.

Claire held it close to her chest, then gently refolded it. "This stays."

"Okay," Bronte laughed. "It's nice to see a touch of defiance, but you might want to reserve your stubbornness for one of your mother's Worth gowns."

Sarah squeezed Claire's shoulder and whispered, "It's lovely, Claire."

That had been two weeks ago. Now Claire was wishing she *was* Mary of Teck, sitting in an enormous tester bed eighty years ago at Sandringham Castle, ringing for hot chocolate in her pale blue bed coat. Alas.

She took a deep breath of Manhattan air and got into the taxi alongside Bronte.

"Okay. So, obviously, I can't go in with you," Bronte began her pep talk. "But Boppy is totally expecting you, and you should basically just throw yourself at her feet."

Claire looked mortified.

"Not literally!" Bronte laughed and grabbed Claire's hand. "Just offer to do *whatever* needs doing. You have such perfect taste. I mean, look at you. You're always so perfect."

Claire cringed at the sound of the dreaded word. *Perfect.* Her mother was perfect. Her mother had demanded perfection. All that proper posture. Proper forms of address. "I am so far from perfect. I'm a wreck."

Bronte switched gears. "Look. Shake it off. You're going in for your first job interview...of your entire life. I get it. It's huge. But you're also a grown woman. You have had parties for hundreds of people in your home. You have raised hundreds of thousands of dollars for charities. You obviously know how to deal with difficult people, between your soon-to-be-ex-husband and your mother—" Bronte caught herself. "Sorry!" She swore quietly under her breath. "I'm trying so hard not to snipe."

It was Claire's turn to play the comforter. "Oh it's fine, Bron. I know Mother has given you a horrible time of it. She's better now, since she's with Jack, but she is just...rigid."

"She is that. I think she's wonderful with Wolf though," said

Bronte, referring to her beloved sixteen-month-old son.

"She is. She's spoiling him. Watch out. Can you imagine what she'll be like with twin girls? The clothes!"

"That's what grandmothers are for, I think."

"I think so too." The taxi stopped at a red light a few blocks from their final destination. "So, just talk to Boppy. You know her style. You've read her books. She's a classicist like you."

"Is that what I am?" Claire wondered.

"Yes!" Bronte laughed again. "Get your story straight. Everybody needs a little mission statement. Yours is all about the bones. You've got history. You've got structure."

"You make me sound like one of the properties in the National Trust."

"You're worse than Eeyore! Cut it out with all this sad sack nonsense. I'm trying to elaborate on your strengths, and all you can do is be mopey!"

"Okay, okay," Claire laughed it off. She probably was like an old pile of a castle anyway. She might as well admit it.

The taxi slowed to a stop in front of a five-story townhouse on a quiet side street in the sixties. A uniformed doorman waited just inside the glass door at the top of the eight or so steps that led up from the street.

"Here we are," Bronte said. "Go get 'em, Tiger. I mean, Tigress!"

"Meow," Claire said quietly.

"Roar!" Bronte cried, and they both started laughing again. The taxi driver was beginning to fidget in the front seat. "All right. Off you go. Knock 'em dead and all that. Call me as soon as you get out of the meeting. I'll be at my office for a few hours then at the Mowbray apartment with Wolf and Max, but you can reach me on my cell either way." Bronte practically had to push Claire out onto the sidewalk.

Claire leaned back into the car before shutting the door. "Thanks, Bron."

"Sarah made the introductory call, but you're welcome. Now go!"

"Okay!" She smiled, shut the door, and took a deep breath before looking up at the stately townhouse. "Here goes nothing," she whispered to herself, then took the first step toward her possible future.

Chapter 4

A MIDDLE-AGED DOORMAN opened the tall, narrow door and gestured toward the small front hall. "May I help you?"

"Yes, I am Claire—" Twenty years of introducing herself as Claire, Marchioness of Wick, caused her to stumble. She smiled at the nice-looking gentleman. "I'm Claire Heyworth. I have an appointment to see Ms. Matthews."

"Please wait in the sitting room." He showed her into a small front parlor that was—predictably—beautifully decorated.

Boppy Matthews had been a protégé of Sister Parish and then struck out on her own in the 1980s. She favored traditional European styles, with particular hints of American whimsy. Claire had spent the past two weeks reading up on everything she could find about her work. Matthews had published seven books, mostly picture books showing her clients' homes, and one that read like a country diary about her renovation and preservation work at a large farm in Pennsylvania where she and her husband spent their weekends and holidays. Claire had been particularly taken with the diary, finding much in common with the way Matthews had created a long-term plan for the home and surrounding gardens. The way she planned certain projects that would take decades to complete—trellised fruit trees, allées of original American specimen trees—reminded Claire of what she had been trying to accomplish with the castle in Wick. She suppressed a sigh.

Claire sat with her hands clasped lightly in her lap. She made no move to pick up one of the many magazines that were piled neatly on the coffee table (definitely Georgian by the look of it) next to a cluster of hothouse peonies in a black-and-white creamware vase (Creil, Claire noted). She tilted her head slightly and resisted the temptation to lift up the pottery and check the maker's mark on the bottom.

"It's Creil, but I'm sure you can tell." The deep voice was almost mannish. The large woman walked into the sitting room, and Claire quickly stood up. "I am Boppy Matthews."

"Claire Heyworth. It's such a pleasure to meet you. Thank you so much for taking the time to speak with me."

"Well, when Sarah called, I couldn't resist." Boppy smiled, but it was a little sad. "Her mother was one of my dearest friends, as I'm sure she told you."

"Yes, but thank you just the same."

"Let's go out to the back garden. It's one of the last sunny days for many weeks, I think." Boppy started to lead them down the hall, then stopped briefly to speak to the doorman, who it seemed was really an all-round everything-man. "James, please have Hilary bring us—" She turned to look at Claire again. "Do you prefer tea or coffee?"

"Oh, coffee please. If it's not too much trouble."

"Two coffees, please, James." The man nodded and walked quietly up the stairs to the upper floor.

The two women walked in silence toward the back of the house. The hallway was lined with photographs of different projects, some of them yellowed with age and looking a bit dated, but the styles were enduring. Claire was tempted to slow down and take a closer look. The hall ended at a matching pair of tall, glass-paned Victorian doors like the ones at the front of the townhouse. Boppy pushed open the right-hand door and held it for Claire. A set of narrow, black wrought-iron stairs led down the side of a tiny, perfect secret garden.

Claire gasped with pleasure. "What a lovely spot."

"Thank you," Boppy said. "I love it. It was my husband's gift to me. I am terrible with growing, living things." She looked momentarily perplexed, like it might have been a more meaningful statement than she had initially intended, then she shrugged her shoulders and smiled at Claire. "It's funny how statements like that seem so ominous as we get older. Have you noticed that?" Boppy gestured to two large wicker chairs with chintz cushions and waited for Claire to sit first.

Claire sighed, deciding she was just going to talk to this woman and hope that would suffice for an interview. When she thought of it as a proper interview, she got too nervous to speak normally. "I know exactly what you mean. Lately, I feel like everyone is being particularly careful about everything they say to me. It's tiresome."

Boppy laughed a full-blown, deep, throaty laugh. "Oh, you are so right."

They both looked up when a pretty woman in her twenties came down the stairs with a silver, oval-shaped tray holding two mugs of coffee and a small Limoges plate of madeleines.

"Thank you, Hilary."

"You're welcome." The assistant clasped her hands in front of her. "Do you need anything else?"

"No, I think we're all set. Please come back in thirty minutes, will you?"

"Of course." Hilary nodded.

"Oh, forgive me. Hilary Rattner, this is Claire…Heyworth."

"Nice to meet you, Hilary," Claire said.

"Oh, so nice to meet you," Hilary beamed.

"Thirty minutes, Hilary," Boppy said, in a more impatient voice.

Hilary's face went back to a professional mask. She nodded, and quickly left the garden.

Claire reached for one of the coffee cups and tried not to be a part of whatever little scuffle she had just witnessed.

"They're all gaga over your brothers," Boppy said.

Claire almost choked on her coffee. "Excuse me?"

Boppy smiled. "You must know Max and Devon are the stuff of dreams here in the beating hearts of New York City's pretty young things."

"I guess I just think of them as my annoying younger brothers."

"Good. That answers my first question. I don't have a lot of time for that nonsense. I know it appears that we're all lounging around here, but it's not at all the case. I mean—" Boppy took a sip of her coffee and looked up at the back of the townhouse, then continued. "I have obviously tried to create a feeling of ease and luxury for when my clients come to meetings here, but the real work is happening up on the second and third floors, where my nine assistants are fighting with fabric wholesalers, Turkish carpet manufacturers, a terribly ill truck driver in Palm Beach, an angry client in Santa Monica, and seventeen million other things that require immediate attention."

Claire nodded again. "I can understand that."

"What? The facade?"

"Well…" Claire said, holding her mug in both hands. The October sun was bright, but the air was cool, and she had always suffered from freezing fingers. "I didn't think of it as a facade when I did it. I don't know if Sarah told you about my place in Scotland?"

"Yes, a bit. I know it of course, from the National Register, but I've never been."

Claire smiled. "It's really an incredible place." Her face clouded. "I mean, I'm not saying I made it incredible. That probably sounded horribly arrogant—"

Boppy reached across the space between them, holding up one hand, but not touching Claire. "Relax. Tell me about Wick Castle."

"Oh, okay." Claire took a deep breath and tried to relax. She liked this woman already and she wanted to impress her. But she got the feeling that if she actually made an effort to impress her, that would very much *not* impress her. "So, when we moved there twenty years ago…" Claire shook her head. She didn't even feel the press of tears anymore, just the press of time…of all that time. "Sorry, let me begin again. It's all very new to me, speaking so boldly about myself. It feels very odd."

"I'm very interested. I'm asking. Please go on."

"Okay, when we moved there twenty years ago, I simply fell in love with the place. It had been so neglected. So unloved. Does that make any sense?"

"Of course, it's exactly how I felt about my place in the country. Why didn't anyone see what a diamond it was? I loved that moment. I think that's also when I fell fully in love with my husband. Because I saw he felt the same way." Claire suspected that Boppy had initially mentioned her husband in an offhand way, but she was now looking more carefully to see how Claire responded to talk of husbands in general. The last thing Boppy Matthews needed was some watering pot of a divorcée junking up the place.

Claire sat up straighter. "Funny. I might have taken a page from your book. Because my husband's utter lack of interest in the renovation and preservation of his ancestral home should have sounded all sorts of alarms." Claire waved her hand. "But that's neither here nor there. In fact, his disinterest really gave me free rein. It was my money, well, again, another story for another time, but I had the resources at the time to really…" Claire paused, trying to think of the right way to say it, how much it had meant to her. "To really bring it back to life. I felt like the buildings and the gardens were on the brink of death, and for once in my young life, I could actually do something about all the hopelessness. Maybe something that didn't matter as much as feeding the hungry or teaching a child to read, but maybe caring for a physical place did have a meaningful…" Claire trailed off, noticing that Boppy looked almost angry. "I'm sorry. I was yammering."

"No! No, you were saying exactly what I feel. I don't listen to my detractors, not now at least. After forty years of doing what I do, I think I'm finally confident enough not to care. I've seen enough people happy with my work—and maybe even happier in their lives from something that I've done, to make their lives more beautiful or comfortable—but it still rankles, doesn't it? That little naysaying voice—usually our own—about the absurdity of our lives? Unless you are, oh, I don't know, curing cancer, I guess, I think everyone must have those moments of wondering…what's the point?"

They both took a quiet sip of coffee.

Boppy spoke first. "When Sarah's mother died, that was really the final turning point for me. I had been so concerned with what other people thought of me and my work—I mean, let's face it, in this business, as in most businesses, *it matters*. But Elizabeth James was so strong, so clever, so beautiful, so *everything*, really."

Claire smiled. "Sarah hardly ever talks about her. It's lovely to hear."

"I think it must be horrendous for Sarah. Her father pretty much shut down after he lost her. And the second wife is abominable. I mean, that's probably too harsh. Let's just say she's not my cup of tea. Anyway…" Boppy shook her head. "All of that is simply to say, when I lost my best friend, who really was not just my best friend, but one of the best *people* I've ever known, I reached this place of not caring. In a good way, of simply putting myself out there and saying: *This is me. Take it or leave it.*"

"I like the sound of that," Claire said.

"The only catch is that some people will leave it. You have to be prepared for that. Just not focused on it."

"I guess I am nearing that place. Trying to figure out what it is I am going to do and just doing it."

"Yes, which brings us to the supposed purpose of this meeting. What are you aiming to do?" Boppy asked.

"Well, anything, really. I am so willing. With two of the most accomplished sisters-in-law on earth, I feel a bit of an underachiever." Claire smiled. "But I do have something to offer. I think. Maybe…" Her voice trailed off.

"Confidence not being one of them, I see." Boppy chided, but it was supportive somehow, as if that was something she could remedy.

"Alas, not quite yet. I'm a bit off kilter." Claire smiled again. "But I'm steady, I promise. I am, according to my family, damnably reliable. And so eager. I could sort fabrics, answer the phone, do paperwork. I am very meticulous and detail oriented. I pursue workmen and craftspeople rather like a terrier pursues a rat. And I'm a terrible perfectionist, which Sarah thought was somehow marketable. So she suggested I mention it."

Boppy was the one smiling this time. "Okay. Let me think about the best way to use you. I notice you're not introducing yourself as the Marchioness of Wick. How does that stand? Are you going to be called away to speak to men in wigs about the sordid details of your marriage, or are you divorced?"

Claire was falling in love with this woman. She was smart and confident and demanding and strong. Her mother had been all those things, but there had been a lack of joy about the Duchess of Northrop, as if bringing up Claire had been akin to training a prized show animal, rather than raising a daughter. Boppy seemed like she might work Claire hard, but might also be interested in being along for the ride.

"I am legally separated. It's just a matter of time until it's official. The castle has been shut down, except for the barest bones of the public areas, and I've called upon my brother to provide the necessary funds to keep the heat and water running."

"I'm surprised he hasn't offered to do more."

"Oh," Claire laughed. "Of course, they both offered to buy the whole thing and give it to me. But I couldn't have that. I think everything will be sorted in the end. My husband—soon-to-be former husband—was a rascal and terrible businessman, but I don't think he was really cretinous. More vain and careless."

Boppy nodded. "Go on."

"Once all of his investors finish pressing charges and everyone gets their money back—which could take years, of course—I think the place will come to me. The property's not entailed, and the marquisate is finished anyway. The title will die with my husband. Unless he remarries, I suppose." Claire looked at the ivy-covered brick wall across from where she was sitting, as if the thought hadn't really occurred to her.

"Anything's possible." Boppy raised an eyebrow.

Claire took a deep breath. "You know, I'm not sure it would be the worst thing that ever happened."

"Good. Okay, why don't you come upstairs and I'll introduce you to everyone? I think I'm going to have to come up with a special title for you. *Intern* sounds odd." The older woman put her coffee mug back onto the silver tray, then looked at Claire.

"Are you offering me a job?" Claire asked, stunned.

"Of course I'm offering you a job."

"A paid job?"

Boppy laughed again. "Yes, Claire. A *paid* job. I can't offer you a huge salary. There are too many others who've put in their time and worked here for years. It would be bad for morale if I paid you too much. And that sort of thing tends to get around. If you're willing to forego a benefits package, I can pay you as a consultant—" Boppy snapped her fingers. "Perfect. That will be your title. Claire Heyworth, Project Consultant. What do you think?"

Claire had stood up as soon as Boppy had, so they were facing each other in the crisp autumn sunshine. "I think I might faint."

Boppy pursed her lips. "Well, don't."

"Okay." Claire smiled. "Thank you."

Boppy turned toward the metal stairs. "I think we'll be thanking each other. There are a few clients in particular that I can already think of who will thrill to the fact that I have a peeress on staff."

Claire cringed. She despised the idea of being marketed as the resident aristocrat. "Ms. Matthews—"

"Boppy. It's a ridiculous name, but everyone calls me Boppy. Including you."

They were standing in the quiet front hall by that point.

"Boppy." Claire looked at the floor, then up at her new boss. Her first boss. "I was rather hoping not to put too much emphasis on my…"

"On your bloodline?"

"Well, I guess you could call it that. Yes."

"Look here, Claire." She gestured around the hall. "It's just a facade, remember? All the work takes place up here." Boppy pointed at her temple. "Let people think what they want, and you just be you. Leave the rest to me. Please."

"Okay." Claire swallowed.

"Okay." Boppy said with boundless confidence and then led the way up to the offices on the top two floors.

From the moment they reached the second floor and Boppy began showing her around, Claire felt like she was simultaneously drowning and taking her first proper gasp of air. She nodded and smiled and shook hands with the other people who worked for Matthews Interiors. There was a receptionist who sat at an immaculate, petite desk, with a sliver of a laptop and a telephone and nothing else. Not a scrap of paper.

"I like to keep it clean…at least at first glance. You'll see how it gets progressively more unwieldy the farther we get."

Claire nodded, terrified at the idea of sitting at a desk without a mug full of her favorite blue pens and several perfectly sharpened pencils and a black notebook with a red spine.

The second floor had been gutted to create an opened-up communal work area. Eight desks lined the walls, four on each side. Luckily, there was more evidence of old-fashioned work methods. One man even had a yellow pad.

Boppy did a cursory introduction, too quick for Claire to retain everyone's full name, but she repeated their first names three times over as she had always done since her mother had first trained her for the life of a peeress or—more to be hoped for—the wife of a peer.

Claire must have sighed aloud because Boppy turned to look at her over her shoulder. "Oh, don't worry. I won't expect you to remember all their names."

"Ned, Emily, William, Kim, Allison, Skylar, Henrietta, Marni."

Boppy turned around to face her full on. "Nicely done."

"Old habits die hard. My mother was a strict taskmistress when it came to introductions."

The older woman continued up the next flight of stairs to the top floor of the townhouse and paused at the upper landing. "I can imagine it wouldn't do to forget the ambassador's wife's name."

"Exactly. Though, I'm beginning to realize it might be just as egregious to forget Allison, Skylar, Henrietta, and Marni if you expect to get your projects done on time."

Chapter 5

Boppy rested the palm of her left hand on the brightly polished mahogany bannister. "I have just the project I want you to work on. And there's a dishy ex-husband."

Claire's face clouded. "Oh, I don't think I'm in the market for dishy just now. Maybe ever."

"Oh, that's just ridiculous. I didn't meet my husband until I was forty. What are you, thirty-five?" Boppy was walking again.

"You're too kind. I'm going to be forty in a little over a year."

"Well, for god's sake, don't say it like that! If anyone asks, you're *just* thirty-eight. Free at last and all that." She turned into a bright open studio space. Four large countertops were covered with fabric samples, carpet samples, paint samples, wallpaper samples, all being mixed and matched and pondered over by four designers. Two were already standing, and they stopped what they were doing to look at Boppy when she entered the room. The other two were sitting on tall work stools. One of them looked up from a piece of fabric; the other remained rapt in what she was doing.

"Up, everyone. I'd like you to meet our new consultant, Claire Heyworth. I haven't figured out exactly what she'll be doing for me, so for a start, I'm going to throw her at everyone who's been giving me a royal pain." She smiled and turned to Claire. "No pun, darling." She patted Claire's upper arm. "This is Simon Connolly, Edwina Sneed, Celine Delaney, and Milt Rubenstein."

One of the women looked skeptical and set down the piece of

fabric she'd been handling, then walked to where Claire stood. "I'm Celine. Nice to meet you. Good luck." There was a hint of malice, or maybe exhaustion, but whatever it was, it wasn't a hug. Edwina, Simon, and Milt introduced themselves in turn.

"So who should we sic on her first?" Boppy asked, as if Claire weren't even in the room.

All four of them spoke in unison: "Pinckney."

They all started laughing. Claire was momentarily terrified. *How bad could this client be?*

"That's exactly what I thought." Boppy smiled.

"Dead in the water," Edwina said as she returned to her worktable.

"Totally unfinishable," Simon concurred.

"Come into my office and I'll fill you in." Boppy turned back to the hall and then into a lovely room that overlooked the garden where they'd had their coffee earlier. "Have a seat."

Boppy looked at her computer for a second then picked up her desk phone. "Please tell Mrs. Hamilton I'll see her at the Colony at one o'clock Thursday. Confirm my Friday three o'clock with Mrs. McClintock and let Alice Pinckney know that my new top British consultant, Lady Claire Heyworth, will meet her in Litchfield for the next monthly visit." She hung up the phone without a good-bye and moved around her office while she spoke. "So, I'm just going to assume that you are pretty much willing to work twenty-four hours a day, seven days a week for the foreseeable future."

"Yes, I am." Claire didn't hesitate.

"Good. I need you to go to Connecticut for the day a week from Saturday. It's a divorce situation, always a bit tricky, but it's really been the wife's design project all along. Everything's in her name. Alice Pinckney. That's who you'll be meeting with. The husband never really took much of an interest, until recently. I mean, I've met him, of course." Boppy did a pantomime of fanning herself. "I can tell you, if I were Alice, I would not be throwing that one back in the water anytime soon."

Claire smiled and left it at that.

"They started the project about a year ago. I think Alice thought repairing a house might help repair their marriage—"

Claire was taking notes with a small silver pen on the tiny notepad she always kept in her purse and a little scoff must have escaped her lips. "Oh! I'm sorry. I didn't mean to laugh."

"Of course, it's ludicrous. It's like people who think maybe that elusive third child is really going to keep the marriage together... not!" Both women smiled, then Boppy continued. "Anyway, Alice is contractually obligated to finish the job, but neither one of us is too happy about it. I've abandoned a few projects in the past, and it's always a disaster. My name is attached to it, and then it comes off half-baked. On the other hand, I think they're eager to sell the property and split the proceeds and move on. I don't blame them. But they can never agree on anything or focus on the project at all, so it has dragged out terribly."

"How can I help?" Claire asked.

"The Saturday after next is our scheduled site visit. I'd love for you to familiarize yourself with the history of the project, work on laying out a tight schedule to wrap it up within the next three months, and then go play peacemaker. Maybe encourage Alice to be a little more...amenable...to some of her ex-husband's financial concerns. I think you have that quality about you. You put people at ease."

"Me?" Claire almost snorted. "I think everyone in my family walks on eggshells around me."

"Oh, family doesn't count." Boppy laughed, almost a short bark. "My sister hates me one day and cries on my shoulder the next— that's probably why she hates me the other days, come to think of it. Anyway…" Boppy's attention was being drawn away again by something that popped up on her screen. "Go tell Henrietta to get you a corporate credit card and to show you where to sit and then you can get yourself situated and familiarize yourself…" Her voice was trailing off as her attention returned fully to her computer screen and she sat slowly. "Off you go."

Off to where? Claire wondered to herself. She got up quickly and put her pen and pad back into her purse. She didn't want to interrupt Boppy's new train of thought, but felt compelled to thank her nonetheless. Claire compromised and whispered, "Thank you so much" as she turned and ducked out of the office. Before she shut the door behind her, she heard Boppy on the phone making plans to fly to Houston the next day to personally oversee the third repainting of a top client's dining room ceiling.

Claire took a deep breath, smoothed her palms down her navy blue skirt, and almost burst into tears of joy. She had a job! Twenty-four-seven? She'd work thirty-six-seven if such a thing were possible. She walked down the flight of stairs and reintroduced herself to Henrietta, relaying the information about the corporate credit card and the client in Litchfield.

"Oh, thank God. None of us can deal with Alice anymore. You'll be perfect to wrap that situation up once and for all."

Henrietta showed Claire back to the main entrance level. Halfway between the formal waiting room and the back garden, there was one more room with four desks in it. One was vacant.

"It's not very glamorous, I'm afraid."

Hilary, the young woman who had carried out the tray of coffee to the garden, turned from one of the four desks. "Oh, hi!"

"Hi," Claire said, reaching out to shake hands. "Looks like I work here…"

"Welcome! I'm so glad."

Claire couldn't quite reckon that she'd actually been hired, but she smiled at Hilary all the same, happy someone was happy to have her.

Henrietta said, "I'll get the credit card set up and delivered to you in the next day or two. Hilary, I have to hop. Will you show Claire the rest?"

"Sure. No problem."

"Bye, Claire. Good luck…you're gonna need it!" Again with the backhanded well-wishing. Claire wanted to chalk it up to her own nervousness, but it was obvious that some of the people who worked here were bitter or just worn out. She had a hard time imagining ever being anything but insanely grateful for the chance to do what she basically did anyway, or had done for the past twenty years, but to have someone pay her instead of the other way round.

Hilary introduced her to Erin, who handled human resources and payroll, and then to a rather severe-looking woman with a strong Brooklyn accent. She was a beautiful brunette, with an appealing toughness about her.

"I'm Roberta, the resident bully."

Claire wasn't sure how to respond.

Then Roberta laughed and gave Claire a little shove on the upper arm. "I'm the one who yells at all the deliverymen and painters and manufacturers who try to tell us they're running late or things have slipped through the cracks. I'm the buck…everything stops here." She used her thumb to point at her chest.

Claire smiled. She liked Roberta already.

The room still had the beautiful period details of the building intact: the tall reception floor ceilings, at least twelve feet high, the pale blue walls and bright white moldings, the hardwood floors. Into each corner, a triangular desk, made of practical, no-nonsense white Formica, had been built.

Hilary pointed to the far corner. "Seniority, I'm afraid. You get one of the desks that faces away from the window."

"Oh, I don't mind at all. I'm so excited."

The other three women looked at her like she was a little bit off.

"I mean," she hesitated, wondering if she would be overstepping some unspoken rule by confiding too much. Three faces waited for her to finish. "You might as well know. This is my first job."

"Your first job in New York or in the design business?" Hilary asked.

"No..."

Roberta had taken a sip of coffee and nearly snorted it through her nose. She sputtered, "You mean...this is your first job, *ever*?"

Claire blushed. "Yes."

"That is awesome!" Erin finally chimed in from the far corner. She had just finished with a spreadsheet and had closed out the screen, swiveling to face Claire full on. "You must be so excited."

"I really am. Thanks." Claire turned to the corner desk and trailed her hand along the white surface, pulled the chair out, and sat. "Wow."

The other three laughed, and Roberta and Erin turned back to their work. Hilary brought her chair over to sit next to Claire, then spent the next hour telling her passwords, how to enter orders into the system, how to access Boppy's schedule. She was given a corporate email address, added to email distribution lists, and shown myriad other details.

"That's probably enough for now. I could use some help with inputting all these orders. Why don't we start there, okay?" Hilary asked.

"Sure."

Hilary handed her a sheaf of yellow invoices. "Just be careful, because we have some bulk fabric orders that have to be billed to separate clients. I'm right here if you have any questions."

Claire began carefully, terrified that she was going to make an error. After an hour or so, her stomach growled, and she looked at her wristwatch to see it was almost two o'clock.

"Hilary, may I step out for lunch?"

"Of course, anytime. You don't need to ask permission. There's a good soup and sandwich place right around the corner on Third Avenue."

"Thanks. Do you want anything?"

"Sure. If you don't mind, I'd love a large latte…if it's not too much trouble."

"Of course not."

Claire walked out into the sunny, brisk air and had to repress the urge to jump up and down and squeal like a little girl. Instead, she reached into her purse and got her cell phone. She clicked on the preset for Bronte's New York cell phone number.

"Well?" Bronte answered without preamble. "Why haven't you called me until now? I was going nuts!"

"I got the job, Bron!"

"Oh my god! I think I might cry! I am so eff-ing happy for you! Did she just put you to work that very second?"

"Pretty much. I'll tell you everything tonight. I just ran out to grab a sandwich and then I'm going back to finish inputting some invoices."

"Listen to you! Already invoicing clients!"

"And I get to go out to Litchfield, Connecticut, next Saturday to meet with a client. It's just all too exciting, Bron. I can't even begin to thank you."

"I didn't do anything, silly. You did. I'll talk to you later. Huge congratulations again! Yay!"

And then Claire heard the shuffle of Bronte babbling with Wolf, the eager toddler reclaiming her attention as the phone went dead.

The next ten days flew by in a whirl of learning as much as she could without her head exploding. She'd been especially looking forward to her day-trip out to Connecticut to meet with her first real client. Unfortunately, it was hard to concentrate when every time she opened the Pinckney file, her heart began to race frantically. *It was a silly coincidence, probably nothing*, she kept telling herself. *Probably nothing.*

As she'd been working on the file, Claire had come across digital copies of some canceled checks from Alice Pinckney's joint checking account with her husband from before they got divorced. Actually, the first time she saw the printed names at the top of the check, her heart didn't race frantically at all. It simply stopped.

Alice Pinckney's husband (*her ex-husband!* Claire's—apparently teenaged—inner self shouted) was Benjamin Hayek. *The Ben Hayek!* her shrieking adolescent inner self added.

Chapter 6

AFTER IT RESUMED beating, Claire's heart didn't really recover. She stared at his name right there on her computer screen with the cursor flashing—*just a name*, she reminded herself—but her heart pounded like one of those Japanese war drums. The scanned check looked innocuous enough, with its grainy bits here and there and a man's firm signature slashed across the bottom right. *What were the chances?* she'd argued with herself. It couldn't possibly be the *same* Ben from all those years ago. And even if it was, she was meeting with Alice and she needed to stay focused on doing well at her job rather than mooning over some long-lost blip on her romantic radar. Well, she'd been a blip to *him*, probably.

She'd held off for a couple of days, then finally gave in to her curiosity and Googled Alice Pinckney and Benjamin Hayek. Sure enough. The *New York Times* wedding section showed the happy couple. Well, at least they'd *appeared* happy ten years ago.

Just then, Hilary walked behind Claire's chair and caught her gawking.

"Ah, Pinckney's ex-husband. Quite something, isn't he?"

Claire clicked on the red dot to close out the web page and swung her chair around. "Nice enough, I suppose."

"Are you blushing?"

"What?" Claire's hands flew to her cheeks. "No. Of course not." She turned her chair back around. "Just preparing for my big client meeting this Saturday."

"Mm-hmm," Hilary agreed skeptically. "Preparation is very important, Claire."

By the time Saturday morning rolled around, Claire had probably overprepared, making list after list of what needed to be done to wrap up the project. She was a little worried that Alice Pinckney would hate all of her nit-picking suggestions, and she didn't even allow herself to entertain the possibility that Ben would show up at the site visit for some unexpected reason. Claire wasn't sure she would be able to function properly if he was there, so she had to keep reminding herself he was *not* going to be there and—even in the very very *very* unlikely event he did come—she was *not* a teenager on a beach in France.

Despite all that, there was something about her first real on-the-job adventure that made Claire unaccountably fearless. She woke up at 6 a.m., showered, and changed into trim blue jeans and a crisp white shirt that she starched and ironed to perfection. She wanted to feel put-together; she wanted to come off as reliable.

Just before she left, she contemplated whether to borrow Bronte's disgustingly expensive Brunello Cucinelli shearling jacket. Claire pawed it longingly, then muttered *what the hell* and pulled it out of the closet, taking a moment to savor the exquisite quality and texture.

She allowed plenty of time to navigate her way out of the city and on into the countryside, especially since she was driving into unfamiliar territory on the wrong side of the road. As she pulled into the circular driveway, she checked the time and saw she was a few minutes early, so she decided to wait in the car. Right at the top of the hour, as she looked out the steamed up windows, she saw someone jog past and gesture toward the front door.

Someone tall and wet and handsome and dark and someone definitely *not* Alice Pinckney.

Claire felt her insides turn to jelly.

It wasn't Ben's turn to deal with the site visit, but Alice had rightly assumed he didn't have anything better to do. He was playing guitar in the Village Sunday night, but other than that, he wasn't on call at the clinic and he didn't have any plans. So Ben had agreed to meet with some designer from Matthews Interiors at the house out in Litchfield, while Alice went out of town on business.

He'd driven out late the night before, feeling his boredom and irritability slip away as the city receded farther and farther in his rearview mirror. The whole second-house idea had been Alice's initially, but lately, Ben had really started to cotton to it. It felt good and right to be building something other than his retirement account. Though he couldn't understand why Alice felt compelled to hire one of the most expensive interior designers in the world. The endless envelopes filled with fabric samples and paint chips had driven him mad. He told Alice she could do whatever she wanted. Until the divorce.

Then it turned into an investment protection situation, as far as Ben was concerned. He wasn't going to approve a four-thousand-dollar antique French chandelier for the front hall if they were just going to sell the place as soon as it was done. For the past six months, it had been stalemate after stalemate. Pretty soon, one of them was going to torch the place just to be done with it.

He kept flipping back and forth between wanting to keep it—to put his whole heart into it, maybe even buy Alice out—or to walk away and never look back.

Saturday morning, Ben woke up at six, as he always did. He read for a few hours then decided to go for a run. He threw on shorts and a stretched-out, gray college T-shirt, tied on a pair of his favorite old sneakers, and headed into the brisk autumn morning. His muscles were stiff sometimes, but he'd never let himself get out of shape. When he was younger—like that summer in France all those years ago—he had loved the exhilaration of physical exercise. Later, living in the city and grinding through the early years of building his private practice, exercise had become a sort of antidote, a way to shut down or tune out. Lately, running in Connecticut had begun to feel like that old elation—just energizing and empowering for its own sake—not something to scrape away layers of tension and anxiety.

By the time the light rain started, it felt good to have the cooling sensation against his heated muscles. He probably should have turned back if he was going to be at home in time for the designer—whomever Boppy tried to foist upon them this time—but they all had a key to the house, so it wouldn't be the end of the world if he was a little late. He ran up the last section of road and saw the small Zipcar in the circular driveway. The driver, a blond woman whose face was obscured by the foggy windows, seemed to be looking at her paperwork in the front seat of the car. He gave her a vague wave, then pointed a single finger to indicate he'd be at the front door in a minute.

He slowed to a quick walk and entered the mudroom through the side door. The place was in such a state. The walls were plastered, but so many paint samples had been applied in so many areas that it looked like a horrible version of the Partridge Family bus.

The kitchen was finished—finally—and Ben clicked on the electric kettle as he passed through, suspecting both of them would want a cup of something hot after the rain. He grabbed a small towel from the laundry room and began roughly drying his short hair while he walked to the front hall. Ben's face was still half covered as he pulled open the heavy, original mahogany door.

He mumbled, "Come on in" through the white terry cloth.

"Um, hello. I was supposed to be meeting with Ms. Alice Pinckney. Do I have the right house?"

The lilting British accent with its cool reserve did something strange and slashing to Ben's gut. His heart skidded to a halt and he remembered all the times he had dreamt of that voice. Or one so much like it. A part of him wanted to stand there with the idiotic towel covering his face forever, so he could prolong the momentary fantasy that it was Claire's voice. That it was really Claire Heyworth standing on his rainy unfinished porch in Litchfield, Connecticut.

Instead, he stopped drying his hair and slowly lowered the towel to his neck, fisting the ends of the material into each hand, tensing his upper arms. He stared at the most beautiful face he'd never been able to forget. During the intervening years, he'd convinced himself that no one could have been that beautiful, as he'd tried to erase the memory of her and those wonderful months.

He'd never succeeded.

"Oh my," she whispered.

Oh, Jesus. She was real. "Claire?"

She laughed and turned all professional-like. The stunning face was still there, but as a sort of pale mask of the real thing. "Oh, what a small world. So you're the oral surgeon husband?"

Ben stood back from the door and assumed a similarly casual posture. "Come on in. It's been a long time. Yes, I'm the dentist... ex-husband."

Claire stumbled on the heel of one of her high boots as she crossed the front hall. She'd been unbuttoning her jacket and not paying attention to where she was going. He reached out to steady her. Craft paper covered all of the hardwood floors, one of the only original features he and Alice had agreed to preserve, but they still hadn't been able to agree on how to refinish it. He sighed at the ongoing battle.

Claire must have thought the sigh was for her clumsiness. "Sorry. I'm not used to these heels," she said, sounding a little defensive.

She looked perfectly gorgeous in those heels, so Ben wasn't quite sure why she wasn't used to them. Long (long!) strong legs in fitted blue jeans, a cropped, gray woolen jacket, and all that silky blond hair tied up in a careless bundle. She was taking off her jacket, and Ben had the absurd flash (ever hopeful?) that she was there to surprise him after all these years with a striptease.

"Excuse me?" She was handing him the jacket with one hand as she held her very practical, navy blue leather attaché case in the other. "Would you mind hanging up my jacket for me?"

"Of course." He frowned, at himself mostly for being such a pervert, and then he took the jacket from her and was disappointed that their fingers didn't touch when she passed it to him. It grated that she seemed to be treating him like some sort of houseboy who was there to take her parcels. He reached toward one of the hooks on the back of the kitchen door to hang it up.

"Actually, it was obscenely expensive, if you wouldn't mind putting it on a hanger?"

"Sure. No problem. Let me put it in the laundry room to make sure it dries properly." Ben made a mental note to look into why the precious daughter-of-the-duke was mindful of expense, no matter how obscene. She'd been too good for him then and apparently she was still too good for him now. Her white shirt looked like it had been pressed by her valet, and her hair looked like it had been tousled that morning by her lover. He scowled as he hung up the expensive shearling jacket on one of the hangers on the makeshift pole over the washing machine—the only place to hang anything on the disorganized first floor.

"Okay," Ben said when he returned to the front hall.

"Okay!" Claire agreed. "Is there somewhere we can sit down and go over some of these decisions?"

He stared at her, maybe for a few seconds too long, but he

couldn't help it. Ben took off the stupid towel around his neck that probably made him look like a wannabe Olympian and tossed it on the floor leading back toward the laundry room. *Was she really going to act like they were just random acquaintances?* Maybe to her mind, that's all they ever were.

He tried to slap on a professional face. "Sure. There's a worktable in the supposed living room that the contractor uses during the week. I'm sure Boppy told you what's been going on around here… with all the back and forth."

He watched as Claire pulled her lips between her teeth and bit down, trying to prevent herself from saying what was on her mind—probably something pithy about foolish people and their foolish divorces.

He remembered that, the way she bit her lips to hold everything in. *Damn it.* She was the same woman he had tried—and failed—to seduce twenty years ago. *All that repression just waiting to… To nothing,* he reminded himself. She was a straight-up good girl. No repression waiting to be freed. No deep-seated desires waiting to be let loose. He exhaled slowly, trying to reconcile the reality of her ramrod posture with the panting, bent woman he'd imagined in his arms all those years ago.

She flushed.

"This way," Ben said, and turned back across the front hall to the chaotic mess that would one day be his living room.

Claire was an utter and complete wreck. All she had to fall back on was a lifetime of what amounted to behavioral conditioning. Her mother and husband had trained her well: the more nervous she became inside, the more appropriate and rigid she appeared. Intentionally or not, the Duchess of Northrop and Marquess of

Wick had raised smile-and-wave to an art form; Claire was a master.

And Ben was making her so incredibly nervous. He was so big and sweaty. And kind of breathing heavily from his run. And she couldn't think straight to save her life. He probably thought she was this ridiculous quivering thing. Which obviously didn't make him very sympathetic, because he seemed sort of angry. Or, if not angry, just irritated. Claire didn't know if she had done something specific to annoy him, or if that was just his default setting. Had he always been like that? Short with people? She didn't think so. At least, that's not how she remembered him.

Not that she thought about him all that often. Well, until recently. And maybe before. To be honest, ever since Sarah had pulled up that picture on the Internet, Claire had thought about Ben with an abstract frequency. She wasn't thinking, "Oh, I'd love to reconnect with Ben," precisely. But more of a general "Oh, I'd love to meet the grown-up version of Ben. Someone kind and attentive. Someone who likes me for no particular reason."

But then that just sounded pathetic, so she hived off that sort of thinking as soon as it started. It was so *unrealistic*.

Then, when she'd discovered he was divorced and living in New York—when he'd become *real* in her mind—she'd tried even harder not to think about him. Which had proved impossible. But at least she'd tried.

And obviously she'd been wise to do so, because the real-life version of the grown-up Ben was a bit of a disappointment. He was kind of mean.

What had happened to the man she'd fallen in…whatever-it-was…all those years ago? She was still reluctant to admit that she had actually fallen in *love* with him. How was such a thing even possible, after all? She'd only known him for several months, and they'd never even had sex. As her mother had pointed out all those years ago, one simply didn't fall in love in a matter of months. Claire set aside the realization that her widowed mother had recently done exactly that: she'd met Jack Parnell in Paris last winter and then proceeded to marry him six months later.

But apparently her mother's advice had been sound when Claire was a teenager.

Because this adult version of Ben was rather…grumpy, thought Claire, and he certainly wasn't anything like the man she'd been daydreaming about over the past few months since Sarah first lit the match of her imagination. Or this past week when she'd been doing quite a lot of her own flint-striking, thank you very much.

He gestured toward one of the two metal folding chairs— dented and splotched with various paint bits—that sat next to each other at the long white plastic folding table littered with blueprints.

"So," Claire began, opening Bronte's briefcase. The case seemed stupid now that she was here in Ben's house. Like Claire was pretending to be a professional. She was such a sham. She looked up. Even if he was grumpy, his arms in that sweaty, rain-damp T-shirt were particularly distracting. He was looking around the room, looking more irritated than ever. She pulled her gaze away from his biceps. "Right. So where would you like to begin?"

He smiled. And Claire's stomach dropped straight out of her. That smile changed every single thing. The irritation. The temper. Those disappeared. The wet T-shirt… She wished it would too. Her heart started to hammer wildly, and she straightened the pile of papers she'd withdrawn from the leather case, as if straightening them would straighten her pulse. She hadn't physically *wanted* someone in so many years; it was utterly bizarre. The push of adrenaline. The prickling along the nape of her neck. How foreign it felt, the most basic desire.

If that's even what it was. Maybe she was just nervous—her first job, her first meeting with a client—that sort of thing.

LIAR!

"Right," Claire continued. "Uh…how about we go through the final paint samples…" She opened that folder and started to go down the list, avoiding his intense stare. "Maybe that's one area in which your ex-wife doesn't want something else entirely."

Ben's smile widened. "Yes. She wanted something else entirely…" He paused and stared at Claire. It was unnerving, but she held her seat and refused to fidget. That much at least had been drummed into her by her mother with such frequency, she could sit perfectly still in the face of a firing squad if necessary. "Would you like some tea?" he asked after the long pause.

"Yes, please. That would be lovely."

He got up and left her sitting at the plastic table. Claire tried to settle her shoulders and release the tension in her neck. *Oh dear. They were alone in the house! So what?* Claire reminded herself. She was an almost-forty-year-old dowd. Whatever Boppy said about sticking to thirty-eight, Claire wasn't blind. She was middle aged. Full stop. Whereas Ben looked like he had stopped aging sometime around twenty-five. The skin around his eyes might have crinkled a bit when he gave her that killer grin, but other than that, his body…oh dear. He looked perfect. She looked down at her spreading thighs, then quickly crossed her legs and sat up straighter.

Ben returned a few minutes later wearing a dry, long-sleeved shirt and loose black exercise pants, carrying two mismatched mugs. He set one in front of Claire. "Cream and a hint of sugar, right?"

Now it wasn't just her stomach that was free-falling. Lower, out-of-use areas of her anatomy were beginning to tense and throb. From a silly cup of tea. A cup of tea that he remembered. Exactly. Precisely.

"Yes. Just so." Claire smiled up at him, but it was that thin meaningless smile that her mother had taught her to use at hospital ribbon cuttings. Ben's smile vanished, and he looked stormy. His brow creased and he shook his head.

"Okay. I get it. All business. Let's go then."

Claire wanted it to be all business. Didn't she? This was her first job. Ever.

But, oh, his smile was so divine. What just happened? Where did his smile go?

She was just being polite. Wasn't that the appropriate way to be? Or was she being too stiff?

Oh, dear. Why did he have to be so mercurial? She liked the remembering-the-cup-of-tea part. She liked the way his remembering made her skin tingle.

But not too much.

Oh, feck. She didn't know what she wanted.

"Yes, all business." She smiled, this time with more feeling, but even she knew the feeling was probably regret for what would never be. How could she possibly launch into some playful, romantic walk down memory lane when everything inside her felt so raw and confusing?

They spent the next two hours going over the paperwork. The endless paperwork. Claire was almost maniacally particular. He tried to wave his hand over a few order forms, mumbling, "Fine, fine, whatever you decide on the baseboards in the guest bathroom is fine."

"No, pay attention! It's the little details that will make all the difference!" She hadn't come all this way to have him fade out after a few hours. She wanted to show Boppy and everyone in the office that she could get results.

"What?" He was obviously ready to be finished. With the house. With the lingering attachment to his ex-wife that this renovation had become. And now he appeared to be adding her to his mental list of people who were not living up to his expectations. He almost growled. "Now, see here, Claire. I've had *enough*. I don't know what you're playing at but I'm the customer here. You're here to serve me, remember?"

She flushed horribly. "I— I'm so—"

"Oh, quit it. You know what I mean. I'm paying Boppy Matthews's stupid hourly fee to get you and your nest of vipers up here every few weeks so we can get this stupid job finished and put an end to this entire farce. If someone wanted to buy it as is, I'd sell it this instant." He looked so angry; she wasn't even sure he knew what he was saying. "Just put whatever baseboards in that bathroom that you would put in one of the gamekeepers' cottages at one of your castles and let's call it a day. Cheap and cheerful and all that. I'm done." He stood up abruptly, nearly kicking over the metal folding chair as he did.

Claire felt as though every word was a punch. He didn't respect her job. He didn't respect her past. He didn't respect anything about her. She refused to cry. It would be much easier to channel her shame—like a weak stream redirected with a few leaves and pebbles—right over to indignation. She stood up, leaving a stack of work orders for him to review, and slid her own papers neatly into the blue leather case. She smiled her thinnest, meanest smile. "Very well then. Good day."

She walked out of the cluttered living room with as much dignity as she could muster, which was pretty much, considering. She got to the car and put the key in the ignition, started it up, and felt the chill in the air.

"Damn." She'd left Bronte's jacket. Was it worth six weeks' pay to never speak to him again? If she hadn't seen the price tag, she might have left it and asked one of the other designers to retrieve it in a few weeks' time at the next site visit…or she could send an email to Ben asking him to bring it to New York when he returned. She could send a messenger over to his apartment building and get it back that way.

She slammed her palm against the steering wheel then rubbed her hands together. That actually hurt more in real life than it looked like it would when angry people in movies did it. Claire swore again then turned the car off, got out, and walked back up the wide steps to the beautiful wraparound porch. The wood was primed and repaired and the final coat of deck gray was set to go on next week. From the outside at least, the house was beginning to look finished.

She rang the bell reluctantly.

Ben opened the large door and said nothing.

"I forgot my jacket…my sister-in-law's jacket, actually…"

"You must have closets full of jackets, *Claire*. What's one more?"

She hated how he said her name like a little stab.

You are rich, Claire.

You think you're so great, Claire.

You are nothing to me, Claire.

Or at least that's how it sounded to her.

"May I have the jacket, please?" Her voice was so weak, damn him. She wanted to drive away then pull off to the side of the road and bawl her eyes out. Bronte would have known exactly how to turn this whole meeting into some sort of wild weekend of rekindled romance and no-strings-attached sexual escapades.

Claire felt like she was the walking, talking embodiment of Every String Attached. And she had no idea what a sexual escapade even entailed. Sure, she'd spent the past week and a half dreaming about the *idea* of Ben, but she'd never approached anything even remotely resembling an actual *fantasy*. Perhaps a swing. Fragonard's painting in the Wallace Collection sprang to mind.

"Say my name." Ben was staring down at her, his voice hard.

She was shorter than he was to begin with, but Claire was still on the porch and it was a few inches lower than the front hall, where he was standing. His words knocked the wind out of her.

"What?" She could barely speak. She wanted to cry or hit him or just bury her face in his hard, warm chest. It still felt like he was taunting her or trying to punish her, and she didn't understand why, and the tears were so close.

"Just say my name. I want to hear you say it."

Claire took a deep, fortifying breath. One syllable for a six-thousand-dollar jacket seemed like a pretty easy trade, but she wasn't sure she could do it. She bit her lips between her teeth in the only nervous habit her mother had never been able to fully drum out of her.

"Or just let me stare at your lips while you do that…" His voice was softer, but no less menacing. Maybe more so.

She unclenched her lips and could feel them throbbing as he stared at her mouth. Her heart lurched into a frantic gallop, a terrible mix of fear and something so hot and eager, she wasn't able to name it.

Air. Air. Air. Claire couldn't breathe properly. She might have to abandon the jacket. It had sounded like he wanted to look at her lips, but he looked so cross now, like he resented wanting to.

Claire's heart pounded harder as she worked up the courage to say the single word. "Ben."

Chapter 7

HE STARED AT her lips as she said the one syllable, then he looked into her eyes. Her pupils dilated, nearly filling the pale, pale gray of her irises. He watched her feel it—desire—finally. Decades too late. It soothed his ego to see her response, but he couldn't let it mean more than that. A physical charge, nothing more.

Claire's blood was so blue, Billie Holiday could have sung songs about it. Yes, she'd always appeared a bit formal, but at least Ben hadn't imagined everything from that summer. They *had* shared something real, and the look in her eyes made it impossible to deny. All those years ago, whenever he had kissed her neck or reached for her hand, she would whisper his name like that, so full of desire and almost a strange disbelief. A kind of quivering hesitance that made him feel like a god.

Now, all her quivering hesitance only served to infuriate him. As if *she* were intimidated by *him*. As if she hadn't spent her entire life among the world's elite.

He turned from the door without inviting her back in, got the jacket from the laundry room, and returned to the front door. She was like a statue. He suspected she hadn't moved a particle of air around her in the few seconds while he'd been gone.

"Here." He handed her the jacket.

She reached out to take it, and he pulled it quickly back; he didn't even know why. Maybe to make her look at him again. He couldn't stand the way she was ignoring him, looking anywhere but in his eyes, avoiding saying his name. Something vindictive twisted inside him. "On second thought—"

"Ben—"

"Oh. Good. You're getting the hang of it. I'm going to call Boppy and tell her you're just the thing."

She looked terrified, and Ben almost felt sorry for her, but decided not to. "Just the *person*," he amended, "to help me wrap up this project once and for all. Who knows? Maybe you'll want to buy it yourself when you're done... A little piece of America to add to your vast holdings."

She held her arm out, perfectly steady, waiting for him to put the jacket into her hand. He would figure out a way to bait her. This silly job seemed to matter to her for some reason. Not like she needed the money; maybe she'd decided she needed a little pet project to fill her royal days. Ben gave her the jacket.

Claire slid her right arm, then her left slowly into the sleeves. She pulled her hair out from beneath the collar, closing her eyes for a few seconds as she did it, as if her unruly blond hair was just one more annoyance. Ben wanted to pull her hair so hard and furiously. He wanted to show her...something.

He raked his hand through his own short hair instead.

She spoke softly. "I don't know if I'm the right person for this job after all."

He stared down at her. He knew it was despicable, but he liked her down there on the porch, a few inches below him.

"No, I disagree. I think you're the best person for the job," he said with narrowed eyes, sizing her up. "And it's my job, so I get to decide."

She licked her upper lip with the tip of her tongue, as if she had to do something rather than utter the condescending words that probably sprang to mind. "Very well." She started to turn toward the car, and if Ben hadn't known the extent of her inbred arrogance, he might have even mistaken the softening of her shoulders for a sign of defeat.

"Claire? Not even a kiss good-bye for an old friend?" He didn't know where all of this venom was coming from, but Ben thought he must have an entire arsenal of ill-conceived, thoughtless ideas tucked away in his brain somewhere. He wanted a taste, and he knew it was wrong and laced with spite, but he wanted it. And he hadn't wanted anything for so long, he felt almost entitled. She was made of ice. What difference did it make to her?

She turned slowly back to face him. "You can't be serious."

Ah, there she was. The haughty, confident ice princess.

"Oh. But I am. Just a peck. I vaguely remember you used to like kissing."

She blushed. She probably blushed like most people raised an eyebrow. *On demand*, he thought cruelly.

"And only kissing," he added, wanting to put a stop to any pleasure she might be getting, no matter how twisted. "It didn't mean anything to you then. Why should it mean anything now?"

She stared at him, raw, murderous rage flashing behind those ice eyes. Then she stiffened. "Why not? Show me what you got...Ben." She said his name with cold precision.

Ben let his hand come away from the doorjamb, where he'd been effectively blocking her entrance to the house. He reached around to her lower back, slipping his hand between the smooth cotton of her white blouse—warm from the skin beneath—and the curled shearling of the luxurious coat lining. Claire didn't gasp or respond, but she bent in a way that felt distantly familiar.

She leaned into him, and in that slight give, she took everything from him. Just like she had all those years ago—pulling him out of himself, out of control—lost to her false innocence.

He didn't care. He planted his lips on hers and took. She made the smallest whimpering sound, which he chose to construe as reluctant pleasure, and he began to have his way with her lips. He hadn't been lying when he'd said how she used to love kissing. They'd done it for hours. Under the plane trees outside St.-Remy. Along the canals near Dijon. They'd kissed for days. Eons. He would have kissed her forever if she'd have let him.

Ben released her, remembering that she would never let him. Not really. She always held something in reserve.

He stepped away abruptly to give himself the physical distance from her warm, soft body, before he fell back into that desperate minefield of adolescent thinking that had done so much damage to his heart twenty years ago. He would retreat first this time. He would call the shots.

"Good-bye, Claire." He shut the large door in her face.

He walked into the kitchen without turning back, unwilling to look at her through the glass panes on the upper half of the wide front door. Once he got into the kitchen, out of sight, he slid to the floor and leaned against the wall next to the cellar door. What the hell had come over him? He wasn't a mean person. Even Alice had cited his damnable kindness as part of the reason she could no longer stand to be married to him. Her exact words were, "You've become disgustingly accommodating."

He scrubbed his cheeks with the palms of his hands. Claire Heyworth made him want to pick a fight from the minute she looked up at him with those doe eyes. *False doe eyes*, he reminded himself. She had been momentarily surprised when his face appeared from beneath that towel, but she'd certainly recovered her duchess-in-training ways quickly enough. He thought for sure when he brought her a cup of tea, made just the way she'd always liked it, that she might have softened slightly.

"Ha," he said aloud to the empty room. She appeared as if the last thing in the world she wanted was to be reminded of their former intimacy, what she probably thought of—regretfully—as their brief meaningless dalliance, that summer two decades ago.

Why did it feel so fresh to him? The smell of the lavender in the hilltop towns in the Vaucluse, the dry air and the saw of the cicadas mixed with the sound of her laughter. How he'd lived to make her laugh. She'd been so reluctant to laugh that every time he'd succeeded, it was a sweet victory. How she would cover her mouth in modesty, and the first time he pulled her hand away so he could see the joy spread across her face.

"Fuck." It was as clear now in a rainy kitchen in northwestern Connecticut as it was under the French sun twenty years ago. It didn't help that he could still taste her on his lips. That sweet light scent of lemon and fresh air and…

"Fuck."

Ben stood up and decided to exhaust his body in an attempt to shut off his maudlin, pathetic mind. The stone wall at the far end of the backyard had been crumbling for the past hundred years. He decided that this particular cold, wet afternoon was the perfect time to remedy a century of slow decay.

Three hours later, his hands were scraped, his back was throbbing, his shoulders were numb, and he'd rebuilt about one linear foot of the wall. He walked down the sloping yard toward the back door, then stopped to turn and look at his accomplishment. It was pretty damned satisfying, that pathetic little architecture of rocks. Mostly because he had managed not to think of Claire Heyworth for three consecutive hours. Scotch would take care of erasing her from the remaining waking hours of the night.

Ben woke up Sunday morning with a headache and an urge to punch himself. What in the hell had he been thinking to treat Claire so abominably? He felt like a third grade boy who kicked the pretty girl right in the shin to let her know he liked her. He tried to envision some happy outcome, some scenario that would let him be friends with her or at least be able to be in the same room with her without wanting to whip her to the floor and crush her against him, beneath him.

The vision felt so real, and then he realized he had been dreaming of her moments before. The images flashed in his mind, the naked body he'd never seen all the way naked, but had imagined easily enough after all the hours of the two of them spread on beaches with her lithe, seventeen-year-old body stretched out next to him in nothing but a turquoise string bikini.

He closed his eyes and reached for his hard cock. He could picture her smiling at him, back when they were both young and free—or when he'd thought she was free. The wind along the Riviera whipping her hair around her face and the golden strands catching in her lips and her eyelashes. He increased the rhythm of his hand, remembering how he'd reached out to put a strand of her silky blond hair back behind her ear, and she'd kissed his palm instead, her eyes drifting shut at the pleasure of contact, as if she'd never been touched. He stroked himself harder, wanting those lips on him now. Wanting those lips against his skin, against his—

He groaned at the bittersweet release, breathing hard a few times, then letting his muscles relax. As his thoughts began to reassemble, Ben reminded himself that the blond, tender, loving, innocent girl on a rocky secluded cove in the Calanques was a figment of his imagination. He wasn't sure she had ever existed in the past, but he knew for certain she did not exist in the present. She'd been dead and buried for years, replaced by the cool husk of a woman who'd come into his house yesterday.

Chapter 8

"WHAT DO YOU mean it was *him*?" Sarah cried.

"Look, Sarah, if you're going to call me at eight in the morning on a Sunday after a long week at work, I'm bound to be muddled."

"What? You usually wake up at five every morning. I thought you would have been up for hours by now."

Claire rolled over and stared at the rainy city morning outside Bronte's window.

"Maybe it's the time change."

"You've been in the States for three weeks."

"Okay, fine. It was the best-worst day of my life."

Sarah laughed and then shushed Devon in the background when he tried to ask her a question. "Stop it," she whispered. "I'm talking to Claire."

"Sarah, just go be with Devon."

"Are you kidding? I want to hear every detail! I can't believe you haven't called me sooner."

"I'm so sorry. I always feel like I'm running late in the mornings, and then by the time I get home, it's too late to call you in London. Boppy is so amazing, Sarah. I'll never be able to thank you enough for introducing us."

"You don't think she's too much of a hard-ass? My father can't stand her. He always felt like she was looking down her nose at him."

"Well, I don't know about any of that. But I like her... confidence."

"Very diplomatic, Claire." Sarah laughed.

"Look, she's my boss. What can I say? I kind of adore her. She doesn't take anything from anyone."

"Wow. Listen to you, with a boss."

"Honestly, if I could work all seven days of the week, I would." As long as being insulted by Ben Hayek was no longer on the docket.

"Wait. But go back to the client yesterday. The line was crackling. Who was he?"

"It was *him*!" Claire whispered.

"Why are you whispering? You're alone!" Sarah laughed again, then gasped. "Wait! You mean the hot guy from your summer vacation before you married *Le Bâtard*?"

Claire smiled, loving her sister-in-law's easy dismissal of her rat of a husband. "Yes. The summer fling."

"Oh my. How awkward. What was his wife like?"

"Ex…wife," Claire said softly.

"Ex-wife—" Sarah sounded like she was choking on a sip of something. "How perfect—a man on the rebound—how divine."

"As you Americans like to say…not so much."

Sarah took another sip of whatever she was drinking to clear her throat, then continued. "Uh-oh. That bad?"

Claire tried to hold back the tears, but given the fact that she was alone in the small apartment and wouldn't have to deal with anyone actually seeing her horribly splotchy, tear-stained face, while still getting the sympathy she desperately craved, she began to bawl. "Oh. Sarah. It. Was. So. Awful."

"Oh, sweet Claire! Don't cry! I mean, cry your heart out! Was he just the worst? Hideous and jowly and rude? Some awful pushy jerk?"

Claire laughed as the tears flowed down her cheeks. She grabbed a few tissues from the bedside table and began to pat at her face.

"Even worse. He looked amazing. I mean, it's almost criminal that he should still look exactly like he did at nineteen and I look like this."

"Like what? You look like you did when you were seventeen. You don't have any wrinkles or freckles or gray hair. It's as if you were hermetically sealed up there in Wick."

"Oh, Sar. I'm like a ghost. I look around New York City and everyone is so *alive*. I feel like a shadow, kind of weaving my way invisibly down the sidewalks."

"Enough. That's just too depressing for words, and it's totally not true. Boppy wouldn't have hired a shadow!"

Claire laughed. "I guess you're right. At work, I'm starting to feel like I might have something to offer. I feel alive there. I have a desk and Boppy is so—"

"Stop. Enough about Boppy. She's great and all that, but back to Dr. Perfectly Preserved. Did you know you were going to meet him? Were you prepared?"

"Yes and no. The entire file is under the wife's name, Alice Pinckney. She's the only contact and everything is filed under her name. But I did see one of their canceled checks from when they were married. And it had his name on it…"

"And?"

"And I Googled him."

Sarah burst out laughing. "I love how you say *Google* like a normal person would say *rape*. So, go on."

"I just figured it was the wife's project and he wasn't supposed to be there, so I just put it out of my mind. I was just too stupid to even acknowledge the possibility that of course he might show up at some point—"

"Oh, stop it with the stupid self-insults. I forbid it. Go on—was he so excited to see you? He must have been gobsmacked!"

Claire felt it in her bones, how much she wished he had been happy to see her. How perfect that would have been. How impossible.

"He was gobsmacked all right. He looked like he wanted to smack me right in the gob."

"I just don't believe it. What were you wearing?"

It was Claire's turn to laugh. "Sarah. What does that possibly have to do with anything?"

"Oh, come on! If you were all icy and beautiful, he was probably totally intimidated. Like we all used to be around you."

Claire felt her heart begin to pound. "What in the world are you talking about?" she whispered.

"Oh, Claire. I guess I'm taking liberties or whatever, and Devon is rolling his eyes, but you must know how much you intimidate everyone with your perfect posture and your carefully chosen words, and I bet the handsome doctor was bowled over."

Setting aside the larger issue of Claire's external appearance of cool indifference being the polar opposite of her internal landscape of insecurity and doubt, she tried to imagine if such a thing were even possible. "I don't know, Sarah. He was so…big…and strong."

"Oh! How fabulous! He's all hunky? Tell me every detail."

Claire snuggled deeper into Bronte's down pillows and duvet and told Sarah the details as best she could, from their strained first moments to his bitter farewell. She didn't bother mentioning the kiss. What a travesty that had been.

There were a few seconds of transatlantic silence before Sarah declared, "He's still in love with you! It's so obvious. And you were so mean to him!"

"*I* was mean to *him*! Are you off your nut?"

"Well, you have your brother here to corroborate that I probably am—insane, that is—but seriously, how sweet was that of Ben to remember how you liked your tea—*exactly* the way you like it—and the way you described how he gave it to you with that sweet nod and how he was so obviously feeling like he was going out on a limb to let you know that he remembered after all these years, that he has been *thinking* about you *all these years* and then you say something typically…British…like *quite so* or *very well* and then he probably felt like a total jackass for pining for some cold…woman…who never gave him a second thought."

"Sarah. He was so angry—"

"I bet he was. Like kind of stormy and bossy?"

"Well, yes, I guess, but he was so grumpy—"

"Like he wanted you to stop talking about baseboards and brass hinges and look at him instead?"

Claire's heart began to pound again. It hadn't really stopped pounding since that kiss.

Claire stayed quiet.

"Did he touch you?" Sarah asked.

"Well, I mean, we were working on documents for a couple of hours and we were sitting next to each other—"

"Claire?"

"Oh, Sarah, you're terrible."

"See? That is exactly what I am talking about. You use these little deflections to avoid having a real conversation. Why do you do that?"

Claire thought she might start crying again. Why did Sarah make everything sound so obvious? For Claire, even the seemingly simple act of retrieving her jacket had been an emotional minefield of Bosnian proportions.

The seconds ticked by. Claire finally gave in. "He kissed me. Quite soundly."

Sarah actually squealed. For several long seconds. "I knew it! I knew it!"

Claire smiled into her pillow and allowed herself to contemplate the crazy possibility that Ben's irrational behavior was as much a reaction to his lingering feelings for her as her cool rigidity had been a defense against acknowledging the same about him.

"You have to call him! Right now! Catch him totally off guard," Sarah instructed. "Tell him how taken aback you were to finally see him after all these years and—did you tell him you are single?"

"Well, no. I think he thinks I am doing this as a little pastime or something. He was quite mean about it, now that you mention it."

"Of course, because he's trying to pretend that you're some mean, cold—" Sarah stopped short. "Hey, wait a minute. What ever happened that summer? How did it end?"

"Oh, you know. It was the end of summer. The invitations had already gone out for Freddy and my wedding in September—"

"Oh my gosh, this all happened a month before you got married?"

"It sounds tawdry when you say it like that. But yes. But no. We were just a couple of kids. It felt innocent somehow."

"I doubt it felt innocent to him."

Claire sighed. "Well, I was honest at least. On our last night, I told him I was engaged. I mean, I didn't tell him how soon I was going to be walking down the aisle, of course."

"Of course," Sarah said, her voice sounding dubious. "So you just said *have a nice life* and that was the end of it?"

Claire remembered those exact words. "Well, we both sort of acknowledged it was a one-off kind of thing."

"Really? Why does it feel so unresolved, then? What do you mean by *sort of acknowledged?*"

"Has anyone ever mentioned you missed a very promising career in the law?" Claire hedged.

Claire tried to put together the fragments of her memories, how her mother had called so early that last day and said she was in Nice and it was imperative for Claire to come meet her. According to her mother, there had been some unexpected royal to-do in Monaco and Claire needed to accompany her.

Claire had gone to look for Ben down the hall, in the small hotel in Antibes where they were all staying. His roommate was curled up with his girlfriend, still mostly asleep. Ben and Claire had never slept in the same room, but she'd kissed him good-night just before dawn and promised to say good-bye before she left.

"Where's Ben?" Claire asked quietly.

"He went for a run," Steve croaked. "Before he left, he said to tell you, 'Have a nice life.'"

Claire paled. "Oh. Okay. Well, I'm off then. Great meeting you and all that. Tell Ben I came to say good-bye, would you?"

"Sure, Princess. I'll tell him."

Claire narrowed her eyes at Steve, wondering for the hundredth time that summer why he had taken such a dislike to her. "Okay. Bye, Steve."

"Bye, Claire."

She pulled the door shut gently and went back to her room. Her friend Sally, with whom she'd supposedly been traveling, was packing up her bag, but paused to look at Claire.

"Was Ben there, sweetie?"

"No. Just that jerk Steve. I suppose it's my own fault."

"You should have told Ben you were already engaged, you mean? Bull. You had every right to have a little summer fling. And it's not like you slept with him or anything. You shouldn't even have told him you were engaged."

Claire sat down on her unmade bed with a heavy thump. "He was so angry last night, Sal. I couldn't quite account for it."

"You couldn't account for the fact that he'd fallen madly in love with you?" Sally was folding a T-shirt and putting it into her bag.

"That's preposterous. We only knew each other for a few months."

"You sound like your mother. It only takes a second or two to know you like someone. And only a few days—or even a few seconds more—to know you might love them. It's a spark and all that. Haven't you ever read anything about love at first sight? You and Ben were gaga over each other. Everyone saw it except you, Claire."

Claire wasn't going to cry. She stood and began packing methodically, ignoring the weight against her chest and the pressure behind her eyes that made her feel old and tired. Her life was supposed to be just beginning, so full of promise, and instead it felt...over.

Sarah's voice across the telephone line snapped Claire back to the present. "You never told him you were engaged to Freddy? That whole summer? Until the last night?"

"It was a summer fling. I wanted to be free of...all that Freddy business. My own version of *An Affair to Remember*, I guess. I didn't want to be promised to anyone or spoken for or what have you. I just wanted to be Claire Heyworth. Was that so wrong?"

Sarah sighed, mumbled something impatient to Devon, then started to speak again. "It kind of was wrong, but not in the way you mean. It was wrong of you to get engaged when you were seventeen and married when you were eighteen. What were you thinking? What was your *mother* thinking?"

"Oh, Sarah. I am simply not going to have this discussion. I was a good daughter. Obedient. You know me well enough by now. I thought if I did what was expected of me…well, I just thought I was part of a system, part of something larger than my silly likes and dislikes."

"Well," Sarah said. "Now I'm the one who wants to cry."

"Don't. I mean, if Freddy hadn't been…a jerk, it would have all been quite lovely. Isn't there some statistic about how we all have about a fifty-fifty chance at marital happiness, whether in an arranged marriage in rural India or speed dating on the Upper East Side?"

"Oh, Claire!" Sarah was trying to laugh, but Claire could hear the tenderness in her voice. "That's probably technically true. But what about your own *feelings*?"

The silence fell between them again. "I didn't know my own feelings," Claire confessed. "I didn't know I had a right to them, I guess."

"Oh, dear. I know what you mean. But, still. Oh, dear." Sarah mumbled something to Devon again, then finished speaking to Claire. "Your puppy of a brother is desperate for my attention. You will figure this all out, Claire. You obviously liked this Ben character right off the bat when you met him in the south of France all those years ago. Why not just try to be friends with him? Just call him—it will be much easier over the phone—you won't have to contend with all those muscles and smoky glances."

Claire actually giggled.

Sarah continued. "Good. You sound much better. A good cry and maybe even a laugh. Have a great day, sweetie. And don't make me wait another week for a phone call."

"Okay, Sarah. Say hi to Devon for me. Bye, honey." She hung up the phone and stared at it in her hand. Could she possibly muster the courage to call Ben? Of course she could. As Sarah had pointed out, it would be much easier to talk to him on the phone. It was all that physical immediacy that had made her so awkward yesterday, or that's what Claire tried to tell herself.

She got up and made a pot of coffee in Bron's tiny kitchen. While the water burbled and began to brew, Claire opened the folder for the Litchfield house project. *The Pinckney project*, she thought with mild irritation. She flipped to the inside flap where she'd put the address and telephone of the property and took a deep breath. She checked the time and saw that it was after nine and probably not too early to call. Ben seemed like the type who was up early anyway.

Claire pressed the numbers carefully and took another deep breath. The phone rang several times then the answering machine picked up. Simultaneous relief and disappointment came over Claire in a quick wave. She tried to stay calm and began speaking after the long beep.

"Hello, Ben. I just wanted to call and, oh I don't know, apologize, I guess. This is Claire, by the way. I was so taken aback to see you after all these years, I think I may have come off—"

The phone screeched loudly and Claire pulled it away from her ear.

"Claire? Is that you?"

He sounded sort of breathless, and his voice right in her ear felt far more intimate than Claire had anticipated. Her breathing quickened.

"Yes. Ben, listen, it was so awkward yesterday—"

"Claire, I feel terrible. I just, I don't know what came over me to be so rude. I don't even have any excuse. I was just…I don't know what to say."

Claire breathed and made a mental note to thank Sarah James Heyworth for the rest of her life, every single day. "Oh, Ben. I'm so relieved. I was feeling so awful the whole drive home. I am just a mess, if you must know."

Theresa Capuss

Other ideas:

Do you have any special talents you co

"A mess?" He sounded like he was settling in. "Can you talk for a few minutes? Is this a good time?"

Claire's stomach flipped. A few minutes? She could talk to him forever. His voice was so deep and optimistic. Tentative, but hopeful. "Of course. I called you, remember?"

"Ouch," Ben said quietly. "I swear I was waiting until I thought you'd be awake and then I was going to call and apologize—"

Claire laughed. "No! I didn't mean it like, *I called you, damn it!* I just meant, I have plenty of time to talk, because I called…I mean, oh, I don't know what I mean. I was just so happy to see you yesterday and then I got all nervous and I tend to act a bit…cool…apparently."

It was Ben's turn to laugh. "Oh, Claire. Listen to you." He sounded so happy to listen to Claire, and her hand shook a little as she poured the freshly brewed coffee into the white mug.

"I know. I'm a shambles."

"You must be joking. If you're a shambles, the rest of us are catastrophic."

She laughed, a wonderful release of a laugh, deep and satisfying. "God, I've missed you," she let slip through her laughter. Then they both fell silent. Oh, dear. Why had she said that? What a horribly inappropriate, overly intimate—

"Oh, Claire, you have no idea," he blurted. "I never knew what happened to you. I came back to the hotel in Antibes, and Steve told me you'd popped your head into our room to let us know you were leaving. I couldn't believe it."

"You were so angry the night before. I didn't think you'd want to see me. Ever again, really."

She could hear the hiss of Ben's exhale. "I think letting you go without a fight might be the greatest regret of my life."

Claire almost dropped the coffee mug on the white tile floor. "Ben. What a sweet thing to say." She had to get this new upbeat…

friendship…on the right track. She wanted to be around Ben, just to be near him, to sit at the folding table and laugh and be his friend. Was it even possible? "Do you think we might be friends? Now that we're so much older and wiser."

Ben hesitated, and Claire worried she'd pushed too hard. Then she tried to remember Sarah's advice, that Claire's idea of pushy was the rest of the world's idea of humble solicitude.

Chapter 9

HOLDING THE CHIPPED blue-and-white mug in his left hand and the cordless phone in his right, Ben weighed the pros and cons of being friends with Claire Heyworth. Was it even possible? When the mere thought of her got him hard. Like right now. The sound of her voice worked on him like an erotic caress. He'd practically torn the pantry door off to get to the phone in time to interrupt her voice message. "Friends. What a concept. I think we might."

She sounded relieved as she exhaled into the phone. He wanted so much more, but if that's all she had to offer, he'd take it. She was probably madly in love with the marquess, after twenty years of marital bliss.

"So. What do friends do?" she asked, with that optimistic innocence that threw him right back to their time together in France. Her eyes had been so bright. She had been so easily amazed. At first, he'd thought she was putting him on. His backpacking buddy Steve had thought she was a frigid tease. Ben had thought she was an angel. He still did, come to think of it.

"Oh, I don't know. How long are you in New York? We could go to dinner or a movie."

"How long? What do you mean? I live here."

"Oh. I thought you lived in a castle…I mean…I thought—"

"Ben. My marriage is over. My husband absconded with my entire fortune. If such a thing still existed, he'd be going to debtor's prison. Unless he can find more of my money to pay for his sins."

"Wow. I had no idea. I'm so sorry, Claire."

"I…I don't even know if I'm sorry or not. I mean…it was pretty awful…"

Then why do you only want to be friends? Ben wanted to yell. Instead, he asked her to come hear him play in the East Village that night. "It's just a small jazz band in a dirty old bar. But it might be fun. Friendly-like."

She smiled through the words. "I'd love that. What time?"

They finished making plans, and Ben said they could grab a bite to eat after his set, which usually ended around nine. He hung up the phone and thought maybe life wasn't as dismal as it had seemed the night before. A chance to remedy all those years of what-ifs and what-went-wrongs. He could be a friend. In fact, Ben would be the best friend Claire ever had.

He spent the rest of the day going through all the items that he'd pretended he didn't have time to think about when he'd been so rude to Claire the day before. He looked at baseboard samples, paint samples, doorknobs, and hinges. He made tons of notes that he would send to Claire's office Monday morning, so she could move forward on the project. He was grateful they had something physical to work on together. Like friends. Maybe eventually it wouldn't feel like an approximation. Or maybe Nora Ephron was right, and all men not-so-secretly wanted to sleep with all their female friends. Maybe it was just pheromones. Ben could deal with that. He wasn't a teenager after all.

The thought of being a teenager made him think of Claire, which made him hard as a lead pipe, which led him back up to his bedroom to rub one out, then back to his to-do list before driving back to the city that afternoon. He put his car in his Upper East Side garage and went to his apartment to drop off his weekend bag. He took a quick look around his place before he picked up his guitar, wondering what Claire would think of his bachelor pad. He shook his head at all of his dreaming about the future and was on the number six subway heading downtown with plenty of time to be at the club by seven.

Ben had been playing with the same three friends for the past ten years. It had started as a way to blow off steam when they'd all been working in the same hospital. Jenny was a plastic surgeon now and played the drums like a maniac, incredibly controlled and nearly militaristic one moment, then volatile and free-form the next. Wendell was on keyboards. He was a pediatrician and lived with his girlfriend and two daughters in Chelsea. Ivan played stand-up bass and was an ENT specialist who had recently gone into private practice in Brooklyn, where he lived with his boyfriend of seven years. The quartet played a schizophrenic mix of mid-century classics like Art Blakey and MJQ, then trotted out souped-up versions of pop singles by the likes of Taylor Swift and Kelly Clarkson that they transformed into lighthearted instrumental pieces.

Ben felt Claire before he saw her. She looked lost, in that elegant way of hers, poking her head into the darker part of the club, beyond the bar. He continued playing the selection he'd been riffing on as he watched her wend her way through the narrow spaces between the café tables. There was an empty spot along the banquette that ran the length of the exposed brick wall. He smiled when she looked up at him. She smiled back.

He was so screwed. Her smile was like one of those absurd shaft-of-light Hallmark cards when the Holy Spirit descends upon some unsuspecting sot. He must have missed a beat or picked up his pace because Jenny took it as a musical cue and launched into a crazy drum solo. Ben chanced another peek at Claire and tried to keep his fingers moving. He knew all the songs like he knew how to breathe. But since breathing seemed complicated, maybe that wasn't saying much. It was much easier when he didn't look at her.

Ben looked down at his own fingers, as if he needed to see the strings and his fingertips touching in order to play the notes. He could have played blindfolded with the guitar behind his back, but she didn't need to know that. They played the full hour and a half without a break, and his three friends gave him a couple of leading glances as they put away their instruments to clear the small stage for the next group.

"Who's the babe?" Jenny asked casually.

Ben looked across at Claire, who seemed as far from a *babe* as a woman could possibly be. He wanted to bark at Jenny that Claire was the daughter of a duke until he realized he was being completely ridiculous. "An old friend. Come have a drink with us." He looked across to Wendell and Ivan, to include them in the casual invitation.

"Sorry, Ben. I'm on call tomorrow and Tuesday. Maybe next week. She looks charming." Ivan winked. Wendell also said his regrets, so Jenny accompanied Ben and his guitar case over to where Claire was sitting.

Claire tried to stand, but she was tucked in behind the cramped table and it was an awkward business.

"Nice to meet you!" Jenny smiled. "I'm Jenny Donovan. The drummer."

"You were amazing!" Claire cried. "Come sit."

Ben was almost jealous—*why did Jenny get to sit next to her?*—then smiled, loving that Claire was genuinely excited by the music. He had spent so many years with Alice tolerating it, at best. Alice had always seen Ben's guitar playing as an eye-rolling hobby to be borne. Claire seemed fired up. Her cheeks were flushed. She was speaking quickly, almost breathlessly, to Jenny.

"I mean, are you thinking? Or does it just come over you? What does it feel like?"

Jenny burst out laughing. "You're a musician's dream come true. Look at you! So turned on by the music."

Claire flushed. "Oh. Sorry. Am I being inappropriately enthusiastic?" Ben almost dove across the table to get back that flushed excitement. Damn the person who ever made Claire feel like her enthusiasm was inappropriate. Whether it was her mother or her ex-husband or her whole damn circle of friends, Ben decided that a big part of his new position as her Very Good Friend was to fan the flames of her enthusiasm. He certainly hadn't helped matters by being a moody bastard the day before.

Jenny laughed again and grabbed Claire's upper arm. "Are you for real? You're from another world. So upper crusty. I love it. Isn't she divine, Ben?"

God. If Jenny only knew how divine he thought she was. Instead of mooning all over her, Ben reached out and took one of Claire's nervous hands in his and patted her like an older brother would. "Yeah, she's the best. We haven't seen each other in over twenty years and we just bumped into each other yesterday."

Jenny stayed for another twenty minutes, laughing with Claire about her first impressions of working in New York. Ben tried to act normal.

After Jenny left, he moved around to the banquette to sit next to her and tried to act like it was because the music from the next act was a little too loud and he couldn't hear what she was saying. Of course, he was just trying to get as physically close to her as he could without frightening her.

She had pulled her hair back into a practical ponytail and was wearing a long-sleeved white T-shirt and a pair of blue jeans. She couldn't have looked more pedestrian if she had tried. Ben had the distinct impression she had tried.

"I'm starving. Have you eaten dinner yet?" Ben asked, forcing himself to look away from the curve of her fitted white T-shirt and away from the train of thought that made him question why she was trying to make herself nondescript. It was impossible anyway. His stomach lurched with desire at a white T-shirt and jeans. What would he do in the face of a black thong and bra? Or just a pair of shorts. He shook his head and scowled at himself.

"Are you okay?" Claire asked. "You look a little…"

"What?"

"Angry."

Ben shook his head and tried to shake off his irritation with himself. "No. I'm just trying to shake off a week's worth of irritation, I guess."

"Oh." Claire looked down at the soggy napkin beneath her wine glass. "You looked like that yesterday, and I thought you were aggravated, you know, with me."

Ben was totally out of his depth. He wanted her, obviously. She didn't want him. Obviously. Or so he thought. He smiled, the big one, which seemed to put her at ease. "It's all just work and the usual crap," he tried. "Let's go get something to eat and forget about life for a while."

Claire smiled, but there was something wistful and disappointed when she did. Ben stared at her gray eyes.

"What is it, Claire?"

She shook her head and tried to look away and then stared into Ben's eyes, as if it were a dare. "You used to say that. Do you remember? When we were in France. When we were so young?"

"What, that I was hungry?"

Claire's face clouded, as if she'd gone too far and the world would never really understand her. "No. Oh, forget it. I sometimes think the world is full of a million memories and most people remember five hundred thousand particular memories, and I remember the other five hundred thousand." She shook her head again. Her long, blond hair swung against her shoulder. "I sometimes think I should try to remember the other five hundred thousand, to be a part of the world." She smiled—a sad, lost smile—then shrugged. "But I guess we can only remember what sticks, you know?"

Fuck, Ben thought. He was a mess.

He stared at her lips. Why did they have to be so plump? If she was a hard, cold, strident woman, it just didn't make sense that she would possess a pair of kissable, red, trembling lips.

"Ben?"

"Yes," he answered firmly. "Sorry, I was just remembering…the same things. I remember it. I remember how you and I could forget everything," *when we kissed*, he wanted to add. "You aren't the only one who remembers that…those…the memories. I mean, well, let's go get something to eat, eh?"

Claire smiled and Ben recognized it for what it was. The full, real one, not the cool stubborn one she used as a mask to protect herself from the world. "Yes. Yes, please."

Ben put a few bills on the table for the two beers and Claire's wine, and they walked out of the bar and into the cool night.

They went to a Japanese noodle shop on Second Avenue and laughed about Claire's first two weeks of work and how ridiculous it was to be almost forty years old at her first job.

"I keep forgetting I'm not supposed to say I'm almost forty! Thirty-eight!" Claire cried, then laughed. "Boppy ordered me to say just thirty-eight!"

They laughed through most of the next hour and ate spicy food and drank lots of water and Claire asked about the band and how they'd all joined together and about Ben's job and his apartment. And they kept it…friendly. By eleven-thirty, Claire was starting to fade, so Ben got the check and insisted on paying for it. It wasn't much, but he felt like—friends or not—he wanted to pay or be the man or something stupid like that. Claire shook her ponytail, not quite understanding him, and then said thanks. They walked out to the sidewalk and plenty of available cabs were cruising by.

"How did we do?" Ben asked.

"Good, I think. What do you say? Can we be friends?" Claire asked. She reached up to settle a strand of hair behind her ear that the wind had pulled, and Ben had the fleeting moment of thinking she was reaching up to touch his hair instead of her own. Wishful fleeting moment of thinking.

"I say yes," Ben said.

"Good!" Claire said, relieved. "I'm so glad. I hated the idea of…whatever that was yesterday. That was awful. And I could use a friend."

Ben must have looked frozen, trying to hold himself together as best as he could. He was beginning to despise this whole friend concept.

"I mean," Claire added quickly, "I don't want to *use* you. Oh dear, that came out all wrong. I am so awkward around you!" She laughed, then took a deep breath. "I think I'll get a cab. Thanks, Ben. I'm so glad we got together."

"Claire."

She had turned toward the avenue to hail a cab then turned back at the sound of his voice. "Yes?"

"I'm so sorry about yesterday, about everything."

"Oh."

She stared at him in the most all-encompassing manner, taking in his shoulders and hips. It was disconcerting in that adolescent way; he felt horribly aware of his physical self, as he rarely did as an adult.

"I'm the one who should apologize." The street noise seemed to quiet around them. "I'm just…" She looked around, as if she might find assistance. "I'm out of practice…of being with people. I'm a bit rusty." She smiled, and Ben felt his heart crack a bit.

She was so tender, so fragile. And not in the manipulative, bitchy way he'd totally misconstrued every bit of her coolness the day before. She kept her distance because it had become a form of self-preservation.

"Oh, Claire. I'm—I'm so happy you moved here. I'll call you this week. We'll do more friend things. Okay?"

She looked so deeply relieved. It appeared that anything more than friendship was entirely beyond her range of motion just now.

"Oh, Ben. I'd love that."

He reached out to pull her into a fraternal one-armed hug. "Here's a cab, Princess—"

She looked stricken at the moniker.

"I meant it kindly," Ben said, his arm still hanging loosely around one shoulder. "You kind of are a princess. So just think of it as a nickname. Okay?"

He was holding open the taxi door, and Claire was looking up into his eyes.

"Okay. Just don't make fun of me…or not too much. Okay?"

He kissed her on the crown of her head. Brotherly. "Okay. Now get in the cab. I'll see you soon."

"Okay. Bye, Ben."

Chapter 10

CLAIRE FELL ASLEEP in a fog of pleasure and anxiety. Ben had been so kind and attentive. She'd only seen a few moments of that stormy gravity pass across his face, and now that Sarah had planted the seed of the idea—that his bouts of temper were really a screen for his attraction—Claire didn't know if that made it more or less disturbing. She rolled over a couple of times. She could still smell him on her shirt and dipped her nose to her sleeve to inhale more of him. It was faint but it was there. She slept in her long-sleeved T-shirt and dreamt of an imaginary time when the man and not just the scented hint of his memory would be wrapped around her.

She got to work early, feeling ready for anything. There was a package from a messenger service waiting for her on her desk. She was the first to get there, and she looked at it with wary concern before she saw it was from Ben. Claire's heart sped up, and then she realized it was probably the samples she'd asked him to take a look at while they'd been arguing on Saturday afternoon. Rather than something…romantic.

Claire shook her long hair away from her face and set her large paper coffee cup down on her desk. She'd decided to give up straightening her hair and she felt entirely liberated. It gave her an additional thirty minutes in the morning to lounge around and read the paper. At first, she'd worried she might look a little unkempt, but then decided she didn't really care. Everyone in the office was coming to see that she was meticulous and precise in any assignment they gave her. If her hair wasn't equally fussy, then so be it.

"Hey! Great hair!" Roberta called as she sat down across the room. "You look hot."

"Thanks. I think." Claire smiled and continued to withdraw samples and signed purchase orders from the packet Ben must have put together yesterday and sent over first thing this morning.

"How did it go with Pinckney?" Roberta asked without looking up from her own work.

"Surprisingly well." Claire smiled to herself as she tried to sound casual.

Roberta swiveled slowly. "Reeeeally...you and Ms. Pinckney hit it off? I wouldn't have expected that."

Claire turned to face her new friend. "She traded her weekend...I got the dentist husband."

"Ex-husband," Roberta clarified with a suggestive waggle of her eyebrows.

Claire blushed uncontrollably.

"Oh my god!" Roberta cried. "Did you screw the dentist?"

"Ew, Roberta! Stop that. You're so crass."

Roberta burst out laughing. "You're such an easy target, Claire," she said as she turned back to her computer screen. "I mean, god forbid I said something about blow jobs or a bit of rough—"

"Stop it!" Claire was laughing. "We're supposed to be working!"

"Exactly. We work hard to keep our clients satisfied. You know that, Claire." Roberta lost her Brooklyn accent and did a splendid impersonation of Boppy's waspy, precise voice. "Boppy is 100 percent committed to client satisfaction." Roberta took a sip of her coffee as if she were giving a lecture on proper corporate behavior.

Claire smiled and looked at the last sheet of paper she pulled out of the envelope. It was a piece of pale blue stationery folded in half. She opened it.

The blue ink looked like it was from an old-fashioned fountain pen. His quick strokes were beautiful across the page. Claire traced the tips of her fingers on the words and smiled.

> Dear Claire,
>
> Here are all the purchase orders we discussed on Saturday. It's a pleasure working with you.
> Your friend,
> Ben

Oh, dear. *It was nothing*, Claire tried to chastise herself. A silly inserted memo that she would pass on to the lead designer on the project, and then it would be put into a file and stored and then archived and then destroyed in a few years. But.

"A love note from your new boyfriend?" Roberta asked from across the room.

"You're a pest," Claire said with mock sternness. She folded the letter and set it aside. "It was just a quick thanks for helping him get all that work done on Saturday."

Roberta burst out laughing.

"Oh my lord, Roberta. You are an infant. Get your mind out of the gutter."

Hilary walked in just then, two large tote bags over one shoulder and a large cup of coffee in one hand. "Someone's mind is in the gutter? Yay!"

Claire rolled her eyes.

"Claire helped the dentist get all that *work done* over the weekend," Roberta said.

Hilary spoke as she put down all of her project bags and settled into her desk. "You met the husband on Saturday?"

"Ex-husband," Roberta corrected.

"Oooh, yes. Ex-husband. Isn't he a dish?" Hilary asked.

Claire blushed again.

"Oh my god, you like him!" Hilary clasped her hands together. "How perfect."

"You two are impossible. It turns out we knew each other briefly when we were teenagers. It was all very funny."

The other two women stared at Claire for a few moments. Hilary spoke first, "How…charming. A long-lost reunion."

"Please. He's a client."

Roberta rolled her eyes and gave Hilary a suggestive eyebrow raise. "Mm-hmm. Right. A client."

Claire laughed. "Okay. So he's attractive. I'm sure lots of Boppy's clients are attractive. Anyone who can afford Boppy can probably afford an expensive haircut and a personal trainer."

"So his hair looked good, huh?" Hilary asked.

"And his abs?" Roberta smirked.

"Enough!" Claire laughed. "I'm going to get all these purchase orders approved by Edwina and Boppy, then logged into the system. Some of us are here to work." Claire picked up all the samples and paperwork Ben had put together, but left the blue notepaper on her desk.

Ben finished looking at the screen with the X ray of his patient's impacted molar and wrote an email back to his assistant asking her to set up surgery as soon as possible. He clicked out of his email program and stared at his phone, then looked up at the industrial wall clock. It wasn't even noon yet, and he wanted to call her. And it was only Monday.

He was a forty-year-old man. Wasn't there some sort of papal dispensation for not having to wait to pretend that you didn't really like someone in a weird stalkerish way but just felt like calling her in a normal hey-how-you-doing sort of way? The phone rang, and he had the crazy hope it was Claire. He cleared his throat and tried to make his voice sound warm and inviting.

"Ben Hayek."

"Why do you sound so charming all of a sudden?"

Alice. Fuck.

"Hey, Alice. What's up?" The smooth voice was history.

"That's more like it. So why do I have to hear from Boppy Matthews's office that you've signed off on a bunch of stuff that I haven't even looked at for the house?"

"Jesus, Ali, this is so boring."

"Just buy me out if it's so boring."

"Okay."

"What?" She sounded like she might have spit her coffee across her enormous desk.

Ben looked out the window of his tiny, thirty-eighth-floor office to the oranges and reds of the autumn trees across Central Park South. What had he just said? He didn't have half a million in cash lying around, and he certainly didn't need to be the sole owner of a colonial-slash-Greek-Revival farmhouse in northwestern Connecticut.

"Let me think about it. It might just be easier," he hedged.

"Well…okay," Alice said with slow skepticism.

Ben almost laughed. It was so typical of Alice to be suspicious of someone giving her exactly what she'd always wanted. She saw pitfalls and hurdles at all times. It was her job, but it was also just *her*. He'd have to maintain the pretense that he was going to be saddled with the annoying prospect of traveling to Connecticut every weekend and finishing the project before he could put it on the market. Otherwise, she'd think he was trying to pull one over on her.

"Listen, neither one of us wants this to drag on like it has been, and we just don't agree." *What else is new?* Ben wanted to add, but he was trying to be a grown-up. "Let's get a couple of real estate agents in there to give us a price, and I'll give you half."

"Now wait a minute. We bought it at the top of the market. There's no reason I should take a hit just because you don't have the patience to see it through."

Ben knew this trick. No question asked. No reason to answer. Silence.

And more silence.

"Ben?"

"Yes?"

"Well?"

"Well, what? You didn't ask me anything. You said, *Buy me out*, and I said, *okay*. Now you're trying to twist it around like—" He caught himself before he slid down that rabbit hole for the nine millionth time, trying to show Alice how she might be a teensy tiny bit…litigious.

"Like what? What were you going to say?"

Here we go, though Ben dismally. "You know what? Forget it. Just forget I offered to buy you out—"

"Wait, no—"

"Better yet," Ben interrupted, "why don't you just name any old amount you want. How about a million? Why not two million? Don't forget to add in your sweat equity. I think you went to Kmart in Torrington that one time, didn't you? To get towels? Don't forget to add that to your list."

Alice burst out laughing. "Oh, Ben. I love you."

"What?"

"I mean, I don't *love you* love you, obviously. I can't stand you. But at least I remember why I loved you enough to marry you. You're the only person who ever called me on my shit. Anyway, look, we bought it for one-point-four…and we've probably put in three, but with the slump I doubt we'd get more than a million."

"That sounds about right," Ben answered slowly. She was sounding much too reasonable.

"But when it's totally done and the market recovers, you'll be able to get way more than what's in it." That sounded more like Alice.

He sighed but didn't say anything.

"What's fair?" she asked, almost to herself. "You want to give me five-fifty and we'll call it a day?"

She was being fair. Ben wasn't used to it. He would have asked for that much if she'd offered to buy him out of his share. Half of what it was worth now.

"Let me see what I can get my hands on."

"Oh, I don't care when you get it to me. I'll be happy to have it off my books. I'll call the attorneys and tell them we worked out a settlement. They'll be thrilled. Let's say you've got five years to pay me off?" Alice laughed lightly. "I sound like a mafia wife!"

"You kind of do. So, what changed your mind?"

"What changed yours?"

He hated when she answered his questions with questions. "Never mind, Ali."

"Oh, sorry, I forgot that you always hated that about me, the answering questions with questions thing. If you must know, I've met someone. And getting that call from Boppy Matthews's office today just reminded me that, even if this guy turns out to be nothing special, I just want to be free, you know? In case? So"—Ben could practically see her shrugging across town—"I figured it was time to cut my losses. I mean…that sounds mean, calling you one of my losses, but you know what I mean, right?"

"I know what you mean," Ben said over a laugh. "I'll call my lawyer, and you call yours. They can draw up the paperwork. Five hundred and fifty thousand over five years shouldn't be a problem. And then we'll be done." Ben thought about asking Alice about the new guy she was seeing and then realized he really didn't want to know.

"Okay. I'll wait to hear back from both attorneys, then I'll call Boppy's office and tell them they can go ahead with all your choices and take my name off the project." Alice exhaled into the phone. "Wow. Done. Right. I'll see you around, then. Bye, Ben."

"Bye, Alice." He put the receiver back in the cradle of the black desk phone and stared at it. His marriage was really over. There had been so many parts of the ending. The beginning of the end—the long silences, the skeptical looks. The middle of the end—wrangling with the lawyers and the physical dividing of objects, the moving out. Maybe it was all that Churchill nonsense, but that conversation really felt like the end of the end.

Ben got up and went to see the next patient waiting in room four. With any luck, he'd be able to put off calling Claire for another few days.

Chapter 11

FRIDAY AFTERNOON, BOPPY stormed into the group office on the main floor of the townhouse. "Claire, what did you do?" Her voice was full of disbelief.

All four women looked up from their desks. Claire felt the blood drain out of her face. She stood up at her desk. "I—I'm not sure. Whatever it is, I'll try to fix it. Is it something terrible? I'm so sorry—"

Roberta, Hilary, and Erin quickly turned their attention—or at least their gazes—back toward their computer screens and pretended to be furiously interested in what they were working on.

Boppy shook a sheaf of work orders in her hand. "This is unbelievable. This project has been the thorn in the side of this organization for nearly two years. And you stroll in and—POOF!" Boppy snapped her fingers. "It's all resolved."

Claire still couldn't tell if Boppy was angry or pleased.

"I—I'm sorry. I still don't know—"

"The Pinckney project, you wonderful fabulous woman, you!" Boppy's face bloomed into a picture of relieved happiness. "I was on the verge of telling that horrible woman that it was just not going to happen, and then I come back from one of the most frustrating meetings in Houston to find this on my desk. You are a miracle worker. I've made reservations for a table for you—and a friend, if you like—at The Spotted Pig for tonight. Go have fun. On me. Take Monday off. Hell, take the whole week off. Great work."

Boppy tossed the pile of approved work orders onto Claire's desk and strolled out of the group office with a happy shake of her head.

After all four women listened to Boppy's footsteps climb the stairs and once they were sure she was out of earshot, Roberta made a soft wolf whistle. "What the hell?"

Hilary jumped up. "What'd you do?"

Erin smiled and swiveled in her chair to face Claire. "Well?"

Claire looked down at the work orders she and Ben had gone over last weekend. All of them were stamped with Boppy's approval and a printout of an email from Alice Pinckney to Boppy Matthews was clipped to the whole bundle:

Boppy,

Ben has offered to buy me out. For all future correspondence, he is the sole owner of Rockledge Farm. Legal docs to follow.

Best,

Alice

Hilary read over Claire's shoulder. "Wow. Maybe you have a future in divorce arbitration."

Claire laughed and tried to keep the seemingly ever-present blush from her cheeks. "I don't think it had anything to do with me. Just lucky timing. Maybe Alice Pinckney finally had enough or something." Claire continued to stare at all the work orders and reread the email in stunned silence. A call was coming in on the general line that all four of them shared. Roberta picked it up.

"Boppy Matthews Interiors. May I help you?"

Hilary returned to her desk and started straightening things up before leaving for the day. It was after five, and Claire thought she might convince Bronte to have the celebratory dinner with her before her sister-in-law headed back to London in a few days.

"Yes, Dr. Hayek. As a matter of fact, she's sitting right here." Roberta's voice had the slightest hint of provocation.

Claire's stomach fell to the floor as she turned to face her colleague.

Roberta was swiveling back and forth, smiling broadly. "Of course, just one moment. I'll put you on hold and patch you through." All three women stared at Claire as the small black dot on the phone blinked patiently, showing that Ben was on hold waiting to speak to her.

"Call for you on line seven," Roberta added with a wicked grin then burst out laughing.

Hilary and Erin started laughing quietly.

"Will you all quit it?" Claire pleaded in a hoarse, desperate whisper. There was no stopping the blush this time. She tried to ignore her juvenile coworkers and took a deep breath. She tapped the phone line and picked up her receiver. "Claire Heyworth."

"Hi, Claire. It's Ben. Hayek."

"Oh. Hi, Ben." Damn it. Why did she have to sound like such a cold fish?

"Oh. Is this a bad time? I thought since it was the end of the day, you might be able to talk for a few minutes, but you sound busy. And you just started working there, so you're probably trying to make a good impression. Sorry. Let's catch up later."

Nooooooo! "No!" Well, that came out a bit stronger than Claire had intended.

"Oh, okay. Maybe some other time then—"

"No," Claire laughed. She decided to ignore the Greek chorus of eavesdroppers behind her. "I didn't mean *no* like that. I only meant, oh never mind. Thanks for sending over all those work orders. Boppy just brought them all down, all approved and everything."

"Yeah, I'm not sure if you've heard, but it looks like I am going to be the sole owner of Rockledge. So—"

"Yes," Claire interrupted to prevent him from going on when she already knew. "Boppy copied me in on the email from…Ms. Pinckney." *Ugh.* Why was it so awkward to say his ex-wife's name? So immature.

"Oh. Okay. Well, good. So…"

"So." *Come on, Claire. Go for it.* "Right, so, I have reservations at someplace called The Spotted Pig tonight and—"

"Oh, so sorry. You must be running late. Sorry again to bug you at work."

God. Could Sarah be right? Was he just as nervous as she was? He was so broad and confident…looking. "No." Claire cleared her throat. "I meant, Boppy Matthews made the reservation, as a little perk."

"Dinner with the boss. Look at you rising up the corporate ladder in a flash. Have a great time."

Were they ever going to be talking about the same thing at the same time? "Oh, no, no." Claire laughed lightly, probably sounding as nervous as she felt. "She told me to go with a friend…and take Monday off."

"Oh. Okay. I was just calling to see if you wanted to go to a movie or something, but sounds like you're all set."

He'd been calling to ask her out! Her heart hammered and the inner girl in her head screamed, *HE LIKES YOU!*

"Actually, I hadn't asked anyone yet. I just found out…so… do you want to go?" Silence. "With me?" Oh. God. What was she? Twelve? She was a grown woman inviting a friend to dinner. Preposterous, but his silence—

"Yes! Sorry. My assistant just handed me some X rays, and I was momentarily distracted. What time should I meet you?"

Just like that? Yes? "Oh. Okay. Right. Eight o'clock sound good?"

"Perfect. I'll see you then. Bye, friend." Click.

Ohmyohmyohmy. Claire put the phone back into its cradle with slow precision.

Roberta coughed. "Well?"

"Well, what?" But Claire was smiling despite herself.

"Oh, man. He's going to make mincemeat out of you."

With all her newfound professional success and womanly confidence, Claire replied, "Maybe I'll make mincemeat out of *him*, so there!" The other three started laughing again, and Claire turned to her computer screen and began inputting all the work orders.

An hour later, the office empty of her distracting coworkers, she input the final order and stuck the paperwork into a neat manila folder with the rest of the orders for the Hayek account.

She tried to hold onto that thread of assurance she'd felt earlier, but the mere mention of his name, the mere sight of the word *Hayek* on a piece of paper, made Claire a little loopy. *Enough.* She powered down her computer and cleared up her desk.

When she left the office and felt the cool October wind against her cheeks, Claire felt a physical reminder of all her years in northern Scotland. She tugged her knee-length coat a little bit tighter around her neck and enjoyed the bracing feel of the air. She remembered how she'd welcomed that cold harshness when she'd married Freddy. Some of her friends had balked at the idea of leaving high-flying London to molder away in the wilds of Caithness. Claire had loved it.

Wick Castle had felt like another planet—a nearly abandoned one—when she'd first arrived, but it was hers, so she didn't care. All of her short life until then had been spent in her mother's shadow. It had been a very luxurious shadow—Claire wasn't complaining—but her life had never felt like her own. When her mother and Freddy's mother introduced them at Claire's seventeenth birthday party that spring, it was pretty much a known fact that they were meant for each other. Claire had been modest, attractive, soft-spoken. She had been trained.

Freddy had been plain old fun. He drank and didn't care if his bawdy stories were a little too loud at Annabel's. He was a fabulous dancer. The way he pulled Claire into his arms with that casual possessive strength of his had made her feel, if not swooning in love, at least able to contemplate the idea of spending her life with someone who fit into her world, who would take charge. He might not have been the most reliable of men, but Claire never could have anticipated the depth of his conniving in those early years.

Her own parents had spent plenty of time apart during their marriage, so that hadn't seemed very odd to Claire. When she'd become pregnant with Lydia almost immediately after their wedding in September, Claire didn't find it terribly unusual that Freddy was frequently called back to London for business meetings or social obligations. In a way, it helped her put the emotional confusion of her time with Ben more firmly behind her. She was married. She was pregnant. She lived at the opposite end of the earth.

After Lydia was born, Claire more or less convinced herself that the summer before with Ben had been nothing but a youthful aside. It was easy in a way. Less than a year later, she was the mother of a beautiful baby girl, a marchioness left almost entirely to her own devices. In many ways, she felt quite free.

Claire focused all of her attention on renovating the castle and starting her family. For many years, that was more than enough. As her mother used to say, she'd always been a grateful little thing.

She shook off the memories and stared out the bus window as she headed down Lexington Avenue. One of her favorite parts of New York City was riding around on the public buses. It made the feeling of being a ghost among the rest of humanity a little less pronounced. She could be regular. She could be a normal person who had a normal job and rode around on normal buses. It wasn't slumming either. She remembered how her mother used to drill her about the importance of who she was and how she was to behave. The Duchess of Northrop was not in the business of raising a slapper.

Claire smiled and hit the call button to indicate her stop was coming. The bus slowed, and she stepped out the back door and walked the two blocks to Bronte's apartment. At some point, she needed to think about getting her own place, but for now, she couldn't afford it, so she called Bronte as often as she could to voice her gratitude.

Just then, her cell phone rang, and it was Bron.

"I was just thinking about you," Claire said.

"What are you doing? No moping around at home on a Friday night. I won't allow it. I demand you come out on the town with Max and me and no argument—"

"I have plans."

"What? With whom? Oh my god, are you going out on a date? Who is it? You're such a player!"

Claire laughed into the brisk night air. "I'm about as far from being a *player* as one person can be."

"Apparently not. Well?"

"Well, what?" Claire was nearly to the building and the doorman saw her coming and opened the front door for her. She smiled and walked into the lobby as Bronte persisted.

"Well what?" Bronte mocked. "Well, who's your date, duh?"

"Oh, just an old friend I bumped into—"

"Oh. My. God. It's the oral surgeon, isn't it?"

After spilling everything to Sarah on Sunday morning about bumping into Ben, Claire had decided to take a wait-and-see attitude before telling Bronte anything. At the time, it had seemed like a whole lot of nothing. Or at least that's what Claire was trying to tell herself as her heart pounded every time she thought about him. Lately, her mind was particularly inclined to picture his long, strong fingers on the strings of his guitar, the way he had pulled and strummed—

"Claire!"

"What?"

Bronte laughed again. "Where are you? I've been asking you a million questions, and it's like you aren't even listening."

"Sorry, Bron. I'm in the elevator and I need to get ready, so I should probably hang up."

"*N. F. W.* There is no way you're going to leave me hanging like this, especially now that it's too late to call Sarah in London to find out what has gone on while you've been avoiding me."

The elevator doors opened and Claire stepped out into the narrow hall with the old, but practical, tile floors from another century. She tucked her cell phone into the crook of her neck and reached into her bag to take out her key. "At least let me get into the apartment and put my bag down so I can give you my full attention."

"Ugh. Oh, all right. But hustle—the suspense is killing me."

Claire smiled and pushed open the door. She put her bag down on the small kitchen counter along with the cell phone, then clicked it onto speakerphone.

"Can you hear me, Bron?"

"Sure. This'll be fun. You can get ready while you tell me how dreamy he is."

Claire rolled her eyes as she took off her jacket and then her boots and set them neatly by the front door. "He is kind of dreamy now that you mention it."

"Listen to you…not a hint of ice."

It was starting to hurt less and less, Claire realized, when Sarah and Bronte would rib her for her old way of behaving so coolly. She realized it was partly the shyness she had thought it was, but it was also a weak fear. As much as her mother had taught her to behave in certain ways and how to be a lady in all situations, the duchess's training had also instilled a strange isolation. Claire had worked with her therapist for the past few years to break it down, but it was so ingrained, it hadn't been easy. Claire didn't want to feel apart from the rest of humanity any longer.

"Claire!" Bronte cried again. "Back to earth! What are you wearing tonight?"

Claire looked down at her work outfit. "Do you think I need to change out of my work clothes? I'm wearing those pretty beige trousers with the creamy silk top. You know, the one with the oversized buttons—"

"Are you crazy? You are going out with the man of your dreams—"

"He's just a guy—"

"The hot oral surgeon—"

"He's just a dentist—"

"Cease!" Bronte laughed her command. "Of course you're going to change into something pretty and flirty. Go tell me what's in your closet."

Claire smiled silently toward the phone and walked the short distance to the closet. "A lot of beige…"

"I was afraid of that. What about that emerald green satin top we made you put in? The Catherine Malandrino—"

"How do you even remember things like that?"

"Oh, don't start with me," Bronte said. "I refuse to be questioned when I'm trying to help you. Do you have the top?"

"Yes, it's here." Claire flipped a few hangers in the closet until she was staring at the blouse in question. She hesitated as she touched the slippery fabric. "I don't know, Bron. It just seems so flashy—"

"Oh my god. You sound so much like your mother. *Flashy?* As if you could ever run the risk of being taken for a Vegas show girl?" Bronte started laughing, and it was contagious. Claire was laughing within a few seconds, envisioning herself in a gold-spangled bikini and peacock-feather headdress sashaying into the restaurant to meet Ben.

"Oh dear," Bronte said as her laughter abated. "Okay, here's the deal. You have to have a little pizzazz. Either on top or bottom. I'd go for the top, because I'm assuming you'll be sitting—because it's dinner—so why bother with the black satin pants, right?"

Claire groaned. The idea of wearing black satin pants for anything but a formal dinner struck her as ridiculous.

"And no groaning. It's not like you have to procure an engraved invitation to Buckingham Palace to wear a bit of satin."

"I'm too old to be getting all dolled up on a Friday night. I'll look like a teenager. And not in a good way."

"I know it's an act of faith, but I think you need to trust me on this one. Wear your favorite jeans if you must, but please wear something shiny on top and some super high heels."

"Heels with jeans? Bronte. I'm not sure I can do it."

"Do I need to hop in a cab and come down there?"

Claire burst out laughing again. Bronte's tone of voice was exactly the same as when she was disciplining her toddler son, with that hint of don't-make-me-come-in-there.

"No!" Claire cried. "I will obey. And when the dentist catches a glimpse of me in my trollopy heels and jeans and rolls his eyes, I will report back to you and prove my point. I'm a practical khakis and flats kind of woman."

"Are you picturing me with my arms folded and my toe tapping impatiently? Because that's what I'm doing. If he even tangentially suggests that you are trollopy, I will…oh, I don't know what I'll do, but I'll eat my hat and all that. You can think of something gruesome like I have to call your mother and tell her how much I'm looking forward to spending Christmas with her at Lyford."

"Oh, Bron. Is it still so bad with you and Mother?"

"We are not going to get into a Sylvia discussion right now—"

"Okay, okay. So I'm going to jump in the shower and try to get to the restaurant by eight o'clock. Let me hop. I'll let you know how it goes."

"Promise? Let's have brunch tomorrow. We leave for London on Sunday night and we all have to get together before then. Maybe with the dentist?"

"Bronte!"

"What? Bring him to brunch tomorrow. Maybe he'll still be with you. You know, after a sleepover date—"

"Bron! You're impossible."

Bronte laughed lightly. "In fact, I think I'm leaning much more to the possible than the impossible. Have a wonderful night, Claire. You deserve it."

Claire felt the warmth of that kindness spread across her chest. "Thanks, Bron. I think I will have a nice time. It's been a good week."

"Aw, listen to you. I'll talk to you tomorrow. Do *not* avoid me!"

"Okay," Claire said. "I'll call you in the morning."

Bronte said good-bye, and Claire tapped the speakerphone off.

After tying her hair up and taking a quick shower, she stood in front of the flashy green satin blouse. It had hints of turquoise and peacock blue when it caught the light. Claire heard a stentorian phrase of her mother's reverberate through the back of her mind: "A lady does not need to draw attention to herself."

It was a bit of a moral quandary, wasn't it? Claire actually *did* want Ben to look at her, to like her. So was it more dishonest to be reserved? Was it a form of false modesty? Claire hung up her robe and chose her favorite bra and underwear set. It was a smooth, silky pale blue that wouldn't snag against the satin blouse like one of her other lacy ones might. She pulled on the matching thong and realized she hadn't dressed for a man in years.

Oh, maybe once or twice before a fancy party, she'd thought absently that she hoped Freddy might compliment her, but this was different. She actually thought of Ben the whole time she was putting on her lingerie. She thought about what he would think if he was watching her or what he would do...

Claire shook her head and smiled. "First things first," she said aloud to no one in particular. She swallowed to build her confidence and grabbed the bright top. Back in London, she'd reluctantly packed it into her suitcase with the full belief that she would never in a million years wear such a showy thing. She slipped it over her head, and it fell with a sensual caress along her back and arms. The sleeves where made of a lighter, sheer version of the bodice. The delicate fabric bloused out and then came to a tight cuff at her wrists. It didn't feel quite as provocative as Claire had imagined. She pulled on her jeans and stared at the four pairs of Sarah James heels that Sarah had had messengered down from her Madison Avenue shop as a welcome-to-New-York present. Claire took all four out of their boxes and set them in a row, like little soldiers.

Gold. Black. Gray. Red.

Red? What was Sarah thinking? When in the world would Claire Heyworth ever wear a pair of red high-heeled shoes? When Claire had called Sarah to thank her for the lovely gifts, she'd laughed at the possibility of ever having an occasion to which she would feel comfortable wearing bright red stilettos.

"Maybe to a private occasion, then?" Sarah had said suggestively.

Claire smiled at the idea of wearing those red shoes—and nothing else—for Ben one day. Or night.

She looked at her watch and realized she was running out of time to contemplate. It was time to act. She pulled the gray suede pair of shoes on. They were so high. Claire felt tippy.

"Oh well." She grabbed her large tote bag then looked down at the serviceable satchel. Did she really need to lug all that around? She pulled her single apartment key off the key ring and put it in the front pocket of her jeans, then pulled out her credit card and cash and slipped them into her back pocket. She stared at her cell phone, still resting on the kitchen counter. *Why not?* she thought. Why not just go out with a feeling of being totally unencumbered? When was the last time she hadn't been "available" to her daughter or her mother or her soon-to-be-ex-husband or her attorneys?

She cut that line of thought short before it led her into a cul-de-sac of sadness and disappointment. She shook out her hair—which had become even more unruly after the humidity of the shower—and left the apartment with empty hands and a light heart.

Chapter 12

BEN STOOD OUTSIDE the restaurant enjoying the cool night air. Lately, he'd been feeling a bit claustrophobic in the city, like a lab rat going from the box of his apartment to the box of the subway to the box of his office. Even the time he spent in bars and clubs with his band had started to feel like another box. He liked being out. Out-of-doors.

He thought about the expression and realized it described exactly how he felt. He didn't just want to cross the transom of a door; he wanted to be out of *all* doors. Away from walls and windows and doors. Walking in woods and across fields with no doors in sight. He was letting his mind wander along those meandering paths when a taxi slowed, and he saw Claire through the back window as she leaned forward to pay the driver. Ben crossed the few steps to the curb and pulled open the taxi door.

"Oh!" Claire exclaimed. "Thank you." Her long legs came out of the cab first, and Ben felt his stomach drop. She had on a pair of extra-long, fitted jeans that made her legs appear endless, and when she stood up in front of him, she was nearly as tall as he was. He slammed the back door shut and the cab pulled away. The two of them stared at each other.

"Did you leave your bag in the back of the cab?" Ben asked with a hint of worry.

She spread her arms wide. "No. I just slipped my credit card into my back pocket"—she turned slightly and patted her own behind for effect—"and my key into my front pocket. I thought I'd live on the edge."

Ben stared at this new version of Claire and tried to keep steady. Her hair was mussed and loose around her face. She was wearing stunningly high heels with those infinite blue jeans, and he caught a glimpse of something shiny and touchable under her serviceable wool jacket.

"Oh. Good. I didn't want to have to run screaming down the street after that taxi driver."

Claire smiled, and Ben decided the friendship plan was the stupidest idea he'd ever had. There was no way he was going to be "just friends" with this woman if he could help it. And he hoped he could help it as quickly as possible. He didn't care if she ripped his heart out again. It would be worth it.

"I might like to see that, but you're right, no need," she agreed. "Shall we go in?" She tipped her chin toward the entrance of the restaurant.

Ben reached out for her hand then thought she might not take it, so he touched the turn of her elbow instead. "You look lovely, Claire."

"Oh! Oh. Thanks. I mean…thank you."

Ben wasn't sure what to make of the fact that she acted surprised when he complimented her. He'd always imagined her living in a sea of admirers, both public and private. He opened the door for her to pass into the warm, bustling air of the restaurant.

"May I take your coat for you?" Ben asked, lifting his hands toward her shoulders as they stood in front of the podium, where a tall, thin woman in a long-sleeved black T-shirt lifted her eyes to them.

"Do you have a reservation?"

"Yes," Claire answered. "I think it will be under my name. Heyworth?"

Ben took a moment to feel the warmth of her skin as he pulled the shoulders of the wool coat from her arms. His fingers touched the light silk of her sleeve, and he felt it like an electrical current up his arms. He exhaled slowly and brought the coat over to the small coat check area next to the bar. He took off his jacket and passed both of them to the attendant.

When he turned back to Claire, the hostess was holding two menus and looking at them expectantly. "This way, please."

He watched the sway of Claire's hips as she followed the other woman to a table at the far corner of the crowded restaurant. It was a small table for two tucked against the back wall. Claire slid into the banquette, and Ben regretted the distance between them as he pulled out the seat and sat across from her. The hostess handed each of them a menu and left.

Claire caught his eye over the top of her menu then quickly looked down. Her eyes were a gorgeous greenish-gray that turned smoky when she cast her gaze away from him.

"So, what do you like?" Claire asked without looking up from the menu.

You! Ben wanted to shout. He was turning into some sort of teenaged version of himself, overcome with hormones and a desire that felt like something slippery and out of his control. Despite all of his griping about feeling like an urban lab rat, Ben was not a fan of the alternative. Unforeseen, uncontrollable situations were his worst nightmare.

"Ben?" Claire had set her menu flat on the table and was staring straight into his eyes.

"Yes?" he answered quietly.

"Are you okay?"

He took a deep breath and decided to throw it all to the wind. He had a momentary vision of a fistful of wheat being thrown into the air and the chaff flying off in a light breeze. "I don't think I want to be friends, Claire."

"What?" She looked so hurt.

Oh, Jesus. Now he'd done it. "I mean, I think, god—" Ben dragged both of his hands through his short hair and let them rest at the back of his neck. "I feel like I'm a teenager and this is ridiculous and I totally understand how you want to keep it light and friendly but I think…"

Claire's hands were clasped so tightly together that Ben reached for her without thinking, the need to soothe her anxiety overriding his own desire.

"I'm sorry," he whispered.

"It's okay," she said quietly. "I guess it was too much to hope that we could just hang out. After all this time. I was pretty awful, I guess, now that I look back on it. And it was dumb of me to think you would still care for me at all—"

He held her hands in one hand then brought the other up so he could hold both of hers in his. "Claire."

"It's all right. Maybe we should just go. I don't know if I have much of an appetite—"

"Claire," he said with more authority.

"What?" She looked up, startled, then contained. He saw the wall of ice, what he now knew to be the wall of insecurity and fear that he'd mistaken for arrogance.

"I don't want to be your friend because I want to kiss you all the time and I can't concentrate at work because I'm thinking about you incessantly. I thought I could just have dinner and be normal, but you're so gorgeous, and I can't imagine how I'm going to get through two minutes, much less two hours, without reaching out to touch your hair—or your cheek—and how I want to…do things to you, with you, if you'll let me, if you want me…at all."

"Oh, god, Ben." Claire was breathless, her words rolling out of her unbidden.

"It's too much too soon, isn't it? I'm so sorry. It's embarrassing—"

"No, it's just—"

"It's all right." He tried to act normal, matter-of-fact. "I know you just want to be friends, and it wasn't right to push that. I'm so sorry. It was wrong. I just thought—"

"Ben." The air seemed to stop around them. She said his name with a finality that made him stop and really see her for maybe the first time since he'd started this rambling, run-on attempt to unburden himself, to release the torrent of feelings.

"Yes," Ben answered.

Claire took a deep breath and turned her hands so she was the one holding his. "Every time I see your last name on a file at work, I have to remind myself to breathe. Every time someone at the office makes an offhand remark about the dishy dentist, I feel like all my clothes are too tight and something has gone amiss with the radiators in the office." She shifted in her seat as if she were experiencing the same effect right then. "Is it too ridiculous? Are we too ridiculous? I feel like a teenager too. Are we just having some silly walk down memory lane? I can't stop thinking about you…" Her voice trailed off then she continued in a throaty whisper, "Especially about that cruel, wonderful kiss on your porch."

Ben was rubbing his thumbs along Claire's knuckles. He licked his lips before he could speak again. "I don't think I ever stopped loving you, Claire."

"What?" she gasped.

The waiter came over to take their drink order, and Ben waved him away with a harsh swipe of his hand.

"Go," he snapped at the waiter, without looking away from Claire's eyes. When they were alone again—or relatively alone, at least—Ben tried to stay calm, which was proving difficult with Claire looking like she was feeling everything he was. "The timing's all wrong," he started gently.

"I know!" Claire leapt in. "It's too fast." She shook her head with a discouraging back-and-forth. Ben looked momentarily disappointed, until Claire continued. "But then I feel like I just *know* you. And it's already been too long. Do you know what I mean?"

He paused to revel in that, but she mistook it for skeptical hesitance.

"God, Claire. The minute I saw you on my porch in Litchfield, it was like a time warp. There you were, and I was nineteen again and the years had folded into nothing—since that last night in Antibes— and then the next day when you were gone. I was so...destroyed." He added the last word quietly and looked down at the table, as if he were trying to avoid revisiting those feelings.

Eventually, he looked up and they stared at each other for a few long minutes after that, trying to process their delayed good fortune, staring with a goofy half-smile into one another's eyes.

Claire finally broke the silence. "Will you kiss me again like you did on Saturday?"

"I was so sorry about that—"

Claire's eyebrows pulled together in anticipation of him saying he was sorry he had kissed her. But he certainly looked like he wanted to kiss her now, the way he stared at her lips when she talked, the way his thumbs and fingers enclosed her hands and soothed her while simultaneously ratcheting up her heartbeat. She felt saner and crazier all at once.

"I don't know if I can eat," Claire whispered with newfound, thrilling honesty, "if I'm thinking about you kissing me again." Ben made her believe that maybe it wasn't so forward or wrong or crass to simply say what she felt, what she wanted.

The waiter came back, starting to look a bit arrogant and impatient. "Are you ready to order?"

Ben turned to him slowly, and Claire saw a hint of that ragged temper that he wasn't always able to control. It was somehow woven into his passion, and he didn't want that passion to be interrupted. "We'd like your best bottle of champagne, whatever you have."

Claire nearly burst out laughing at the waiter's immediate and unabashed enthusiasm, which had been bordering on snippy impatience only moments before.

"Of course," the waiter agreed. "Right away."

"Hold on, sorry." Ben stopped him before he walked away. "Ice it down for a few minutes, will you? We forgot something in the cab, and he's just coming back around the block to return it. We'll be back at the table in a few minutes. Okay?"

"Of course, I'll ice it down and have it waiting for you when you return. May I suggest a few appeti—"

"No." Ben cut him off without further ceremony. Then he stood up and pulled Claire behind him. She practically danced along, and in a few seconds they were back out on the sidewalk. Neither of them had retrieved their coats, and Claire was confused about the taxi and wondering what Ben had meant—

Ben slammed into her, cradling the back of her head a second before she would have hit her skull against the brick side of the building—and not have cared a jot. They stood huddled into each other, around the corner from the plate glass windows of the restaurant and out of sight of the other diners who'd just watched them stumble out. His other hand was at the small of her back, pulling the lower half of her body flush up against him. The tilting, whirling sensation of her head pushed back and her hips straining forward while teetering on the too-high Sarah James shoes all made her feel completely off balance.

His kiss made her feel…everything. She felt the cold air against her cheeks, the hot press of his lips against hers, the tender, inquisitive touch of his fingers as they found their way beneath her blouse and trailed across her belly just above the waist of her jeans. Claire felt an electric snap, like a transformer blowing.

She gasped his name like a starving person. She wanted to nip and bite at him. He made her feel fierce.

Ben gradually slowed the kiss and removed his hands from against her supple skin, trying to take a few breaths between lighter kisses. He began to smooth her hair where his hand had clutched the loose curls at the nape of her neck. "So lovely," he whispered.

Claire blushed. "Thank you."

Ben laughed loud and it rang down the street. "Come, my little polite sexpot. You're divine."

Claire liked the idea of being a polite sexpot. The kiss had served its purpose and the nearly intolerable tension that had been hovering between them was temporarily tamped. Slightly. Claire felt like she glided back through the restaurant, a couple of people looking up and furrowing their brows in confusion about their coming and going and coming back again so quickly. Claire laughed and sat back down in the seat along the banquette that she'd taken a few moments before. She clasped her hands in front of her. "Well, now that we have that all settled."

Ben smiled in a way that made Claire's stomach flip and her heart sputter and drop.

"You'd best not smile at me like that if you intend to have supper," she said. "I'm not certain I'll make it through a proper meal." She looked down, blushing, and pulled the neatly folded napkin into her lap. She kept her head down, looking to make sure she had opened it and refolded it neatly across her thighs. When she looked up, Ben was staring at her and shaking his head in the tiniest way.

"How did you ever get away from me?"

"Oh." Claire's brow pulled together and she pressed her lips. "Must we really go through all that?"

"Yes."

"Did your wife put up with that sort of monosyllabic nonsense?"

"She's the one who trained me in it. So, yes."

Claire twisted her mouth as she contemplated her reply. Luckily, the waiter arrived with the champagne just then, so she didn't need to launch into a tedious reenactment of her mother and her betrothal and how unalterable it had seemed to her seventeen-year-old self. "Oh! Champagne!"

"Saved by the bell," Ben added with a hint of sarcasm.

As the waiter poured the champagne, Claire opened the menu and made hard work of deciding what she was going to have. She settled on the oysters to start and the crispy pork belly for her main. When she looked up from the menu, Ben was holding his champagne flute aloft and staring at Claire.

"Oh. A toast…" Claire set down her menu and picked up her glass.

Ben tapped his glass with a barely audible clink against hers. "To right now. I want to toast to this very instant with your lips just kissed and about to take a sip. And then, to later."

Her heart began to pound with an unfamiliar, delectable force. "Yes," she breathed. "To right now…and later." Her cheeks must have shone bright red, and she should have been self-conscious, but she couldn't bring herself to care. She loved how he made her feel.

The food came, and Ben ordered a bottle of cabernet to go with it. By the time they'd finished, Claire was warm all over. The last of the wine was swirling in her glass as she twisted the stem and looked into Ben's eyes.

"What happens now?" she asked.

"I take you home and devour you."

Claire stopped twisting the stem of the glass and looked into Ben's eyes; his irises had gone from pale, cool jade to hot, bright emerald during the course of the meal. "I think I'm going to like that," Claire said.

The waiter brought the check, but it was merely a formality as Boppy had already called in the reservation and told the manager that she would be picking up the tab, regardless of the cost.

"I wouldn't have ordered the most expensive bottle of champagne if I expected Boppy to pay for it—" Ben protested.

"You are effectively paying for the whole meal, Ben. You're a client, remember? Boppy pays. No point in getting chivalrous now. She's earned enough off you and your wife to warrant this."

"Ex-wife," Ben added.

Claire looked up and smiled. "Ex-wife. I like the sound of that." She looked down to sign the bill, to make it official that she had in fact eaten there, then closed the leather case and left it on the table. She looked up into Ben's penetrating green eyes. "I don't think I can eat another bite. Shall we?" she asked.

He put his napkin on the table, then stood slowly and reached out a hand to help Claire up from her side of the banquette. "I'm starving," Ben whispered hotly into the curve of Claire's ear.

She stumbled, and Ben took the opportunity to wrap one strong arm around her waist.

"You okay?" he asked.

"Never better." Claire slid her arm behind Ben's back and pulled herself closer in to his hold. "Better and better," she whispered.

They stopped at the coat check to retrieve their jackets and decided to walk the shorter distance to Claire's apartment. The two of them swung their arms in long, wide strokes for a few blocks, then tucked close into each other when the cooler wind whipped down Fifth Avenue.

Chapter 13

"So...THIS IS IT." Claire gestured around to indicate the small, tidy one bedroom apartment, but when she put the single key on the kitchen counter and her gaze returned to Ben, she saw the way his eyes had darkened and his lips had quirked into the sexiest thing she had ever seen. "I mean...this is the apartment..."

Ben took off his jacket and hung it on the back of the kitchen stool to his right.

Claire walked slowly backward, taking off her jacket as she did. "I mean..." She smiled, loving the predatory way Ben was following her, step by delicious step. "I mean..."

He pulled the coat out of her hand and tossed it on top of his.

"Yes?" he asked, still pursuing her slowly. She looked quickly over her shoulder to make sure she didn't trip over the coffee table, then paused.

"I mean...I guess I mean...this is it..." Claire changed direction and dove at Ben. The silky shirt, the high heels, the tight jeans— Claire realized with a rush of pleasure that all of that was for Ben *and* for herself. The smooth fabric of her shirt made her feel like she was skating across his hard, hot chest and stomach. The heels gave her just the right amount of added height to look him in the eye and kiss him outside the restaurant. The jeans...were suddenly quite annoying. Claire groaned through the kiss, or kisses. Then she felt something rumble through him and wasn't sure if it was pleasure or frustration.

"What is it, darling?" she asked.

He reached up and moved a strand of her golden hair, so he could see her eyes clearly. He brought the hair to his nose and inhaled. His eyes closed. "God, when you were standing in my doorway in Connecticut, I almost slammed the door in your face—"

"You did slam the door in my face!" Claire laughed and kept kissing him wherever she could find skin: his neck, below his ear, along his jaw.

"I meant when you first walked up. I thought I was having some sort of hallucination. I just couldn't believe it was really you."

"Kiss me, Ben. Please." Claire had never thought to *ask* Freddy to kiss her—and had certainly never *begged*—because a kiss from Freddy was a quite perfunctory business. Whereas Ben's kisses were so…thorough. She would beg shamelessly for kisses from Ben.

The problem with his thoroughness was that when he stopped to make those tender little comments, Claire was left feeling half-done. She couldn't concentrate on anything he was saying, because her eyes were focused on his mouth: the glistening lower lip, the way his tongue touched the edge when he spoke, the way his teeth flashed in promise. All she could do was wonder how long before his lips were going to be back on her body.

"Are you hearing anything I'm saying?" he asked abruptly, with more force.

"Not a single word," Claire said on a sigh. "But I love watching your lips move when you talk, so it's not a total loss." She smiled shyly. "You're turning me into something wanton."

"God, Claire." His voice was rough and strained. He trailed the pad of his thumb over Claire's lower lip, and she let her tongue taste the salty hint of him. Her eyes closed in the pleasure of it: his smell, and the texture of that bit of skin, and all of him, in her arms, so close, so available. Finally.

"I don't think I ever stopped wanting you either," Claire said quietly into his neck, not opening her eyes as she let her hands rake through the short dark hair that just skimmed Ben's collar. It was easier to be totally honest if she didn't have to look right into those green, demanding eyes. "Maybe that's why my marriage was doomed."

"Oh dear." Ben stood up straighter and set Claire back a few inches. "Let's not spoil everything with talk of doomed marriages. I'm not sure I can take it." Ben tried to laugh it off.

Claire opened her eyes. Her blood had cooled considerably. "Did you just tell me to stop talking about what I was talking about?"

"What?" Ben was trying to pull her close again, beginning to dip into the crook of her neck to whisper more of that unintelligible nonsense about how lovely and gorgeous she was. Claire tried to push him away.

"Did you just tell me not to talk about my doomed marriage?"

"Jesus, Claire. What the hell?" Ben released her and put his hands out in a show of innocence. "My marriage was doomed too. We can talk about whatever you want. But—" She narrowed her eyes skeptically and he lowered his voice. "The truth is, I want to get you into bed. So. Much. I want to feel your supple body all around mine and to touch you everywhere you will let me. I've dreamt of you for so many years. *Years, Claire.* Why in the hell would I want to talk about either of our doomed marriages?"

Claire stared at him. "I... My husband...I just meant that I never..." Claire felt the press of tears and the extent of her foolishness. She collapsed onto the sofa in a heap. "I'm just a mess, Ben. I want all that too." She threw one hand up to encompass his whole existence in a quick flick of her wrist. "Well, who wouldn't? Just look at you." The tears got the best of her and started to fall. "I'm just a rickety old thing."

Ben smiled slowly and knelt down on the floor. "Me too. Ow," he said with dramatic exaggeration, "my arthritis!"

Claire smiled and wiped at her tears. "Seriously, though, don't you feel old sometimes? Too old to be necking on a couch."

"Of course I do," he said. Then, eagerly, "So are we going to neck?"

Claire laughed and wiped away more tears.

"Look, Claire, sweetheart, I'm forty. My nieces think I'm ancient, a relic." He reached out to touch her cheek where a stray tear sparkled in the gentle light of the table lamp. "May I?" he asked, before actually touching her.

Claire nodded.

Ben wiped away the tear and then stroked the edge of her cheekbone and traced her jaw and her chin. He didn't look her in the eye. "I'm terrified, Claire. You broke my heart when you left like you did all those years ago. Just *poof* and you were gone—"

Claire swallowed and felt an entirely new and unanticipated wave of tears coming on. "Oh, Ben—"

"I'm not saying it to get you to forgive me for being an ass just now about the not-wanting-to-talk-about-the-doomed-marriages shutting-you-up comment." He took a deep breath and continued. "You can talk about whatever you want. We can talk about anything. I really believe that." He kept touching her in that gentling way, memorizing her, or reacquainting himself with the details, more like. "I just meant, I want to touch you, to really feel you, because I have wanted—I mean really *craved*—you...*us*, for so long." He inhaled and leaned closer into her, spreading her legs apart so he could kneel in front of her and brush his lips across hers. "Why would I ever postpone what I've been wanting for so long?" His stray touches were beginning to have more purpose. He was tracing the turn of her breasts through the silky fabric. "This shirt is diabolical, by the way. All night I kept getting shadowy glimpses and then, nothing." He cupped her breast fully and squeezed, and Claire gasped at the pleasure that crashed over her. "Come to bed with me, Claire. Please. Now." His breath was hot and demanding between kisses.

She reached her hands around his neck and her legs around his waist. "Yes, Ben."

"Now let me see if I can lever myself up and sweep you into my arms in some stunningly romantic gesture."

Claire laughed and buried her face into the warm, promising scent of his neck. She held on tightly with her arms and legs, and he stood up easily, cupping her bottom and walking toward the small bedroom adjacent to the living room.

"Nice bed," Ben said, gesturing toward Bronte's mammoth mattress covered in beautiful French sheets and enough pillows and bolsters to build a small fort.

"It's my sister-in-law's," Claire said. "I think she's a bit of a sex fiend."

"Good. I like her already." Ben leaned down slowly, placed Claire onto the center of the puffy down comforter, and started tossing aside some of the smaller pillows. Then he looked up at the wrought iron headboard and narrowed his eyes. "Lots of possibilities…"

"Ben!" Claire blushed, caught in some sort of limbo between the sexpot she'd been earlier when he kissed her outside the restaurant and the unbidden memory of the cold, sexless woman Freddy had repeatedly told her she was.

"What just happened? Why did you zone out?"

"I was thinking of some of the mean things my husband used to say to me…about how I was a bit of a cold fish."

Apparently Ben thought that was hilarious. He laughed as he kept up his busy clearing of the extra pillows. Then, he was like a mischievous boy, rummaging around her body. He pushed up her silky shirt and kissed her navel.

"Oh!" she gasped, writhing beneath the intense sensation.

"Cold fish my ass." He growled the words into another kiss, lower on her stomach.

He began to work on the button of her jeans, and Claire didn't know what to do. She'd only been with one man her entire life, and he certainly never came after her like this. Ben seemed so adamant. He yanked her jeans partway down her thighs and stared at the silky underwear, his face only a few inches from the tiny triangle of fabric. Claire had a hand across her face, too embarrassed to look at him looking at her there.

And then he kissed her there, a hot wet possessive kiss right through the thin underwear, and Claire gasped and cried out.

"Ben!"

He kissed her again and inhaled her scent. "Jesus, Claire. You're unbelievable. Your skin is like…perfection." He rubbed his rough cheek against the smooth tenderness of her thigh and hummed his pleasure. "Just perfect."

"Ben," she whispered. It seemed to be the only thing she was capable of. She didn't know what to make of any of it. Freddy had never put his face between her legs. Never.

Ben kept tugging down her jeans until he came to her high-heeled shoes. He stood at the end of the bed, contemplating his options. "I do love the shoes, but the jeans have to come off."

"I'm so embarrassed," Clare said over a laugh. "I don't feel at all sexy."

He took each shoe off slowly. "As you would say, that's daft." He trailed his thumbnail up the arch of one foot and then the other. Claire's back arched in response.

"Oh!" she gasped again. "Okay then…" She rubbed her thighs together in anticipatory glee after he tugged her jeans the rest of the way off. He pulled his sweater and shirt off in one swift motion, and Claire must have whimpered.

"What is it?" he asked, looking genuinely concerned.

Claire pulled one of the pillows from those that remained behind her on the bed and put it halfway in front of her face. "You're just… quite nice."

Ben's smile was the epitome of pure male stroked ego. "Really?" he asked with false innocence, as he kicked off his shoes and slowly unbuttoned his jeans with one hand, rubbing the other lazily along his hard stomach.

Claire squealed into the pillow like a teenaged girl at her first rock concert. His torso was dark and firm, dusted with a fine spray of black hair that led down to where he was undoing his pants with maddening patience. His chest was almost exactly as she remembered it. She had seen it in her mind's eye all these years, just as it had been on those rocky beaches on the Côte d'Azur. Dark and foreign and strong. She'd been mad for his broad chest and ridged stomach. She'd loved leaning her back into him when they'd watch the sunset and she'd nestle into the security of his embrace. He'd always held her with such conviction.

"I've missed you," she whispered more seriously.

He finished taking off his pants and stalked up the length of her body. For some reason, he'd left on his boxer briefs, like he'd done when they were still teenagers, that adolescent concession to safe sex. Thinking back on it now, Claire realized they'd been so chaste. All that kissing and panting and rubbing, but they'd never been fully naked with each other. Her heart started pounding madly at the realization she was finally going to fulfill a dream she'd thought lost forever.

He pulled the pillow from her grasp. "I want to see all of you, Claire."

"Likewise…" Claire reached around and let her hands tentatively hold the firm turn of his ass through the thin fabric. She stroked and reached and watched his eyes cloud and focus as she touched him. "I love your body...it's just so..." She grabbed his hip where the muscles curved like a classical Greek statue across the bones. "Ideal."

"You're going to inflate my ego if you keep talking like that." He was working his hands under her blouse. "Are you ready for me to take this off?"

Claire looked up at the warm light from the small French chandelier that hung over the bed. "Do you want the light on?"

Ben laughed so hard and so abruptly that Claire was momentarily frightened. "What do you think?" he asked, incredulous.

Shaking her head to let him know she really didn't know what he thought, he stopped laughing as quickly as he'd started.

"Oh, Claire," he said softly. "Did that bastard make you feel like you weren't the most beautiful woman in the world? Because I want every light in New York City shining on this body of yours so I can see your eyes and your lips and your reddening skin and the slick response here—" He'd reached his fingers between her thighs and behind the satin of her underwear. "God, Claire...why wouldn't I want to see you like this?"

Her breasts were straining against the inside of her bra and her hips were rocking of their own volition into the touch of his fingers. Claire turned her face away, afraid of how much she wanted this, wanted him. The wanting was dangerous. Very, very dangerous.

"Look at me, Claire." His voice was stern, just like it had been last Saturday when he'd been mean to her, taunting her with that vicious kiss and then dismissing her. When, she now realized, he'd been covering for wanting her. Or maybe not covering at all.

Gathering her courage, and her desire, she reckoned, Claire turned her head back to look him in the eye. That binding look wove them together as much as any copulation or marital rite ever would. He held her with his eyes—daring her to stay with him in those demanding green depths—as one hand began to feel the smooth, slippery evidence of how turned on she was, and the other pushed up her blouse to reveal her bare stomach and bra.

"I don't ever want you to turn away from me." Ben's voice was rough as his fingers were dipping into her. She stared into his eyes and felt her fears, her cold terrors, slipping away. She could really have this. He wanted her in a way she'd never thought possible. She smiled at the realization.

He smiled back, the slow, coaxing rhythm between her legs never ceasing. "What made you smile?"

Claire arched into his hand and sighed her pleasure. "You, Ben. You make me smile. You make me feel...warm and..." She squirmed toward him, putting her hand over his other hand where it rested over her breast.

"And what?" He leaned down and kissed her navel.

"And it makes me happy to think maybe you want me as much as I want you."

His hands froze, and she thought she'd said too much or something wrong, and then he took her mouth with his and turned his fingers inside her in a way that shot bolts of pleasure throughout her body, to the tips of her fingers and toes, up her spine and then tingling across her scalp. She ached for him to be inside her.

Ben pulled away suddenly and stared down at Claire. He was all mussed hair and swollen wet lips; he groaned. "Damn it. I didn't bring any protection."

Claire reached up and trailed her fingertips along his chest, and his eyes slid shut at the simple connection. "I feel like I could just touch you this way for days," she whispered.

He smiled and then slowly opened his eyes, which had taken on a predatory gleam. He took his hand from between her legs and brought it to his lips. "I want to taste you and touch you everywhere, Claire."

His lips, her scent, his fingers, her eyes on his tongue. Claire's mind short-circuited. She had never seen Ben like this, so completely given over to erotic pleasure. Then she whispered, "You're naughty."

Ben laughed, deep at the back of his throat, and then touched his wet fingertips to her lips. "So are you. You just don't know it yet."

She moaned at the feeling of his fingers—and the taste of him and her mingled together—on her tongue. He leaned down and pushed his hard length against her belly. "Is there a drugstore around here where I can go get some condoms?"

"Actually…"

"What?" He stopped moving, thinking she was going to change her mind about everything. They were both still so skittish.

"There are a whole bunch in the bathroom—"

Ben was up and across the room before Claire finished the sentence. She heard him pull open the cabinet and mumble something victorious. She took off her blouse and tossed it across the room, so she'd be lying on the bed in her bra and underwear when he came back. Then she felt embarrassed all of a sudden, like she was laid out in some tawdry pose. She sat up quickly to retrieve her shirt, or put on a nightgown, or get under the sheets, or something. With her back turned, she had one knee on the bed and one foot on the floor when Ben came out of the bathroom.

"Where do you think you're going, sexy?"

She closed her eyes then gathered her courage and looked over her shoulder. "Nowhere," she smiled hesitantly, pulling her foot off the floor so she was kneeling back on her heels near the edge of the bed. "I'm sort of out of the habit."

"Really? Good!" He'd walked around the end of the bed and was standing in front of her. He was right at eye level, as it were.

Her mouth dried, and she licked her lips nervously. She couldn't look away from the straining fabric of his briefs.

"Up here," he joked. "My eyes are up here."

Her eyes flew up to his. "Oh. Sorry."

"I'm joking, Claire." He touched the edge of her cheek. "I love when you look at me like that. Hungry."

She blushed furiously and stared down at the floor. "You're so… graphic."

"Graphic?" He laughed as he opened the box of condoms. "If you think the word *hungry* is graphic, you are in for some downright filth."

She smiled and reached up to touch his stomach.

He smiled back. "By the way, what's up with the gazillion condoms? Were you expecting someone?"

Claire fell back on the bed and tucked her face into the pillow.

"Not that I'm complaining, mind you! I like it."

She looked up and smiled at him. "They're probably expired. My sister-in-law moved to London a few years ago and doesn't come back all that often. They were in the cabinet when I got here."

"Nice welcome wagon," Ben said. He set the box onto the bedside table and tapped the foil packet against his palm while contemplating something. Then he stopped and looked down the length of Claire's body and back to her eyes with that dark mischief. "Take the rest off."

He had this way of switching gears that made Claire pleased and almost terrified—in a good way—all at once. "Oh. Oh, okay." She began to shimmy out of her underwear.

"Slower," he said, clipped and stern.

The way he was able to use his voice to finesse her reaction was beginning to muddle her brain. Then she realized it was quite the opposite of muddled: everything felt gloriously clear, sparkling almost. When he spoke in that dictatorial way, she felt it between her legs, like a switch had been flipped. She slowed way down, sliding the slippery underwear to her ankles and then fidgeting with her feet until she had it dangling from one toe. "Like that?" she teased in a provocative voice she had not even known she was capable of.

He cleared his throat. "Yeah. Like that."

Claire let the underwear drop to the floor and watched Ben's eyes travel up her legs, pausing at her throbbing center, then continuing languidly up to her breasts. "Now the bra," he ordered.

"Oh, okay." Claire smiled, feeling like she was getting the hang of it, getting the hang of him, and how deliciously satisfying it felt—for both of them—to have him fully focused on her like this. She had to arch her back to reach her hands behind to the clasp of her bra, and she watched Ben's face twitch at the movement.

"Do you like that?" She arched her back more and then let the bra unsnap. She didn't remove it, but the loosened cups barely covered her breasts. She lowered herself back onto the bed, slowly moving the shoulder straps to rest near her elbows, dipping her chin and feeling like a burlesque dancer. She thought she'd be embarrassed when she was totally revealed to him—her breasts weren't as firm as they'd once been, her stomach not nearly as supple—but the way he looked at her made her bold. He made her feel beautiful, not just because he said it, but because he looked at her in that ravenous way of his. She started to reach for her breast, thinking she might tease him—

"Stop it!" Ben snapped.

Claire looked at him and her breathing caught. He was so demanding, so narrowly focused. Almost brutal.

"Ben..." she said, her voice low and wanting. "Please touch me." She took the bra the rest of the way off and let it fall to the floor next to the bed. She never stopped looking at him. His eyes were stormy, bordering on angry. His cock was straining behind the fabric of his underwear. "What are you waiting for?"

His breath came out like a hiss. "Claire." He shook his head once. "I have been waiting for this, for you, for so damn long. I think I'm having trouble processing that this is real...that you are real... and that you want me..."

"I do. So much." Claire sat up from her reclining position and got to her knees on the bed in front of him. It wasn't nearly as terrifying as she'd imagined—all this naked business.

She reached her hands to Ben's waist and dipped her fingers between the elastic and his quivering hot skin. "May I?" She looked up at him and began to tug down his underwear. She stretched the elastic so it didn't scrape against the shining tip of him, then she let the boxers fall to his ankles.

"Step out," she whispered. He was staring at the ceiling, breathing hard, still holding the condom in one hand. He lifted one foot and then the other so they were both finally and completely naked. Claire leaned down and kissed the crown of his cock, then wrapped her slim fingers around the base and took him into her mouth.

"Oh, Claire!" His hand was in her hair and pulling hard within seconds. "No—" He choked on the word, but he didn't pull her away exactly. She released her mouth and stared up at him, her lips wet and eyes smiling. She relished the frustration and control he had to exercise when she looked at him like that. Good. Make him feel what she felt. The crazy wanting.

"I wanted to taste you too..."

A few seconds later, he'd torn open the condom and pulled it on, pushed her back onto the bed, and the two of them were smiling and touching and scrambling to get as much of their bodies in contact with one another as possible. Claire's legs were tangled around his. Ben's lips and fingers were caressing Claire's neck. Her hips were tilting and rising to meet him.

Ben paused and held Claire still, gripping her upper arm with one hand and the turn of her hip with the other. "Yes?"

She whimpered. It sounded preposterous, but there was nothing for it. She nodded and whispered, "So much yes."

Claire put her palm up to his cheek as he guided himself into her. She marveled at the pale tone of her skin against the dark beauty of his. She wanted to tell him that she loved him just then, but she held it back; it felt juvenile or injudicious. But she *felt* it, and she loved that she loved him, expressed or not. Her eyes must have gone moist at the realization, because he mistook her joy for sad tears.

"Are you okay?" He was entering her slowly, taking his time to go inch by heavenly inch.

She lifted her head to kiss her answer. "Yes. I am just so very happy. I keep thinking *finally…finally…*"

Ben pounded into her on that second *finally* and whispered, gruff and raw, into her ear, "Finally."

Chapter 14

CLAIRE AND BEN spent the rest of that night in a restless joining. Sleeping intermittently. One or both of them waking up enough to touch or kiss the other, and the whole wonderful cascade of pleasure firing up between them all over again. By ten on Saturday morning, Claire was nearly drunk on the happiness of it. She started laughing, tucked into the hold of Ben's strong arm, her lips dragging across the turn of his biceps. She kept thinking how perfect he was. *Perfect for her*, she amended. Strong and lean and reliable. And he wanted her.

He tightened his arm around her back. "What's so funny?"

"I think I might be punch-drunk or something. I keep closing my eyes and dozing and then I smell you or touch you and this little voice inside me squeals, *He's real! He's real!* and I need to—I get to—reach out and kiss you and touch you and it's just all so…lovely."

He kissed the top of her head. "Exactly."

She continued her travels across his upper arm then kissed his neck. She leaned up on her elbows and her face took on a pragmatic cast. "So. What shall we do today? I want to see you outdoors. I want to see you in shops. On streets. In the city. I want to see you in the country."

"I want to see you in bed. Naked." He grabbed her bottom and squeezed.

"Well, that too." She smiled and kissed his chest. "But seriously, I want to be with you out in the world. I want to be all hand-holding and strolling and all that."

He smiled at her. "Okay. Do you want to stay in the city or should we head out to Litchfield? I'm not playing with the band tomorrow night and I don't have appointments on Monday, so we could stay in the country for a couple of days…if you think Boppy was serious about you taking off Monday."

Claire closed her eyes and relaxed her cheek against Ben's chest. Just that. His thinking about her plans. Her job. That was probably sexier or more alluring than all the other mischievous attention he'd paid to her body in the past twelve hours. He was mindful in a way that Freddy had never been. Or really, that anyone in her life had ever been. Maybe even herself.

It was probably her fault as much as anyone else's. She had uttered the phrase, "Don't mind me" with such regularity, it was almost a tick. *Perhaps*, Claire thought, *if you tell people to ignore you often enough, they start to obey.*

"Yes," Claire said. "Let's go to Litchfield. I'd love that."

They showered together, and Claire got dressed and packed a small overnight bag.

"Oh, drat. I totally forgot my sister-in-law invited me out to brunch." Claire looked up at Ben, all scrubbed and gorgeous, his shirt from last night perfectly rumpled. He would be quite the day-after door prize at brunch with Bronte. No. Way.

"We can do that if you want," he offered.

She shook her head. "I don't think I'm ready to share you just yet."

Ben smiled and turned to pull on his coat while Claire made a quick call letting Bronte know she wasn't going to be able to make it after all. Ben could probably overhear Bronte shrieking across town, a loud patter she kept up until Claire was finally forced to say, "Okaaaaayyyy. Byyyeee." She turned off the phone and pretended to ignore the fact that the person on the other end of the line had still been talking. "All set," she said as she turned off the phone all the way, ignoring a bunch of voice mail notifications from London—probably her solicitor and a bunch of other tripe she had no interest in thinking about just then—and slipping the device into her purse.

After a quick stop at Ben's apartment, they were on the road. Ben's car was small and fast.

"Is this a divorce car?" Claire asked.

Ben laughed. "Is it that obvious?"

She nodded and looked out the window. She wanted to hold his hand, but it was a stick shift (of course) and he didn't have a free hand to offer. "You should have chosen an automatic."

"Why? I like the power and control of the stick."

"The hand-holding." Claire pouted in mock consternation.

He smiled, slipped the car into fifth gear, and switched into the middle lane of the highway. "For a few minutes, I can maintain this speed and hold hands." He reached out his right hand for her to take it. Claire felt tingles all along the palm of her hand as she took his and kissed it.

"Thanks," she whispered, holding his strong hand like a treasure.

They turned onto Route 7 a little while later, the curves and speed variations making him pull his hand away. "Sorry," he said.

They made it to the farmhouse in two hours flat.

After they got out of the car, Ben opened the front door of the house and stood aside for Claire to go in before him. "You remember this door, right? The one I slammed in your face?"

She looked down at the craft paper over the front hall floors then up into his penitent green eyes. "Yes," she said quietly. "I remember. You'll have to thank my other sister-in-law, Sarah James, for explaining how that might have been a sign of your...er...ardor, rather than mere cruelty."

Ben dropped his duffle bag and pulled Claire into his arms.

"When will I get to meet all of these fairy god-sisters to thank them personally for all of their good works on my behalf?"

Claire tilted her face to his, a little startled. "Oh, anytime, I guess." She shrugged. "Do you want to meet them? Meet my family?"

He loosened his hold on her, mistaking her hesitance for a desire to keep him separate from her family, as he'd always suspected she'd been trying to do all those years ago. "First things first, I guess." He let go of her and picked up both of their bags. "C'mon. Let me show you everything I did last weekend to punish myself for treating you so abominably."

They spent the late afternoon walking through the forest that ran back and away from the property line behind the house. He showed her his pathetic attempt at rebuilding the stone wall, and she made a note in her project to-do list on her phone to call the local stonemasons and get them out here to remedy his…enthusiasm.

Ben's cell phone rang a couple of times while they were walking. He glanced at the names and then slid his thumb across the screen to silence the calls.

When they were back in the house, cheeks red and cool from their walk, they talked about what they wanted to do for dinner. His phone rang while they were talking; he looked at the screen and held up one finger.

"This one I have to take. Sorry." He stood up from the makeshift kitchen table and looked out the window behind where Claire was sitting.

"Hey, beautiful! How's it going?"

Claire was momentarily tormented and put her face in her hands, until she felt Ben's hand rub her back and his hot breath whisper in her ear. "It's my niece, at boarding school a few towns over."

Claire made a mental note to avoid being jealous of sixteen-year-old girls and looked up into his face with a smile. He kept rubbing her neck absently while he dove into the conversation.

"Sure, but I'll need to check with my friend, Claire." He smiled at his niece's reply. "Yes, she's a girl." He smiled again. "Yes, I like her like that." His smile was really wide. "Yes, she heard me say that. She's sitting right here…okay, let me ask her."

He held the phone against his shoulder and said, "Nicolette Hayek-Milton requests the pleasure of your company for dinner tonight and-or lunch tomorrow. What that really means is she's going stir-crazy in her dorm, and she wants us to swoop in and take her off campus. Are you up for it?"

Claire nodded enthusiastically. She had been totally remiss with her own daughter lately and she saw this as a chance to do a good deed. Ever since she'd arrived in New York, Claire had decided no news was good news as far as her wayward Lydia was concerned. The girl was going through what was euphemistically known as "a bad patch," and Claire was perfectly happy to leave the twenty-year-old troublemaker to her own devices for a few weeks at a stretch.

"I'd love that. Let's go get her now and have supper together."

"Yes," Ben said over a laugh. "Yes, she said yes…she has a daughter, that's why…she probably knows that you won't stop bothering us until you get what you want. We'll see you in an hour. Bye, Nicki."

A few minutes later, the sports car was taking the tight turns of the northern Connecticut roads with gripping confidence.

"You're a great driver," Claire said.

"Thanks." Ben turned to look at her profile in the glow of the dashboard. The late autumn evening had come on quickly, and it was already dark at half past six. "What're you thinking about?"

She turned back to face him. "Oh. Nothing, I guess. It's beautiful here, but I think I'm missing Scotland a bit. Everything feels a little on top of each other here." Claire turned back to look out at the small town they were passing through.

"Why don't we plan a trip?" Ben offered.

Claire's head swung around. "To Scotland? With you?"

Ben tried to fob off the slight with a shrug. What was it with this woman being the most giving creature in bed and the most uptight, withholding woman in other areas of her life? "Yes, Claire. To Scotland. With me." He shook his head, unable to conceal his frustration this time, and stared straight ahead.

After a few seconds, Claire said, "Wow. I would love that."

"What?" he asked in astonishment.

"I said I would love that. Before when you asked when you had to meet my sisters-in-law, I figured you wouldn't want anything to do with my snooty family. I figured the longer we could postpone it, the better it would be for you. I mean—"

"Claire. This is ridiculous. I *want* to meet your family. I *want* to meet everyone who matters to you, just like I want you to meet everyone who matters to me. We're not seventeen anymore." His eyes skimmed suggestively down to her long legs in their snug blue jeans. "Even though you might still look like it to me."

She smiled up at him and pushed his upper arm. "You don't have to say that."

"What? It's true. You're gorgeous. Whatever, I'm not going to waste time trying to convince you. I have all night in bed to do that."

"Ben!" Claire cried.

"You know I'm right. Anyway, all I was saying about when we were teenagers is that it was all that love-in-a-vacuum stuff. You know what I mean?"

Claire nodded. "Totally."

"But now we're grown-ups. And I have to confess, I love being a grown-up. No one can make my decisions for me. I mean, sometimes that sucks, when I do something stupid like stay married to the wrong woman for nine years, but you know, even that, it was mine. You know what I mean?"

"I know exactly what you mean. I think that's part of my whole midlife...I hate the word crisis, but...as they'd say in Wick, part of my going mental."

"I like that. We are both going mental."

Claire reached out and rested her hand on his strong thigh. "Going mental together, I like it too."

He paused for a few seconds. "So, go on about what you were saying about your family, because I think I'm pretty screwed up about the whole thing."

"What whole thing?"

"Oh, you know. Your mother probably hated me and that was why you never said good-bye that summer and why you never wanted to see me again. Touch of the tar brush and all that."

"God, that's such an awful expression."

"Well? It's not like it never came up. It's bad enough that I wasn't even British. Much less some working-class American. To top it all off, your mother probably thought I was some Middle Eastern parvenu come to take you to my harem."

Claire burst out laughing. "Harem?"

He smiled too, despite himself. "You know what I mean. Your roommate...what was her name again?"

"Sally Musgrove."

"Yeah, Sally. She always looked at me like I was from the wrong side of the tracks."

"What tracks?" Claire tried.

"Jesus, Claire, if we can't talk about this now, as adults—who just screwed all night and professed our undying love for one another..."

She stayed silent, staring out at the passing trees.

"Claire?"

"What?" She still didn't look at him.

"You can't just not answer."

Her lips firmed.

"Wow." He downshifted the car into a tight turn. "I guess you can. This should be interesting. So…let me get this straight. We only talk about what you want to talk about?"

She pulled her lips between her teeth then exhaled as if it hurt her lungs to do it. And then the dam broke. "I hate my family sometimes—"

"What? Claire, no. That's not what I meant—"

Her voice rose uncontrollably. "I know it's not what *you* meant. It's what *I* meant!" She slapped the palm of her hand against her chest. "I've hated them for so long…my cruel, cold, calculating mother, my life-of-the-party, insulting bastard husband, my spoiled, ungrateful daughter, all products of a society that I withdrew from decades ago, but that you—and everyone else—think I embody or represent or something."

He slowed down and pulled off to the side of the road. It was rough gravel and sloped away from the pavement. "Claire, honey. Come here." He reached for her and felt the way she leaned into him. He stroked the back of her hair and kissed her temple.

"I just sound like a spoiled shrew, right?" Her voice was muffled into his coat and she was crying stupid tears again.

He lifted her chin so their faces were inches apart. "Stop. It wasn't the right time for me to bring it up. I'm sorry. It's my hang-up. It's my thing. We'll work it out. I always felt like you thought I wasn't, I don't know, a good enough person or something, because I was Lebanese."

"Why would you think *I* would think that?"

"Because I thought that was the reason you didn't stay with me all those years ago. That I didn't measure up. Socially or something."

"Oh god. What a stupid mess." She took the handkerchief he offered. "Thank you."

"You're welcome. I'm really sorry, Claire. I guess it was dumb to think it was something we could joke about. Like, *Hey, wasn't that bit of passive racism hilarious?*"

She ended up laughing at that after all. "Oh, Ben. My mother is a horrible snob, but I don't think it's about race or anything. But none of that matters. To me, I mean." Patting her eyes dry and letting out a long breath, Claire tried to collect herself. "Now that sounds stupid too, like I don't respect your heritage or something. I only meant—" She groaned and leaned in to kiss him.

He felt it like something constricting around his chest, her tenderness, her vulnerability. "Claire…" he whispered as she pulled away.

"Ben. I can't…" She turned to the window again. "There's just so much crap in my life." She looked back into his eyes. "I want to keep you perfect for a few more weeks or months, uncontaminated by my messed up past. Is that so bad?"

He caressed her cheek. "No. It's not bad at all." His warm fingers snaked around her neck and sent a shiver down her back when he rubbed his fingers into her hair. "Do you trust me, Claire?"

Her eyes widened. "What kind of question is that? Of course I trust you. After what we did last night…and this morning…even the way you are touching me right now. How could you ask such a thing?"

"I don't mean do you trust me with your body—"

"You're making me angry," she interrupted. "Of course I didn't mean I trusted you only with my body. I'm madly in love with you. Isn't it obvious?" Her voice was raised in a way that bordered on shrill. His hand was still resting on her neck, but she'd turned away again.

The silence in the car was suddenly profound, and their shallow breathing cut through the thick air.

"Not really obvious," Ben replied quietly. "You sound kind of pissed off about it, actually."

Her head whipped around to look at him. "*Not really?* Whatever do you—" She clenched her hands into fists and kept them resting on her thighs. The silence settled around them again.

"What are you doing right now, Claire?" Ben finally asked.

"I'm containing myself."

"Well don't!" He tried to lower his voice, but now he was angry too. "I don't want you *contained.* I want you splattered all over the inside of this car. I want you mad and frustrated and crying and joyful and furious. I want all of that. All of you."

Claire thought the pressure inside her chest might be a heart attack. The weight of it, of how much this man wanted from her, his persistence. "Ben, I…"

He'd withdrawn his hand from her neck, keeping one hand on the wheel and one hand on the stick shift, even though they were still parked on the side of the country highway and they weren't going anywhere. He wasn't touching her or trying to soothe her feelings away. He was waiting.

"Okay. Well." Claire took another deep breath. "I…that will take some getting used to…on my part…I've never splattered. Ever."

He turned his head just enough so he could look at her out of the corner of his far-too-perceptive eye. "You've never just totally lost your shit?"

She shook her head.

"Never yelled at anyone in the grocery store?"

She continued to shake her head.

"Never given someone the finger for cutting you off in traffic?"

She shook her head one last time. "Not that I recall."

"Why not?"

"A display of ill-temper is fatal to harmony," she parroted.

"Is that so? Who said that? The Dowager Duchess of Northrop, I presume?"

"Some etiquette book that she always cited. But I kind of agree, regardless of the source. How does lashing out solve anything?"

He shook his head in frustration.

She wiped away a slow tear that trickled down her cheek and almost laughed. "What are you doing to me right now? I think I might prefer the door being slammed in my face. I'm trying to keep it together, Ben. We should really go pick up Nicki. She'll wonder what's become of us."

"No she won't. She's probably Instagram-ing half her classmates and has already forgotten we're on our way to pick her up." He gripped the steering wheel harder. "Claire, sweetie, look." She kept looking at her lap. "Look at me, please."

She met his eyes. For a few seconds, she was back in Scotland in her mind, reliving the moment she said those same words to Freddy. Only her husband had refused to look at her. She had finally uncovered his greatest lie—he'd had a vasectomy shortly after Lydia was born. And he hadn't even had to decency to look her in the eye. She had ignored his financial indiscretions. She had even ignored his occasional sexual indiscretions. As long as she didn't end up reading about them in *Tatler* or the *Daily Mail*, what difference did it make? But when she'd accidentally happened upon that old medical file, she realized Freddy had robbed her of far more than money or reputation.

"Neither one of us is keeping it together, Claire. We're going mental, remember? I'm here for you. I love you. That's what I'm doing to you right now. Loving you."

"I don't even know what that *means*, Ben!" She looked away again. "I know I want to be near you—I couldn't even bear to be apart from you when you got in the shower this morning—but is that love? Really? Or is it some, oh I don't know, some grasping after something that both of us have built up in our memories to be this hugely romantic thing?" Like she had built up her marriage? Pretending everything was fine. Pretending she knew what was happening.

As soon as Lydia was born, Claire had wanted more children. For years, Claire had wanted more children. She'd become pregnant with Lydia on her honeymoon, so she was confused when she didn't get pregnant again right away. After a few years of unprotected sex and no baby, she had begun seeing specialists. On each of her monthly trips to London to visit her mother, she secretly started seeing a fertility expert. Freddy was tested and his sperm count was fine. It was something to do with Claire.

Eventually, she flew to a world-renowned expert in Geneva. She and Freddy still had sex on a regular basis—when she knew she was ovulating—but the more stressed out Claire became, the more Freddy implied that her barrenness was a result of her neurotic desire to have more children. He told her to relax and enjoy life. He shrugged it off.

The ups and downs of her cycle began to dominate her existence. For those two hopeful weeks when she *might* be pregnant? For those two weeks, her life seemed so full of hope and promise. Maybe this time. Maybe this time.

Then. She would get her period. Like clockwork. Practically down to the minute. And she would bawl her eyes out and wait a few weeks until the whole cycle of hope and despair could start all over again. Freddy had robbed her of so much.

But Ben was *not* Freddy. In fact, he was so far from being Freddy, she felt guilty for even letting thoughts of Freddy enter her mind when Ben was sitting right next to her. She cleared away all those wretched memories and lifted her eyes.

She looked at Ben and waited for him to speak.

"Listen to me." He touched her cheek tenderly. "I am a forty-year-old man, Claire, and I am sitting here right now, in the present moment, telling you, I *know* what love is. And for me, love is what I feel for you."

She gave him a watery smile. "I am dogged by fear, Ben. I've not been good at this. In fact, I've failed miserably. I did what everyone expected of me. I did what my mother told me to do—"

"Well then stop doing that! It didn't work!" His temper flared.

She laughed, really laughed, deep in her belly. "Oh, Ben." She reached for him and pulled him to her for another kiss. When her lips were right next to his ear, she whispered, "I love you, Ben Hayek. I know that what I feel for you is love." Then she bit the lobe of his ear.

"Ow! What was that for?" He sounded angry but his eyes looked sexy as hell.

She smiled, feeling happy and slightly devious. "Don't badger me. I don't like it."

"Good," he said as he revved the engine back to life and pulled onto the highway. "I like it when you give me a little what-for."

"You do?"

He was concentrating on the dark road. "Yeah, I do. You can bite me anytime. That's all I was asking about trusting me…I want you to trust me enough to be uncontained, you know?"

"Ok. I'll try to be a real mess."

"Let's start with ear-biting and work our way up."

Chapter 15

SHE SMILED AND rested her hand on his thigh again, letting it stay there until they pulled into the entrance of the boarding school. They stopped in front of a brick building with white shutters, just like eight other brick buildings with white shutters that were dotted around the campus.

A tall teenager came running out, long dark hair flying behind her, waving her hand. Claire and Ben both got out of the car.

"Hey, Uncle Ben!" she cried and threw her arms around his waist.

He hugged her back in a way that made Claire melt. He would be the best dad. The idea was just right there. She tried to scrap that thought as quickly as it flew into her brain. *Bad bad bad thought. Good good bad thought? Totally unrealistic. Totally——*

"Claire?"

She had zoned out. "Oh, sorry! Hi, Nicki. It's so nice to meet you." Claire reached out to shake the young woman's hand and was surprised when Nicki hugged her instead. She was stiff at first, for a second, then hugged her back.

"You're so British! It's adorable. Thinking I would shake your hand. Priceless." Nicki smiled and turned back to Ben. "So where should we go for dinner? It's so boring around here. Can we drive up to Great Barrington?"

"Sure. You want to pack a bag and spend the night?" Ben asked.

"No, I have an early rehearsal tomorrow, but thanks."

"Okay, let's go." Ben pulled open the passenger side door. "Hop in the back, Legs."

Nicki smiled and pretzeled herself into the cramped backseat of the sports car.

As Claire was about to get in, he dipped his head near her ear and whispered, "Thanks for doing this," and kissed her neck. She sat and looked up at him with a grateful smile right before he smiled back and shut the car door. She had no idea what he was thanking her for, but she was happy about it.

They chatted about nothing in particular as they drove the half hour to Great Barrington. Nicki played guitar in a three-piece jazz band, and she and Ben were laughing about some new band that Claire had never heard of.

"What kind of music do you like, Claire?" Nicki asked.

"Oh, I don't really listen to much music."

"What? Oh my god. That's like...sacrilegious or something. Ben is one of the best guitarists ever."

Claire smiled at Ben, who shrugged as if truth was truth. "I went to hear him play last week. He is really good," Claire agreed.

"But you don't listen to music at work or when you're at home?"

"Not really, no."

"Wow." Nicki was stunned into silence. "I can't really even imagine what that would be like."

"Maybe you should try it sometime," Ben said. "Just for the novelty."

"Very funny. I'd die."

Ben and Claire laughed at the same time, then Ben said, "I think you'd probably survive it. So which place do you want to go to in Great Barrington. That unpronounceable Mexican place or the tavern place?"

"It's Xicotencatl, Ben. It's not unpronounceable; it's Mexican. Seriously, you are so narrow minded."

Claire smiled again, then her face fell. She missed Lydia. "You sound like my daughter. She thinks I'm horribly narrow minded."

"You have a daughter?"

"Yes. She's twenty."

"Where is she?"

Claire had a pang of guilt. She wasn't precisely sure where Lydia was. Claire had finally checked her voice messages after she and Ben came in from their long walk, and one of the calls she'd avoided earlier in the day had been a message from her sister Abby. She'd said she was done baby-sitting and Lydia had quit the charity project in Nairobi.

"She was doing some volunteer work in Kenya, but I think she's going to stop soon."

"She is?" Ben asked. That was news to him.

"Yeah, Abby left me a message this morning."

"She sounds cool," Nicki interjected. "What's her name?"

"Lydia...Lydia Barnes."

"Why have I heard that name before?" Nicki clicked on her phone and tapped a few times. "Oh my god! You are Devon Heyworth's sister? Ben!" Nicki reached up between the car seats and punched her uncle on the shoulder.

"Ow! Cut that out!" he said as he rubbed his shoulder.

"Seriously, dude! Claire is related to one of the hottest guys... on...the...planet."

"Nicolette Hayek-Milton. Your manners are appalling. I'm calling your mother to tell her. Did you just Google my friend while she's sitting right here and then talk about her in the third person... as if she weren't here?"

She was properly chastised. "Sorry. And sorry, Claire. That was rude. I apologize."

"Oh, no worries." Claire turned back to face Nicki and gave her a little smile. "Devon's never done anything to limit his exposure, if you know what I mean." A few weeks before, in fact, Devon had been sunbathing naked in the Bahamas and the partially obscured photos were all over the tabloids. "I don't blame you for taking an interest."

"Thanks. Still, that wasn't nice of me." She put her phone back into the pocket of her hoodie. "So. Is he really hot in real life?"

"Nicki!" Ben was trying to keep a stern tone in his voice but having a hard time of it.

Claire laughed. "I think he's sort of ragtag and foolish. But I'm his older sister, so that's how I'm supposed to think of him. His wife thinks he's very dishy."

"Oh," Nicki said on a girlish sigh. "Just the word...*dishy*..."

"Did I just fall into some sort of estrogen time warp?" Ben asked.

Claire looked over her shoulder again and smiled at Nicki. "Maybe if we think of someone not in my family I can jump on the estrogen bandwagon. Roger Federer?"

"He's okay. But he's so old."

"Old?" Claire cried. "Never say!"

"Ben! Don't you love how Claire says, *Never say!*, just like Lizzie Bennet?"

Ben smiled so only Claire could see in the glow of the dashboard as he answered Nicki. "I do love it."

Claire felt her heart swell, as foolish as it made her feel to think so. Ben loved her, for whatever crazy inexplicable reason. Maybe she had finally found a slice of happiness.

"How about Bradley Cooper?" Claire tried.

"Still pretty old. But I'll give you the blue eyes. How about Adam Levine?"

"Who?" Claire asked.

"Oh my god. What planet are you on?"

"Planet Claire?" Ben tried.

"That's just lame, Uncle Ben. Seriously." Nicki sighed at his weak attempt at a joke. Then she snapped her fingers. "I know! Ryan Gosling! Isn't he the man no one can hate?"

"Ah, someone we can all agree on," Claire said. "Mr. Gosling to the rescue."

Both women sighed in unison.

"Are you two for real? What's so great about Ryan Gosling?"

Nicki was still in Ryan-dream mode. "Don't even bother…"

Claire agreed. "Just…not worth questioning greatness…"

"Thank god we're at the restaurant. I don't know how much more swooning my V12 engine and I can stand."

Claire and Nicki laughed as they got out of the car. The three of them went into the restaurant, which was crowded and loud on Saturday night, with a live band playing contemporary Mexican music at the back. They were shown to a table in a separate room, a little bit quieter.

"Okay fine," Nicki said, picking up the conversation where they'd left off in the car as if they'd never stopped talking. "Just for gender equality's sake, and Ben's enjoyment, who do you think are the sexiest women, Claire?"

"Oh…let me think…sexy? I guess I think of women differently. I think they're more beautiful than hot, you know what I mean?"

"Okay, sure. So who do you think is the most beautiful woman?" Nicki dove into the chips and salsa as soon as they were set down on the table.

"So many…Vivien Leigh…Keira Knightley…" Claire was having a hard time concentrating as Ben's hand came to rest on her thigh, unseen beneath the Formica tabletop.

"Claire," he said.

"Yes?" she answered.

Ben turned from her to look at Nicki. "No. I meant my answer is Claire. I think Claire is the most beautiful woman I've ever seen."

"Aw, that's so romantic!" Nicki said over a crunchy chip. Then she looked at Claire more objectively. "You are really gorgeous, now that I look at you in the light. Great bones."

"You two are so strange." Claire took a sip of her water to do something other than feel them looking at her like a butterfly pinned to a bit of felt.

"Yeah, totally strange," Ben said as he gave her thigh a little squeeze. "Let's stop tormenting her, Nic. She's from a place where speaking plainly means *pass the tiara.*"

"Oh, god. Then don't ever bring her home for Christmas! Can you imagine if Sitti starts asking her about her orgasms?"

Claire was unable to swallow properly and choked. "Oh dear. So sorry," she tried to gasp out.

Ben patted her gently on the back. "Sitti is my mom, by the way. Are you okay?"

"Sure, sure. Fine." She patted her chin with a paper napkin to absorb the liquid that had escaped from her mouth.

"Oh my god! You're not kidding? Have you ever even said the word *orgasm?*"

Claire looked at Nicki then at Ben. "Out loud, you mean?"

Nicki burst out laughing. "This is going to be *so* awesome. Ben, your mom and all your sisters are going to go nuts."

Ben smiled and put his arm around Claire's shoulder. "Claire can handle herself. I'm not worried."

But Claire was. If Ben's family was filled with strong, confident, outspoken women who talked about their orgasms over the *bûche de Noël,* she was going to feel even more ridiculous than she already did.

"Don't listen to her, Claire. She's just trying to scare you."

"No, I'm not!" Nicki defended after taking a big sip of her Coke. "I'm trying to prepare you. My mother and all her sisters are like a bunch of militant feminists. Ben, you need to give Claire a heads-up. Seriously!"

"Nicki, I want her to like me. You think I'm going to tell her about my six sisters?"

"Six?" Claire nearly choked again. "How could I have forgotten that?"

Ben shrugged. "I probably didn't tell you on purpose. It's more or less horrifying. They're like a pack of wolves." He took a sip of his margarita.

"Well," Claire said. "Then I owe you a debt of gratitude, Nicki. Thanks for the warning. What are their names?"

"Olympia. Sanger. Joumana. Cady. Hoda. And my mom, Betty."

Claire started laughing. "You're joking!"

Both Ben and Nicki shook their heads and widened their eyes in a doleful way. Nicki spoke first. "Can you imagine? My poor mom… having to be named after Betty Fucking Friedan."

"Nicki! Language!" Ben snapped.

"Sorry. Bad habit." Nicki smiled, and Claire noticed neither of them were any the worse for it. Claire had given up trying to chastise Lydia years ago—the slightest correction was immediately seen as a horrible slight.

"And where do you fall into the birth order, Ben?" Claire asked.

"The baby. It's your basic birth-order disaster."

"Ok. Give me the one-sentence description of each one," Claire said to Nicki.

"Oh, fun. All right, let me think. One sentence. Here goes… Olympia lives in Paris and is a curator in the Islamic Art Department at the Louvre, married, no kids. Sanger is a painter and lives with her husband and four dogs in Santa Fe. Joumana teaches Arabic at

U. Penn. and she's single, supposedly, but we all know she lives with some Republican econ professor Sitti hates."

"Go on."

"Cady and Hoda went into business together and now run a software development company in Northern California. Cady has a girlfriend; Hoda has a boyfriend. Then Boring Betty, my mom. The housewife from New Jersey. One kid. She doesn't do anything."

"Ouch." Claire felt the sting.

"What? It's just so boring. I have all these relatives who are doing all this cool stuff and what did my mom do?"

"She had you," Claire answered with something bordering on despair.

"I know, I know. I respect that. But seriously, what did that take? Like a day or two? To push me out?"

"Nicki…" Ben realized what was happening, but it was too late.

Claire put her hand on his. "No, I want to hear this. A day or two to deliver you, you mean?"

Nicki looked like she knew she was probably insulting Claire somehow, but she wanted to be honest. "I don't mean to be disrespectful, but my mom just sort of threw in the towel. Her sisters joke that she was the smartest of all of them—perfect performance on the National Latin Exam when she was twelve. Piano prodigy. That sort of thing. She could have done anything!"

Claire stared at this glorious, bursting young woman. "She did do something, Nicki. She raised you."

"But I'm just a by-product. Don't you see? Who is *she*?"

"Wow. Is that really how you see it?"

Nicki shrugged. "Yeah. Again, I don't mean to be rude or dismissive. I just don't really get it."

Claire narrowed her eyes and tried to think how to explain her feelings. "Look, I'm in no position to talk about what it means to be a good mother right at the moment. I'm failing miserably—"

"Oh, I'm sure that's not true!" Nicki exclaimed. "You're probably just being modest—"

"No. I'm being honest."

Ben took a sip of his margarita and watched Claire as she spoke. Nicki stayed quiet.

"But when Lydia was born…" Claire's voice trailed off and she twisted the stem of the margarita glass absently. "It was like the greatest love affair imaginable. I felt like I had finally found my purpose on this earth. She was such a precious, beautiful thing. And so tiny and vulnerable and lovable. And she was so easy to satisfy. Everyone in my life up until then had been so mysterious and confusing to me, you know what I mean?"

Nicki and Ben nodded, both listening intently and watching Claire relive the memories.

"Lydia was so happy. I had never seen anything like it. She would just play in her crib and kick her chubby feet and reach for the mobile, or if she wanted company, she might bark a small cry, but the minute I came to the edge of the cot, she would…" Claire was back in that wonderful place in time. "She just beamed that gummy smile, and her eyes lit up. It was amazing."

The three of them were quiet for a few seconds before Claire continued.

"It's a really deep, powerful human relationship, Nicki. It's not *nothing*. And it's certainly not something that takes a day or two. I'm still doing it. Or trying." Claire looked up and realized she had been lost in her own memories. "Oh, sorry to be so maudlin."

"No!" Nicki was smiling. "I loved that. You were so right there. I could totally picture you with a baby. You know, you're still really young—you should have another one! I bet you're an awesome mother."

Claire stared into her margarita glass, and Ben took a sip and looked toward the band.

"*Awkward.* Totally sorry." Nicki's face was bright red. "Seriously. You guys are just starting to date, and I'm talking about you having babies together."

"Nicki," Ben said in a warning tone.

"What? It's not like you never thought about it, Uncle Ben. Mom says you've wanted to have kids ever since you came back from France that summer you were at Cal Tech. Remember?"

Claire was biting her lips into her mouth, and Ben was rubbing the flats of his hands on his jeans. "Nicki, enough with all the talk about babies. All right?"

"All right, all right. What are we going to eat?" Nicki whipped open her menu and hid her face behind it.

Ben turned to look at Claire and mouthed *sorry* and touched her cheek. She smiled and slowly opened her own menu. She was sorry too. But for what, she wasn't exactly sure. For secretly wanting Ben's babies? Or for feeling like she shouldn't entertain such dangerous thoughts in the first place?

The rest of the meal passed in much lighter conversation. Claire told stories about her own family, about her responsible brother Max and her wild brother Devon. About her sister Abigail, who ran the organization in Africa. Over dessert, Claire looked up at Nicki and smiled. "I guess I'm sort of the Boring Betty of my family. Maybe your mother and I should meet?"

Nicki laughed. "Totally. You both have that weird peaceful thing going on. Like everything's going to be okay no matter what. I don't think I'll ever feel like that. Will you, Uncle Ben?"

"When I'm around Claire, I feel like I might have a chance."

"Man, you two have got it bad. It's like crazy-love-town all up in here. You'd better take me back to campus, so I can remember what bitter disappointment and teenage angst are all about."

Ben paid the bill and they drove back through the mountainous winding roads. Nicki hooked up her cell phone to Ben's car stereo and gave Claire a crash course in contemporary music. They got back just before midnight and Ben made sure Nicki got into her dorm safely before curfew.

When he returned to the car, he let his head fall back against the headrest and exhaled for what seemed like a full minute. "She is utterly exhausting."

"She's charming. I loved meeting her."

"You did?" He turned to look at Claire.

"Of course I did. I wish Lydia had an ounce of her... enthusiasm."

"Enthusiasm, huh?" Ben put the car in gear and drove through the dark natural arch of leafless trees.

"Yes, enthusiasm. She's so full of life."

"So full of uninformed opinions, you mean."

"She's not uninformed. She's going on her own experience. I think she's wonderful."

"Well, the feeling's mutual. As she was saying good-bye at the door, she told me she hopes I don't bungle the whole thing, because she can't wait to see you again at Thanksgiving or Christmas."

Claire felt her stomach go all fluttery again. "What's on for Thanksgiving?"

"Oh, nothing. The usual. Family overload at my parents' place in Pennsylvania. Would you come?"

"I don't know...family..." Claire felt a shot of fear and delight snap through her. He was so sure of them as a couple.

He almost snorted. "Why? You scared?"

"Of your mother and at least five out of six militant feminist sisters? What would possibly give you that idea?"

He laughed. "Okay. Thanksgiving is a bit soon. I won't subject you to my family just yet. I think we're both wary of that for different reasons. What did you call it earlier? Contaminated, right? I'm not going to let my family contaminate what we have. I like the idea of spending Thanksgiving alone with you in Litchfield. Just the two of us…and no clothes."

Claire smiled and exhaled.

"But there's no way you're getting out of Christmas."

Chapter 16

CLAIRE WAS RIDING home on the Lexington Avenue bus a few weeks later when her phone rang. Normally she didn't answer her phone in public, a silly etiquette rule that had never left her, but she looked at the number and was simultaneously excited and worried when she saw it was Lydia.

"Hi, Lyd," she answered quietly.

"Hi, Mum. What are you up to?" It was loud and busy wherever she was calling from. Definitely not an African village, that was for sure, with the unmistakable street sounds of London punctuating her words.

"I'm riding on the Lexington Avenue bus, on my way home from work. Where are you?"

Lydia burst out laughing. A little too giggly. A little too loud. "You're riding on a *bus*?...*Yes, Daddy, she is actually riding on a city bus...*" She laughed, and a male voice said something loud in the background.

"Is your father with you?"

"Yes, he's been such a doll since I got back from that tedious trip to *Africa*."

The way Lydia said *Africa* reminded Claire of the way Boppy said *polyester*: perish the thought.

Lydia continued, "He's made tons of time in his schedule to go out and do fun things with me."

Claire heard Freddy's deeper voice in the background, but

clenched her teeth together to prevent herself from saying something insulting about how fifty-year-old men shouldn't be escorting their twenty-year-old daughters into Mayfair nightclubs. Instead, she glanced at her watch and saw it was nearing midnight in London. "So you're back in London then? Where are you staying?"

"Yes, I'm back, but it's ludicrously *boring*. I'm staying at Grandmother's and I need a change." Lydia's voice was hitting that pitch that always made Claire worry, the voice that begged for someone else to just *do* something. Lydia carried on without any encouragement. "So…I was thinking New York City might be a fun change of pace. Daddy was just saying he thought that sounded like a lovely plan—" Lydia declined a cigarette from someone in the background. "Is there room in Bronte's place for me?" She inhaled. "Or do you think James would let me use the Mowbray corporate apartment again?"

Claire took a deep breath. The combination of Freddy's blasé encouragement and Lydia's carelessness was simply too much. Having spent the entire week working ten-hour days, Claire felt simultaneously angry and deflated. "Can I call you in fifteen minutes when I'm home? I can't really talk now."

"What do you care what the people on the *bus* think of you?" Lydia laughed through the words, and Claire could have sworn she heard Freddy's deep, malicious laugh chiming in.

Claire stayed silent. The line crackled a few long seconds, then Lydia exhaled on an impatient sigh. "Oh. All right. Fine then," she huffed. "Call me back whenever you get around to it. I just thought it might spice things up a bit to come for a visit. If you don't want me there, just say so."

Claire closed her eyes. "Lydia, I didn't say that at all. I would love to see you. I just meant…" She looked around the rush hour bus and resented her daughter for making her have this private conversation in public. Then she felt guilty she was never available for her daughter, that she wasn't fun and dashing like Freddy. Then she tried to dismiss both waves of emotion as far too complicated to resolve on the rush hour bus. "Darling. I'll call you back in fifteen minutes. I promise."

Of course, fifteen minutes was a lifetime in the breakneck pace of The World According to Lydia, and when Claire finally got back to the apartment after hustling from the bus stop—in the too-high-heels she never should have worn to the office in the first place—too much time had passed, and Claire's call went straight to voice mail.

"It's your mum. We should talk more about you coming to New York for a visit…" She wanted to add that what she'd really love would be if Lydia came to New York *to get a job*, but she knew her oversensitive daughter would take it the wrong way—that she would see it as Claire being controlling or dictatorial or something—and not call her again for another month. "So. Call me back, and we can talk about it. Call me back, okay?" She ended the call and stared at the phone in her hand. *Call me back*, she repeated to herself as she sat down on the sofa. She didn't even know how to tell her own daughter she loved her. It would have sounded awkward and stilted, especially on the recorded message. *I love you, Lydia.*

Claire repeated the words over and over in her mind and hoped they transmitted through some metaphysical pathway into her daughter's distant heart. She loved her daughter, loved her laugh and her frivolity and her razor-sharp wit and how she didn't give a fig what anyone else thought of her. But she worried for her for all the same reasons. She was a loose cannon, and Claire couldn't help feeling she might detonate. Again.

The first time, the change had come upon her so gradually, Claire had missed it entirely. Mother and daughter had been inseparable during Lydia's childhood. While Claire had been overseeing the renovation of Wick Castle, Lydia had toddled around with her, pointing at paints and fabrics, making drawings that she would tape to the walls. She always traveled with her on their monthly forays to London.

By the time Lydia was thirteen, Claire realized that history had repeated itself. Just as Claire and her mother had formed an unhealthy intimacy, to the exclusion of everyone else, so had Lydia and Claire. When they all decided it was time for Lydia to go to boarding school—or rather Freddy had decided it and Claire had reluctantly agreed and Lydia had screamed and cried wretched tears—something broke between them.

Freddy tried to tell Claire it was the natural order of things— adolescent girls and their mothers fought, full stop—so Claire had forced herself to refocus her energy on her charity work in Wick and the ongoing maintenance and renovations of the castle and land. Claire's stewardship of the land and the historically important building had seemed honorable. Her father had always instilled a sense of cultural responsibility in each of his children. Claire convinced herself she was living an honorable life. Freddy stayed in London more and more frequently and Lydia only came home on holidays.

Near the end of Lydia's second year away, on a glorious April afternoon when the land was full of new life—pheasants and grouse and lambs everywhere—Claire walked in from the stables and picked up the ringing phone on the kitchen wall. Lydia's housemaster was on the line to let Claire know her daughter had overdosed on Adderall.

When the phone rang in her hand, Claire was startled back into the present. "Hello?"

"Hey, sexy, it's me. You ready?" Ben's voice sent a warm comfort through her that began to smooth away some of the anxiety and worry that always lingered after she spoke with Lydia. She had already told Ben all about Lydia's struggles, as she called them.

"Oh, dear. I just got home. And I had a rather disappointing call from Lydia. She's back in London. Partying with her father."

"Do you feel like you need to go see her?"

"No. I mean, I don't know. I have a job and a life, and I don't think it's being entirely selfish to let her realize that. I don't know." Claire sighed into the phone. "I'm just exhausted, I guess. It's been a long week." She stretched her shoulders and took a deep breath, and decided she would call Lydia again in the morning.

"Why did you leave the office so late?"

Claire smiled to herself. "There's this one client in Litchfield, Connecticut, who has become so demanding. I had to stay late and make sure all the final orders went through for the wallpaper in his front hall and the carpets in his guest bedrooms."

"He sounds *deplorable*."

She loved how Ben made his voice sound like some version of hers, British and appalled. "He makes up for it in other ways…"

"Really? Like how?"

"Well," she said as she got up from the couch and walked across the living room. "He's a really good kisser."

"Mm-hmm. Go on."

Claire went into the bathroom and turned on the shower. "And he drives a really fancy car, very fast and powerful."

"Sounds like my kind of guy. Handsome too, right?"

"Oh, he's all right to look at, I suppose."

"You suppose?"

Claire laughed. "I have to jump in the shower, darling. Let me get cleaned up, and I'll meet you at the movie theater, okay?"

"You sure you don't want me to come pick you up?"

She took her clothes off while she talked to him. "You know if you come up here, we'll never even make it to the cinema."

"That sounds like an awesome plan to me."

She stood naked in the bathroom. "Ben, stop. I want to see this movie. Abby's friend made it, and I promised her I'd go. Plus, I want to."

"I know, I know. But after the movie?"

"Good-bye!"

"Bye. Love you."

"I love you too. Now I'm hanging up." She ended the call and realized Ben made it so easy to say *I love you* all the time. *So why with Lydia did it seem nearly impossible?* she wondered. Claire pulled back the shower curtain, stepped into the tub-shower, and tried to forget about her flibbertigibbet of a daughter and to focus instead on her loving boyfriend.

Ben set the tray on the bed and smiled down at Claire. True to his word, they'd made an entire Thanksgiving supper—prepared, served, and about to be eaten—with both of them naked the entire time.

"I like this whole American Thanksgiving idea," Claire said a few minutes later, between bites, when they were both tucked up in Ben's big bed in Litchfield. "It's very festive without a lot of pressure."

"Especially *naked* Thanksgiving," Ben said. "I think we should make it an annual tradition."

Claire smiled and looked back down at her tray, almost shy.

"What?" Ben prodded.

She looked back up into his eyes. "When you say things like *annual tradition*, it makes me feel all wobbly inside."

"Why?"

"You know. It sounds so permanent."

He burst out laughing. "It sounds permanent because it *is* permanent. If you think I'm ever going to let you go again, you're nuts." He shook his head and took another bite, never taking his eyes off her.

"Well, I probably am a little. Nuts, that is." She took a sip of wine and smiled.

"Not any more than the rest of us. You're really quite sane, you know that?"

She shrugged it off. "You make me feel sane. Grounded, I guess."

They finished eating and did the dishes, still naked. When Claire was filling the dishwasher with liquid soap, she shivered. "This whole naked thing is a bit impractical after a while."

Ben came up behind her and ran his strong hands along her bare thighs and hips. "That better?"

Claire snapped the dishwasher closed and pressed the buttons to start it running, then leaned back into him. "Much better."

He wrapped his arms around her waist and pulled her in tight. "Let's go back to bed. I know just the thing to warm you up."

She shivered again, but this time it was from the press of his body and the thrum of his voice. "Mmm, I can't wait." She turned in his arms and kissed his neck. "Happy Thanksgiving, darling."

He put his lips to hers with a tender hesitance, then gradually began to kiss her more passionately. As usual, Claire was swept into the torrent almost immediately. A few minutes later—without really knowing how they'd moved from one room to the other—they were on the newly delivered velvet couch in the living room.

"Damn it," Ben grumbled as his kisses worked their way down Claire's neck, between her breasts, into her navel.

"What is it?" Claire asked.

"The condoms are upstairs. Hold on—" He stood up to go fetch them.

Claire grabbed his hand before he could escape her reach. "Don't."

His eyes narrowed and he stared down at her. At first, he was looking into her eyes, as if he could bore directly into the center of her mind with his intensity. Then his gaze flickered down the length of her flushed naked body. "Why not?" he asked, looking at her lips and reaching out to touch the pulse that was fluttering along her neck.

"Because I…because we…need to talk…" She started to sit up and Ben was on her—pinning her to the couch—before she could get to an upright position.

He was caging her face between his elbows and settling his hips into the welcoming embrace of her spread thighs. "What do we need to talk about?" he asked, his voice low and suggestive. He was playing with her hair and looking at her face in that studious way again. The way he'd positioned himself over her wasn't erotic, exactly. They were both naked and he was totally turned on, but his stomach was against her pelvis and his erection was pressing into the cushion of the couch while he waited for her response.

Her eyes shifted, as if she were looking for a quick escape. He held her cheeks between his palms to steady and soothe her. "Look at me, sweetheart." She stilled and stared right into his eyes.

"I am afraid to say it out loud, I guess."

"Why?" he asked softly.

"In case."

"In case what?"

"In case it's not what you want."

Ben felt his heart pounding in his chest. God, what he wanted. He wanted so much. And he suspected Claire knew, on some deep, unspoken level, how desperately he wanted them to start a family. But he wanted—he needed—to hear Claire say it, to hear her beautiful voice frame the words that would bind them to each other forever. He kept silent.

"Ben, darling…"

"Say it," he whispered. "Please."

"I want to have a baby…" He watched as she smiled and cried all at once. "Our baby," she added, her voice cracking on the words.

Leaning down to kiss the trail of one tear, Ben whispered in her ear, "You have just made me the happiest man in the universe."

He made love to her then, with all the patience and ardor and passion and conviction that he didn't even know had been germinating, lying in wait, during all those years of their separation. The moment his body joined hers, Ben realized his entire life had been leading him to this fulcrum point. Increasing his pace, he watched Claire's face as her climax approached, he watched the joy and love and—

"Oh Claire!" he cried out, throwing his head back and seeing her face behind his closed lids and feeling her inner muscles clamp around him as his own body left him and raced to join hers in the most primitive, elemental way.

When he came back to himself—barely—he opened his eyes slowly to see Claire was crying again. "Oh, darling, what is it?" He caressed her cheek and tried to smooth away her distress with gentle kisses on her cheek, then down along her neck and shoulder.

"I'm just—" She was hiccupping and stuttering with emotion. "I love you so—" She moved her hands from his back where she had been gripping him and scratching him moments before. Snaking her arms around his neck, she took a deep breath and continued. "I love you, Ben Hayek. That is all."

By December, they had become inseparable. Claire was either at work or with Ben. They'd already started talking seriously about moving in together. Meanwhile, Claire had tried repeatedly to get back in touch with Lydia. When all of her calls had gone unanswered, she'd finally resorted to communicating with her by text. Lydia didn't always answer those either, but it was something.

At least Claire had been able to convince Lydia to come to the Bahamas for Christmas with the rest of the Heyworths. Lydia had texted something unintelligible like *blerrrgggh but ok fine*. For now, that had to be enough. In a few weeks, they'd be together in person and Claire would tie Lydia to a chair in order to have a conversation if she had to.

In keeping with their typical romantic enthusiasm, Sarah and Bronte had been thrilled about Claire's budding relationship with Ben. Especially at first. But lately, Claire had been sensing a bit of wary caution seeping into their voices when she talked about how she and Ben were getting more serious, spending much of their time planning for the future. Together.

It all came to a bit of a head when Sarah called from London early one morning in mid-December.

"Well, that's great you guys are starting to talk about the future," Sarah said.

Claire looked out at the way the delicate snow dusted the fence and shrubs of Gramercy Park. Maybe she and Ben could move into another apartment in the same building. She was becoming attached to the neighborhood.

Sarah pressed on. "But…you've only been in New York, what, a month and a half?"

"Three months this week, actually. My first Christmas season in New York. It's glorious."

Claire adored everything about the cold air and the shimmering lights and the bustle. She didn't even mind the throngs of tourists who were responsible for grinding every street to a halt. She felt like she was part of something grand.

"I know! Isn't it the best?" Sarah agreed. "I love New York at this time of year. But going back to the whole moving-in-together thing…don't you want to spread your wings and all that? You've been cooped up in Scotland for so long. This was supposed to be your big independent chapter, remember?"

Claire wasn't sure how to respond to that. From the October night that Ben had come back to her place after their celebratory dinner at the Spotted Pig, she had completely lost the plot on the whole independent-woman-about-town scenario. Her reply was knee-jerk, fire with fire. "If memory serves, you and Devon certainly didn't waste any time moving in together. You were reunited about two nights, weren't you, when you began shacking up? The weekend of the christening?"

"That is so low. I always kept my room at the Connaught."

Claire laughed at the absurdity of that statement.

"Okay fine," Sarah conceded. "Point taken. But still! Just because I was a foolish idiot doesn't mean you have to be one too!" But she laughed, and it made Claire feel better.

"The weird thing is… I don't feel foolish or idiotic when I'm with him, Sar. I feel like I'm right where I'm supposed to be in the universe. Does that make any sense?"

Sarah sighed into the phone. "Of course it makes sense. I'm just worried for you. It seems so fast to the rest of us. On the outside looking in."

"I know, and I totally appreciate it."

"Yeah right!" Sarah snapped.

"No, I mean it. I haven't felt this connected to my family in… well, ever, if you must know. You and Bronte are like the sisters I never had, giving me fashion advice and letting me know I'm not crazy for wanting to do all those, you know, things in bed."

"Oh my god. *Things*? Can you still not say the words? You are so adorable. So, I'll take that to mean you finally got him to—"

"Anyway!" Claire interrupted and then blushed even though she was alone in the apartment. Ben had done so many *things* in bed this morning before he left for early rounds at the hospital at 6 a.m. "I love all of that."

"I bet you do!" Sarah joked.

"Stop! I'm trying to be serious. You and Bronte have helped me so much over the past few months. And I love how you've been there for me."

"We love you, sweetie. Of course we want what's best for you. Speaking of which, are you divorced yet? When is that going to be official? Enough already."

"Any day now…"

"It's been any day now for the past year."

"I honestly don't know how these solicitors stay in business. They're really horrendous in terms of dragging everything out."

"You know our offer still stands…"

"What offer?" Claire asked after she took a sip of coffee.

"The offer to have Devon hack into the tribunal documents."

"Sarah!"

"What? You know it's a good idea. Freddy wouldn't think twice about doing it if he could rub two brain cells together to think of something so clever, or rub two pence together to hire someone devious enough to do it."

"You're terrible!"

"Fine. We won't do anything rash. But really, what does Ben think about you still being married?"

Claire didn't say anything.

"Oh, it's like that, is it? You haven't told Mister-I-can-tell-you-anything that piece of info yet, have you?"

"I didn't see the point at first…"

"Oh god. What is it with you Heyworths and your selective disclosure of information? Like Max didn't think he needed to tell Bron he happened to be a duke—"

"Well, technically he only had his courtesy titles when they first met—"

"Claire! You have to tell him. What if he's planning on proposing or something equally insane…" Her voice petered out into the silence. "Oh my god. Has Ben already proposed?"

"Would you look at the time? I need to be at work in—"

"—like two hours! I know Boppy doesn't even open her doors until ten. You are stuck with me for at least a few more minutes. Did he propose or not?"

"No."

Sarah muttered something that Claire could have sworn sounded like *thank God,* but she wasn't certain.

"Look. We're trying to do everything…differently," Claire said. "Ben's not going to propose in any traditional sense of the word, because it just seems silly for him to get down on one knee when it's such a mutual decision… I mean, we both just know…"

"Wow." Sarah breathed deep then let the air sift through her lips. "You both *know?*"

"Yes. We both know."

"Okay. Just wow. So, you're like together-forever and carving your initials in trees and all that?"

Claire didn't have the courage to tell her Ben actually had carved their initials into one of the two-hundred-year-old beams that formed the central support of their house in Litchfield. His house. Their house. Whatever.

"He didn't!" Sarah burst out laughing.

"Why do I even bother talking?" Claire asked. "You always know what I'm going to say anyway. So, yes. We are just that immature and totally in love with each other, and yes, Ben may have, perhaps, possibly put our initials…somewhere."

"Oh my god! Did he get a tattoo?"

"What? No! He carved our initials into one of the crossbeams in the basement of the country house."

"Aw, that's adorable. He sounds wonderful, Claire, honey, he really does, but…so much so soon…"

"The way we look at it, we've been waiting twenty years, and that's long enough."

"Okay, okay. I'll quit harping. Just don't go do something crazy like have a baby…"

Claire's silence could have filled the entire space between North America and Europe.

"Oh, Claire. No."

Lately Claire had been feeling so many new feelings, she was often overwhelmed, but she tried to ride it out. If she felt anger or frustration, she was trying to actually feel them and not scurry away like she had for most of her adult life. Avoiding her feelings had become second nature. It was a hard habit to break.

Ben hated it, especially in bed. He always said and did the most outrageous things—partly to bait her, but it was so much more. All of his joking and teasing made her feel safe. Of course, everything he did was outrageously pleasurable to boot, but it was about far more than the physical release and sexual freedom. Ben always told her he loved seeing her open up, bit by bit. To feel everything. Good or bad, joyful or angry.

And just now, Claire was really angry with Sarah James. And she wasn't sure what to do about it.

"Claire, are you still there?"

She went for the bald truth. "Sarah, I'm really angry at you for saying that, and I'm trying to figure out the right way to tell you how I feel."

"I think you just did. Serves me right, judgmental thing that I am."

"I'm sorry, I don't mean to be cross, but—"

"But you are, and it's wonderful to hear you say it flat out. Brava. I take it all back. This is all happening because you trust yourself to be a blubbering mess with him, isn't it?"

"I think it is. I mean, who knows, maybe I would have become… better, eventually, at just being myself and not being afraid of consequences all the time. I'm seeing a wonderful therapist too. But maybe just being away from Freddy and all of his horrible lies. I don't know." She shrugged and smiled to herself. "Ben just loves me, you know, any which way."

Sarah hummed her agreement. "Go on."

"I never feel like I'm waiting for the other shoe to drop, like I always did with Freddy, or even before that, with my mother. But with Freddy, it was so keen, the waiting-to-fail. Like I would forget something important or say something that annoyed him to no end. It was so…exhausting to be so mindful all the time. I didn't realize it, I guess, that I had come to live my whole life like that, on eggshells."

"Oh, I wish I could be there right now to hug you. Ben sounds simply perfect for you, protective and daring you to…be you."

"That's it. Exactly. I feel like being myself might be enough, that I might be okay."

"You're so much better than okay, Claire. You're fabulous. And apparently the mysterious Ben Hayek thinks so too."

Claire took another sip of coffee and smiled again. "He's not mysterious."

"Then when do we get to meet him?"

"Actually, he's going to come to Lyford Cay for Christmas after all."

"Oh my god. You're going to subject him to all of us at once?"

"I know. He's a brave man."

They finished up the conversation and, just as Claire was saying good-bye, Sarah said, "I'm sorry again for saying that about thinking of having a baby. Whatever you decide, you know I will totally support you."

"Thanks, Sar. It always helps to hear it. We're not planning anything…" She hesitated, wondering how much to say. "But sometimes in life the best things are unplanned, right?"

"All right. That does it. You are way too happy for me. I'm hanging up now."

"Love you," Claire said, now accustomed to it from always signing off her calls with Ben that way.

"I love you too." Sarah stopped. "I'm not sure I've ever heard you say that."

"I'm trying to get in the habit."

"I can tell already I'm going to love this guy."

"I think you will."

They said their good-byes, and Claire set about getting ready for work and straightening up the apartment before she left for the day. She went into the bedroom and tidied her things, smiling all the while. She'd taken the pregnancy test that morning after Ben had left for work, and—other than her brief tiff with Sarah—Claire had been smiling like a fool ever since. She looked at her watch and calculated that she had about nine hours of delicious anticipation until she could tell him the results in person.

Chapter 17

BEN FINISHED UP with his last patient of the week and smiled at his dental assistant as he handed her the burnisher he'd been using.

"You're all set, Mrs. Richardson," he said. "The root canal is done."

The patient looked up at him and smiled as he raised the seat into an upright position.

Ben patted her on the shoulder. "Let me or Deborah know if you have any problems in the next few days."

"Thank you again, Dr. Hayek. I was so worried."

"That's why we're here. Call anytime."

He left the examination room and went into his office and shut the door. Everything was tidy, the way he liked it. Everything in his office was running smoothly, as it always had, probably. But lately, since Claire really, everything at work just seemed...better.

He sat at his desk and booted up his computer. While he was answering a few emails, his cell phone vibrated in his pocket and he pulled it out to take a look. A text from Claire.

want to meet for happy hour?

He clicked out a reply.

ready and waiting. where and when?

She sent back the name of a restaurant a few blocks from his office on Fifth Avenue, and he told her he'd meet her there in twenty minutes.

When he arrived at the bar area, he was worried he wouldn't be able to find her in the dense after-work crowd. She must have been looking for him, though, because he spotted her instantly at the far end of the oak bar, waving one graceful arm.

He pushed his way gently through the sea of people until he reached her. Claire was sitting on a barstool with her long legs crossed and a frosty glass of something pink at her elbow. She had on a soft, pale yellow silk blouse, which made her look nearly angelic.

"Look at you...the marchioness of Manhattan."

"Stop. I'm just a working girl having a well-earned rest after a long week in the coal mines."

"The silk-curtained, French-wallpapered coal mines?" he teased.

She took a sip of her drink with her usual delicacy, but something about her tonight was even more elegant and aristocratic than usual. Ben stared at the turn of her jaw, imagining queens and princesses and duchesses from centuries gone by. Claire's confident posture was the result of something innate, something Ben was reluctant to call breeding.

"What are you looking at? You're making me nervous." She smiled and leaned in to kiss him. After a quick peck, she leaned toward his neck and whispered, "I love you."

He got such a rush out of those three simple words when she said them. No matter how often or how mundane they might have sounded to someone else, his heart hammered...every...single... time. Ben leaned in close to whisper something back but licked her ear instead, then pulled away slowly and reached for her cosmo. He watched as the shiver of sexual excitement ran through her body. He loved how, at first, she always tried to be more controlled, more upstanding, more unaffected, when she was turned on. Especially in public.

She always acted a little shocked when he kissed her in a restaurant or a store or whispered something erotic when they were sitting next to each other on the subway. But her skin's flush told the real story, not the frosty words she used to conceal her pleasure.

"I love you too," he said as he put the drink back down. "What is that? It's pretty weak."

She smiled up at him. "So what were you thinking when you were staring at me just now?" She looked mischievous, like she had a secret and she wanted him to beat the bushes to figure it out.

"Fishing for compliments, are we?"

She smiled again.

"Okay, I'm happy to oblige. You look particularly lovely tonight, just…the way you sit, your posture, your…you." He smiled and she looked embarrassed. "If you want to know the truth, I was thinking terrible thoughts about breeding, about how there must have been duchesses and queens who looked like you." He trailed his finger along her jaw. "So perfect."

"I am so not perfect." She looked away from him.

"You are to me." He drew her chin back, forcing her to look at him.

"Because I'm like a cold statue or an old painting?"

"You know I didn't mean it like that," he snapped.

She looked confused by his quick temper. "I know." She tried to shake it off. "I just meant, I don't want to have to stand up to perfect, whatever that means."

"You know you don't have to stand up to anything with me, sweetheart." He reached his hand around her neck and pulled her in for a deep kiss. She made a slight protesting moan at the back of her throat then softened and bent into him. When he released her, she looked stunned, her lips slightly parted and her eyes sparkling.

"Anyway," she grinned. "You always say I look lovely, so I'm not quite sure when to believe you."

"Well, tonight I said you look *particularly* lovely, not just your regular old stop-my-heart lovely. So, what's up?"

She smiled again.

He took another sip of her drink while she smiled that tempting smile at him. He frowned at the glass when he put it down. "That is the worst cosmo I've ever tasted. It's like straight cranberry juice."

She kept looking at him with that beatific grin, and he felt his skin begin to tingle at the back of his neck, then along his spine, at the roots of his scalp.

"You're pregnant."

"I knew you would know right away," she whispered, almost to herself.

He pulled her off the stool and hugged her so her entire body was flush against his. He spun her around and bumped into all the people near them and kissed her again as he set her back down. He turned quickly to apologize to everyone. "Just got some good news. Sorry for the disruption!"

A few people grumbled and a few others smiled, as if they already knew what the news was. He dragged both of his hands through his hair and stood there staring at her. Dumb struck.

"Claire." He reached out and held her cheeks in his hands.

"Ben. I'm so happy," she said softly. Her eyes gleamed, and she looked like she was about to weep.

"Let's go. I want to hold you for days without letting go. I think we should stay in the city after all. I won't be able to have my hands off you for the drive out to Litchfield." He threw a twenty-dollar bill on the bar and smiled at the bartender, then pulled Claire's coat off the back of her stool and held it for her to slip her arms into the sleeves. Everything about her exuded a fluid warmth, the way she slipped her hands into the silk lining of her jacket, the way she bent to pick up her work bag.

"I'll get that," Ben offered, taking the bag before she could.

"You okay?" she asked, adjusting the bright red cashmere scarf around her neck and tilting her head to one side.

"Home," he growled, pulling her hand into his and tugging her behind him through the crowded bar.

It was just starting to snow. "You all right to walk to the subway?" he asked.

She laughed, loud and free into the open air of the city sidewalk. "Oh, Ben. You are glorious. I can walk. I can run. I can do all sorts of *things* to you in bed in about fifteen minutes when we get back to your place or my place and I get you all to myself."

"Stop talking about the *things*, or I'll have to get us a room at the St. Regis instead of walking the rest of the way to Lexington Avenue."

She gasped.

"What?" he asked, concerned.

"Let's!" She turned so she was standing in front of him, blocking his way.

"Let's what?"

"Let's go check in to the St. Regis! Right now! I've always wanted to do something totally spontaneous like that. Let's order room service and watch movies and do all the *things*."

He thought his face might split from his smile. "Yes. Now."

He pulled her a few yards, and they stepped into the exquisite hotel lobby. Fresh bunches of roses sat atop marble tables. Shiny, polished brass sparkled under the chandeliers. Ben asked the woman behind the desk if they had any rooms for the weekend.

She typed onto a keyboard and then looked up. "I'm sorry, sir, but we are completely booked. It's such a busy time before Christmas."

"Oh, what a shame," Claire said, noticing the woman's name tag. "Not even for one night, Melanie?"

The woman tapped her keyboard again, then shook her head with genuine regret. "I'm sorry, but no."

Claire turned to Ben and whispered something in his ear, then turned back to the woman. "Thank you for trying. Maybe something will open up. I think we'll have a drink in the bar and hope for the best."

"I really don't think—"

"I'm feeling very lucky today." Claire's smile was contagious, and Melanie smiled in return.

"I wish I could help."

"No worries. Thanks again." Claire put Ben's hand in hers and they walked across the lobby into the bar, finding a table in the corner that had just opened up. "See? Lucky," Claire said as they sat down.

"You are so bad. All your talk about not wanting to use your title to impress or manipulate and then you go and call your brother to bring in the heavy artillery for a hotel room at Christmastime. Maybe you're not such an angel after all—" He reached for her but she swatted his hand away.

"Oh, hush," she said on a light laugh. "I'm certainly not using it for any nefarious deed."

"You might not be thinking of any nefarious deeds, but I certainly am," Ben said as Claire tapped a text into her phone. "By the way," Ben grumbled, "this delay is defeating the whole purpose of slaking my raging lust, remember?"

"Patience," she chided. Her phone vibrated within a few seconds. Her smile was smug.

Ben shook his head. "These terrible relatives of yours…"

A waiter came over to ask what they'd like. "I'm not sure we'll be staying after all—" Ben said.

Melanie from the front desk had walked quickly into the bar and was standing at the entry looking for them. When she saw them sitting in the darkened corner, she schooled her worried features back to professional calm. "Lady Wick, I am so sorry about the confusion. Lord Heyworth just phoned from London to release his suite. I am so sorry I didn't think of it immediately, that I didn't recognize you—"

Claire stood up slowly. "No need to apologize. It wasn't like I told you who I was... I didn't want to take his suite if I didn't have to." Claire smiled and continued. "But this is an emergency of sorts, so for all of Devon's misdeeds, I thought he could spare his older sister a room at the inn for a few nights."

Ben was still shaking his head as he stood up and wrapped his hand possessively around Claire's waist. "Unbelievable," he muttered close to her ear, making the single word sound like a sexual promise.

"Do you have any luggage?" Melanie asked.

Ben was still holding Claire's work bag—a utilitarian canvas tote that was filled with fabric samples and project folders—and Melanie practically wrestled it from his hand. "Please. Allow me." She handed it to the bellman with a tight smile. "Lord Heyworth's suite."

She led them to the elevator then turned back to Ben and Claire as she pressed the button and the shining brass door pulled open. "I've already taken the liberty of sending up a bottle of champagne at your brother's request. Please let me know if there's anything else you would like."

Claire and Ben stood in the elevator with the bellman.

"This is wonderful. I'm sure everything will be perfect," Claire said.

Melanie gave a professional nod and released her hand from where she was holding the elevator open. "Enjoy your stay."

"Thank you!" Claire said as the doors slid shut.

A moment later, the front door of the hotel opened and a blindingly handsome couple walked in with several carts of luggage following behind them. The man was tall, immaculately dressed, and his black hair was slicked straight back away from a high aristocratic forehead. His cheekbones were slashed beneath bright blue eyes. The young woman with him was a porcelain doll of a redhead, but with full, sultry red lips that removed any hint of innocence. In fact, she might have even been a high-class hooker.

"May I help you?" Melanie asked politely.

"Lord Wick. I have a reservation." He didn't look at Melanie when he spoke, but tossed the words rudely in her direction as he kept staring at the woman who looked up at him in return with blatant sexual invitation.

"Welcome to the St. Regis, Lord Wick." It wouldn't be the first time married people checked into separate rooms—with separate people—and it certainly wouldn't be the last. Melanie kept her professional smile in place and did her job.

Chapter 18

CLAIRE'S HEART POUNDED as Ben's grip around her waist tightened, then softened and he began gently pulling her closer into his hold. The presence of the bellman in the elevator was maddening. The floors sped past, but not fast enough. They finally reached the private ninth floor and were led into a large suite that looked far more like a Manhattan apartment than a hotel room.

"Would you like me to show you around the suite?" the bellman inquired politely, after setting down Claire's tote bag.

"No," Claire and Ben answered in unison.

The three of them smiled at each other for a brief moment, and then the bellman bowed quickly and was gone.

Ben released his hold on Claire and walked back toward the door, bolting it and turning slowly to face her. She had started taking her coat off, undoing the clasps slowly while she watched him walk toward her. She turned to the closet in the small hallway and reached for a hanger to put away her coat and was startled when he grabbed her wrist.

"Nefarious, remember?" He tore the coat from her hold and tossed it across the room, following it quickly with his own.

She became more arch in the face of his aggression, taunting him with her haughty disinterest. "Really Dr. Hayek, I have no idea what you're talking about…" Her words trailed off as she slowly undid the tiny pearl buttons of her blouse.

His mouth went dry watching her long elegant fingers

methodically unbuttoning, then separating the front placket of her yellow silk top. She reached for his tie, loosening the knot and focusing on her fingers as she worked the silk. He stared at the golden strands of hair that had come out of her professional chignon at the base of her neck.

"Oh, Claire…" He reached up to touch the tender skin just below her ear and marveled at how she sighed and warmed to his touch.

She kept her eyes on his tie until she'd finished getting it undone, then proceeded to undo each button on his dress shirt while he caressed her nape and the turn of her shoulder, her jaw. "I think I love everything about you. It's almost debilitating," she said. Her eyes closed, and she leaned in to kiss his exposed chest. "I love this part of you…" She kissed him again on his stomach. "And here…"

He snapped out of his reverie, hauled her up into his arms, and carried her the short distance to the bedroom. She burrowed into his neck, kissing him along his jaw, then nibbling at his ear. "And here…and here…" she whispered, continuing to enumerate the tender kisses.

He laid her down on the bed and slipped off her blouse as he did. She was wearing a pale yellow lace bra he'd bought her a few weeks ago. "How does someone working in the coal mines afford such expensive lingerie?"

She squirmed on the bed, watching him remove his shirt and unbuckle his belt. "My lover buys them for me."

He smiled at her, with a devilish gleam in his eye. "He sounds generous."

She shimmied out of her skirt and tights and lay there in nothing but the bra and matching lacy boy shorts. "He is. Incredibly generous."

By then, Ben was naked and stalking up the length of her body, until they were face to face and he had her lovingly trapped beneath him. "Is he generous in bed?" he whispered.

She swiveled her hips against his. "Very…very…generous…" She kissed him between each word. "But sometimes he talks too much."

Ben growled and plundered her mouth with a forceful kiss. She battled his tongue with hers and arched her body up into his.

"You're going to pay for that…" he whispered when he pulled away to catch his breath.

Claire was already slipping into that dreamy place Ben always took her, somewhere between profound need and the blissful knowledge it was about to be met.

"Oh, really? Promises, promises." She loved when he was rough with her body. The way she responded so eagerly to his more forceful lovemaking had been a surprise to them both.

Initially, he'd taken a little convincing. They'd had their first real fight when she accused him of being too careful with her, of that being one more example of him putting her up on some unrealistic pedestal instead of just loving her full stop.

"I'll be right back," he said, then continued in a deep, commanding voice. "Take everything off the bed except the fitted sheet," he ordered as he stalked out of the room, stark naked and glorious.

She smiled as she leapt from the mattress and began tossing all the pillows and bedding onto the floor. Moving quickly, she was slightly winded when he walked back into the room a few minutes later. He stopped by the door and stared at her. She was holding a king-size pillow in her arms, and the white mattress was an empty canvas between them. He was holding his tie in one hand and her red scarf in the other.

"We're going to need to improvise." His smile was deadly and

Claire nearly shrieked in delight, but it came out as part-moan, part-cry.

Once Ben had overcome his hesitance, they both thrilled to the extremes of their passion, agreeing that it was the final expiation of everything that had held Claire in purgatory for most of her life: the delicacy, the perfection, the caution. When he tied her to the bed or took her from behind or grabbed her hair in a greedy tug, Claire felt a sense of elation and freedom she never could have imagined.

"Drop the pillow."

It fell from her arms before he finished saying the words.

He narrowed his eyes, contemplating her. The flush of pleasure spread across her chest and up her neck as he stood there watching her, rubbing the silk tie absentmindedly between his fingers. Her gaze dropped to the movement of that hand, and her pulse raced.

"Ben…" she said, turning his name into a plea.

"Eyes up here," he snapped.

She took her time, appreciating the power of his erection, the turn of his hip, the hard ridges of his stomach, the dark hair on his chest, the straining muscles in his neck, then looked up at his gorgeous green eyes, dark and menacing, clouded with desire.

"Feeling leisurely, are you?" he asked.

She nodded and smiled.

"Very well. I'll be taking my time then."

Her stomach flipped with joy and anticipation and a heavy pressure settled low in her belly.

"Sit at the end of the bed."

She did as he said, knees together, hands folded primly in her lap.

"Spread 'em."

She huffed out a sigh of delight and slowly spread her knees a few inches apart.

He shook his head and furrowed his brow in mock disappointment. "All the way."

She looked at the ceiling and spread her thighs until the outsides of her calves were pressed back into the mattress. The move caused a wonderful hint of straining muscles to shoot up the inside of her legs.

"Eyes."

Her head came back down so she was facing him. *Damn him.* He was touching himself. He'd dropped the red scarf and put the tie loosely around his neck. Taking his time, all right. He was stroking his length as if he had all the time in the world. Claire could feel the evidence of her own desire saturating the confining yellow lace between her legs. She reached to touch herself—

"Don't even think about it."

She should have known he'd want to torture her. Beautiful torture. She moaned as she continued to watch his hand. He was leaning against the wall by the door staring at her, his right hand firm and sure around his cock. Long, powerful strokes, over and over. Her breasts felt like they no longer fit into her bra. Her underwear was a wet mess.

She tried to tilt her hips to see if she could sneak a little contact with the lacy fabric against her throbbing center.

"Nice try." He pulled at his balls and took a deep, thoughtful breath. "If you're having trouble sitting still…"

She moaned again as he removed the tie from his neck and walked slowly toward her.

"Ben…"

"Yes, darling…" He was on his knees in front of her, his face scant inches from her needy core.

She kept her lips pulled between her teeth while he knotted one end of the tie around her ankle and attached the other end to the leg of the bed.

"One down…" he said, looking up at her and leaning in close to inhale her, but never touching her.

"You are a devil," she cried.

He looked up at her with a grin that proved her right. "If I am, it's because you made me one."

She reached for his face, and he let her touch him, briefly, then he set her hand back on the mattress.

"No hands."

"I hate you so much right now."

He laughed and stood up. "Your body tells a different story, sweetheart."

He retrieved the red scarf and attached her other ankle in the same way.

"Very resourceful," Claire complimented.

"Eagle Scout, that's me."

She stared down at him, desperate to touch him, but bunching her hands into tight fists instead.

"Feeling a little antsy, are you?" He trailed a single finger up her calf, and she moaned at the contact. By depriving her, even for a few minutes, that single touch sent a fire deep into her.

Her eyes slid shut.

"It's a shame about your underwear." He leaned in and kissed her through the lace and her hips pitched involuntarily off the bed.

"Oh god," she cried through clenched teeth. She could feel the vibration of his rumbling laughter as he kissed and sucked and nipped at the fabric covering her swollen center. "Ben! Please!"

"Patience, Claire."

She felt so raw and exposed, nothing to grab, nothing to bury her face into. Her breasts were heavy and desperate for the weight of him.

He licked the inside of her thigh, then rubbed his rough cheek against the spot. "What to do? What to do?" He kept rubbing against her like that while he weighed his options. His warm exhalations were a maddening reminder of what she was not getting.

"Me," she whispered.

He smiled and looked up at her. "What's that?"

"You asked what to do, and I answered. Me. Do me."

He burst out laughing. "Claire. You have no idea what it does to me to hear your aristocratic voice wrap around the phrase *do me*."

She smiled. "Please."

He didn't say another word as he tore off the yellow lace and pressed his hands with near-painful firmness on her upper thighs, effectively pinning her to the bed. The first slow lick sent wild shocks through her and forced a scream from her throat. Within seconds, she was quivering and shaking on the edge of release.

He stopped and looked up at her and shook his head once, the silent command reminding her that she was to hold off as long as she could.

She took a deep breath, and he started again. The long, slow strokes of his tongue followed by that delicious thing he did with his lips, then more tongue and a bit of teeth. The teeth were going to be her downfall.

"Ben!" she cried out. "I can't!"

"You can," he finally whispered. "Go." Releasing her at last, he sucked so hard, she exploded into a million pieces, her hands flying to grip his skull, holding hard and fierce, as wave after wave crashed over and through her and her screams of joy pierced the air around them.

They stayed in bed all day Saturday, ordering room service, watching movies, rolling around, touching, laughing. Most of the time, Ben kept a hand resting on Claire's lower belly, talking to the baby like he or she was in there with an old fashioned telephone pressed to its little baby ear.

"It's like the size of an apple seed. You know that, right?" Claire pointed out as she sipped a milkshake in bed on Saturday afternoon.

"Apple seeds need love too." He leaned down and kissed the gentle slope of her stomach. She reached her fingers through his short dark hair. He'd had it cut recently, and she loved the combination of bristle-soft silk against the hard turn of his head beneath. He moaned into her touch and turned his head to look at her. "Do you want to find out if it's a girl or a boy?" He rested his cheek on her thigh and then began toying with the hair between her legs with one hand.

"What are you doing?" she asked slowly.

"Nothing," he said with wide-eyed innocence.

She adored him like this, utterly languid, touching her almost thoughtlessly. Slurping noisily on the last drops of chocolate milkshake, she kept looking into his eyes. She set the glass on the bedside table and turned on her side and patted the pillow. "Come up here."

"Okay!" he answered enthusiastically, as if she'd just suggested a round-the-world cruise, leaving in five minutes.

She laughed and pulled him in for a kiss, tracing her fingers slowly along his neck and his hairline as her lips molded to his. They paused, facing each other on the same pillow, their limbs entwined. "We can find out if you want." She gave a small shrug. "I'm just going to be happy no matter what. I already am." She laughed out the last few words.

"So am I. I was just thinking you'd want to decorate or something, you know, for the baby's room."

She looked into his eyes. "Maybe. But mainly I want the baby to have your eyes. How lucky will that be for me to be able to look into your eyes while I hold the little one in my arms?"

Ben made that delicious rumbling sound in the back of his throat and pulled her hard against him. Their faces were nearly touching, so his breath fluttered across her skin. "You're such an angel when you talk about the baby. Your voice takes on this tenderness that makes me…" He ran his hands along her back and shoulders, down her arms. "I can't describe it."

"You don't need to describe it. I can see it in your eyes," she said while she traced the turn of his eyebrow. "And your lips." She caressed him there with the tip of her finger.

"I think we're going to have to deal with my family soon," Ben said. "Before Christmas. They're going to be so bummed if they find out and you're already far along—"

"I'm more like one day along." She tried to make light of it, but something about meeting his herd of sisters was making Claire want to avoid it as long as possible.

"You know what I mean. Technically, you're like four weeks, right?"

"Right…but a lot of people don't tell anyone anything until twelve weeks…"

"I'll never make it that long. I want to tell the whole world. Plus, we need to get married. Obviously."

"Ben." Her voice sounded ominous.

He only pulled his face a few inches away from hers, but it was more like a recoil. "Ben what?" he asked, with the approaching storm of his temper beginning to show in his pupils.

She put the palm of her hand on his cheek. "Relax. We don't need to get married just because I'm having a baby."

He sat up and pulled his legs out from between hers, and it felt like he was ripping off a bandage, at the warm places they'd been adhering to one another. His face was your basic scowl. Claire took a deep breath and sat up a little straighter.

She pressed on. "Ben, you know my marriage was a mess. The last thing I want is to dive right back into—"

"You did not just compare me to that pathetic excuse for a human being you used to be married to, did you?" He was beyond furious.

"Of course not. Stop being so dramatic." She knew she sounded frosty and he wouldn't appreciate it, especially in his current state.

"Dramatic?" He got off the bed and found his boxer briefs behind a chair in the corner.

"What are you doing?" Claire asked, worry lacing her words.

"Putting my underwear on, what does it look like?"

"Are you leaving?" she asked.

"Claire! This is me!" He was standing at the end of the bed, scraping his fingernails through his hair. "I'm never leaving, remember? Never."

"Then why did you get out of bed?" Her voice was shrinking under the assault of his coiled anger.

"Because I can't fight with you naked."

She smiled.

"Don't you dare smile at me!" But he smiled too. "This is serious, damn it." He forced the scowl back into place.

She folded the sheet neatly over her breasts, which had been exposed until then. "Is that better?" she asked.

"Don't try to make a joke out of this. I am not Mr. Right Wing Conservative and you know it, but this is *my* baby—"

"Our baby," Claire whispered.

"Fine! Our baby, but you know what I mean. I want the baby to have my name—"

"Well, what if—"

"Stop!" He held up his hand like a crossing guard. "I was raised by feminists, not misandrists! I know my rights. You will never win this argument. I don't care if it's Heyworth-Hayek or Hayek-Heyworth…" He smiled despite himself. "Has a nice ring to it, actually."

She looked down at the bed. "Of course the baby will have your name, but even so, that doesn't mean we have to get married. It's just so…"

"So what, Claire?" He was still angry, but his tone was softening around the edges.

She kept avoiding his eyes. "I just dread it."

"Oh my god. You still don't… I'm not even going to say that. It's too ridiculous."

"Say it." She looked up at him.

"You're still ashamed of me in some way."

"That is absurd. I love everything about you. And what do you mean by still? I've never been ashamed of you."

He kept staring at her. Fuming.

She pressed on. "You're coming to meet my entire extended family over Christmas and New Year's in the Bahamas—God save and keep you—and I don't think there's anything more I could do to declare to the world that you're mine."

"Really? You can't think of *anything* more?"

"You know what I mean. Marriage is not necessary."

"Necessary?" He crawled up onto the bed, pulling her hands into his. "What's come over you? What does necessity have to do with how we feel about each other? Is it the money? I'll sign any prenup you want. I don't want anyone to think—"

She barked a laugh that was almost the beginning of tears. "Money? I'm a portrait of financial ruin. If anyone should draw up a prenup, it's you, to protect yourself from my husband's creditors."

"Ex-husband," Ben muttered as he stroked the backs of her hands with his thumbs.

There it was. The Big Lie. Claire took another deep breath. She just couldn't bring herself to tell him outright that she was still—technically—married to the most reprehensible man on the planet, otherwise known as the Marquess of Wick. She shut her eyes to avoid revealing too much. Ben would probably figure it out soon enough with all of her hedging.

"Claire?"

"Yes?"

"It's fine."

She opened her eyes. "It is?"

"Yes. You're right. If it's terrifying or awful or just the whole idea of matrimony is"—he tilted his head while he looked at her—"*not on,* as you would say, then I'm okay with that."

"You are?" She reached up to touch his face.

He nodded. "Not forever, I hope. I mean." He shook his head and gave her a baleful look. "I guess deep down I do have this sort of caveman desire to imprint myself on you in some codified, legal way. It's my hang-up. I'll deal with it."

"Oh. It's not a hang-up," she said softly.

"It's just a piece of paper," he added. "I know you love me."

"So, now that we have that bit sorted—" She sounded so relieved to be done with the discussion that Ben almost felt sorry for her. Almost, but not all the way.

"Temporarily sorted—"

"Okay. Temporarily sorted. So, in the meantime, will you take your smalls off again?"

His sly grin was all the answer she needed.

"Allow me," she offered with a saucy wink, letting the folded sheet drop away from her body as she crawled toward him and slowly took off his fighting gear.

Chapter 19

By Sunday morning, they were both raring to go. They'd spent thirty-six hours in bed, and—as romantic as that sounded in theory—the reality was that they both adored the outdoors and were craving a big dose of cold fresh air and winter sunshine.

They showered and changed into the clothes they'd arrived in Friday night. Chatting in the elevator about what time Ben's band was playing in the Village that night, they weren't paying attention when two people got on at a lower floor.

"Claire?"

The elevator wasn't big to begin with, but with the entrance of Freddy and his redheaded…companion… Claire felt immediately short of breath and claustrophobic. She froze.

"It's like something out of Oscar Wilde, darling," Freddy continued without missing a beat, almost chuckling. "Is this your lover?"

Ben tried to lunge at the marquess, but Claire stepped between them at the last second. As the elevator doors opened at the lobby a few seconds later, Freddy maneuvered himself out first, holding the woman's hand in his. "How delightfully *brutish* your man seems." The redhead laughed, a deep husky roll, and the two strolled out of the hotel as if the four of them bumping into each other was nothing more than a pithy joke.

"Take me home," Claire whispered. She didn't realize Ben was practically holding her upright until he tightened his grip around her waist and steered her to one of the couches in the lobby. She felt like her feet were barely touching the ground. "Ben."

"Claire, sweetheart." He was touching her and saying soothing nonsense, anything to erase that look of stricken horror on her face. Her usually diamond-bright eyes were a cold shade of dull steel.

"He's such a bastard," she whispered, her jaw clenched. Ben realized he'd never heard her sound vicious before.

"Claire darling, look at me. He's nothing. He's less than nothing."

"What is he doing here? He was supposed to be broke…and under indictment by now…" Her voice trailed off, and she shook her head in angry confusion. When she looked up into Ben's eyes, he barely recognized her. Her lips were pressed together, angry and stubborn. "I need to go." She stood up quickly, as if she thought he'd let her sally off by herself.

He pulled her back to the couch. "Sit down for a few more minutes. You're in shock. Think of the baby."

She gasped. "Oh god. The baby. I need to call Max and Devon. Right away. They'll know what to do."

"Do? Claire, he's your ex-husband. He's not your mortal enemy. You don't need to *do* anything." She lifted her eyes and the cold hatred there said he might be wrong about the mortal enemy part. "Okay. Let's go. I don't want to have this conversation in public." He helped her up and placed her hand on his arm. "My place, okay?" he asked kindly.

"Sure, that sounds great." But she sounded like she would have given the same response if he had suggested they jump in the East River.

He hailed a taxi, and they were back in his apartment about fifteen minutes later. Claire had been silent the whole trip. Before he'd finished locking the deadbolt, she was on the phone to her brother, Max, the Duke of Northrop.

Ben followed Claire into the living room, where she sat down heavily on one of his two brown leather sofas. ("Divorced-Man Furniture," she'd declared when she first came to his place a few months ago.) Veering to the left, Ben went into the open-plan kitchen and set some water to boil. He pulled out a box of chamomile tea and a tin of hot cocoa. He held them both aloft while she told her brother Max about Freddy being in the United States. She pointed at the hot chocolate and smiled, then turned her attention back to the call.

"But he is *not* supposed to be here, Max. I did everything the solicitors told me to do. I provided years of records. Years of evidence. I did everything they said. He should be in *jail!* He shouldn't be staying in expensive hotels in New York City with some...*trollop.*" Her voice was strained, but measured. Ben had noticed that she always had a certain controlled resistance about her whenever she spoke to anyone in her family, other than her American sisters-in-law. She hummed her assent to a few things Max was saying on the other end of the line, then cried out, "No!"

Ben stopped what he was doing in the kitchen and went to sit beside her, but she turned her shoulder, effectively cutting him out of the conversation. He touched her arm softly; she looked up and shook her head no. He stepped back to the kitchen and gave her the space she needed.

"Pay him? No, Max!" Another silence. "But why should anyone pay another dime? This is so wrong!" She hummed again and tried to keep it together, but Ben saw the slow tear roll down her cheek. The kettle whistled, and he pulled it quickly from the heat to silence it.

"Okay." She nodded as if Max could see her. "Okay. Anything to divorce him once and for all."

Ben almost poured boiling water on himself as he listened in shock. *No*, he thought. He must've said it aloud because Claire turned to look up at him. She was devastated, and he probably should have been supportive or empathetic or something, but all he could think and feel and say was, "No!" He put the kettle down so he didn't add first-degree burns to all of his other problems.

"Yes, I'm at Ben's," Claire answered. Max started talking again and Claire stared over the back of the couch at Ben. Whatever Max was saying forced more tears from Claire's eyes. "Okay," she whispered. "How much does he want?"

Ben gripped the edge of the marble kitchen counter. *Alice's marble kitchen counter*, he thought, out of nowhere. He was so tired of living other people's lives. He and Claire deserved their own damned life together.

Claire ended the call and sat staring out the windows of Ben's apartment. "I have to go back to London after the New Year," she said to no one, as if she were alone in the room and thinking aloud. "I need to call Boppy." She reached for her phone, but Ben grabbed her wrist.

"Claire. Stop. What is going on?" He sat down next to her, keeping her wrist in his firm hold.

"It's such a mess, Ben. I don't even know where to begin. Freddy is now saying he is going to sue Max. As the current duke, Max is technically responsible for fulfilling the terms of my marriage contract."

"Marriage contract? What the hell? Are we in Elizabethan England or something?"

Claire tried to smile at his black humor. "Nearly. It feels that way sometimes. Freddy and my father drew up a traditional marriage contract before we got married. I just thought of it as a prenup, I guess. You know, the usual bits about the Heyworth money going to our children."

Ben kept looking at her. "And? What else?"

"Well," Claire said, "I guess it was more than a regular prenup. Apparently it contains all sorts of arcane language that my father's attorneys must have thought was some sort of medieval boilerplate or something."

"Fucking Brits."

"Thanks a lot." She gave him a weak smile, but her brow knit almost immediately.

"So it's about protecting Lydia's inheritance then? Max wants to make sure…"

Claire stared at him and bit her upper lip. "Not exactly…"

"Well, what then?"

"He wants *my* money. Lydia's trust from my father is ironclad."

"But how can Freddy come after you now…after you're already divorced…" he said. She stared into his eyes and shook her head slowly. He felt it like a pummeling into his chest. "Claire. You're divorced," he repeated, as if saying it often enough would make it true.

Sobs racked her shoulders at that point and she spoke in choppy, desperate words. "My solicitors—kept saying—any day now, any day now," she gasped out between inhales.

He didn't know whether to comfort her or crush her. "Why couldn't you just tell me?" He supposed he should have been angry, but after a few seconds, once the initial shock abated, all he could feel was sorrow that she was still so alone. He pulled her against him.

"I don't know…it sounds like I was being all secretive and withholding and all that, but honestly, when I moved here, when I decided to take back my name, I just sort of made this mental swipe." She gestured with her forearm to indicate a sweeping motion and rested her cheek against his chest. "I wanted a fresh start. I was willing to work and do whatever I had to do to begin again."

"But with me? You should have told me, Claire."

She stood up abruptly and pulled her hair into a knot at the base of her neck with the rubber band she pulled off her wrist, then began pacing around his living room. She stopped near the fireplace and glared at him. "Don't you think I know that? Especially now?"

"I'm not trying to punish you or anything, I just meant, you *could* have told me. Because you can tell me anything, remember?"

She tilted her head slightly to one side, assessing him, then let out a long sigh. "How in the world did you get to be so kind?"

He gave her his best arrogant-man smile. "I'm just that good." He patted the empty sofa next to him. "Get over here."

Claire crossed the room and curled back into the space he made with his spread arm. The two of them sat quietly for a few moments in each other's arms.

"But there's nothing else, right?" he asked.

She looked up at him with a slow smile. "Hmm. Let me think. Other than the bastard husband, the recovering drug addict daughter, the racist mother, and the meddling siblings?"

"Yeah, other than that," he added, slowly tracing his fingers along her neck and cheek.

She leaned up and kissed him. He felt the slight touch of her lips like a match to an oil spill, like her love was spreading through every part of him. She pulled away slightly and whispered, "No. That about covers it. I'm a real prize."

He looked into her soft gray eyes. "You are." He kissed her hard and then pushed her back onto the sofa and let his body show her what his words had only begun to convey.

After, Claire rested against his chest. Good, strong, wonderful Ben, whom she'd dragged into her sordid, disgusting life.

He took her head in his hands. "Claire. Look at me." She sniffed a few times, then straightened.

"Yes?"

"I will never leave you. It's just a piece of paper, remember? Same thing applies to the piece of paper that Freddy is using to manipulate you, right?"

She nodded and took a calmer breath. "But it's bad, Ben."

"My ex-wife is a divorce attorney. I've seen bad, I promise."

"British law is…difficult."

"So we'll get you a new team of lawyers—the most contentious, difficult, vicious team we can assemble."

She gave him a weak smile. "You're unbelievable." She leaned her forehead against his shoulder. "I can't believe I lied to you. I know it sounds terrible, and I'm so sorry, but I just… I think I was lying to myself more than anyone. I didn't want to admit it to myself most of all, but I am technically still married to Freddy…" Saying the words aloud actually fortified her. Claire sat up straighter, rebuttoned her shirt, and looked at Ben, then leaned in and gave him a tender kiss of gratitude. "Thank you."

"I know, I'm pretty amazing."

She gave him a light punch on his upper arm.

"What?" He smiled then looked up at the ceiling. "But I'm really not at all. I'm really a bit of a violent mess right now because all I want to do is go back to that hotel and beat the crap out of that guy."

"Oh god. Don't even joke about that."

"Fine, I won't, but I'm just saying, with you, it's true I feel this really deep well of understanding or forgiveness or whatever, but when I think of anyone else coming between us, I feel a bit like the Hulk with my seams straining and my skin taking on a faintly greenish hue."

She kissed his neck, then near his ear, on his cheek, then full on the mouth with a promising wet kiss.

When she pulled away and they were both breathing a little harder and pressed up against each other a little tighter, Ben's voice had a hint of wonder as he said, "That seems to set everything to rights, doesn't it?"

"It does," she agreed in a soft voice. They lay in each other's arms a few minutes longer, then Ben suggested he start a fire and order in some Chinese food for dinner. After he'd made the call and got the logs and kindling going, he sat back down beside her on the sofa.

"So why don't you just stay here in New York and let him try to extradite you or something? Let's be fugitives! I've always wanted to be a fugitive. We could be like Billy Joe and Bobbie Sue."

"Who?" Claire asked, looking at him with a curious, tentative smile.

"Never mind," Ben said, slowly wrapping his strong fingers around the base of her neck.

"It could get a lot worse," Claire whispered, somber again. "Max said if I got pregnant, Freddy could try to claim the baby, since we're still technically married."

That put Ben over the edge. His raw anger and disbelief somehow morphed into a fit hysterical laughter. When he finally started to calm down, he sputtered, "I'll kill him before he ever declares any rights to our child."

Claire's eyes widened.

"I don't mean I'll actually kill him!"

"Oh. Okay."

"I mean, unless you want me to?" Ben offered, wiping his eyes and settling down.

She shook her head. "Too risky," she said with a wink. She took a deep breath and relaxed into him. "And, trust me, he wouldn't want to declare the baby as his. He would just use the legal snafu to threaten Max with as much public humiliation as possible so he can extract more money from my family." Claire shook her head at the irony. "He hates children."

"Really?"

"Well, since we're putting it all on the table, as you like to say, that's the real reason I petitioned for the divorce. Because obviously, I'd put up with the questionable visits to London and the depleted bank accounts for years without considering it."

"What happened?" Ben asked, the concern showing in his eyes.

"It turns out Freddy had a vasectomy right after Lydia was born."

"But I thought you always wanted more kids?"

"I did. He lied and told me his sperm count and everything were totally normal. For years, he led me to believe the fault was mine..." Her voice trailed off.

"Oh dear god. This man is such a pathetic excuse for a human being. Why in the hell would he do such a thing?"

Claire shrugged. She'd come to accept Freddy's bland form of cruelty many months ago. "He probably wanted to make sure he didn't leave a trail of his illegitimate brats in every posh neighborhood between Chelsea and Hampstead." She let her head lean back on the sofa and exhaled. "I was his wife in name only, I guess. He never loved me or cared about me. It was an arrangement, nothing more. To him, at least. Lydia and I basically played house all those years while he popped in whenever he felt like it. I just trusted that his work in London was his work in London."

Ben shook his head again. "What a prick."

"I mean, if we're really being honest, it wasn't entirely him." She reached for Ben's hand and held it. "I'm not going to wallow or blame myself or anything, but the truth is—now that I can see the past twenty years for what they really were—there was a part of me that was perfectly happy to be left alone. I had my house. I had my daughter. I desperately wanted more children, but even that…I convinced myself that I was an ingrate, that I needed to accept my life as *enough*. I thought hoping for more was a form of spoiled grasping."

He leaned in and kissed her again, then said, "I kind of know what you mean. I stayed with Alice all those years for a lot of the same reasons. I just kept thinking, *this should be enough* or that I had unrealistic expectations of something. I guess it's a natural response to a lifetime of being taught to be grateful for what we have and all that."

The doorbell rang and he got up to pay the deliveryman from the Chinese restaurant, then set out the food on two plates and brought it into the living area. They ate on their laps and talked about the week ahead. Claire had been given two new projects to work on and Ben listened and smiled as she imitated Boppy's commanding voice telling her, "Just fix them like you fixed Ben Hayek!"

After they'd cleaned up and settled into bed for the night, Ben turned to Claire and asked, "Do you want to tell Max about the baby?"

"No. I really don't want to tell *anyone* just yet. Do you mind? I know you're probably dying to tell your parents next weekend when we're down there."

He smiled. "I am sort of bursting with it, but I totally understand."

"Please let's try to get my divorce settled before we tell either of our families. I'm sure they'll understand."

He was stroking her shoulders and calming her into sleep with the light, consistent touch. "Of course we don't have to tell them. I'm just worried all my nosy sisters with their voodoo intuition are going to suspect the truth regardless of what we say or don't say." He let his hand trail down to Claire's belly—as he had for most of the weekend—reminding them both over and over about how much they had to be grateful for.

"Oh lord," Claire said, her voice already laced with impending sleep. "I'm so nervous about meeting them all." She rested her hand over his. He loved the feel of both of them cradling the new life growing inside her body.

"Come here," Ben whispered as he pulled her closer and kept up the rhythmic soothing motion until she fell asleep in his arms.

Ben looked down at her elegant profile. She was breathing gently, the slow rise and fall of her naked body a balm to his jangled nerves. Whatever happened, they would figure it out together. He leaned deeper into his pillow and Claire nestled more comfortably against him. He shut his eyes and smiled at the irony: even in the face of the thousand-year-old British court system coming down on their heads, Claire was almost more worried about whether or not his persistent—if loving—family would find her wanting.

Chapter 20

"SO, IS THIS okay?" Claire gestured down at her practical outfit of pressed gray trousers and a pale blue cashmere sweater. "Do I look too conservative?" Claire was a nervous wreck. It was the Wednesday before Christmas and they were getting ready to take the train down to Philadelphia to spend a few days with Ben's family before heading to the Bahamas to be with the Heyworths for Christmas and New Year's.

"You look gorgeous as always."

Claire pulled the door wider to let him into her apartment. She'd slept alone last night, needing the time to pack and get all her things together before being away for the two-week holiday. Having Ben in her bed had become the norm, and she'd felt the empty space around her all night long as she tossed and reached for his warmth, only to have her hand fall into nothingness. As a result, she'd woken up a jittery mess.

He pulled her into a tight hug, enveloping her in his strength. "They're just my stupid sisters. You have to stop worrying."

She spoke into the front of his navy blue overcoat. "They're not stupid. That's the problem."

He held her a few inches away from him to look into her eyes. "Claire, honey. Let it go. You're not in love with my family—you're in love with me, remember?" His face bloomed into a delighted smile. "I love saying that. *You're in love with me*... It's such a wonderful fact, don't you think?"

She nodded and stood on the balls of her feet to kiss him slowly on the lips. It quickly changed from a tender bit of gratitude to the usual leaning and moaning mess that landed them in bed for six hours.

She wrenched herself away. "We have to get to the train station." He was kissing along her jaw, then near her ear, ignoring her words.

"What train station?" he whispered.

She contemplated the temptation of seducing him in order to avoid their family obligations, but she hadn't quite reached that level of sexual manipulation yet. "If I were a truly selfish cow, I would let you get carried away so we would miss the train and have to spend the next three days in bed…" she said softly, rubbing her fingers greedily through his short hair.

His eyes were glassy and full of desire when he pulled reluctantly away from her neck, then dipped back in for more light kisses. "Yes, you should. Be a selfish cow, I mean. Three days in bed sounds perfect. I missed you last night." He continued kissing down her neck until she gave him a firm pat on the cheek.

"Snap out of it. If I'm going to meet the Hayek sisters, I want to get it over with. Let's go."

He sighed dramatically. "Oh, all right." He pointed to her single piece of luggage. "Is this it?"

"Yes, I tried to pack light." She pulled on her overcoat.

He extended the handle from her wheelie bag and held the door open for her. "Off we go then. I left my bag down in the lobby."

Claire picked up her handbag and took one last, longing look into the apartment. What she wouldn't give to spend the next two weeks under the covers in that bed.

"Keep it moving, Chi-Chi," Ben joked, giving her a little shove out into the hallway.

"Oh, very well. Here goes nothing," she said as she pushed the elevator button.

They took the train from Penn Station to Philadelphia, then rented a car to drive an hour west to the rural town where Ben had grown up. The roads had been plowed, but the snowstorm a few days before had been pretty heavy, so most of the trees and surrounding ground were still covered in a blanket of white.

"It's so beautiful here." Claire admired the stark grace of the passing trees as they wended their way the last few miles into the countryside.

"So boring, you mean. Growing up here was about as exciting as watching paint dry."

"No! I love it. I guess I'm a country mouse at heart. You know that."

"I know." He turned his attention from the road for a second to catch her look. "I could be a happy country mouse if you were there, I think."

She smiled and looked at his strong profile when he turned back to face the road. "I'm glad. I'd love to live in Litchfield full time. I'm sure it's totally impractical for both of our jobs, but I already miss being part of the seasons and the earth, you know what I mean?"

"When you say it like that, it sounds wonderful. I just pictured the two of us in the garden in the backyard next summer. You're going to love it." He reached his hand across the armrest to rest on her thigh, then let his hand rise up to her belly. "The three of us…"

She felt a wave of pleasure and a flutter of anticipatory joy. Resting her hand over his, pressing him into her, Claire leaned her head back against the headrest. "Won't that be a wonderful turn of events?"

"It will."

They were both silent.

"But Ben, honey…"

"Yes?"

"Please don't say anything in front of your family. You promised."

"So stop acting like I'll break my word. You know I won't. But they'll probably ask. They're nosy and persistent. It's a terrible combination." He lifted one side of his mouth in an apologetic half-smile.

She sighed in resignation. "I don't want to lie. Can't we say something lame like *we're trying* or something like that?"

He laughed. "I won't initiate the conversation, how about that?"

"Okay. I just don't know what to think. After listening to you and Nicki, I'm expecting an inquisition."

Ben smiled again. "You're going to love my mom and dad. You'll love them all, I bet, but Mom especially. She always hated Alice. She said she didn't have a heart."

"Ouch."

"Yeah. Alice just laughed it off."

"You told her your mother said that?" Claire asked, shocked.

"What do you mean?" He looked at her quickly then focused on the turn in the road. "My mom said it to her face."

Claire put both of her hands over her face. "Oh my god. This is going to be hell."

As they turned into the driveway of the three-story, white clapboard colonial, Claire took another deep breath.

"Quit it with the deep breathing. You're going to start hyperventilating," Ben ordered.

"Okay."

He turned off the ignition and unbuckled his seat belt so he could pull her into a deep kiss. Her head fell back into his waiting hand, and he took her roughly against him. "I love you, Claire Heyworth. Nothing else matters."

She was breathless, barely noticing a movement of someone coming out the front door. He tried to pull her into another kiss.

"Ben! Your mom will see us."

He barked another laugh and planted a firm kiss on her lips. "So?" He laughed again and got out of the car to hug his mother. She had bustled out of the front door and down the front path to greet them.

Ben lifted the petite woman into a big hug, pulling her from the ground and shaking her from right to left. No question that there was enough love to go around. The woman exuded wave after wave of affection. Claire had walked around the front of the car and was standing quietly, waiting for them to finish saying hello. When Ben set Mrs. Hayek back down on the neatly shoveled path, the woman reached for Claire.

As with Nicki, Claire was extending her right hand to shake, and the other woman burst out laughing and hauled her into a hug. "Claire! I've heard so much about you! I feel like I know you already!"

Claire wasn't at all sure what to do during that hug. She caught Ben's look as he opened the boot and took out their two bags. The rat. He'd been talking all about her to his family. Claire patted Mrs. Hayek's back a couple of times, but hugging strangers had never been her thing.

"Oh, but you are a brittle branch, aren't you?" Mrs. Hayek said matter-of-factly. "Let's go inside and get to know each other better." Ben's mother didn't release Claire's hand as she led her up the path and into the house.

After the front door had shut behind them, Claire was overwhelmed with the overpowering sense of...love. The feeling of family and intimacy and togetherness that filled the air of the house. Voices were chattering from every direction. A deep, older-male voice from the kitchen that must have been Ben's father. More raucous female voices from the living room to the right.

"They're here!" Ben's mom cried into the house.

Claire felt Ben at her back, warm and supportive. He whispered into her ear, "Ready or not, here they come" as he removed her coat. He kissed her neck, and she tried to swat him away. When she looked back toward the living room, about a dozen people were standing there staring at them.

After a beat of silence, the onslaught began. "Ben!" Everyone sort of dove at them. "Claire… This is Olympia… Hi, I'm Sanger… Hey, I'm Cady and this is my partner Jen… Don't worry; we'll wear nametags at dinner… I'm Hoda…"

Claire was pretty sure she'd figured out which one was which, but Ben never left her side. He hadn't seen Olympia in nearly two years. He began speaking French to her husband, and Claire answered in the same language when the man introduced himself. He looked to be about fifty and smiled when he realized she was also fluent in his native tongue. Ben had grown up speaking French at home, but none of his sisters' partners were fluent except Georges, Olympia's husband.

"Into the kitchen or the living room. Out of the front hall," Ben's mother commanded. Everyone began to disperse into the other areas of the old house.

Ben led Claire into the kitchen, where his father and Olympia had been making supper.

"Oh, may I help?" She hoped keeping her hands busy would help avoid unwieldy conversations about the Syrian conflict or Chechnya, which, for some reason, she assumed everyone in the house would be entirely well-versed about and she would say something revealingly ignorant.

"Yes, please," Olympia said in French. "Do you want to make the salad?"

"Sure." Claire pulled her hair back into a functional ponytail, then went to the sink and washed her hands. Olympia set out the big wooden bowl and heads of lettuce and tomatoes.

"Not very inventive, I'm afraid."

Claire smiled. "At this point, it's probably more like a mess hall than a kitchen, right?"

"Exactly. Feed the troops." Olympia went back to buttering several baguettes.

"So Ben tells me your mother lives in Paris. Is that right?"

Claire filled the sink and began cleaning the lettuce. "Yes. She met her second husband there."

"Is he French?"

"No. He's an ex-pat American, but he's lived there for nearly fifty years."

"I could totally see that happening to me," Olympia said.

"Do you ever miss America?"

Olympia tilted her head to one side, just like Ben did. "I can't say that I do. When I'm here like this, with everyone's voices and hugs and all that, I miss that. But I don't really long for America."

"I've only been away from the UK for a few months, but I could see that happening. I love my job. I love New York. I love…"

"Ben?" Olympia was reaching for a drawer to get the foil to wrap the bread and gave Clare a sweet little nudge on her upper arm.

"Yes. And Ben." Claire blushed.

"You're adorable." Olympia grabbed the foil and shut the drawer. "He's lucky to have you. That Alice was such a twat."

Claire choked and started to cough.

"What? Are you okay?" Olympia smiled. "Oh, I forgot. You're not accustomed to the Hayeks' colorful language. Betty told me."

"Oh, right, Nicki totally sold me out, huh?" Claire asked.

"Pretty much."

As if on cue, Nicki burst in the back door. "Hey, Aunt Olympia! Hey, Claire!"

"Hi, Nicki!" Claire dried her hands on the kitchen towel and reached out to hug the exuberant teenager after Nicki had hugged her aunt.

"I'm so glad you came," Nicki said. "I thought for sure I would have scared you off." Nicki was unwinding a red-and-white scarf that looked to be endless.

"You almost did," Ben added. He'd just come back into the kitchen. "I had to forcibly remove her from her apartment this morning."

"That's not exactly true," Claire said.

Ben looked at Claire and winked.

"Ew. You're obviously still in that syrupy lovey-dovey phase, I see," Nicki observed.

"Yep. Pretty much," Ben replied.

"Well, are Sanger and Hoda here? I know they'll give me a good dose of snark and skepticism."

Ben pointed into the living room with his thumb. "Thataway. Where's your mom?"

"Helping Dad out of the car. He's not feeling well." She shrugged and continued into the living room.

Ben looked at Olympia, who shook her head, letting him know she didn't know what was up. Even though the two of them were the bookends in terms of birth order, oldest and youngest, they were the most similar in many ways. Intuitive. Aware in a way that the rest of their sisters simply were not. Claire picked up on it too.

"Why don't I go see what's up with Betty and Paul?" Ben suggested and headed out the back door.

A few minutes later, a younger version of Ben's mother came in with a tall, blond man in his mid-forties. He looked exhausted.

Ben set down their luggage and made the introductions. Betty and Olympia hugged, and it seemed to go on a little bit long. Claire was worried.

Paul extended his hand. "You must be the princess."

"Oh dear," Claire said, "I certainly hope not."

His smile was so endearing, but even Claire could see the poor man was in pain. He reached out to shake her hand and, for once, Claire was the one to pull him into a hug. He chuffed a laugh and hugged her back. "I see you've already been drawn into the Hayek hugging factory."

She stepped back and smiled up at him. "I have."

Betty had finished hugging Olympia and moved on to Claire next. "You made quite an impression on Nicki a few weeks ago," she said.

"She made quite an impression on me. She's so full of life."

Betty let out a quick laugh. "That's one way to put it. She hates me just now, but that's why I'm the mom, I guess." She turned and grabbed a bottle of wine out of the refrigerator. "Anyone want a glass?"

All four of them raised their hands.

Betty took down five glasses, and Ben opened the white wine while Olympia and Claire finished preparing dinner. Olympia put the two baking dishes of lasagna into the oven to cook, and Claire set out the huge bowl of salad. Paul sat down carefully at the enormous farm table made of reclaimed barn boards, then the rest of them in the kitchen joined him.

Betty leaned back to crane her neck into the living room, making sure that Nicki couldn't hear them. "So." She looked at Paul. "Do you want to tell them or shall I?"

Chapter 21

"GO AHEAD. I'M sick of talking about it."

"Paul's been diagnosed with stomach cancer."

Claire felt Ben reach for her hand, and they squeezed each other beneath the table. "What can we do?" Ben asked.

"Nothing for now. We're still trying to decide how to tell Nicki."

Ben looked at Claire. "What would you do?"

Claire's eyes widened. "What would I do?"

"Neither Olympia nor I have children…you do. How would you tell Lydia?"

Betty's eyes connected with Claire's. "Yes, would you tell her right away or wait until you had more test results and a treatment plan and all that?"

"Oh, it's so hard to say," Claire hesitated. "I think I would tell her right away. She would be so furious if she'd been kept in the dark. But Lydia tends to be furious by nature. If I were Nicki, I would want to know. Wouldn't you?" She turned to look at everyone at the table.

Paul squeezed Betty's hand. "You and I both know we need to tell her."

Betty started weeping, holding her husband's hand against her cheek. "I feel like…" She took a deep breath. "I feel like if we tell her, then it's actually really happening."

He reached up with his free hand and touched her cheek. "It is really happening, love."

Claire squeezed Ben's hand hard. It was so bizarre for her to be thrown into the midst of all this raw family drama. The way she'd grown up had been so completely different. It wasn't that her family had been loveless. It was more that the love was very compartmentalized.

Her parents loved each other, and her mother loved her, and her father loved her, but it had all been very separate relationships. Her father would take her to the opera when she was a little girl. That was their time together. Her mother loved to dote on her with fancy clothes and trips to visit starchy grandes dames in Mayfair. Her younger brothers and sister were so very much younger, she'd never really had this level of integration with them at all.

The Hayeks were so tight.

Ben's mom walked into the kitchen, still laughing at something Nicki had said in the living room. She turned the corner and stopped short when she saw Betty wiping her eyes.

"Hi, Sitti," Paul said with a sad smile.

"Oh Paul." She came around fast, like she did everything it seemed.

She was so tiny and he was so tall, they were almost the same height when she stood hugging him while he stayed seated. "No more oh-Pauls, okay?" He said into her hug.

She took an almost military breath, fortifying her little body into rigid attention. "You're right. None of that." She patted his cheek in that loving, maternal way.

The next few days were a revelation to Claire. An education. When she and Ben had their child together, this was the type of home she wanted them to have. This was a real family. Everyone was so deeply invested in the success of everyone else, so hopeful and joyful on behalf of one another. Their happiness always multiplied and their sadness was lighter for being shared.

The thought gave Claire pause. It made her wonder how Lydia would fit into her new life with Ben and the baby. Would she be full of resentment? Resigned? Altogether absent? When Claire allowed herself to imagine what she really wanted—her dream scenario— she envisioned all of them living in New York, with Lydia happily employed and enjoying a productive life. She pictured her coming over for Sunday dinners, like supposedly normal people do.

Claire sighed and reminded herself that neither she nor Lydia had ever been "normal people" and that too many things would have to happen for that dream to come true. She tried to rein in her enthusiasm for some unlikely mother-daughter happily ever after and focused instead on getting to know Ben's real family instead of the imaginary one in her head.

The upstairs bedrooms were very small—almost dorm-like— and the walls were paper-thin. Later that night, everyone could hear Nicki's wail of misery when her parents finally told her about Paul's diagnosis. The extremity of his condition lent a poignancy to the next few days. Claire was honored to be there.

All of her worry about not being smart enough, or independent enough, or cool enough, or something enough, was utterly dispelled. Paul continued to call her princess, teasing her like Ben, in a way that made Claire feel like a part of some loving inner circle, rather than a source of ridicule.

Ben's sisters were fierce—that much of what Nicki had said was true—but their ferocity was about loyalty and love, not about confrontation. They all talked. All the time. Whether it was about the local political uproar over replacing the stop sign with a flashing light or reproductive rights in China. They were all so familiar with one another, but it never bred contempt.

And Nicki did ultimately make Claire say the word *orgasm* out loud. At the dinner table.

They'd all been talking for hours as usual and Sanger, the painter from New Mexico, had just started talking about Georgia O'Keeffe and vaginas just after dessert was set out on the table. Claire must have blushed, and Nicki cried, "Stop saying *vagina*, Aunt Sanger! You're making Claire go all red in the face."

"I must just be a little flushed," Claire said defensively. She covered her cheeks with her hands as a very atypical silence descended over the table.

"She's never said the word *orgasm* out loud," Nicki continued. "Isn't that priceless?"

Sanger narrowed her eyes across the farm table in Claire's direction. "You're joking, right?"

Ben leaned back to get a better look at Claire; he'd been resting his left hand on her right thigh for most of the meal. Now, he folded his arms and grinned.

Claire shook her head. "It's just never come up."

Hoda and Cady burst into gales of laughter. "*Come up*! Get it?"

"You all are being mean," Ben's mother said, looking to make sure Claire wasn't getting her feelings hurt. "It just can't be true. Tell them, Claire."

"Well…" Now everyone was so quiet, Claire felt like she should stand up and recite a few lines of poetry, as her parents had always made the children do on special occasions. Olympia took a sip of wine and gave her an encouraging wink.

"Just say it, Claire," Nicki said.

"Nicolette!" Betty chided. "Stop being so…loud." Obviously, Betty wasn't going to chastise her for content, but delivery.

Claire took a deep breath. "So you want me to just say the word, for no reason."

Ben's other sister, Joumana, who was the professor at Penn, had arrived just before dinner with The Republican Boyfriend, as Ben's mother introduced him. His name was Rob, and he sat to Claire's left. He raised his glass. "Orgasm!" he yelled.

Ben's father, usually quiet, especially in the face of the full battalion of female energy roaring around him at holiday times, raised his wineglass next. "Orgasm!" And around the table it went until all the glasses were raised and all eyes were gleaming with jolly expectation at Claire.

She took a deep breath and raised her glass. After a moment of hesitation, she yelled at the top of her lungs, "Orgasm!"

They all clinked their glasses and laughed and were enjoying the return of the usual melee when Ben's mother raised her voice. "Wait!"

"What?"

"What is it?"

The table of people quieted again and Ben's mother looked at him with a crease of worry in her brow, then shifted her eyes to look at Claire. "Just because you don't say the word, you still *have* them, don't you? I raised my son to know better—"

"Oh my god!" Ben shouted. "How am I even related to you people?"

His father smiled as all the sisters started talking and laughing again, and Claire worried she might never return to her normal skin color, but instead remain in that permanent state of beet red. Ben's mother was still looking at the two of them, waiting for an answer.

"Mom!" Ben barked. "Stop! Yes, of course. I mean, good god, just get off."

Hoda and Cady and Nicki all burst out laughing again. Wiping her eyes, Hoda said, "You did not just tell Mom to *get off*, did you?" Everyone started laughing again.

Ben raised his eyebrows and shook his head in complete defeat. He put his arm around Claire's shoulder and pulled her toward him.

"I tried to warn you. They're crazy." Then he leaned in and whispered hot and close, "And they adore you." He kissed her cheek.

During the days, Claire took a few long walks with Nicki. Lydia was going to be spending Christmas and New Year's in Lyford Cay, and Claire wanted so much to rebuild their relationship. And for Lydia to get along with Ben. And she hoped Nicki could help.

"I feel like I'm using you," Claire said at one point, when she and Nicki were plodding through the snowy trail.

"As the song goes, use me up. What is it about your daughter that makes you so…upset?"

Claire tried to think if that's what it was, if Lydia upset her. And if so, why. "Well, it's just that she's so…useless."

"Ouch."

"You asked me to be honest, didn't you?" Claire felt instantly guilt-ridden.

"Yeah, but that's…really honest." Nicki gave her a rueful smile. "I mean, nobody's *useless*."

"I didn't mean it literally, Nicki!" Claire tried to remember she was seeking advice from a human being who thought 1990 was *olden days*. She took a deep breath of the cold air. "It's just a British expression that means, oh I don't know, kind of lazy and unambitious."

"Okay, so you mean you want to help her figure out what she wants to do with her life?"

"Yes, exactly."

"First of all, I don't think you should use words like *worthless* and *useless*."

"Ouch," Claire mimicked.

They both laughed, then Nicki continued. "I mean, not like I know what I'm talking about but, you know, she must have something, some *thing* that she loves...that inspires her?"

Claire shook her head and looked down at the path as they walked on. "I don't know. It's a terrible thing to admit, but I don't feel like I did a good job helping her foster anything unique like that."

"Well, what do you love? What inspires you?"

"Oh," Claire sighed and looked up at the trees. "Everything. The branches. The color of the snow. Patterns. Fabric. How things are made. Your uncle—"

"Enough with the goo-goo love stuff. I mean, what else out in the world? What does Lydia do that she loves? Like you love design and color."

Claire hadn't really thought about it like that, but it was the truth. She had loved color and shapes and objects long before she ever thought of that as the foundation of a career. "I guess that's a good place to start, isn't it? I'll ask her. It's terrible that I don't already know."

"Maybe she doesn't know either." Nicki shrugged. "My roommate's such a great singer, but she didn't even know she had a good voice until she got with this one teacher."

"You're fabulous, Nicki. I can't wait for you and Lydia to meet each other."

"Oh, I would love that. I bet she's wonderful."

When they said good-bye very early on the morning of Christmas Eve, everyone hugged and squeezed and whispered encouraging words about babies and happy couples and second chances. Claire felt filled to the brim with the outpouring of love from Ben's family.

Chapter 22

"BE CAREFUL WITH that!" Lydia barked at the porter as he removed one of her six pieces of luggage from the van she'd been forced to take from the grubby airport in Nassau. She scowled as she saw Devon and Sarah pull into the front circle of the hotel in their glitzy convertible. She doubted they'd flown commercial either.

"Hi, Lydia!" Sarah called as she got out of the car and walked toward her.

"Hello, Sarah." *Little Miss Perfect*, Lydia thought snidely. "Have you just arrived?"

"No, we came in a few days ago to spend time with my parents."

"Oh. Your mother and father are here?" Lydia had met the aggressive wench and the stuffed shirt at Devon and Sarah's wedding. How tedious if Mr. and Mrs. James were going to be here too.

Sarah's face pinched. "She's my stepmother. And no, they were here until this morning, but they've flown back to Chicago. Did you just get in?"

Lydia sighed. "Yes, the flight was horrific. So crowded and miserable. Hi, Dev."

Devon had come over after talking to one of the men who worked at the tropical resort. He was always trying to pretend he was so egalitarian all the time.

"Hi, Lyd. Are you going to be a twat again this year or are you going to have a nice holiday in paradise for once?"

"Bugger off."

"I'll take that as a twat."

Lydia smiled despite herself. "Look. The last thing I want to be doing is hanging out with a bunch of pie-eyed lovebirds like you two. And now my own mother sounds all lovey-dovey too. And grandmother! It's like goddamned Fantasy Island or something."

Sarah laughed. "Maybe you'll meet someone?"

The young Bahamian man who was loading the last of her luggage smiled to himself.

Lydia snapped. "What are you smiling about?"

"Nothing, miss." He tipped his chin down and caught Devon's eye as he walked past with the luggage cart piled to high heaven.

Lydia stomped her foot. "You are all ganging up on me as usual. Seriously. What did I do to deserve that?"

Devon grumbled something into Sarah's ear and turned toward the front entrance of the main building. "Bye, Lydia."

Sarah lingered. *Perfect. Now the lecture*, thought Lydia.

"Your mom is really nervous about introducing Ben to everyone. You could try to be nice."

"What do you care?"

"Lydia. Grow up. Devon and I have been married a year. I'm part of this family now."

"You and everyone else, it seems."

"What's that supposed to mean?"

"Oh, never mind. I'll try to play nice in the sandbox."

"Why do you have to *try* in the first place? What's so hard about being Lydia anyway?"

They started to walk into the lobby.

"I've already got a shrink in London. I certainly don't need you analyzing me, Sarah."

"You should get a new shrink, then, because he or she is doing a crap job of helping you appreciate your life." Sarah turned from the front desk, then turned back. "We're meeting for drinks at six thirty. Dinner's not until eight. We'll be down at the beach before then if you want to hang out."

"Oh, twats welcome, then?"

"Whatever, Lydia." Sarah turned away and walked out the large French doors and onto the path leading to the bungalows.

When Lydia returned her attention to the front desk, the porter who had transferred all her luggage from the van was already gone to deliver her things to her villa. In his place was a distractingly handsome young black man standing tall and serene behind the desk.

Now, Lydia wasn't one to stare, but he happened to be one of the more attractive blokes she'd ever laid eyes on. Dark, smooth skin that pulled across sharply defined, high cheekbones, long black lashes that should have made him look feminine but didn't. And a mouth…lips that were…sinful. He was everything intense and masculine compared to the pale toffs she'd been partying with in London lately.

Her mind wheeled through the possibilities, then screeched to a halt. Lyford probably had some stupid rule about not letting him *fraternize* with the guests. Nor did she fancy being some absurd hot-for-the-help cliché, either. Still, there was something about him, something unfamiliar—because it felt real—that pulled at her.

"Please sign here, Lady Lydia." He turned the registry book toward her and pointed to where she was supposed to sign. His hands were particularly elegant. Strong and confident.

She got distracted by the way he tapped the page with that long, strong finger. "Quit tapping!" she snapped.

But when she looked up, he was still smiling. He tapped one more time, just to let her know he could. She couldn't help it. She smiled back. Maybe she'd be having a fun holiday after all.

"What's your name?" She bounced the pen against her palm while they stared at each other.

Before he could answer, an older Bahamian man, the general manager of the resort, came out of a door behind the desk. "Alistair?"

"Yes, sir," he answered respectfully, all hint of mischief gone.

"Please show Lady Lydia to her villa."

"Yes, sir."

Yes, Alistair, do show me.

Once she had signed the registry and they were out of earshot of Mr. Grumpy Boss, Lydia asked, "So what time do you get off work? Is there any fun to be had around here?"

He shook his head. "No, miss."

"Oh, please, don't *no-miss* me. *No*, you don't get off work? Or *no*, there's no fun to be had?"

"There's horseback riding or parasailing—"

"Stop! You know perfectly well that's not what I mean. I'm going to be bored to tears!" She kept trying to get his attention, to force him to look at her instead of keeping his back so straight and the set of his jaw so firmly forward. "Look," she continued, "the nearest relative to my age is that goody-two-shoes Sarah James, and even though she's only about six years older than I am, she acts like she's the most mature woman in the world. Boor-ring."

"This way to your villa, Lady Lydia."

"Oh, why thank you, *Lord* Alistair," she answered in a mimicking tone.

He repressed a smile.

"Seriously!" She blocked the path, now that they were out of sight of the main hotel building and she wouldn't get either of them in trouble if she were seen impeding his duties. They were hidden in one of the winding narrow paths that ensured everyone had privacy. He stood still, waiting for her to let him pass. He raised his eyebrows and looked over her shoulder.

"Take me out on the town, *Alistair*." She liked saying his name.

It sounded all buttoned-up, but she suspected—she hoped—there was a very unbuttoned Alistair lurking very close to that all-business surface. "Come on. There must be some fun to be had in Nassau. It's like a prison here at the hotel."

He looked up at the bluest blue sky and then over his shoulder at the most turquoise of turquoise seas. "Some prison."

"You know what I'm saying."

He shook his head. "Honestly, I really don't." His voice had changed. He was no longer the luggage-toting, registry-tapping employee. He was a confident man. "What *are* you saying?" he challenged.

She inhaled, having a moment of shock, thinking of words her grandmother would have used, words like *impertinence* and *insolence*. And then she paused, because for once in her life, she didn't want to deliver a setdown. She wanted this tall, strong, beautiful man to like her. Her heart started pounding, and she turned away. "Oh, never mind. Which way to my luxurious cell and golden handcuffs?"

"This way, please." He was back to being an officious member of staff.

She followed quietly and tried to shake off the feeling that he saw right through her. When they reached the pale pink bungalow a few minutes later, he held the door open for her. "Your room is to the left."

Lydia tried not to visibly shudder when she turned sideways to pass by him in the doorway. He was about six inches taller than she was, and broad. His muscled chest was…right there…in her face… *How was she supposed to* not *notice it?* she wondered. Her inhale was probably superfluous, but he smelled divine.

She exhaled when she was fully inside.

There was a central living room and small kitchen, all white clapboard with lovely, lazy fans spinning in the high rafters. He walked toward the bedroom where she was going to be staying. One of the other porters had already set all of her bags near the closet and on the luggage racks. Claire and Ben were going to take the larger suite on the other side of the communal space.

"Ugh." She dropped her handbag on a chair with a disappointed toss.

The room was gorgeous, thought Alistair. Not that he was being boastful, but it had just been used for yet another magazine photo shoot. So Lydia's existential boredom with it all simply made him laugh.

She turned quickly, like she was going to scold him. Then, surprising them both, she laughed as well. After a few seconds, she flopped into one of the oversized chintz armchairs. "I'm terribly spoilt, am I not?"

Alistair set the room key down on the armoire near the front door, dodging the question. "Please let the front desk know if you need anything else."

"You know I do. Relief from boredom."

He dipped his chin and started to leave.

"But in the meantime," she raised her voice slightly to stay him, "I'll start with a pitcher of rum dums."

"Very well." He bowed more formally and left.

Something in his voice made her feel chastised, then, very quickly, defiant.

Chapter 23

As HE WALKED back to the main building, Alistair tried to figure her out. Initially, he'd dismissed her out of hand as one more worthless heiress come to complain about the bad cell phone reception and the tedium of having *nothing* to do. Sure, she was a little immature and petulant, but…

But nothing. Despite himself, after a few paces along the shady path, his mind was circling back to her eyes. Pale, pale blue, so frosty and distant, until she focused on him and he thought he saw her blasé shell crack a bit. That moment when she was signing the register, then again, right there on the path when she'd tried to block his way, he saw something spark to life in her, something more than the low simmer of aristocratic boredom, and he was damned if he didn't want to get in there and bring her up to a rolling boil.

Ludicrous. He shook his head to dismiss any thought of *Lady* Lydia. He passed a waiter on the way into the main building. "Pitcher of rum dums to Lady Lydia Barnes, please."

"Yes, sir."

When he crossed back to the front desk, his uncle was checking in Lydia's grandmother. "Oh, Alistair," he called. "There you are. Please come introduce yourself."

"Oh my!" the former Duchess of Northrop—now Mrs. Jack Parnell—said. "You look so much like your father."

"Nice to see you again, Mrs. Parnell." Alistair's father had been one of the youngest members of parliament in the Bahamas and was now the minister of foreign affairs. He'd gone to Eton with Mrs. Parnell's first husband, the eighteenth Duke of Northrop, long before there'd been any indication either man would amount to anything. Alistair had been his late-midlife child.

"And how is your mother?" Mrs. Parnell asked.

"She's very well, thank you. I'll tell her you asked."

"Please do. I'd love to see them both if they are here."

"Yes, they'll be here tomorrow for Christmas lunch. I'll make a point of finding you."

"Very well. That sounds lovely." She leaned down to sign the guest registry. "Alistair, your uncle tells me you've completed your studies."

"Yes, Mrs. Parnell. I received my degree in hotel management from Cornell."

"So the political life is not for you?" She set down the pen.

"Well, I told my father that running a hotel requires its own form of diplomacy."

"Quite so," she said.

"He's keeping up the tradition from his mother's side of the family," his uncle said proudly, as he turned the registration book back around.

"Very true," she said on a smile, then she looked around the lobby with aristocratic inspection. "Has everyone else arrived?"

"Everyone except the marchioness," Alistair's uncle replied.

"Not the marchioness for much longer. At this rate, none of us will have a title anymore." She looked up at her untitled husband and laughed lightly. "The things we do for love, right, darling?"

Jack touched her cheek. "Right, my dear."

Just then, another van pulled in from the airport and Claire stepped out, followed by her tall, attractive companion.

"My, oh my," Sylvia whispered.

"He's much too old for you, darling," Jack teased.

"Stop. He's quite divine. Look how happy Claire looks. I've never seen her…" Something sad and brief passed over Sylvia's face, then she was forcing a smile again.

"She does have something more about her, doesn't she?" Jack agreed, facing in the same direction.

In a simple white T-shirt and pale green trousers, Claire reveled in the warm sunshine of the West Indies, looking up to the clear sky to feel it on her face before turning from the front of the hotel to enter the familiar main building. She supposed she should have been worn out from the flight from Philadelphia, but instead she felt energized. She was excited to see Sarah and Bronte. She was really excited to see Lydia. She was even excited to see her mother, who was there waiting by the front desk when Claire and Ben crossed the lobby.

"Claire, dear!"

"Mother!" She was trailing her wheelie bag behind her with one hand and holding Ben's hand in the other.

"Where's the rest of your luggage?" Sylvia asked.

"This is it!" Claire beamed, as if even that small victory was something she treasured about her newfound self-sufficiency. Letting go of the handle and releasing Ben, she reached out for her mother and pulled her into a firm hug.

"Oh my!" Sylvia reached up to prevent her wide-brimmed sun hat from falling off. "What was that for?"

Claire shrugged. "Just happy to see you, I guess."

Ben and Jack had already introduced themselves to one another, both staring at the two beautiful blond women in front of them.

"What?" Sylvia and Claire both said at the same time, reaching up to adjust a stray bit of blond hair in exactly the same way.

Claire laughed at their unconscious, identical gestures, then turned and said, "Mother, please allow me to present Dr. Benjamin Hayek."

Ben extended his hand. "It's an honor to meet you, Mrs. Parnell."

"We're so glad you could join us. Please call me Sylvia. I've heard so much about you, Ben."

"Thank you again for including me."

Claire hugged her stepfather as well.

"So much hugging," he said quietly.

"Yes," she said in an equally subdued voice. "I've become a hugger. Who could have known?" Her smile felt like it was radiating all of her joy.

They agreed to meet up for cocktails in the main lobby at half past six, then Sylvia and Jack said their temporary good-byes and walked toward their villa.

"That wasn't so bad, was it?" Claire asked quietly, more to herself than to Ben.

He pulled her in for a quick kiss. "Wasn't bad at all. She's so much more relaxed than you led me to believe."

Claire reached for her bag and turned to Alistair. "You don't need to show us out. I remember where it is." She smiled, and he nodded. Claire had been coming to Lyford her entire life and knew every inch of the place. Even some of her rare happy times with Freddy had taken place here.

Ben walked beside her as they headed back out into the bright tropical sunshine. "My mother's changed," Claire said softly. "In the best possible way."

"I have to admit…"

"What?"

He shrugged. "I guess I always sort of blamed your mother for your abrupt departure that summer in France. I thought she got wind of our little romance and was there to put a stop to it."

Claire took a deep breath. "She probably was. But it wasn't anything to do with you, per se."

"How could breaking us apart not be about me?"

She looked up at him and they both stopped in the turn of the path. It was shady and a light breeze rustled through the palm fronds. "Ben." She reached up one hand to his cheek and he closed his eyes.

"It still hurts sometimes," he said. "All the time we lost. I want to blame someone. Usually myself, for not trying harder, for not believing it was real—"

"Ben, stop," she interrupted, then stood up on the tips of her sandaled toes and kissed him lightly, barely tracing his lips with hers.

He moaned into her, wanting more, but she pulled away gently. "Ben?"

He opened his eyes. They were stormy with a mix of desire and something harsh or angry. "Like even that," he said with mild irritation. "We could have been doing *that* for the past twenty years. Don't you ever feel it boil up in you? I get…angry—"

She smiled and licked her lips, repressing a laugh.

"What? That's funny?"

"Sort of."

"Why?"

She shook out her long blond hair then met his eyes again. "Because I think we both know you *get angry* and it's not just because we were star-crossed lovers torn asunder by the wicked witch."

He smiled despite himself. "So I feel strongly about things." He pulled her against him. "You like that about me," he whispered near her ear, almost growling, "remember?"

"I love everything about you," she whispered in response. "I guess I'm so overwhelmingly grateful we found each other again—at all—that I don't even think about the lost time. Or resenting mother. Or even hating Freddy...much. We're together now."

He kissed her again, along her neck, then her jaw. Both of them were still holding their wheelie bags with one hand, and Claire used her free hand to push him gently away. "Stop. Or I won't want you to."

"Good," he grumbled, pulling away reluctantly.

Her voice was slightly rough when she continued. "I'm not excusing my mother—oh, I don't know; maybe I am—forgiveness feels so much better than resentment. Don't you think?"

Ben looked up to the trees and sky then back into Claire's eyes. "Of course, in theory. But if I still feel the resentment, I can't very well pretend that it doesn't exist."

"I don't want you to pretend anything. I just mean, look, marrying me off to Freddy was my mother's *job*. It was her purpose in life, to get me to that altar. If that makes any sense."

"I know it here," he tapped the side of his head, "but I still feel it with a lot of boiling anger here." He rested his palm against his heart.

"You are so beautiful," she said out of nowhere.

"Thanks. I think." He furrowed his brow. "Maybe another kiss would make me feel better?"

She laughed lightly and was about to do his bidding when there was a rustle behind them, where a path joined theirs from another direction. One of the waiters came upon them, carrying a silver tray with a pitcher of something alcoholic and heading in the direction of their villa.

"Good day, Lady Wick."

"Oh, hello, Georgie. How've you been?"

"Quite well, thank you. Just bringing this to your villa, per Lady Lydia's request."

Claire's nose pinched. "I'd rather you didn't."

Georgie smiled, relieved he wasn't going to have to be there to see the wrath of Lydia being deprived of her hourly rum infusion. "Very well. Please let me know if you need anything else."

"I will do. Thank you again."

Georgie turned back toward where he'd come from, and Ben and Claire continued in the direction they were going.

"Are you ready?" Claire asked a few minutes later, her hand resting on the knob of the front door of the villa.

Ben reached up to touch her cheek. "I'm sure Lydia's wonderful, sweetheart. Don't be so concerned. Even your mom seemed to approve of me. How hard could Lydia be?"

Claire tried to smile but it wouldn't really come.

"Other than my…angry outbursts"—he winked and she smiled in earnest—"I tend to get along with people, remember?"

Raising her eyes to the heavens, Claire tried to wrestle with the unexpected wave of emotion. "I know. That's why it's going to be so mortifying when Lydia's rude and terrible to you, and you finally meet the one person on the planet with whom you cannot *get along*…"

"Just open the door, darling. Give us all the benefit of the doubt. Yourself included."

Before Claire could turn the knob, the door swung open with Lydia nearly singing, "Alistair, is that you with the drinks—" Then her voice dropped an octave and she put a hand on her hip. "Oh, Mother."

"Hi, darling." Claire let go of her luggage handle and reached to hug her daughter. Lydia held on to the doorknob and more or less permitted her mother to hug her. When Claire pulled away, Lydia stretched her neck a bit to see Ben.

"And you must be the dentist." Her tone was bored and dismissive.

"And you must be the fuck-up."

Claire looked at the ground and wished she could crawl a few feet under the nearest gardenia bush. She was certain Lydia was going to snarl at his rudeness. How could Ben possibly—

And then the most miraculous sound in the world—Lydia's spontaneous laughter—spread through the gardenias and the palm trees and floated free into the Caribbean breeze. Claire looked up to see Ben and Lydia smiling at one another.

"An honest man," Lydia said. "How utterly refreshing." She pulled the door wide to give them room to enter. "I took the smaller room to the left, obviously."

"Do you want the bigger room?" Ben offered. "Your mother and I don't need much space between us."

"Ew! You don't need to be *that* honest!" But she was still smiling. "Take the better room already."

And just like that, Claire felt so many terrible wounds begin to close. *An honest man.* Freddy had never been an honest man. The thought clung to her as she went into the beautiful, high-ceilinged white room and unpacked her small bag.

Ben and Lydia were sharing a Coke when she came out a few minutes later. Claire had changed into her bikini and put on a sheer, lightweight cotton tunic. "Why don't we all go for a swim in the sea?"

Lydia shrugged. "I think I'll stay here. I ordered some drinks and I wouldn't want the guy to go to the trouble of delivering it and all."

"Oh, we saw him on the way and canceled the order. Too early in the day to be getting bombed, Lyd."

If Ben could be honest, why couldn't Claire? She waited for the usual confrontation that would follow that type of interference, but it never came.

Lydia shrugged. She looked younger somehow, like she might be slightly relieved to give up her usual occupation of always being on the lookout for someone trying to pull one over on her. Followed by a row. A cigarette. And a stiff drink. "Okay, then. Let me change and we can head down to the beach."

Lydia got up and went into her room.

Ben put his soft drink on the coffee table and stood up. When he reached the door to their suite, he put his hands on Claire's hips and held her in a firm grip. "I love you to distraction," he whispered. "I think I love everything about you."

She softened against him, her back to his front. "Everything?" she teased.

Chapter 24

HE DIPPED HIS head so his lips were close to her ear. "Yes, everything. Your stiff mother. Your angry daughter. And I especially love this bikini." He let his hand ride up her thigh and under her cover-up, then dipped two fingers beneath the triangle of stretchy fabric at the apex of her thighs.

She shuddered against him. "It's just an old bathing suit…" But her voice petered out when he started kissing her neck and the turn of her ear. "Oh, Ben."

He pulled away reluctantly. "Let me change into my swim trunks before I do something embarrassing like haul you into that enormous bed and tell your daughter she's on her own for a few hours."

"Mmm," she hummed. Her eyes were still closed, even though he was no longer kissing her. His hands were steady at her waist. "A few hours in bed…doesn't that sound divine…"

"Back, temptress." He gripped her harder then released his hold. She opened her eyes, glassy and wanting. Ben tapped the tip of her nose. "Go put on some sunscreen. I don't want this beautiful skin getting any damage."

The three of them made their way down to the shore, where Devon and Sarah were already spread out on big towels with a couple of straw bags around them. Devon was lying down and Sarah was using his bent knees as a backrest. When she caught sight of Claire, Sarah leapt to her feet and bounded across the sand.

"How are you?" she cried, pulling Claire into a quick hug, then releasing her. "And is this the infamous Ben Hayek?"

Lydia rolled her eyes at all that absurd enthusiasm and kept walking toward a chaise a few feet away.

"Yes," Claire beamed. "My one and only."

Ben reached out to shake her hand. "You must be Sarah James."

"Yes, I must!" Her enthusiasm was infectious. Ben smiled widely in response.

"Aren't you something?" Sarah widened her eyes flirtatiously.

Devon was standing by then, looking like he might rip Sarah's hand from the other man's grip. "And I'm Devon. Sarah's husband."

If possible, Ben's eyes sparkled even more. "Playing according to type, I see?"

Sarah burst out laughing. "Priceless!" She clasped her hands together. "He's horribly jealous!"

Devon tried to look put upon, but he realized he was the only one who wasn't making light of his insane jealousy so he plastered on a polite smile. "Pleasure to meet you, Ben."

"You too, Devon."

They shook one last time, and Sarah grabbed Devon's hand in hers. "When are you going to remember I married *you*, you idiot?"

"Remind me," he growled, dipping into her neck to steal a kiss.

"Oh dear god. Here we go with the lovey-dovey shite," Lydia muttered as she inserted her earbuds and pulled her sun hat farther down to avoid all the tedious family around her.

Claire smiled. She didn't even know why. It should have made her flutter around and try to make sure everyone was getting along and see if there was something she could do to make Lydia feel more a part of everything. But it was fine. Everything was really fine. Ben was here and Sarah and Devon *were* being pretty annoyingly lovey-dovey, after all.

"What are you smiling about?" Ben sat on the towel Claire had just set out for him.

"You. Everything." She gestured around. "It's beautiful here. Everyone I love is here." She looked at the sand between her feet. "And Freddy is *not* here." She looked up at Ben to make sure it wasn't going to upset him that that was part of what was making her feel so...light. "Is that okay?"

Sarah and Devon had gone into the sea and Lydia was lost in her MP3 world.

"Of course it's okay." Ben reached for her hand and they both leaned back on their elbows and faced out to the calm sea, watching Devon pester Sarah, splashing water in her face and driving her mad. "They look happy."

"They're infants." Claire hadn't meant to sound so judgmental, but it came out that way.

"Maybe we should all try to be a little more infantile then." He raised an eyebrow to challenge her.

Claire looked at him for a few seconds, then flopped all the way back onto her towel and shut her eyes behind her sunglasses. Ben turned on his side so he could stare at her nearly naked body sparkling in the sun. She spoke quietly so only he could hear. "It's been a lot of years of them all...not liking me..."

Ben squeezed her hand. "That just can't be true."

She smiled up at the sun and rubbed the back of his hand with her thumb. Claire had a moment of pure happiness. How wonderful—how imperative—to have someone who didn't see you like the rest of your family did, someone who hadn't been there every minute to catalog a lifetime of petty infractions, every childhood cruelty. Every adolescent bit of spite.

"It's true. I promise."

He brought her hand to his lips.

"Not you too!" Lydia barked, pulling one earbud free. But—again, miraculously—she was smiling.

Ben looked over his shoulder. "We'll keep it PG, Miss Chaperone."

She lifted her chin. "Good." After reinserting the earbud, she started bopping her chin to the beat of whatever she was listening to.

"Do you want to talk about it?" Ben asked.

"It's all the regular things I've already told you. It's just—" Claire took a deep breath and it pushed her chest into an unintentional arch.

"Don't do that." Ben's voice was low and almost angry.

She smiled, tilted her sunglasses up, and squinted at him. "Do what? This?" She arched her back as if she were stretching out a crick in her neck.

"Seriously. Stop it right now or I'm going to toss you in the ocean."

She put the sunglasses back in place. "I'm too perfectly happy to taunt you further just now. But later, I'd love a toss." Her smile was promising.

"Anyway." He hissed out a breath and tried not to stare at her tiny bikini top.

"Anyway, I was the spoiled one. Or at least, that's how I was always made to feel. Like I'd been trotted out on the town by my mother and the other three were...well, the *other three*."

"That's true in every family. You know that. Look at Hoda and Cady. Some siblings are just naturally closer than others. And your differences in ages certainly didn't foster any real friendship."

Claire shrugged deeper into the sand. "I'm also just not like them."

"Oh stop—"

"No. I know part of my feeling like an outsider in my own family has to do with my"—she swirled her index finger around in a circle near her temple—"delicate nature, but trust me. Seriously.

They were like a little posse with my dad. And I was with my mom. Separate."

"Well, you don't need to be separate anymore if you don't want to be."

"I know. That's why I was smiling. And oddly, Freddy always came to Lyford for Christmas. He hated all my family obligations; he didn't even come to Max or Devon's wedding for goodness' sake. But he always made a point of spending Christmas here. So…I don't know. It just feels that much more special. Finally being in this beautiful place with you…and knowing he is no longer in my life."

"No matter what the courts say."

"No matter what the courts say," she agreed.

After they'd bumped into Freddy at the St. Regis and Claire had spoken to Max, Ben put a call in to his ex-wife and asked for legal advice. She had been sympathetic and blunt. "Follow the money. He's got to be paying his legal team somehow. Nobody works for free. Find out where or how he's getting his money, and you'll have him right where you want him."

Over the course of their holiday in the Bahamas, Claire intended to sit down with Max and see what they could figure out.

Claire and Ben spent a few hours in the sun, swimming a couple of times and settling in with their books. The hotel staff came over to see if they wanted anything to eat or drink. Claire caught Lydia's eye before she ordered something alcoholic. "Just a few pitchers of water and some finger sandwiches would be great."

Lydia pursed her lips but didn't fight it anymore than that. Around four, Ben asked if they wanted to go for a walk down the beach. Devon and Sarah had left a little while before ("Probably off for a predinner shag" Lydia quipped), so Ben directed his gaze at Claire and Lydia.

"You two go," Claire suggested. "I'm a little tired from the flight."

Ben had promised he wouldn't appear overprotective about the baby in front of her family. "You okay?"

"I think I'll take a short nap before dinner."

"You sure?"

"Yes! Go. You two can talk about me behind my back. It will be much easier that way."

Lydia had pulled out her earbuds and was coiling them around her MP3 player. "Sounds good. I could use a walk. Or maybe I'll race you. Mother says you run?"

"I do," Ben answered then looked to Claire one more time. "You're absolutely positive?"

She lifted her chin. "Go already!"

"Okay, okay."

"I'll take our things back to the villa."

Lydia looked at her straw bag for a second and furrowed her brow.

"Don't worry. I won't look into your bag, Lyd." Claire may have narrowed her eyes. And she may have sounded a bit peeved.

Lydia pulled her lips between her teeth and bit down, trying hard not to lose her temper. "You *would* think I was hiding something!" she flared.

"Lydia…please don't act like I wouldn't have had good reason to think so." Claire sounded tired, and Ben wished he could do something to make the whole situation better. Claire had voiced her concerns about Lydia's drug use, and Ben had hoped she was exaggerating, expressing the worry of a loving mother over something that might have been nothing. Now that he'd met her, he thought Lydia certainly didn't *look* like a drug addict.

Ben wanted to kick himself for thinking something so idiotic. He'd seen more than his share of cases, of people who had become addicted to painkillers or other prescription medications—as Lydia had—while maintaining an immaculate facade. He forced himself not to get involved. Yet.

Lydia almost snarled. "I was going to ask if you would charge my phone for me. But you know what? Just forget it."

Claire took a deep breath and counted to five. "Lydia. I would be happy to charge your phone for you."

Lydia took a deep breath that was almost identical to her mother's. "Thank you, Mother. I'd appreciate it."

Ben clapped his hands together. "Excellent! Phones will be charged! Walks will be had! Naps will be taken!"

Both women kept staring at each other, then slowly turned to face him.

"What did I do?" he asked innocently.

"Nothing," they answered simultaneously.

Lydia shook her head then looked at her mother. "I'm trying."

"So am I." Claire reached out and slipped a loose strand of her daughter's hair behind her ear. Lydia shut her eyes as if the touch nearly hurt. "I love you, Lydia."

Lydia swallowed or nodded or flinched, or a little bit of all three. Ben wasn't sure. *Could they really be so unaccustomed to one another?* he wondered.

"Off we go then."

Claire watched as the two of them walked away and continued along the shore. If anyone could help repair all the years of damage, it was Ben. The man simply knew how to love.

Chapter 25

BEN AND LYDIA started at a brisk pace. The sand was the sugar-soft, coral-pink for which the island was renowned.

"Do you like to talk when you walk or are you more broody?"

Lydia burst out laughing. "Do you even know what that means?"

"What, *broody*?"

"Yeah, *broody*."

His legs pumped and he looked at the distant turn of the beach where the dunes seemed to touch the edge of the sea. "Um. Thoughtful. Contemplative."

"Maybe where you're from."

"What does it mean where you're from?" he asked.

"Pregnant...or nearly."

It was Ben's turn to laugh. "So. Are you broody?" he asked abruptly.

"God! I hope not!"

"Why?"

"Why don't I want to be a single mum at twenty? Hmmm." Lydia tapped her lip in mock contemplation. "Let me think."

Ben kept walking. And smiling. Lydia was like the completely uninhibited version of Claire. She said whatever popped into her mind. For better or (usually) worse.

"The ankles."

"The what?" he laughed out the words.

"The ankles, for starters. Look at Bronte's ankles."

"I haven't met her yet."

Lydia rolled her eyes. "Boy, are you in for a treat. She's a bitch on her best day, and seven months pregnant with twins?" Shaking her head to show the desperate nature of the situation, Lydia left it at that.

"Poor thing. She's probably a little uncomfortable."

"Oh my god, are you really that sympathetic by nature? It's unbelievable."

"Well. I am in a profession that tries to help people."

"Then why do so many people have to take a Xanax before they have an appointment with you?"

"Touché."

Lydia shrugged then sighed. "Oh, Xanax. My old friend."

"Do you really miss it?"

"I suppose Mother told you everything already."

"Well, if by *everything* you mean that you were hospitalized for an overdose when you were fifteen…then yes. She told me everything."

Quirking her mouth—like that was all there was to it—she kept walking.

"But that's not everything, is it?" he asked.

"Oh, god. Are you going to analyze me, with all your dental psychiatric expertise?"

"What do you have against dentists, anyway?"

"You're right. Such a lost opportunity." Lydia snapped her fingers like she'd just thought of a great idea. "Why didn't I ever date a dentist? All those prescription pads lying around. I could have been awash in a sea of pharmaceuticals by now. I can totally picture it: some sort of campy Damien Hirst meets classic Horst P. Horst photo shoot, with me all glamorous and naked in a bathtub full of pills."

"Cut it."

"Cut what?"

"Cut all the joking about it. Do you miss it or not?" Ben asked.

"Of course I miss it. And it's not just an 'it'...I miss everything... the oblivion...the lead-up...the desire..." Her voice trailed off. "I shouldn't be talking about it."

"Why not? We're not anywhere you can get any?"

She snorted. "If you don't think I could have a bottle of pills or a gram of coke or an ounce of weed in that villa by midnight, you're an idiot. And I was so hoping you weren't an idiot."

"Wow. So, what would you do? Ask one of the guys who work here? The attractive Alistair who failed to deliver your pitcher of rum punch?"

"He is attractive, isn't he? Unfortunately, he appears to be moderately intelligent. I prefer stupid."

"No you don't."

"Okay fine. I don't. But this is starting to feel like an interrogation. So. Moving on. What else?"

"What else what?"

"What else do you want to know? About my father. About the castle in Scotland. You must have questions."

Ben shrugged and they both kept walking. "I don't really. Your mom seems to be happy in New York, so I'm happy."

"No curiosity at all? Seriously? That sounds perverse." She glanced at him, a quick head-to-toe. "You look like the settling-down type. Don't you want to know the particulars? The entail? The inheritance? What you stand to *gain*?"

"I think I might prefer your fond reminiscences of your good old days in the gutter to this line of questioning." Ben's voice was completely devoid of the playful banter they'd been sharing up until then.

"What? You seriously expect me to believe my mother's fortune isn't the least bit interesting to you?"

He stopped then. She walked on for a few more paces then turned to face him, hands on her bare hips. He tried to remember she was still young, but she wasn't so young that he couldn't speak his mind. She wanted to be treated like an adult. Well, he was happy to oblige.

"Lydia. I love your mother. I know that is absurd to you. Since you don't love her, you can't believe anyone else would?"

He hit his mark with that one. Her lips twitched in a defensive little snarl. "I love her."

"Good. At least we have that established. Beyond that, as far as I know, your mother makes $35,000 a year as a design consultant and lives month-to-month in her sister-in-law's apartment in Gramercy Park. And that's more than enough for me."

Lydia rolled her eyes. "Yeah. Right. Whatever, Ben. You're a saint. Her siblings are three of the richest people in England and that doesn't even interest you in the least?"

He resisted the temptation to grab her upper arm and shake her. "Yeah, as far as sainthood, we both know that's not true. I'm an irascible, selfish pig a lot of the time, but…" His voice petered out as he looked toward the darkening clouds that were beginning to come in from the east. Then he turned and stared right into her now-familiar silvery gray eyes. "But, here's the crazy thing: your mother makes me a better person. We care about each other. I love her. And that's all I hope to *gain*. That connection."

She pulled her hands from her hips and crossed her arms in front of her chest. "Nice speech."

"It wasn't a speech." He sighed and then relaxed the tension out of his shoulders and tried to redirect the conversation. "Look, Lydia. You enjoy taunting people until you piss them off so much, they move along and then you can solidify your impression that they're selfish and uninterested in you."

"That sounds spot on." She narrowed her eyes at him. "And it's amazing how quickly people prove me right."

"Well, I'm not going to prove you right. Not in that at least."

"Everyone proves me right, Ben. No one gives a shit about anyone."

"What about lovey-dovey Devon and Sarah?" Ben asked, starting to walk again. Lydia turned slowly and met his pace.

"Ugh. The worst kind. Sarah loves Devon because Devon loves Sarah—it's like a sickening mirror of I-love-how-you-love-me. That's just narcissism pretending to be love. I hate it."

"Wow. Sounds like you've got it all figured out," Ben said in a tone that let her know she hadn't figured out anything as far as he was concerned.

She slapped her forehead. "Oh! Right! I'm a twenty-year-old recovering drug addict. I know nothing. What was I thinking?"

"Do you see how you do that? You derail every conversation."

"I didn't derail anything," she said quickly, but she looked surprised that Ben sounded as if he actually wanted to converse rather than spar. Not knowing what to make of that, she defaulted to her usual defensive tone. "You just think what I have to say is worthless, so you insult me instead of listening to what I say."

"Wait a minute. Let's go back. You were off on your love-is-a-crock-of-shit rant, and I asked what you thought of Devon and Sarah and you dismissed their relationship out of hand. Do you seriously believe they are happy because they feed each other's selfishness?"

Lydia looked a little deflated. She wasn't used to people actually listening to what she said. "That seems to be the way of it." She tried to make her voice full of bored acceptance, but he could tell her heart wasn't in it anymore.

"Not where I'm from it doesn't. That sounds like an awful *way of it*."

"It is." Lydia said it so softly—with such desperate conviction—Ben wanted to hug her.

"I'm sorry, Lydia."

"Oh god. Don't go and get all sentimental. That would be dreadful. My parents' marriage was a shambles. My father is a complete douchebag…but he's still my dad, you know?" Her voice trailed off. "What? Not going to find something nice to say about the marquess? Your crown is slipping."

Ben quirked his lip. "Your father and I have had only one very brief, very regrettable meeting."

"Fair enough. So let's go on to more enjoyable topics. What kind of music do you listen to? The Beatles?"

He burst out laughing. "Yes. Because I'm seventy."

She smiled too, and he began to reel off a bunch of bands that he'd been listening to over the past few months.

"Mom said you were into music, but I just thought she meant you had regular seats at the opera or something. This is great news. You play the guitar? Like in a band?"

"Wow. Did you just approve of me?"

"Reluctantly. One small part of you." But her smile was forgiving, and Ben thought he might be able to see a crack in her hard shell of bitterness, and a glimpse at her kind center. Whether he wanted to or he had to, Ben believed such a thing existed inside Lydia.

They all met up in the lobby at half past six. Claire hugged Bronte and patted her cheek. She wanted so much to tell her she was also pregnant, but knowing Bronte's boundless enthusiasm, she feared it would have been impossible for her to keep it a secret.

"You look so beautiful, Bron."

"I'm a fat cow. Please."

"Stop it. You look splendid. So round and glorious."

"You know, from anyone else, I would take that as the worst veiled insult, but I think you really mean it."

"Of course I really mean it. I think pregnant women are the most beautiful women in the world."

"Oh Claire." Bronte sighed. "You should talk. You look so wonderful. And Ben is absolutely dreamy." She glanced across the seating area toward Ben. "Even better than his picture on the Internet." Bronte nudged her elbow into Claire's upper arm.

"Ow. Stop that." But she looked across at Ben and Devon talking on one of the pale pink-and-green chintz sofas and sighed. "But he is, isn't he? Dreamy, I mean."

"Look at you." Bronte let the dreamy go on for about two more seconds. "But."

Claire laughed. "I knew I wouldn't get much a reprieve."

"Why is everyone always acting like I am such a trial?"

"Because you are! But that's why we love you."

"Oh well, thanks. I guess. Anyway, what is going on with work? Are you still Boppy's grunt? Are you starting to take on your own projects?"

"Well…" Claire tore her gaze from Ben, who had just looked up and smiled at her while Devon continued talking. "Okay. Well, here's the thing. I can't very well fall in love with *every* client in order to resolve postdivorce spats about interior decoration. But I have got a bit of a name for myself as this peacemaker or something."

"Oh, I fucking love that. It is so you!"

"Bronte." Max's deep voice was more of a heads-up than a chastisement. "Wolf is on his way over to say good-night."

"Oh, thanks, darling." She put her arms out as the little boy toddled over to his mother.

He dove at her, and she nearly toppled onto the floor. "Let

me sit!" She laughed and settled him into her lap. She whispered something in his ear, and he kissed her stomach twice then looked around at all his aunts and uncles and then saw his grandmother and smiled just for her. He wriggled out of his mother's lap after a few more bedtime kisses then weaved through legs and chairs and coffee tables to reach his grandmother. Bronte watched as Sylvia hugged the little boy close and Jack Parnell patted him on the back.

Max rested his hand on her shoulder. "It's good, right?"

She put her hand over his. "Yes. It's good," she answered quietly.

The nanny was there a few minutes later, scooping up Wolf and taking him back to their villa for bath and bedtime.

Claire watched the whole scene and felt a wave of warmth, anticipating next Christmas, when both Claire and Bronte would have new babies with them. She was about to join Ben on the sofa when she saw a familiar face across the lobby. An older, white-haired man named Julian Stembridge was escorting his aging wife toward the dining room. Claire had met them both many years ago. They lived full-time in the Bahamas, expatriate Brits who'd never wanted to return to the rain and fog of London after their first visit to the islands in the 1950s. He and Freddy had also had some business dealings at one time, but Claire didn't remember seeing the Stembridge name on the list of Freddy's creditors. She set down her drink and crossed the lobby.

"Julian?"

He looked somewhat startled, but she thought it might be the hesitance of old age, the need to cull his memory bank before the lights of recognition came on. Still, he said nothing.

"It's Lady Wick…Claire?"

His wife remembered her then. "Oh, Claire dear. How are you? It's been so many years. Since you and Freddy were first married, I believe."

"Yes," Claire said kindly, "I think that was the last time we saw each other. Maybe twenty years ago."

Julian Stembridge looked perplexed, and it didn't seem to be from a loss of memory.

"Is everything all right, Mr. Stembridge? I hope I wasn't too familiar calling you Julian?" Claire tried.

He shook his head. "No, no. Of course not. I'm just so flummoxed. How did you get here so quickly?"

"Quickly?"

"Did you just fly in today?"

"I did, yes." Claire smiled, worried the old man had gone a bit senile, poor thing. "From Philadelphia, actually. I've moved to New York. Late last summer. It's been quite wonderful."

"New York? I—you must forgive me. We spoke this morning and you told me you were in London."

"We what?" Claire stood up straighter and felt the blood draining from her face. She rested her hand over her abdomen, then let it drop, not wanting to draw attention to her spontaneous, protective gesture.

"I spoke to you and Freddy this morning. You said you had a cold, because your voice was a bit froggy."

"I'm sorry, Julian…Mr. Stembridge. You must have me confused with someone else. I haven't been back to London since September. And I, well, if you must know, Freddy and I were legally separated many months ago and we are going through a rather acrimonious divorce right now. Perhaps you are thinking—"

"Oh dear. Oh dear." Julian shook his head and his wife looked up at him with concerned, pale blue eyes.

"What is it, Jules?"

He patted his wife's knobby hand against his forearm. "Nothing that should be discussed on such a lovely occasion." He forced a cheerful smile. "Christmas Eve is no time to worry over such things." His smile faded when his gaze slipped from his wife to Claire. "Lady Wick. Please accept my deepest apology for greeting you so shabbily just now. Will you be staying in the Bahamas long? I would very much like to meet with you at my offices on the twenty-seventh if you are free?"

Claire felt the frisson of dread creep back up her spine. She tried to tell herself it might just as easily be good news as bad. "Of course. We are here through the New Year."

"Very well. We are closed for Christmas and Boxing Day, but please come in at nine o'clock on the twenty-seventh. Again, I'm so sorry to have been so thoughtless earlier."

Claire felt the press of Ben's hand against her lower back. "Everything all right, sweetheart?" he asked kindly.

She took another deep breath, but she felt like she couldn't quite fill her lungs. "Yes." There was an awkward pause as the four of them stared at one another. "Oh!" Claire realized it was up to her to make the introductions. "Ben Hayek, this is Julian and Amanda Stembridge. Old friends. Julian and Amanda, this is my…"

Ben smiled.

Claire looked at him then finished speaking with a slow, sure smile. "This is my fiancé, Benjamin Hayek."

Mr. Stembridge tried to hide his shock as best he could. Ben was likewise pleased and confused to hear Claire introduce him as her future husband.

"Pleased to meet you both," he said.

"Would you like to join us for a drink before supper?" Claire asked. "I know my mother and brothers would welcome the chance to say hello."

Julian looked down at his wife, who nodded and smiled. "Very well," he said. "We'd love to join you."

Chapter 26

After Christmas Eve dinner, Devon and Sarah ended up coming back to Claire's villa. Lydia had not overserved herself, for a change. She was bubbly and snarky as always, but without quite the spike of meanness. Or maybe Claire didn't feel the need to monitor her so closely. Either way, she was funny and charming when the five of them returned to the villa for a nightcap.

Ben had managed to rustle up a guitar from the hotel somewhere, and they sat out on the porch while he played some Spanish flamenco music. Near midnight, Alistair knocked on the door to make sure they had everything they needed and to wish them a happy Christmas.

Lydia leapt up to say hello to him. She shut the door to the villa and didn't return right away.

Sarah raised an eyebrow. "Who was that?"

"Handsome Alistair," said Ben, without missing a chord of the complicated music he was playing into the night air.

"Quite," said Sarah.

"Sarah…" Devon warned then kissed her cheek.

"I can't even look at the bellman?"

"No. You cannot even look at the bellman."

Claire smiled at the two of them, then watched Ben as his fingers moved over the guitar strings, his head bent and his neck tensing and flexing as he brought the notes from the instrument. She sat next to him on the outdoor sofa, her knees pulled up to her chest. Sarah and

Devon were on the opposite sofa, leaning into one another.

"This is heaven," Claire whispered.

Ben smiled but didn't take his eyes from his hands working the more complicated notes on the frets. "Do you remember the first time you came to hear me play in the Village?"

"Of course I remember. I loved it."

"So did I."

"You did? You didn't even look at me. I thought you were sort of ignoring me."

He finished the complicated Flamenco song and started into something simpler, a Mozart minuet. Claire knew it was like child's play for him, but he still didn't look away from the instrument. "I couldn't look at you because I was so blown away that you were even there. Like I am now. Before we met up again…" His voice was harsh and soft at the same time. Almost desperate. "You blind me, Claire. You really do."

"Oh, Ben." She reached up and rested her hand on his shoulder, feeling the muscles work beneath her fingers. He finished the easier song then set the guitar down carefully. He turned and kissed her. A simple declarative kiss. An I-love-you kiss.

"Oh my god! Is this like a kissing parlor game or something? Stop!" Lydia was standing in the doorway, watching with horrified eyes as the two couples disentangled themselves. "What is *with* you people?" She reached for a cigarette and lit it while Sarah sat up a little straighter and Claire adjusted a strand of her hair.

"I wish you wouldn't smoke, Lyd," Claire·said on a sigh.

"I wish you wouldn't make out with some guy in front of your daughter."

"Ouch. Now I'm 'some guy'?" Ben asked, sounding wounded.

"All right, fine. You're too old to be a boyfriend. Beau? Partner?"

"Fiancé," Claire said.

"What?" Sarah leapt from the sofa and darted around the coffee table to hug Claire. "Oh my god! You're engaged? When?"

Lydia narrowed her eyes. "How can you get married when you're still married to Daddy?"

"I won't be married to your father much longer. You know that. I just want what's best for you, Lyd. You have rights too, you know." Claire's voice was somber. She hated that her happiness seemed to be forever compromised by a man she never wanted to clap eyes on again. She hadn't wanted to put it quite this way, but it came out just the same. "I'm staying married to your father until I make sure he's not hiding your inheritance."

"What?" Lydia furrowed her brow. "Daddy would never steal from me. He's maybe a bit reckless, but he's not…"

Devon and Sarah looked at their clasped hands and tried to be invisible.

Ben held on to Claire's hand. Claire looked straight at Lydia.

"Lydia."

"I don't believe you." Her voice was cracking. She was cracking. "Just because you hate him doesn't mean I have to!"

A mantel clock in the villa began to chime the twelve tolls of midnight.

"Happy fucking Christmas." Lydia stamped out her cigarette and turned back toward the villa. "I'm going for a walk on the beach," she said, pulling the door shut with a dramatic slam.

"Well," Devon said. "That could have gone worse."

Claire smiled because it was easier than crying. "Oh, Devon. Can you imagine if we learned Father was stealing from us, from his own children?"

Devon lifted a careless shoulder. "We would have made our way, because he raised us to make our own way, regardless of our inheritance."

"Oh please." Ben regretted it as soon as the sarcastic words slipped out.

"Please what?" Devon asked coolly.

"Never mind."

Sarah bit her tongue.

"No. Say it," Devon challenged. "You think we're a bunch of spoiled wankers and you're the only one at this party who knows how to earn a buck?"

"Devon—" Claire wasn't quite sure what to say after that. She was afraid that was precisely what Ben thought.

"What, Claire?" Devon continued. "I'm sick of it. I know we were all born with silver spoons and all that, but we're not wastrels and it's tedious. I work. You're working now. Max works his ass off. Abby isn't even here because of some damn pestilence in Kenya. Honestly."

"Look," Sarah interjected. "Let's not have this turn into some pissing match."

Ben kept looking at Devon. "I only meant…Lydia just took a huge emotional hit and I don't think expecting her to pull herself up by her bootstraps is really the best strategy just now."

Devon was about to say something then shut his mouth.

"This is the last thing I wanted to happen," Claire said. "I wanted us all to get along. But I can't pretend with Lydia anymore. You know that, Dev. She's going to have to see her father for what he really is. And we need to be a little sympathetic, all right? Can you manage that?"

Devon shrugged again, as if he'd give it a shot but he wasn't going to guarantee any results.

"Please?" Claire asked.

Sarah shoved her husband.

"What?" he grumbled.

Sarah widened her eyes at him.

"Okay fine. But she's just such a spoiled brat."

"Lucky you two have so much in common, then." Sarah kissed him on the cheek to soften the blow.

"What did I do?" He kissed Sarah on the cheek then said, "Sorry, Ben. I didn't mean to snap."

"No problem. It's not my business."

"But it will be…" Claire added.

Ben smiled at her then turned back to Devon. "I don't have any of my own children…yet…" Sarah's eyes focused on Claire like a laser, as if to say *don't even!* "But I sympathize, you know. We were all twenty once, and trying to find our way in the world. No matter how rich or poor or happy or miserable our parents were. That's all I was trying to say."

"I get it," Devon said. "But I've seen a lot of shit over the years with Lydia. I've seen how she's hurt her mother and manipulated people and I just…" Sarah gave him another elbow in the ribs. "Okay. I'll try."

"Good," Claire said. "Well, now that we've solved the problems of the known universe, I think I'll beg off. Are we all meeting at Mother's villa in the morning?"

"Yes, presents at ten," Sarah said. All four of them stood up. Sarah hugged Ben and then Claire. Devon shook hands with Ben then hugged his sister. He held on to her hand a moment longer and said, "I also want to talk to you about Stembridge. I saw you talking to him and I have some ideas about that."

"You do?" Claire asked, surprised.

"I do."

"Excellent. Thanks, Dev. Happy Christmas."

"Yes, Happy Christmas."

Devon and Sarah held hands and wandered off into the balmy

night, wending through the tropical paths back to their villa.

"So."

"So?" Claire asked.

"You want to go find Lydia?"

"Where can she go? No. Just let her walk it off. I'll talk to her when she comes back."

Walking down toward the beach, Lydia was torn between getting a taxi and heading into Nassau for a night of debauchery, or just lying on one of the stacked beach loungers and staring at the stars. Both offered their own form of oblivion, but the debauchery would be far more effective, she decided rashly, and turned toward the main building with renewed conviction. She sped up her pace before she lost her nerve and slammed into a wall of hard flesh.

"Whoa! Where are you headed in such a rush?"

She could barely see him in the darkness, but his voice was unmistakable. "Of course it would be you." She pulled a cigarette out of her slim clutch and held it unlit near her lips. "Well, are you going to light it for me or not?"

"Not. I can't stand cigarette smoke."

She returned it to the pack and closed her bag with a sullen *snap*. "Aren't you all pure and perfect."

"No, my dad had lung cancer last year. I used to smoke. Now, I just can't be around it anymore."

"Sorry." She let out a sigh of resignation. Apparently, the more she tried to find something to dislike about this guy, the more she ended up liking him.

They stood in the dark, there at the turn of the path, neither one saying anything. The sound of the lizards and the whisper of night creatures settled around them.

"Are you lost?" he asked.

She was not going to burst into tears. That was simply not on. But the way he asked—not trying to be a jerk or prying, probably just trying to show her back to her villa—made her want to wrap herself around him like a vine. She felt *so* lost. And he seemed so solid, so sure of himself. So grounded.

"I am, a bit," she answered softly. "Are you?"

"No, actually. I know my way around." He smiled, a welcoming, inviting smile, and reached for her hand. "You were probably headed to the beach for a walk, right?" When he spoke to her like that, he made it seem fine, that he was holding her hand and sort of leading her away from that bad, bad decision she was about to make. That he must have known she was about to make, the way she'd been barreling around, probably wild-eyed and looking like she was craving trouble.

She looked down at their clasped hands. "Will you get in trouble for...*fraternizing?*"

He burst out laughing, and it was probably the most wonderful sound Lydia had ever heard. It was deep and rich—the sound of rolling pleasure—and it held her to the earth like an anchor. "You are quite something, Lydia. *Fraternizing?* Hilarious." He shook his head. "I don't really even work here. My mum's brother is the general manager. He asked if I could help out this weekend, with it being so busy, and"—he shrugged—"I tend to be the helpful sort, I guess."

Lydia exhaled, and it was so obviously the sound of relief that he laughed again.

"Does that put an end to your cabana boy fantasy?"

She looked up at him, her pale eyes sparking with mischief. "Thankfully, yes. I was having a hard time getting my mind around the whole cabana boy part of the fantasy." Her breath hitched when she said that last word, such a blatant admission.

"Busted," he said softly, squeezing her hand in his.

They spent the next two hours staring at the stars, holding hands while they lay on adjacent lounge chairs that they dragged down near the edge of the sea. Lydia's heart was a fluttery mess when he caught her out in that whole fantasy business, but he never pushed her.

Well, he did push her verbally, he taunted her and made fun of her in some ways, but he never let go of her hand when he did. He never pulled away. And it was such a remarkable, lovely feeling, to talk to someone in the dark, with all those stars and the lapping waves, and no *pressure*.

Lydia realized she'd been one big pressure cooker for the past three years. Trying so hard to have more fun, more adventures, more drugs, more guys in her bed. She'd been trying to outrun her own life.

"It's almost two. You okay?" Alistair asked, after one of those lovely silences when he breathed evenly and held her hand, and she could stare at his profile and wonder how she could fashion herself into the type of woman he might want to be with. Or the type of woman some good man like him would want to be with.

"Thank you, Alistair." She was on her side, staring at him instead of the stars.

He turned his head slightly. "What for?"

"You know what for. I was so angry and frustrated when I bumped into you a couple of hours ago, and you haven't asked me any annoying, prying questions. You're just…lovely."

"That doesn't sound very promising."

Lydia levered herself up onto one elbow. "What do you mean it doesn't sound promising? That's probably the nicest thing I've said to a man in years."

He smiled and turned his head back to the dark sky. "I mean, *lovely*? Come on. It sounds like a flower or a frock. Real men don't want to be called *lovely*."

"Ooh, so you do have an ego after all. You're a real man, eh?" she teased. "And here I thought you were all consideration and selflessness."

"Hardly."

She loved his voice, some high-low admixture of plummy Etonian and Bahamian patois, with some American slang thrown in. He'd lived in England for a few years when he went to Eton, like his father. Lydia wasn't even sure what to make of that, what it must have been like to be one of only a few black students at a school so steeped in white tradition. Still, she didn't want to ask about it in that way, as if he were some sort of sociological science experiment in her mind. He talked about Eton matter-of-factly, like so many of her friends talked about it: it was the place where his father went, so it was the place where he went. Nothing more.

When she asked him about his time at Cornell, he brushed her off a bit. She sensed it hadn't been what his parents had been hoping for, but she didn't press him.

"So if not *lovely*, then how shall I describe you? *Brawny?*"

He laughed again, low and rumbly, and she loved to see the way it enlarged his chest. She wanted to reach across the small distance and rest her hand on that chest of his, but it felt wrong, too soon in some strange way. If she'd had a few more drinks in her, and they'd met on a sweaty dance floor near Leicester Square, she would have been on her knees and undoing his pants by now. But he was clear and direct, and it forced her to be the same, rather than some drunken girl who wanted to get laid. She turned away from him at the realization that that's what she'd become. Her first year at St. Andrew's and then these past months in London, that's all she'd wanted—the oblivion, the forgetting that she usually found after a few stiff drinks and a meaningless shag with some guy she picked up at a dance club or a party.

"*Brawny* makes me sound like a cartoon hero. What else?"

"Are you actually asking me to think of words to compliment you?"

"Yes, I guess I am." He smiled at the idea, turning to catch her eye for a second then looking up again. "Tell me what you like about me."

Her heart started flipping around. She wanted to tell him that lying there under the stars with him was the finest thing she could recall. She wanted to tell him that his hand holding hers was like a tether to the earth, saving her from flying away and self-destructing like one of those wispy paper lanterns that are so lovely until they are consumed by fire and disappear. Instead, she said the very thing that she used to think—as recently as that afternoon—was so despicable. That thing she'd always mocked as the narcissism everyone mistook for love. Because it happened to be true, and she finally had a tiny glimpse of what it really meant. She said, "I like the way you make me feel. I like how you look at me." Her heart was pounding from the unfamiliar honesty. "I like you," she whispered.

He squeezed her hand and smiled to the stars. "I like you too," he answered with that low-slung confidence of his.

Chapter 27

Sometime after three that morning, Claire woke to the murmurs of Lydia talking to a man outside the villa. She took a deep breath and tried not to imagine the worst. Had she gone into Nassau and picked someone up? Had she wandered on the beach and found some stranger?

"Do you want to go talk to her?" Ben whispered.

"You're awake…" She sidled up against him and wrapped her arms around his neck. They pulled their bodies together, and she felt the sheer relief of him, the blessed feeling that she wasn't alone in her bed worrying about Lydia, as she had been for so many years. They were starting to knit together, so their worries didn't feel so hopeless. The two of them could figure it out.

"Do you mind?" she asked quietly.

"Of course not," Ben said. "I mean, come back to bed soon." He winked. "But go talk to her." He kissed her forehead and then held an extra beat. He let go of her and watched as she got up to pull on a robe. "Good luck," he whispered.

"I love you," she whispered back as she left the room.

Claire crossed the living room and rapped lightly on Lydia's door. No answer.

She opened the door a crack, seeing the light on beneath. Lydia was on the bed with her earbuds in and watching something on her smartphone. Claire knocked louder and waved one hand to get her attention. Lydia pulled one earbud out and tapped the screen to pause whatever she'd been watching.

"You okay?" Claire asked.

Lydia shrugged and pulled the other earbud out. "Not really."

"May I come in?"

She sat up straighter and put her device on the bedside table. "Sure. Fine."

Claire shut the door and sat at the edge of Lydia's bed. She tried not to fall into the old pattern of looking at her eyes to see if she was high or drunk, but she must have been doing it anyway.

"I'm not buzzed, if that's what you're wondering," said Lydia.

"I wasn't— Oh, I don't know, maybe I was…" Claire faltered.

"It's okay." Lydia's voice sounded softer somehow.

"I've always—no, I don't want to talk about *always*."

"Nor do I," Lydia agreed.

"So."

"So."

"So how can we move forward? I mean, is there anything I can be doing better, for you?"

Lydia stared at the ceiling and took a deep breath. "Mother…" When she hesitated, it was hard for Claire to resist filling in the silence, but she stayed quiet.

"I've been so lost," Lydia faltered, her voice cracking.

"Oh darling." Claire reached out and pulled her into a fierce hug. "I'm so sorry. Please talk to me. We're all lost, you know."

Lydia was weeping in her mother's arms, and Claire was soothing her with all the strange and unfamiliar words she'd never been able to express when Lydia was an errant teen. Freddy had always said she'd never grow up if Claire continued to coddle her, even as he accompanied her to drunken parties and late nights in London. As if partying and gallivanting around Mayfair were the hallmarks of adulthood.

"Oh Lydia. I don't want you to hate your father. But I can't—"

Claire hesitated to collect her thought. "I can't cover up for him anymore either. He's been quite terrible to both of us."

"Please." Lydia pulled back and wiped at her face with a rough pull of her fist. "Don't. It's not about Father—"

"But it is, darling." Claire kept her voice soft. "It is for me. And if we're going to start being honest with each other, I need you to see me for who I am. He weakened me, Lyd. He belittled me for years. Forever, really. I don't want you to think that is okay."

"I know it's not okay how he treated you." Lydia took a trembling breath, then whispered. "But you could have been stronger. You should have been."

Claire took it. It was true, and she had asked for the truth, but she still felt it like a slow poison spreading through her veins. Cold and penetrating. "Lydia."

"I know. It's a terrible thing to say." She looked down at her hands on the tropical bedspread. "It's a terrible thing to feel," she added softly.

"Oh dear. We are quite a mess."

Lydia's expression lightened slightly. "Well, that's sort of a relief, isn't it?"

Claire smiled too. "Yes. It's a relief to be a mess. Quite. So." She hesitated, then reached out to place a strand of hair behind Lydia's ear.

"I hate when you do that."

"What? Why?" Claire was taken aback, but it felt different. Lydia's accusation was more of a sad revelation than her typical sniping.

"I feel like you look at me and want to adjust me or clean me up or something. I'm never going to be perfect like you."

Claire toed off her slippers and pulled her legs up on the bed. "I do that because I want to see your beautiful face and your hair gets in the way."

"Oh."

"Darling, look at me."

Lydia was still hugging her knees against her chest. Not looking.

"Okay. You don't need to look at me. I want to be here for you. On the phone. In person. Whatever you need. But if you want me stronger, this *is* me stronger. I'm going to tell you when I think you're not doing your best. I'm going to be honest about your father. I'm going to be honest about me."

"Do you love Ben?"

"I do. Unequivocally."

Lydia finally looked at her mother. "How do you know?"

"How do I know I love him?" Claire tilted her head to look at the ceiling. "How do I know?" She dropped her chin back down. "It probably sounds silly, but first off, he tells me all the time how much he loves me."

Lydia wanted to find fault with that, but then she thought how it might feel if Alistair—in some imaginary future—ever got around to telling her he loved her. All the time. How *lovely* that would feel. But still. "I didn't ask if *he* loves you, I asked if *you* love him."

"Isn't it the same, if you both feel it?" Claire asked.

"I don't know."

Claire recognized her own skepticism reflected there in her daughter's eyes. How impossible it had all seemed even just a few months ago, that two people could find each other and open their hearts to each other, and not destroy each other. "I know. Finally. It's so hard to trust. I haven't had any practice at it, really." Claire smiled at Lydia. "But I trust Ben so completely. So when he tells me he loves me"—she shrugged—"it feels real to me. The love is real."

They stared at each other, Claire trying hard to hold on to whatever tentative emotional cord was pulling taut between them. "I guess I think of it as the place where we meet. It's not an arrangement or an agreement or a negotiation. I think that's always how I felt about your father. Maybe that wasn't his fault, really. We had been sort of thrown together by our families from the start. But with Ben…" Claire took another deep breath. "With Ben, it's like we've walked into the same room and there we both are…together. I don't really know how to explain it. We feel like we're part of each other. Does that make any sense?"

Lydia's chin rested on her knees. "A little. I guess." When Alistair held her hand, there'd been the incipient hint of something like that. Then she shook her head. "It just sounds so highly unlikely. I'm so cynical."

Claire patted her daughter's feet through the coverlet. "Lydia, sweetheart. I want to tell you something."

"Oh god. What now?"

"Lyd."

"Sorry. Go on."

"Okay." Claire took another breath then gave a small laugh. "I didn't reckon this would be so hard."

"Just out with it."

"I'm having a baby."

Lydia froze. No snark. Not even the slightest twitch of her mouth to indicate anger or disgust or joy. Nothing.

"Lydia?"

"What?"

"Are you okay with that?"

"Why? Would you have an abortion if I wasn't okay with it?"

"What a horrible thing to say. Of course not. I only meant— You know what? Never mind. I wanted you to know before anyone else. We haven't told anyone and I was really hoping…"

Lydia stared down at her feet where Claire's hand still rested.

"Sometimes I think I'm a very bad person, Mother."

"Oh darling—" She pulled her into another near-painful hug, all knees and elbows and awkwardness. "You are a wonderful person. You're smart as a whip, funny. But sometimes you don't remember to filter. Or maybe you're just mean as a snake."

They both started laughing through the tears. "I am!" Lydia laugh-cried. "I didn't mean that at all about you having an abortion. I just meant, oh I don't know, I guess I felt like, what does it matter to anyone what I think?"

Claire grabbed her shoulders. "It matters to me! I want you to be a part of my life. I want to be part of your life. You're going to have a sister or brother. Do you remember how you used to beg for one?"

Lydia smiled at the ancient memories. The endless pleading. "I remember."

"Well, I'm a little late, as usual." They both smiled, then Claire continued more seriously. "I want you to move to New York or, if we move back to England or Scotland, I want us all to be together. We've been apart too long. Forever, really. And I hate it." She pulled Lydia's hands into hers, feeling her tremble, wanting to relieve her somehow.

When they had both settled, Claire reached up to rest her palm against Lydia's cheek. "You're so beautiful. Inside, I mean. All that fire, from both your grandmothers."

Lydia quirked her mouth, unable to see any beauty in herself. "If you say so."

"I'll quit while I'm ahead. You okay to sleep?"

"Should do. I'm exhausted."

"Me too. I love you, Lydia. I don't say it enough. Or I haven't until now. I love so much about you. Your spark and wit. Please think about what I said about moving to New York."

"I will."

"Okay. And mum's the word about the baby, okay?"

"Okay."

"See you in the morning. Sleep well, darling." She leaned down and kissed her on the forehead, like she'd done when Lydia was a small girl and still allowed it. "Happy Christmas."

"You too. G'night, Mother."

As she was pulling the door closed, Claire could have sworn she heard her daughter whisper, *Iloveyoutoo.*

Chapter 28

BEN WAS READING in bed and set the book down when she came in. "How did it go?"

"I don't even know. Fine, I suppose. I think all this fence-mending is going to take a while. At least now she knows about the baby and we didn't kill each other."

"Get in here." He pulled back the sheet and patted the pillow.

"I should wash my face and brush my teeth. I fell asleep so quickly at midnight."

"You're exhausted. Just get into bed."

"You wouldn't care if I didn't bathe for weeks."

He grinned. "You're right. I'd probably love that."

She took off the robe. "Men are so bizarre." Then she slid into the cool sheets. "Oh. This is heavenly."

Ben reached across the bed and pulled her body into the turn of his. Claire was already breathing steadily with her eyes closed by the time they settled into each other.

"I love you, Claire."

"I love you, Ben," she whispered. "I love you so…"

He stared at her, tracing the turn of her jaw, the rim of her ear. He stretched over her to turn off the lamp on the bedside table then pulled her closer against him in the darkness. The ceiling fan made a faint clicking sound as the two of them fell into a deep sleep amid the unfamiliar tropical night noises.

When Ben woke up early the next morning, a few hours later,

neither of them had moved from that position. Claire was still snug in his arms, her even breaths creating a soft rhythm against his forearm. In the past few weeks since she'd discovered she was pregnant, Claire had been particularly...eager...in the mornings. They'd laughingly agreed that making sure she had an orgasm straight away was the best method to avoid morning sickness.

He let his hand caress her breasts, which were already feeling fuller to him, but not enough for anyone else to notice the changes that were beginning to take place in her body. He toyed with her warming skin, circling and teasing until her sensitive flesh puckered. She hummed her sleepy approval. Keeping one hand at her breast, he trailed the other down her bare abdomen to rest over the slight roundness of her belly. She softened her back against his front, still asleep but rousing just enough to register his touch. Her half-waking moan was all the welcome Ben needed. He rubbed the flat of his hand lower and lower on her stomach, feeling the deep flutter and twitch of her arousal beneath his palm.

He removed his hands from the front of her body and gripped her hips, positioning her exactly where he wanted her. Keeping her on her side, he tilted her at a steeper angle until he was able to slip right into her. "Oh god, Claire. You're already so wet for me."

He could practically hear the smile in her answering purr of agreement. Her hips were beginning to move in counterpoint to his, slow and easy, inviting him deeper into her body. She reached her hand around to his hip and scraped her nails lightly along his taut muscles there. Drowsy and sexy all at once.

Unable to maintain the slow rhythm, Ben began to move faster, loving the increasingly higher pitch of her soft exhales. He moved one hand from her hip and slid down to cup her, then began circling her swollen clit. A few seconds later, she pushed her face into the pillow to stifle her dreamy cry of pleasure.

"So beautiful." His voice was a hoarse whisper, hot and close to her ear, as his orgasm followed quickly on hers, their insides gripping and pulsing in time with one another. "So beautiful," he whispered again, before both of them fell back to sleep for another blissful few hours.

When Ben awoke next, Claire was sitting up in bed wearing one of his oversized white T-shirts, reading a design magazine. "How are you this lovely morning?" he asked.

Without looking away from the article, she said, "Quite nice. I had the most delectable dream earlier. I can't remember the particulars, but I was in some medieval castle with some brute of a man plundering into me from behind." She licked her finger and turned a page of the magazine. "It was so lifelike."

He scraped his nails through his short hair and then settled his clasped hands behind his head and looked up at the ceiling, then askance at Claire. "What a strange coincidence. I dreamt I'd grabbed ahold of a scullery maid and had my way with her in the pantry, in just the same way."

"The scullery maid? How terrible. You took advantage of your position as lord of the manor? You probably terrified the young lass."

"Who said I was lord of the manor? I was the strapping stable boy and she was my sweetheart. And she loved it when I grabbed the turn of her hip"—his strong fingers dug into Claire's flesh to demonstrate what he meant—"like this."

Her eyes lowered involuntarily as she pretended to keep her attention on the magazine. "I bet she did," Claire murmured.

There was a light tap at the bedroom door, and Claire swatted his roving hand away. "Until we meet again, stable boy," she whispered. "Now go shower off all that rammy stable stench." She shoved him out of bed and waited until he was closed up in the bathroom.

"Come in."

Lydia leaned her head in. "I hope I didn't wake you."

"Of course not. I was just reading the latest *World of Interiors* and Ben's showering. Come sit with me." She patted the bed in invitation.

Such a simple gesture—or so it seemed now—that brought back a flood of warm memories from when they'd lived in Scotland and spent so much time together before Lydia went off to boarding school.

"This is lovely," Claire mused as Lydia sat at the end of the bed in her pajama pants and tank top, sipping a cup of coffee. "I'm so glad we get to spend time together this week."

"Me too," Lydia agreed, but she didn't look Claire in the eye. "I've been thinking more about what you said, about everything."

"And?"

"First off, I'm so sorry I even mentioned the word *abortion* after you'd just told me your big news. I didn't mean it at all." Her voice was unsteady.

"I know you didn't, darling." Claire reached out to her arm and touched her gently. "We all say things when we're agitated."

"You don't."

Claire withdrew her hand. "I don't what?"

"You don't ever say things you don't mean. Or have regrets."

"Oh, Lydia." Claire didn't know whether to laugh or cry. "You can't be serious. My entire life—other than having you—has been filled with so much regret. Your father treated me abominably for years, and as you yourself pointed out, I should have been stronger—"

"I didn't mean it like that—"

"I know. We don't need to do this. I mean, I'm happy to talk about everything…I really want to. But if anything is really upsetting you, we can go in little bits and pieces."

Lydia took a deep breath. "Okay. I'm going to need to deal with Father—I mean, he's already called to wish me a happy Christmas and he sent me a lovely necklace from Asprey—"

Claire bit her bottom lip to contain her fury. Where in the hell was he getting the money to buy Lydia lovely Asprey necklaces?

"Look, Mother, maybe we just shouldn't talk about Father. He's been really helpful to me the past few months. He's helping me get my finances sorted, introducing me to all sorts of people around town, helping set up the trust for when I come into my inheritance this year—"

"Lydia—"

"Mother, I know you think he's a terrible businessman, but he just wants to help. He doesn't want me to make the same mistakes he did. You haven't really been around very much, you know?"

So much for feeling like it was going to be a path of rose petals from here on out. "That's not really fair, Lyd. You've called me exactly five times in the past year."

"You would keep count—"

"Don't do that. You know what I mean. I leave you messages. I tried to encourage you to spend the year with Abby in Kenya. You don't really welcome my presence, if you're being honest."

"Father's just so much easier to deal with." Lydia was getting exasperated. "I feel like you're always examining me, trying to delve into something. Like even now, it's like you're—"

"Stop. Lydia, just stop. This isn't productive at all. You are turning twenty-one this year and you are entitled to your inheritance, but—"

"But what? You want to control me. Don't you see?"

"Lydia. You stand to inherit a tidy sum from your father's side of the family. I have nothing to say about that or how you protect it, but believe me, I will most definitely do everything in my power to control the money you get from the Heyworth side of the family. You know my father set aside a trust for you, and it has been in excellent hands for the past twenty years. I worry—"

"Well stop. Stop worrying. Whatever happens with my inheritance from Father is my business."

Claire shook her head. "Have a care. If you cosign any accounts with your father, he will have access to all of those funds."

Lydia took another sip of coffee and didn't say anything.

"Lydia?"

"What?"

"You haven't cosigned anything with your father, have you?"

"I don't know! Probably! I mean, he helped me set up a few accounts that he said would protect my assets, in the Cayman Islands or something."

"Oh dear god."

"Stop being so dramatic," Lydia snapped.

Claire took a deep breath and set the magazine on the bedside table. "Okay. We won't talk about your father. Just know that you can always come talk to me if you want. About anything."

"Okay. I'm sorry. I don't mean to be so angry, but I hate being in the middle of you two."

"You're right. I won't put you in that position again. What else were you going to tell me, when you first came in?"

"Oh, I don't know. I suppose I need to figure out what I'm going to do…you know, with my life." Lydia took a sip of coffee then continued. "I think I need to go back to school. It was foolish of me to drop out after one year." She kept staring into her cup as if the answers were in there somewhere.

"I'm so glad you think so."

"Do you think I should go back to St. Andrew's and continue there?" She looked up.

"Well, is that what you want?" Claire felt guilty for holding out the slim hope that Lydia might want to move to New York when all of her friends were in England and Scotland. She wanted to let Lydia make her own decision, but she just hoped she'd decide to stay close to Claire and Ben.

"I don't know." Lydia turned to look out toward the ocean through the white slatted Bermuda shutters. "Some part of me loves the idea of making a fresh start in America—like you're doing, I guess—but I don't think it's really me. I don't want to live there for the rest of my life. And I'm a bit afraid of what I might get myself into, if you want the truth."

"I do want the truth. And thank you. So, why don't you come visit for a few weeks in January, if you like? You can live at Bronte's, I'm sure. I can stay with Ben."

As if on cue, the bathroom door opened a crack. "Is everyone decent?"

Claire smiled at Lydia then said, "All clear."

Ben came out of the bathroom in a thick white robe. "Merry Christmas, Lydia." He crossed the coir rug and kissed her on both cheeks. "I hear your mom told you about the baby."

"Yeah, she did. Congratulations. It's going to be cool to have a little brother or sister."

"Cool. I'm glad it's going to be cool." He looked to Claire. "Ready for coffee?"

"God, yes."

"I made a pot," Lydia said. "Sorry I didn't offer sooner."

"No worries. Let's go sit out on the porch and have some delicious fresh fruit then go over to my mother's to open presents."

Lydia slid off the end of the bed. "Thanks, Mum."

Claire was out of bed by then too, and gave her a warm hug. "I love you, Lydia. Happy Christmas."

The three of them sat on the covered terrace for another hour, reading the paper that had been delivered and enjoying the fresh local papaya and mango that had been brought in for breakfast. The rest of the day passed in relaxed comfort. Bronte tried not to be too churlish about her swollen ankles; Devon tried not to be too fixated on Sarah's every move; Abby called from a crackling landline in a remote village two hours west of Nairobi. Claire felt like she was part of her family for the first time in decades. She was no longer cruising along the surface, hoping she'd be able to avoid any probing questions.

It was so different now. She wanted to talk about what she was doing at work. She wanted to talk about her life in New York. Bronte and Sarah loved chatting about their favorite place for Cuban coffee or the best red velvet muffin in the West Village. Ben and Max played backgammon, Wolf balancing on Max's knee. Ben and Jack played gin rummy, talking about Ben's sister who lived in Paris and worked at the Louvre. Ben and Devon went for a run and talked about some of the new composite materials Devon was developing and how they might have practical applications for dentists.

Basically, Ben simply got along swimmingly with everyone. Even Claire's mother.

Sylvia, for her part, was formal with Ben, but still respectful. At least she didn't treat him with the obvious disdain she reserved for Bronte. Despite having convinced Ben that Sylvia had never intended to break them up that fateful summer, Claire still harbored some doubts about how much her mother knew about the two of them twenty years ago. It had always struck Claire that her mother's timing was a bit too perfect, showing up at the Negresco in Nice ten days before Claire was supposed to finish her summer holiday. Ten days that Claire had had every intention of spending in Ben's bed. Ten days that never happened.

The day after Christmas, Boxing Day, everyone spent the afternoon on the beach, kiteboarding and body surfing. Claire decided to stay with her mother in the villa for a little while. The sun had been a bit strong, plus she was generally more worn down in the afternoons because of the pregnancy. They were drinking iced tea and sitting quietly in the living room of her mother's villa, Sylvia doing some needlepoint and Claire reading a novel she'd brought with her from New York.

"Did you know about Ben, Mother, that summer in France?" Claire asked, looking up from her book.

Sylvia kept her attention on the needle and canvas. "I did."

Claire didn't even feel angry. Maybe Lydia was right. Maybe she just never got mad enough. "How?"

"How what?"

"How did you know? What did you know?"

"Sally's mother and I were in constant contact that summer, of course."

"Sally told her mother about Ben? What did she say?"

Sylvia rested her hands in her lap, on top of the canvas and thread. "It was so long ago, Claire. Does it really matter?"

"Yes. It matters."

Sylvia stared at her glass of iced tea. "I thought I was doing what was best. Freddy's mother was one of my closest friends." She touched the condensation on the base of the glass. "Freddy was handsome. Wasn't he?" She looked up.

"He was handsome. Go on."

"When Sally's mother called and said you were having some sort of assignation with some Arab—"

"He's Lebanese, Mother. Not that it matters to me one way or the other, but he's a Maronite Christian, not *some Arab*."

"You sound like Abigail, trying to paint me as some horrible racist."

"Well?" Claire had never come up against her mother like this. They'd always been allies within the family in some way. After all these years of patient obedience, Claire felt she'd earned herself a good row.

"Oh, come on, darling. It's all worked out for the best."

Claire took a fortifying breath and set her novel—closed neatly with the bookmark placed just so—on the coffee table. "Mother. Twenty years of hell with the Marquess of Wick? Under no circumstances could that possibly be construed as *for the best*...I've been miserable."

"We all have our crosses to bear."

"Now you're just being contrary."

Sylvia's eyes snapped from the glass of iced tea. "Claire. You are with Ben now. He obviously adores you. What more do you want from me?"

"God, Mother." Claire widened her eyes and held her rising temper. Speaking plainly still set her pulse racing. She felt her cheeks reddening. "Maybe an apology? Maybe the slightest concession that you may have possibly been the tiniest bit...wrong?"

"Wrong?" Sylvia never raised her voice, but this was damnably close. Claire watched as her mother smoothed the fabric of her pristine white linen trousers before continuing. "Think about my position then. I was your age. Do you feel so *knowledgeable* right now? Can you solve Lydia's *problems* for her? Don't you wish you could? I would have kept you with me forever. You were my best friend, darling. You know that. It was terribly unhealthy, I'm sure, by today's standards, but we had so much fun, didn't we? Gallivanting around London and going to all the events of the season?"

Claire felt what her mother was saying. In her seventeen-year-old mind, the Duchess of Northrop had been infallible. Sylvia Heyworth was formidable. Silently, Claire stared at her mother, unwilling to answer all those rhetorical questions without the slightest self-awareness on her mother's part.

"Fine," Sylvia finally said on a frustrated exhale, then paused. "I'm sorry. There. Is that what you want to hear? I'm sorry for so much. I'm sorry for all the years I spent away from your father. I'm sorry I was a terrible mother to your younger brothers and sister— no mother at all, really—and I'm sorry for your years of sorrow with Freddy."

"Thank you," Claire said, tilting her chin down. It was a pyrrhic victory to say the least, as if her mother had climbed down into the sad pit of regret with her, instead of either of them rising up to some happy place of forgiveness. "I didn't mean to dredge all that up. I just meant…you know I love you, Mother. It's just that sometimes—and I only say this because I know I do it too—but sometimes you act so certain about everything. Like you've never second-guessed a single thing."

"Well, what's the point anyway?"

"Because sometimes there *are* second chances, better choices. And sometimes it's not too late to grab at them. Look at you and Jack…"

Sylvia poked at her needlepoint absently, but the lift of her lips showed the mere speaking of his name set her heart in a happier spot. "Yes. I see what you mean."

"Anyway, I appreciate what you said about how you were my age. I have no idea what to do about Lydia."

Sylvia picked up her needlework. "Why do you have to *do* anything? She's a perfectly capable young woman."

Claire shook her head and smiled at her mother's downturned head. Right. Perfectly capable.

Chapter 29

LYDIA SPLASHED IN the ocean with Devon and Sarah. They weren't entirely horrible, she'd decided.

Devon whipped more water into her face.

"Noooo!" Lydia cried.

"Admit it! You love it!" Devon dove under the turquoise surface when she tried to splash him in return. Sarah was floating serenely on her back a few feet away. Devon came up to the surface with a sparkling orange starfish larger than his head.

"Cool…" Lydia reached out to hold it.

"Here…" Devon handed it to her. They were standing in about five feet of water. Max, Bronte, and Wolf were building a sandcastle at the shore, while Ben and Jack talked beneath one of the pale pink sun umbrellas.

"So what are you going to do after the holidays, Lyd?"

For once, Devon sounded like he was just curious, rather than getting ready to sling some insult about her worthless existence. "I think I may go to New York for a bit. Mother suggested it." She shrugged like she didn't have anything better to do. "Then I'm going to try to get back into St. Andrew's for the autumn term."

"Really?" Devon had been a bit of an academic disappointment in London, not going in for Oxford or Cambridge like the other men in the Heyworth line. "You miss hitting the books?"

Lydia quirked her lips. "Yeah. Not so much. I just figure I'm less likely to mess up my life if I'm at university. Instead of spending all my time searching for the perfect handbag, maybe after a few years, I'll have a clue about what I want to be when I grow up. How's that going for you, by the way, being a grown-up, I mean?" She handed back the starfish and he dove back under the water to set it on the sea floor. When he came up, Sarah had turned her face toward Lydia.

"Why don't you work at one of my boutiques, Lyd?"

"Twats for hire?"

"Oh, enough of that." Sarah flipped around in the water, dunked under, then stood so the surface of the water came to just above her copious chest. "You all are so mean to each other all the time—all that sniping—I just want everyone to get along."

Lydia looked up at the endless blue skies, a few wisps of clouds beginning to come in from the east, then looked right at Sarah. "Yes. I would love to work at one of your shoe stores."

"What?" Sarah's eyes went wide. "Did you just say *yes*? Oh that's wonderful!" Sarah clapped her hands together and splashed Devon in the face. "See! I told you! People can always surprise you."

Devon smiled at Lydia and gave her a conspiratorial glance, as if he couldn't help it if he'd fallen in love with a golden retriever puppy. "Right again, my love," he said, turning to kiss Sarah on the cheek.

Sarah smiled. "Oh, Lydia, this could be so fabulous! What do you want to do? Do you think you'd be into design or sales or marketing or what?"

"I'm going back to shore," Devon interrupted, "with the men and the alcohol."

"Very well. Go. Go." Sarah gave him a quick kiss and refastened all of her attention on Lydia. "Do you mean it? Would you be willing to be a lowly shopgirl?"

"Well…when you say it like that, it's not quite as glamorous as I'd hoped…"

Sarah looked momentarily disappointed.

"I'm only joking, Sarah! Of course, I'd be willing to do anything you need doing. Honestly, I don't even know what I'm doing in this family sometimes. Am I the only one who inherited the sarcastic gene?"

"Oh. Good." Sarah looked genuinely relieved. "I just…I never know with you."

Lydia dunked under the water again and came up floating. She turned to face Sarah. "You can pretty much assume I'm always taking the piss. I'll try to stop. I'm trying to stop." Her gaze slipped to the beach where the Adorable Alistair (as she'd come to call him in her mind) was bringing a tray of rum dums to Jack, Ben, and Devon.

"He's quite handsome, that Alistair, isn't he?" Sarah sighed.

Lydia didn't feel like being prickly for once. "He is. Quite."

"Why don't you ask him out?"

Lydia swam a bit then stood up again, loving the feel of the soft wet sand between her toes. "We did have a bit of a hand-hold, if you must know."

"Really? Lucky you." Sarah looked at Alistair's strong back and legs as he walked away, up the beach path.

The two blond women looked like a pair of wide-eyed schoolgirls. Lydia nodded. "He's really sweet, actually. Initially, I'd hoped he'd let me tag along to some local den of iniquity, packed with pot smoke and a bunch of reggae locals hanging out and getting high." Lydia shrugged. "But we ended up holding hands on the beach like a couple of twelve-year-olds." Then Lydia frowned. "But what can ever come of it, really? Now I just have to satisfy my lust by looking at him and making him bring me things on a silver tray."

Sarah started laughing. "You do not!"

"I do." Lydia was still watching his retreating form as he wove his way through the dunes, the bright white of his uniform creating a lovely silhouette against the tropical greens and blues of the grass and sky. "Just this morning, I called the lobby and specifically asked for Alistair to bring me eye drops. On a silver tray." She didn't bother mentioning that they'd kissed behind the hibiscus hedge. Alistair seemed to fancy her calls to room service as much as she did.

"You didn't!" Sarah was still laughing. "That is so genius. Does he know?" Her laughter was settling down.

Lydia turned to look at her. "Does he know what?"

"That you *fancy* him, of course."

"Hmmm."

"What do you mean, *hmmm*?"

"Oh, nothing." Lydia turned her attention back to Sarah. "Just… well…never mind about Alistair. Which shop of yours were you thinking you'd like me to work in? I'd go wherever you need me, of course. But…"

"Yes?" Sarah asked.

"Well, New York would be lovely. I think my mother and I are finally reaching some sort of rapprochement, and I'd love to be with her, you know. But I'm trying to be a little less…brittle." She smiled in a self-deprecating way. "So if you'd prefer me to be in Chicago or London, I would totally do that."

"Who is this new Lydia? I love her. So accommodating."

"Don't let's get ahead of ourselves. I'm still a bitch, and you know it. But I'm also feeling the press of Twenty-One with a capital *T* and a capital *O*, and I don't need to be tossing up my accounts on my twenty-first birthday on some beach in Ibiza or some sidewalk near Oxford Street."

"Oh, Lydia. You are so much funnier than I ever realized."

Lydia's face pinched. "I think I'm completely offended, but I'm trying to see the compliment in that somewhere."

Sarah laughed again. "Okay. New York it is. And I want you to use my apartment. Devon and I can always use his ridiculous apartment at the St. Regis—"

"I'm happy to live at the St. Regis if you'd rather be in your own apartment—" Lydia tried.

"Yeah, no. Thanks, Lydia, but I think you living at the St. Regis is right up there with you puking in Ibiza. As my father would say, let's try to avoid the occasions of sin, shall we?"

"Oh, fine." But Lydia's capitulation was nearer a happy resolve than her typical sulk.

Sarah stared at the young woman who seemed to be transforming before her eyes.

They swam out a bit farther, then Lydia turned on her back again. "Wouldn't it be grand if a few days in the Bahamas could set my life on a course that might not be entirely rubbish?"

Sarah didn't know if Lydia was being her snarky, sarcastic self or actually hoping that her life might be taking a turn for the better. A bit of both, probably. She decided to let it slide.

The two of them floated quietly for a while longer then started to swim back toward shore.

"So." Sarah dunked under one last time and stood in the shallow water, dragging her hands over her long blond hair to squeeze out the excess water. "New York then."

"Yes. New York. Wow. That's actually really exciting. Thank you."

Sarah stared at her. "Did you just say *thank you*?"

"I think I did." Lydia smiled. "No need to point out how rusty I sound. But I'm really grateful for the offer. Thank you, Sarah."

"Oh," Sarah said, waving a hand in front of her face. "I'm happy to do it. It's great, actually. At least I know you won't steal from me."

Lydia tilted her head and widened her eyes as if she were considering the possibility. "Well…now that you mention it…"

"Don't even joke about that." Sarah's face turned serious. "One of my closest employees—I thought she was my friend—stole from me. Devon helped figure the whole thing out."

"Devon did?"

Sarah's smile was sort of secretive and knowing. "Yeah. He's not the silly rake he'd have us all think."

"Interesting."

"Anyway," Sarah continued as they started to walk up onto the beach. "New York offers so many…possibilities…" They reached the lounge chairs and Sarah wrapped herself in one of the large towels.

"What kind of possibilities?" Lydia asked, flopping onto her towel without bothering to dry off. "You sound like you have more in mind than getting me to sell a few shoes while I'm out and about hobnobbing."

Sarah's eyes lit up at the idea. "Oh, I hadn't even thought about using you in that way!"

"You're hilarious. Go on."

"Just think, you can be a party girl with purpose at last."

"The *at last* wasn't entirely necessary."

"Sorry. You know what I mean. You can wear my shoes out to all the hottest parties and get lots of press. All of us working *en famille* and all that. Everyone will love it. Bronte will get you on all the invite lists." Sarah's face lost some of its perennial animation.

"What?"

"No falling out of nightclubs drunk and half-dressed if you're there representing Sarah James Shoes, okay?"

"So you saw that, huh?" Lydia tried to act as if the pictures on the *ToffsGoneWild* website were never seen by anyone…even though they got ten thousand hits a day. Her tumble out of Loulou's earlier in the month had been a howler.

Sarah tilted her head to one side. "Everybody sees everything, Lydia. Best to remember that if you're serious about coming to work for me."

Just then, Alistair appeared. He stood a bit too close to Lydia's lounger and she loved how he was sort of playing along with her flirtatious impertinence. "Oh there you are!" Lydia sang. "Perfect timing. I'd like a pitcher of water and a planter's punch."

He nodded and stared down at her nearly naked body, still wet from the sea and prickling a bit across her bare stomach.

"Oh, and maybe a bowl of cashews." She also loved how his eyes trailed across her mouth when she spoke.

"Anything else?"

She stared at him then, right in the eyes. She'd been looking slightly away from his face while she was listing all of her bossy demands. His eyes were a lovely amber, with bits of copper and gold and chocolate sparking from the pupil, with those insanely long eyelashes. He was disarmingly gorgeous. He somehow managed to smile without moving his lips. But his eyes smiled.

"No," she snapped. "That's all for now."

Sarah was watching the whole interchange, eyes narrowed behind her sunglasses.

"Would you like anything, Lady Devon?" he asked politely.

"No, thanks, Alistair," Sarah said. "I'm all set."

He nodded professionally and walked back up the beach.

"He totally fancies you," Sarah whispered as she began to flip through the pages of French *Vogue*.

"No he doesn't. He thinks I'm a stuck-up bitch," Lydia said. "Because he's right."

"You're not that stuck-up." Sarah's face was hidden beneath the enormous floppy hat she wore to protect her fair skin and the big black sunglasses she always had on these days. "You just got into the habit of being stuck-up."

"Habits. Very true. It's just harder to break something inside."

"Mm-hmm," Sarah agreed.

"It's not like I can quit being me like I could quit taking diet pills."

Sarah looked up from the magazine. "I know what you mean. It's all so tedious, like me trying to manage this body." She gestured down the length of her full figure. "You and Bronte and Abby and even your mother, you're all a bunch of skinny bitches."

Lydia burst out laughing. "I love when you swear. It's so out of context. It's like driving down a quiet country lane and all of a sudden Pussy Riot jumps out of the hedgerow."

"Oh my gosh. What the heck is Pussy Riot?"

"Never mind. It's just a great band from Russia. Anyway, I'll try to keep my head screwed on when I move to New York. Maybe just a soupçon of bitchiness to keep things lively? Would that do?"

Sarah nodded and went back to flipping through the magazine. "A soupçon of your cynicism sounds just about right."

Alistair came back a few minutes later and set the water, punch, and bowl of nuts on the little table next to Lydia's lounge chair. "Thank you, Alistair," she said softly.

He looked at her and winked, then mouthed the words *you're welcome*.

Holy hell. Lydia watched his lips wrap around those unspoken words and felt exactly as if he was pressed up against her and kissing her.

Sarah pretended she was still reading. "So, Alistair, what's this I hear about your new job?"

He tore his attention away from Lydia and stood up a tiny bit straighter to answer Sarah. "As I mentioned last night, I've just been accepted into the management training program at Small Luxury Hotels of the World."

"Tell us more. I don't think Lydia was there when you were explaining the details."

Pretending not to care, Lydia took a deep pull on her planter's punch and tried not to feel so naked. She lay there in her teeny bikini, and Alistair stood over her in that immaculate white uniform that needed to be ripped off. Obviously.

"Oh." He looked at Lydia for a split second then back at Sarah. "They've offered me an assistant manager position at the Lowell in New York City. So, that's where I'll be."

Lydia began coughing uncontrollably, while Sarah smirked and flipped to the next page in the magazine. "Watch out, Lyd, those drinks are strong." Then to Alistair, "I love the Lowell. It's just around the corner from my shop on Madison Avenue. Perfect location. Right near my apartment. Close to everything."

Chapter 30

THE LAST THING Claire had anticipated was spending any part of her Christmas and New Year holiday in a stuffy bank office in Nassau. But there she was, feeling underdressed in white trousers and a pale blue tunic and surrounded by oil portraits of British and Bahamian bankers who'd been doing business since the eighteenth century. Devon, Max, and Ben had accompanied her on the mysterious errand, all four of them sitting at the mahogany table, meeting with Julian Stembridge.

"Thank you for coming today, Lady Wick. Gentlemen. I am hoping this is perhaps a slight mishap, but I must confess, I fear the worst." Stembridge sat at the head of the table, with a stack of folders piled neatly in front of him. "These are the records of your investments here at the Grand Bahama Private Bank."

Claire stared at the paperwork and clasped her hands tighter in her lap. She'd never had any accounts at Grand Bahama Private Bank. "You mean my husband's investments?" she tried.

Stembridge looked at the top folder then rested both hands flat on the olive green surface. "These are all your *joint* investments, Lady Wick."

"I have no joint investments in the Bahamas, Mr. Stembridge."

"Please, call me Julian."

"I have no investments in the Bahamas. Julian." Claire felt Ben's hand come to rest on hers, beneath the table, and she relaxed.

"May I?" Max asked, pointing to the pile of papers.

"Of course." Stembridge passed all the documents to Max, who was sitting to his right. "Why don't you take a look while I give a brief history of the accounts to Lady Wick."

Claire had never been particularly focused on her finances. She was very careful, as her mother and father had taught her to be, but never tightfisted. The fact of the matter was that she had inherited so much money and it was held in trust at Coutts, and she never really gave it much thought. She gave generously to charities and always chose the finest fabrics and wall coverings for her projects at the castle. About ten years ago, Freddy had begun to comment that her spending on the castle was bordering on excessive. She tried to economize, not wanting to be foolish, and also began keeping very careful records of her domestic spending. Even so, her Coutts account was draining faster than her interest dividends.

When she had finally worked up the courage to leave Freddy, she had sent Max the records, for what little they were worth. Freddy had claimed that Claire had been spending massive sums, depleting their joint resources, and forcing him to invest in wilder and wilder schemes in the hopes of recovering some of their losses.

Stembridge explained that Claire and Freddy had been making monthly transfers, and occasionally additional transfers of much larger sums at infrequent intervals, into the shelter trusts they'd set up many years ago. "I have all the signed documents, Lady Wick. This past year, however, we've been trying to tighten up all of our security measures, meeting with clients in person whenever possible, especially long-term, loyal customers like yourself."

Claire kept shaking her head as the potential implications of the details began to sift into a clearer picture of Freddy's treachery.

"When we spoke on the phone last week—"

"We did not speak last week!" Claire cried.

Ben patted her hand again. "It's okay," he whispered.

"I know that now," Julian agreed. "It's not usable in a court of law, but I took the liberty of recording my conversation with the woman I thought was you. Perhaps there's some way you can use it in a civil case, but these things tend to go on and on. Very public, you know."

"May I see?" Devon asked Max, pointing to the paperwork.

Claire squeezed Ben's hand, feeling the bittersweet satisfaction that—one way or another—the end of her loveless first marriage was in sight. Perhaps she could confront Freddy directly, let him know that she knew what he'd done, and give him the chance to walk away. No need to involve the courts and a civil suit that would drag them all through the papers. Especially given Lydia's precarious loyalties, Claire wanted to avoid anything public. "I'd rather not pursue anything that would be in the papers…for the sake of my daughter…and my family." She squeezed Ben's hand again under the table.

Devon spoke up. "I might have a few—" He looked at Stembridge and stopped speaking. "May we have a few moments alone?"

"Yes, of course."

Claire watched as her brothers behaved in ways she'd never seen. She marveled at how she'd pigeonholed them into their juvenile stereotypes—Max the little band leader, Devon the imp. Instead, she looked across at two accomplished, grown men. While Stembridge was out of the room, Devon whispered something to Max and then they both looked at Claire.

"We can solve this, Claire, but you probably shouldn't be a part of it."

"I don't think it's right for me to be in the dark," she protested. "I'm sick of being rescued."

"How are you at breaking through World Bank firewalls?" Devon asked.

Claire smiled. "Are they plaster or drywall? Wood construction or masonry?"

Devon winked. "Leave it to me. Think of it as delegating, not rescuing. I'd actually love to do it. Freddy deserves a bit of his own medicine, don't you think?"

Stembridge came back just then, and Claire nodded at Devon to show she agreed wholeheartedly.

"Very well," Julian said as he sat down and opened a small laptop computer. "Here's the recording of the conversation. I can't advise you in any way, but once you know the nature of the situation, perhaps you can proceed…in a new direction."

They all listened as he clicked on a digital recording of a telephone ringing. The ringtones were distinctly European. Freddy answered the call with a cheery *hel-LO*. *The cheery bastard*, thought Claire. He always maintained that jaunty nonchalance while everyone around him suffered miserably. The conversation was a professional exchange, with Stembridge explaining the nature of the call, to touch base personally with all of their clients in light of the new higher security measures being implemented at the bank. When Julian asked to speak to Lady Wick, Freddy didn't even hesitate.

"She's right here. Happy to chat." The phone was passed and a plummy-accented English woman said, "This is Claire."

Claire stared at the back of the laptop, narrowing her eyes and feeling the last bit of tenuous hope slip away. Up until that moment, some tiny thread of optimism had held on. Perhaps Freddy was a compulsive gambler who could get help? Perhaps he was investing with a dangerous group of Mafiosi who were blackmailing him?

But the second Claire heard that voice—and pictured the arrogant redhead that went with it—all of that vanished. Freddy was a greedy little beast. Nothing more. He didn't deserve an ounce of her attention, much less her compassion.

The conversation continued, the imposter hitting her stride. She even laughed at one point, slightly deeper than Claire's, but a pretty good approximation.

"Turn it off!" Claire snapped.

Julian hit the pause button immediately. "You think you know her?"

"We're done here, Julian." Claire stood up quickly, all four men jumping to their feet as soon as she did. "I don't want to say anything that would put you in an uncomfortable position, Julian. As far as I'm concerned, we never had this meeting. I"—she pointed at her chest—"may be making some changes to my account. It's been a pleasure doing business with you *all these years*, but for personal reasons, I may be transferring the bulk of my assets at some point. Please don't be alarmed. And please don't make any notes to the records or any changes to *our* account."

Stembridge smiled and reached out to shake her hand. "Very well, Lady Wick. It's been a pleasure."

She smiled. "I don't know about that, but there may be a bit of justice yet."

Devon was reaching down to take a few documents from the files. Julian turned to him. "Unfortunately, none of the documents can leave the bank."

Devon looked slightly disappointed, but Claire had the strange impression her youngest brother had already committed much of the necessary information to memory.

"Oh that's a shame—" Devon started.

"On the other hand"—Julian looked at his watch meaningfully—"I have a meeting starting just now and hate to leave, but you are all welcome to use this conference room for the next half hour. Do you happen to have a phone with a camera?"

Devon nodded and smiled, and Julian nodded once. "Very well.

Lady Wick. Gentlemen. Thank you for taking time to come to the bank this morning. Happy New Year."

With that, the older man left the room with his laptop tucked under one arm and shut the door quietly behind him.

Ben whispered, "Do you know what just happened?"

"I've got an idea or two," Claire whispered back.

Max was flipping through the sheets and handing them to Devon. "This one...this...these two...god damn it...this one...these four..." After about fifteen minutes of Max's culling and Devon's snapping images with his smartphone, her brothers reorganized the papers into the neat stacks, exactly as they'd been when they first entered the room.

"All right, then." Devon looked excited.

"You don't have to be quite so happy about it," Claire joked, but she hugged him to her. It was a bit awkward, what with Devon trying to repress his smile. "Okay, fine then. Be happy about it."

His grin spread. "Excellent. This is going to be *fun*."

The four of them rode back to Lyford in Devon's sports car and spent the rest of the holiday never once mentioning the mysterious trip to the bank. Devon told everyone he had an important work project that had come up unexpectedly and spent a few hours on his computer in the mornings and at night. In the following days, Claire felt as though the walls within her family were finally coming down.

Claire burst into tears when Lydia came to tell her she'd accepted a job with Sarah James in New York City.

"Mum?" Lydia pulled her into an awkward hug.

"Oh darling." Claire held her tight. "I'm so pleased."

"I'm glad you're glad"—Lydia chuffed a small laugh—"but I wasn't even sure you'd be glad. I felt like you were sort of inviting me to come visit because you felt like you had to. And that time I called you when you were riding on the bus, I wasn't even sure if you wanted me there at all."

Claire smiled a watery smile and wiped her eyes with a tissue she pulled from the bedside table in the villa. "I didn't know what to expect or what was best for you. I wanted it to be your decision and not me telling you how desperately I wanted us all to be together, making it some kind of emotional obligation, but I'm so happy, sweetheart. You're going to love New York."

"I think I am." Lydia's smile held more than a tourist's interest.

"Wait." Claire cleared her throat. "What else are you not telling me?"

Lydia looked like she was having to relearn how *not* to be paranoid, always hearing the suspicious undertones of her mother's voice from her drug days.

"I didn't mean it like that!" Claire backpedaled.

"I know you didn't. I'm trying."

"So? Other than my lovely company, what are you looking forward to in New York?"

Lydia looked at the floor. "Turns out…"

"What is it? This is so unlike you to hesitate. Usually you just blurt everything out and demand I accept it."

Laughing at herself and at the joy of her mother's newfound honesty, Lydia began to appreciate the possibility that her future might not be a total disaster after all. "Well. It looks as though handsome Alistair is taking a new job at a hotel in New York."

"Really?" Claire smiled in a conspiratorial way she'd always dreamt of sharing with her daughter, but had lost hope they ever would. "How interesting."

Smiling in return, Lydia flopped on her mother's bed. "He's so adorable, isn't he?"

"He is."

They talked for the rest of the afternoon, about Alistair and New York and what Lydia was hoping to do at the Sarah James store, maybe eventually working on some of her own designs for belts and bags. If Claire had been a praying woman, she would have believed nearly all of hers had finally been answered.

Nearly all.

Chapter 31

BY THE MIDDLE of January, Claire had officially moved in with Ben. She only had her suitcases, so it wasn't much of a monumental event, but it *felt* monumental. Devon and Max assured her that she would be getting great news from Freddy's lawyers before the month was up. They never spoke of the particulars, but she trusted her brothers so much more than her former attorneys, so she was finally beginning to accept that her life would soon be her own. Freddy's hold on her would be over in a matter of weeks.

Lydia had moved into Sarah's small apartment on Sixty-Seventh Street and was loving her job at the shop. They'd even had Sunday dinner together last weekend, at the noodle place down in the Village where she and Ben had gone that first night. Alistair and Lydia had come to hear Ben's band, and then the four of them had walked the few blocks to the restaurant.

Claire had spent the whole meal gripping Ben's hand beneath the table as the two of them listened to Lydia and Alistair talk animatedly about each of their new jobs. Something about the way her twenty-year-old daughter rattled on about "possibilities" and "new ideas" made Claire's heart feel like it was going to burst out of her chest.

"Apparently pigs really do fly," Bronte said on a laugh, when they were speaking on the phone a few days later. "Lydia has a paying job and Abby has fallen in love with a man."

"What? Abby's in love? When did that happen? I'm so out of it."

"You've been a bit preoccupied the past few months," Bronte

agreed. "But we're all pretty much clueless. It seems she's been secretly pining for this guy, Eliot Cranbrook, ever since Devon and Sarah's wedding last year." Bronte's voice turned thoughtful. "Or maybe even since Wolf's christening way before that, now that I think about it."

"Really? They've been dating this whole time and no one knew?"

"Not dating exactly."

"Sounds complicated."

"I don't know the details." Bronte became more pragmatic. "Sarah just called me and we're all meeting over at her and Devon's place to have dinner with Abby in a little while."

Claire was sitting in her favorite coffee shop on Third Avenue, having a cup of soup for lunch. She listened to Bronte talk while she pictured them all together at Devon and Sarah's lofty apartment in Mayfair. "Oh, I miss you all even more when I think of you having dinner together."

"Me too. Would you and Ben ever consider moving back?"

Claire looked out to the avenue and the bustle of people walking by with their winter coats and hats and all that American purpose. She was starting to feel like this was where she belonged. At first it had felt like she was unmoored. Now it felt like freedom. "I don't know, Bron. I think I'm falling in love with New York almost as much as I've fallen in love with Ben."

"I miss it too. I totally know what you mean."

Claire took another sip of soup, then asked, "So when did Abby get back from Africa?"

"After the New Year, I think. Apparently she's been in Paris for a few days visiting your mother and trying to get some professors to back one of her projects or something. We're just all excited to see her and…catch up."

"Oh, sure. So what you really mean is that you and Sarah are going to gang up on her."

Bronte barked a laugh. "Just being helpful. It worked for you, didn't it?"

"I suppose it did," Claire agreed happily.

"For some reason, you Heyworth women are big into postponing your joy. Sarah and I are just here to give you a little push in the right direction."

Claire smiled into the phone and shivered slightly. "Speaking of joy…"

"Oh my god…don't even tell me…"

"Okay, then. I won't tell you I'm preg—" Claire teased.

Bronte screamed a wild flood of ecstatic obscenities across the transatlantic phone line.

When Bronte had worn herself out, Claire asked, "Are you quite finished?"

Bronte began swearing again. Then she started crying. "I'm just so fucking happy for you. You're going to have a baby! Oh my god, we're both going to have babies this year. I'm so excited!"

"I know, me too. I was dying to tell you in the Bahamas, but it was all so new and there were all these stupid complications with Freddy and his lawsuit."

"I understand." Bronte was still catching her breath. "It's just the *best* news."

"I want to tell Sarah and Abby myself," Claire said in a more serious tone. "Do you think you can keep it quiet a little while longer?"

"Yes. Absolutely. I mean…"

"Bron!"

"Yes! Yes! I totally will. I promise."

"Okay." Claire took a deep breath. "Give Abby a hug for me when you see her tonight. I'll be back in a few weeks to sign the final divorce papers, and hopefully that will coincide with the arrival of your twins—"

"Oh, wouldn't that be perfect?"

"We'll make it work. You've been such an angel, Bron, really. I don't know how I would have made it through the past six months without you."

"Oh, stop. I'm going to start crying again. This whole pregnancy has turned me into such a watering pot. I'm a mess."

"It's lovely. You're lovely."

"Thanks, sweetie. So...can I tell Max?"

"Of course, please tell Max."

"Oh, good! He's going to be so pleased. Five grandchildren. Oh my god. Your mother is going to be beside herself." Bronte took a deep breath. "So when are you and Ben going to get married?"

Claire melted a little inside. "We're getting married as soon as the divorce goes through. Really soon, I hope."

"Oh good. So you've been able to move things along with Freddy, then?"

"I think Devon and Max have totally painted him into a corner. We'll see, but I'm pretty sure he's going to sign the documents this week or next. And then we're free."

Claire heard the door open in the background on Bronte's end of the call.

"It's Max! Oh dear, what's the matter, darling?" There was some shuffling and then Max's strong voice came down the line. "Claire?"

"Yes. Max, what is it? You sound so serious?"

"Has anyone called you yet?" he asked without preamble.

"No. What about?"

"I just got a call from my attorney that Freddy's...shit..." Max sounded tired and old. She barely recognized her own brother's voice.

"What is it?" Claire whispered. "Just tell me."

"I should have known he'd pull one last thing before he gave up." Max exhaled with impatience. "Turns out he drained all of the accounts that he had cosigned with Lydia in the past few months. It wasn't even that much money, in the grand scheme of things—a hundred thousand pounds or so—but I guess he just couldn't resist stealing one more thing from our family."

"What a bastard," Claire said under her breath. She was unaccustomed to swearing, but whenever she thought of Freddy and his complete lack of morals, she wanted to swear to high heaven. Instead, she took another deep breath. "So where does this leave us? If he's run off, I guess that means he didn't sign the divorce papers…"

"No, that's the unexpected good news."

Claire felt her skin begin to tingle all over. "What—"

"Apparently that trampy girlfriend of his made him sign the divorce papers and agree to marry her before she would leave the country with him."

"Oh my god, Max."

"I know. It's really fabulous news. I suppose we should be grateful that she's just *that* trampy."

"Max!" But Claire was laughing and crying all at once. She reached for one of the paper napkins and patted her eyes.

Max's voice softened. "Still. I'm just sorry about Lydia. She's going to be so upset—"

"You know what, Max? I don't want to tell her."

"Really?"

"What's the point?"

"Well, the point is that he can't take advantage of her again if she sees him for what he really is."

"I know. But not right away. Not like this, all right?"

Max sighed. "All right. I'll leave it to you to tell her. If and when you want. Meantime, as I said, it's a relatively small sum of hers he took anyway."

"Relative to what?" Claire asked.

She could hear the smile in her brother's voice. "Relative to the amount that's sitting in an account in the Bahamas with your name on it. Devon was able to, er, *transfer* all of the funds Freddy stole over the years and put them back into your name without Freddy having any idea. Until…" Max's voice trailed off.

"Until what?"

"It's kind of wonderfully horrible. Apparently, Freddy had written checks all over town on those secret accounts and over the past few weeks, he's been blackballed everywhere—"

"Oh Max, that's terrible!" But Claire knew her words were brimming with joy.

"I know. Perfectly awful. Devon said he watched him get turned away from Mark's Club just the other night."

"Poor, poor Freddy."

"How true!" Max laughed.

Claire took a deep breath and looked into her empty soup bowl. "I don't really know how to thank you, Max."

"You don't need to thank me, Claire." He was silent for a few moments. "I wish we'd all known sooner how unhappy you were, how bad it was. Maybe we could have done something before now."

"Oh, don't think of it like that. I mean, now that Ben and I have found each other, everything feels like it's exactly as it's meant to be."

"I'm happy for you, Claire."

They said a few more words then ended the call. Claire stared at the cell phone in her hand and felt her bones melting at the joyful realization that she could marry Ben in a matter of days. She left a ten-dollar bill on the table and said good-bye to the waitress. She called in to work to see if it was busy and asked if she could swing by a couple of fabric showrooms that afternoon. Hilary said no problem and Claire picked up her pace.

She reached Ben's office about twenty minutes later, her feet cold and her heart bursting. He was just coming out of one of the examination rooms when he saw her sitting in the waiting room with a grin that could have lit up the city. He turned to his receptionist and said he'd be a few minutes late for his next appointment, then pulled Claire into his office.

Turning the lock on the door, he stayed with his back against the smooth wood. "What is it? You look like you're about to burst with good news."

"It's done," she whispered. "Freddy signed. Max just called me. We can get married"—she hesitated and glanced at the ceiling to count the days in her head—"in four or five days. Or sooner if we fly to London."

Ben was crossing the short distance between them. Claire smiled and took a step back so she was leaning against his immaculate desk. He was right up against her.

"It's very tidy." She dragged her hand along his desk. "Very smooth."

He lifted her up onto the desk and pulled her into a kiss. "I love you so much, Claire." He continued kissing her, pulling at her scarf to get deeper into the warmth of her neck.

She wrapped her arms around his neck. "Oh, Ben. Can you believe it?"

He pulled his face back a few inches. "No." He shook his head gently. "I really can't. But I was never much of a believer anyway."

"Really?" She smiled and kissed his cheek. "What will convince you?"

He hummed into her skin. "I'm more of a scientist. I'm going to need a lifetime of physical evidence."

Acknowledgments

This book would not exist in any form had it not been for the affectionate prodding of Janet Webb; she believed in Claire and her story long before I had any idea who Claire really was, much less how I was going to write her book. So many writer friends helped me along the way: Mira Lyn Kelly explained why it might not be such a good idea to have Lydia kill her own father; Grace Burrowes shared heart-wrenching insights into why vengeance is never clean; Miranda Neville was a genius with all things British and motivational (Miranda: "Why would that character do that?" Me: "Uh, no reason." *delete-delete-delete*); Catherine Bybee offered her continued kick-ass support; Jen Talty let me talk her ear off; Lexi Ryan listened to me hem and haw and fret and wring my hands about self-publishing; Anne Calhoun listened, full stop. Lisa Dunick was an incredible editor: fast, attentive, precise; thank you for being my Editrix Extraordinaire. Allison Hunter and Lisa Vanterpool helped me figure out a Middle Way to self-publish this book while still having the power and expertise of InkWell Management behind the project. Regan Fisher proofread the final manuscript, and if I get any sleep at night, it is thanks to her meticulous attention. Thank you to Deb Werksman, Beth Pehlke, and everyone else at Sourcebooks who supported my efforts to integrate this book into the Unruly Royals series. Alexandra Haughton was supportive and kind and lovely. Ross Beresford and E. M. Tippetts formatted all the files with precision. Kimberley Van Meter set up the cover beautifully. My husband and children do everything all the time, so it's hard to thank them for anything specific when my gratitude for their patience and understanding is woven into every word I write. Most of all, hugs and thanks to my mother, who always reads my books with a mother's love and a reader's honesty. This one's for you.

About the Author

Megan Mulry writes sexy, stylish, romantic fiction. Her first book, *A Royal Pain*, was an NPR Best Book of 2012 and *USA Today* bestseller. Before discovering her passion for romance novels, she worked in magazine publishing and finance. After many years in New York, Boston, London, and Chicago, she now lives with her husband and children in Florida.

Website: www.meganmulry.com

Twitter: @meganmulry

This paperback interior was designed and formatted by

www.emtippettsbookdesigns.blogspot.com

Artisan interiors for discerning authors and publishers

CPSIA information can be obtained at www.ICGtesting.com
Printed in the USA
LVOW06s2038310314

379680LV00005B/634/P